LADY HARTLEY'S
HUSBANDS

LADY HARTLEY'S HUSBANDS

Written by

Andrea Emblin

First Published in 2023 by Fantastic Books Publishing

ISBN (ebook): 978-1-914060-50-2
ISBN (paperback): 978-1-914060-49-6

To Richard, my husband

Acknowledgements

My first thanks go to a fellow traveller on the Truro to Exeter express train. This was when I heard her answer her phone just behind me: 'You need to be careful, Elizabeth – people are beginning to talk.' It was the spark that ignited *Lady Hartley's Husbands.*

But I do need to thank others for their guidance, support and encouragement without which my novel would not have emerged. A big thank you to Cornerstones Literary Agency who put me in touch with Terri Nixon (author of the Penhaligon Saga) my first mentor/editor who helped to push the story into shape, so my thanks, too, go to Terri for her invaluable guidance. My thanks also to Wight Writers and my long-suffering family and friends, especially John Nicholson and Jean and Robin Dynes, who read my manuscript and gave me advice, putting up with all my repetitions and conundrums. My deep thanks go to Ellen Weeks who gave me unstinting support through my final edit.

Finally, my greatest thanks go to the Fantastic Books team for believing in me and repeatedly pointing me in the right direction for the completion of *Lady Hartley's Husbands.*

Chapter 1

Cornwall May 1938

Something was brewing, but Reenie was determined to make the most of the day. She stepped outside the cottage and breathed in the scent of hawthorn. It was a bright morning and every tree defined its new-found growth with a rich vibrancy against an azure sky. A stiffening breeze promised a bracing walk across the bay and filled her with longing: at sixteen years old she deserved to be free of her mother's fussing, free to feel the sand between her toes and the shallows washing round her ankles. She slipped back inside, put on her costume, then pulled her blouse and skirt over the top. She was ready.

'Going for a swim on your own?' said her mother, frowning.

'I won't be long! It's as safe as houses down there.'

Her father lowered his newspaper and peered at her. 'Be careful, my love. There can be an undertow, depending on the currents.'

Reenie sighed. 'I'll be careful! I'm only paddling anyway.' She blew them a kiss before further argument kept her inside a minute longer and made her way to the path zig-zagging down to the beach. The nearer she drew to her destination, the stronger the wind blew, tossing her long, wavy hair in equal rebellion. Salt flavoured her lips, gulls wheeled overhead, their raucous cry mocking her as her feet soon ploughed through soft sand. Deciding on the spot where she should leave her clothes, she kicked off her sandals and stripped down to her costume, her favourite with the colours almost matching the sea. Then she padded across sandbars emulating the ripples that had formed them and splashed through broad pools left behind by the tide.

A turquoise sea, with headland to her left and sand dunes petering out to her right, merged with the horizon, glimmering in the sunlight, beckoning to her. Two other bathers had beaten her to it, though only one had dared to immerse his shoulders. Reenie strode towards the foam curling on the shore, determined to leave at least a damp line on her costume. With one deep breath, she inched into the sea, until the numbing swell smacked against her thighs. There was nothing for it, but to do her usual – an instant plunge, then a mad crawl, front, back, sideways … anything to re-circulate her frozen bloodstream. Once sensation returned to her body, she relaxed into a less serious breaststroke, swivelling to make for the beach. So … why was someone shouting? Were they pointing behind her?

She turned.

A vast green wall towered over her, froth boiling at its crest. Reenie's heart skipped. Was there time to make it to the shore? In the next second an ocean of water seethed and pounded overhead. Frantically, her hands struck out in an effort to rise above the turmoil, but it was hopeless. She tumbled over and over, a rag doll shaken by a hound, utterly at its mercy. The roaring in her ears terrified her as much as the impossibility of one vital gasp of air. In the darkness of this underwater world, all other sound was eclipsed. Panic swept through her, squeezing her lungs tighter, dizzying her head, sucking out the strength to fight … for her life.

One more breath – that's all I need!

Her thoughts spun like the foam itself until hands suddenly gripped her. Up, up and out of the spume she burst, gulping at the air, spitting salt water and gulping again. The sky reeled, and the air scorched her lungs, but its sharpness brought unimaginable relief. Sand grains stung her cheek as the wind slapped her face. Was it scolding her for taking the natural world so lightly when she first dipped into the sea? A frenzy of goose-bumps surged from her head to her toes as she leant into the protective chest of her rescuer. Losing its power, the rogue wave churned ahead of them, as if cursing her for her narrow escape, while her hero tightened his grip round her waist, carrying her to safety.

He panted with exertion: 'Where have ye left your clothes?'

Pushing her bedraggled hair from her eyes, Reenie attempted to scan the beach.

'O-ov-er there,' her voice wobbled. She pointed to her pile of clothes with sandals on top, her head still spinning until he lowered her beside them. Uncontrollable shivering set in as she realised her life had almost been snatched from her.

He dropped the towel round her shoulders and rubbed vigorously. 'My God, I thought you'd gone! I yelled, but you were too busy splashin' about.'

A concerned face stared down at her. As her head stopped whirling, Reenie found herself focusing on the amber flecks dappling his brown eyes.

'Never thought I'd make such a good catch today. 'Twas pilchards yesterday!' He gave her shoulder a squeeze. 'Proper boiler, that, but—'

'But you came j-just in time,' said Reenie, her teeth chattering. She burst into tears and her rescuer wrapped his arms round her again.

'You cry all you like, my lovely; you've just had a fearful shock.' He stroked her arms, pushed her hair from her face and wiped her tears tenderly with the corner of the towel. 'Thought I couldn't get any wetter,' he teased.

Still trembling, Reenie nevertheless appreciated an attractive young man when she saw one. The hands, like his arms, now tucking the towel round her, were sturdy and tanned. Water dripped from tousled dark hair and trickled over the striped swimsuit clinging to him.

'Do I know you?' he asked.

She shook her head, struggling to iron the quiver from her voice. 'Might I ask wh … who my life-saver is?'

'Certainly can. Mawgan Pedrick, at your service, ma'am. I've a flask of tea up with my things. If you'd slip your clothes back on, that'll give me time to fetch it.' He smiled at her. 'Second thoughts – I've a picnic to share. Might as well go for the whole thing. Watch where I'm goin' and catch me up there. You'd need a little cheerin' up after such an argument with that roller.' He stood, all six foot of him, and tipped his head towards the dunes. 'We'll be out of the wind then. You're sure you're all right?'

She nodded and he left her to pull on her skirt and top. Reflecting on how tiny she was next to him, Reenie thought of all her mother's warnings about tall, dark strangers … then headed straight for the dunes. Mr Pedrick looked like the best discovery for any girl in Cornwall.

There he was, dressed and signalling to her from the dip in the sandhills. She gladly settled on to the jacket he'd spread for them, hugging her knees in an effort to warm herself.

'Sorry, there's just the one cup, but we can take it in turns,' he said as he passed her a welcome cup of tea. She smiled her thanks and sipped the over-sweet brew, while he beamed in return and opened his knapsack. ''Fraid I didn't catch your name.'

She pushed her hair behind her ears, wishing she wasn't quite so dishevelled. 'Irene Meadows. But everyone calls me Reenie.'

'Then Reenie it is.' He cleared his throat. 'Are ye feelin' better now?'

Rarely short of anything to say, under Mr Pedrick's spell, Reenie's words stacked on the tip of her tongue and froze. 'I ... I think so ... but Mr—'

'Please – call me Mawgan.'

It seemed curious that moments before, he'd clutched her entire body and she'd been in no fit state to savour it. Now they sat side by side, sun-dried sand sticking to their bodies, goose-bumps still prickling Reenie's limbs, though less feverish by the minute.

'Let me see, ah, cheese first.' He unravelled a cloth holding a roll, which he presented to her. 'Drowning do make you hungry!' he laughed, watching her demolish his offering as if she'd been starved for a week.

She chuckled with him in agreement. She had the chance now to soak up the rest of his appearance: a strong face, yet kind. Definitely handsome. Older than her by a few years? She glanced round. 'It's almost like a room, isn't it? A "window" framed by swaying marram grass overlooked a shimmering sea now belying its savagery a mere half hour ago.

5

'A private one,' said Mawgan, tucking into his meal. He followed her gaze. 'Who'd have thought it could be so calm now. Tell me, are you from these parts?'

She shook her head. 'Falmouth. I'm a townie.'

'Falmouth! Well, aren't I the lucky one? Our farm nudges the last terrace. So, how come you're here?'

'Spending the weekend with my cousin. Only she's poorly today and I came down—'

'On your own. You know what they say about swimming on your own, but 'twas a double lucky for me.'

Reenie's hopes soared.

Their "room" gave them a closeness beyond the every day. Or was it the circumstances in which they'd met? Or even … that they were meant for each other?

No, she thought, that's a bit fast.

She quickly established that Mawgan was three years older than her, the son of a tenant farmer living in the small tied cottage not far from the coastal path. He, too, was visiting family. How she wished she didn't have to reveal she was still at school.

'Matriculatin'!' he said wistfully. 'In the next couple of month. So, brains as well as beauty! Wish I could've done the same, though didn't think so at the time. I'm just a farmhand, working with my Pa. But I don't mind. I like the outdoor life. I got plans for that place, too. There's a lot can be done with it.' He smiled again. 'What do ye think you'll do when school's over?'

'I'd love to be on the stage. Films even better! And I like drawing – wouldn't mind being an interior designer, but none of that's possible. My parents are expecting me to take up a secretarial course.' Reenie shrugged. 'I don't mind, though it don't sound very exciting. What else can a girl find round here? I do want more than simply being like my mother, moaning at the daughters who don't dutifully do as they're told. Well, one of them doesn't or she wouldn't be straying into the dunes with a life-saver.'

Mawgan stole his arm round her shoulders. 'Would ye mind …' She heard him swallow, 'if I …' She closed her eyes and leant towards him. Her head giddied as his lips met hers, a salty kiss that lingered, drawing out emotions, even sensations, she hadn't realised existed. They separated to gaze at each other, then clung together as if Mawgan carried her in that first embrace out of the surf. Could a kiss get any better? How had she never known it could be like this? For a moment, a twinge of guilt teased her: should she be so intimate with a complete stranger? But he'd pulled her from the waves and was surely trustworthy.

Gently, he released her. 'Won't somebody be missin' you by now?'

'Don't worry, they know I'll be all right.' She wove her fingers through his, still wondering how she could be quite so forward. Yet, what could be more faultless? She sighed, 'You're right, I'd best get home. I'm much later than I said I'd be.' She knew her mother would blow a hole through the rafters, but it had been worth it. She'd swing her way round the eruption, especially with her father on her side. Her sister Lizzie might come to her rescue, too.

'When can I see you again? Without dashin' into the surf!'

She shook out her hair. *How dreadful I must look.*

But Mawgan pressed on. 'I can call round for ye late next Sunday mornin'?'

'Can't manage then, I'm afraid – always chapel at ten. An'

you best not call on us. I … I'd have to kind of break Mummy in first. I mean, she won't be keen on me going out with somebody when there's studying to do.'

She pictured their house, half way up the hill. With her father's improving prospects at the docks her mother was expecting to, metaphorically speaking, climb further. It didn't take much to guess that Mawgan wouldn't reach her mother's expectations.

His eyebrows rose. 'So—'

'Come on Sunday afternoon, if you can. My friend Jenny'll be my alibi. We can pretend … oh, I'll think of something.'

'That'll do me nicely! Pa'll let me take time off a couple of hours at least.' He stood and helped her up, brushing off a half-chewed sandwich stuck to his trousers, chuckling simultaneously. 'See what effect you've had on me – it's not often I'd miss my lunch!' His mouth puckered. 'But how'm I to wait eight whole days?'

Reenie took the liberty of brushing her lips over his cheek. 'It'll come.'

She wasn't going to let on so soon that her pulse was racing.

Chapter 2

'Exams – I hate them!' Reenie hurled her book across the bedroom. She'd been walking out with Mawgan for almost two months now, and revision took second place. Lizzie put an enquiring head round the door. 'Please don't ask,' groaned Reenie.

Lizzie glanced at *History of the Tudors* on the floor. 'I can see the studying's going well! It's Saturday. Take a break.' She gazed sympathetically at Reenie. 'Mother would have you buried in books all day if she could.'

'I've got an invitation from Mawgan's parents. Tomorrow. Do you think—?'

'No, I can't. Not again!'

'Go on. You know I daren't tell Mummy.'

Lizzie sighed. 'He does mean a lot to you, doesn't he? I can see why. Apart from his good looks, he's a breath of fresh air. Well, to this household he would be, if you could let him.'

Reenie stared out of the window, as if to summon him with a twitch of her nose. 'He's such fun. And he's kinder than anyone else I know, apart from you, of course!'

'So, how are we to work it this time?'

'Thought I could nip out the back door when Daddy switches on the wireless. Maybe you could distract them and when they ask say that I've slipped down to Jenny's. You know, swotting together.'

Lizzie's frowned.

'Please! Just for me.' She hugged Lizzie.

9

'Never thought my little sister would be so passionate. You know I'm a hopeless liar, but ... I'll try.'

'As long as I see him, I can face the reception when I get back. I promise I won't let you down.'

Lizzie attempted to put on her stern face. 'Make sure you're not late,' she said as she left.

Reluctantly, Reenie retrieved her revision but she couldn't concentrate, knowing she would be with Mawgan tomorrow. She folded her arms and swore to rule her own life in a future, which she hoped would include Mawgan. She was worried her parents might discover their romance. There were so many gossips about. Keeping a secret in her part of the town was as difficult as holding water in a leaky pail. She grimaced at her reflection in the mirror. If only her mother hadn't become such a snob.

*

On Sunday Chapel came first, followed by an all too slow family lunch. Reenie couldn't wait to stack the plates.

'I'll do that,' said Lizzie, taking the crockery from her.

Her mother looked up. 'Aren't you changing?'

'Just going, Mummy.' She headed for her room.

Reenie had no intention of parting with her favourite dress. The pale blue fabric complemented her blue-grey eyes and promising summer tan. She pulled in the belt as tightly as possible to accentuate her tiny waist, opened the door and listened. Soon the familiar crackling and buzzing sound of the wireless rose from the living room. A low hum of her parents' conversation merged with the voices on the programme and then Lizzie joined in. *Dear Lizzie!* Holding her high-heels to change into, Reenie inched her bedroom door further open, willing it not to creek. Then she crept down the stairs.

A sudden burst of laughter made her jump. Arthur Askey – perfect. Far better than the endless news about Hitler's tentacles reaching towards them. Austria was thousands of miles away and so was Hitler.

Now the whole afternoon stretched ahead of them and Reenie quivered in anticipation. But first she was to be introduced to Mawgan's parents. Would they approve of her? She hoped to make a good impression. Her stomach turned over as she knocked at their front door.

'Been waiting for this moment! In you come, my love,' said Mawgan, ever ready to put her at ease. He kissed her cheek and pulled her into a small front room. 'Ma—'

Instantly, his mother was beside him, beaming at her just as Mawgan did. Though shorter, with a rounder face, Reenie could see the likeness. The crinkles at the corners of Mrs Pedrick's eyes suggested humour and kindness.

'We've been looking forward to meeting you, my dear. Mawgan's told us so much about you.' She folded her arms about Reenie and pecked her cheek. 'Come 'n' have a seat over here. The kettle's boilin'. Where's your Pa? Give 'im a shout, Mawgan.'

Reenie made for the armchair with a small quilt thrown over it. She couldn't help noticing the well-worn dip in the middle, into which she sank. *Know just the fabric to make this chair sing*, she thought. From a blackened range, an equally darkened kettle began to sing. A small table had been set with an embroidered cloth and what she guessed was the best Pedrick china. Clearly pennies had to be watched, yet the room had a welcoming, homely quality.

'Oh, please don't go to any trouble—'

''Tis no trouble at all. Now where's that husband of mine? Pa!' Mawgan's father strode in, his arm outstretched to shake Reenie's hand.

'Sugar and milk, Reenie?' asked Mrs Pedrick, with the teapot poised.

'Just milk, please.'

Mrs Pedrick smiled. 'Plenty of milk on a dairy farm. I have to say I've been admirin' your dress, Reenie. Sets you off proper nice. Say somethin', Mawgan.'

'Reenie always looks special to me. It don't matter what's she's wearin'.'

'Oh my! You've stolen his heart all right, my dear. Do have a slice of cake – our own saffron.'

Reenie smiled shyly, a little embarrassed yet delighted at the same time. She couldn't help but notice a flush to Mawgan's face, making him all the more desirable.

Mrs Pedrick tut-tutted: 'Don't you let that son of mine beguile you – him an' his chestnut eyes. S'posed to be our dark secret in more ways than one – a tryst with a cast-away from the Spanish Armada, that's what they say.'

'Well there must have been a lot of such trysts in Cornwall, that's all I can think,' chuckled Reenie. *But none with quite such handsome results.* Reenie sipped her tea, considering how different it was in Mawgan's home compared to her own. Although cramped, how easily she relaxed into the frayed chair with a sense of belonging, though she scarcely knew the family.

'Can't stay, I'm afraid,' said Mr Pedrick. 'There's a cow about to calve in the top meadow. But now you know where we live, you're always welcome, Reenie.'

'We can't stay too long, neither,' said Mawgan. 'We've plans for the afternoon. If you don't mind, Ma, when we've had our tea—'

'No need to lose your precious moments stayin' here. You got to make the most of your time together.'

Mawgan tipped his head towards the door. Then focused on Reenie's shoes.

She grinned. 'Don't worry, I've sandals in my bag, along with my costume.'

'We're off then, Ma.'

'Come again soon,' his mother called as they stepped out to the path.

Reenie wished she could see her own parents in the same embracing light.

*

If only life could stay like this Reenie thought as they rubbed themselves dry from a quick swim and set out for a vigorous walk along the coastal path. The waves sighed effortlessly in the background.

'Do you think Germany wants war? With us?' Reenie asked. 'Everyone's talking about it.'

Mawgan pulled a face. 'Too soon after the first one, isn't it? I don't think it'll 'appen again.'

She pinched her bottom lip between her teeth. 'Would you be called up if war did break out?'

'Might be. I have wondered.'

'I couldn't bear it!' she cried as she flung herself round him.

'So … I do mean somethin' to you!'

'Mawgan Pedrick, you *know* you do!' She slapped his shoulder in mock scolding.

'With a bit of luck somebody'll finish Hitler off before he gets started. Then you'll be stuck with me. Let's think of nicer things.' He clasped her hand. 'Come on, let's—'

Reenie suddenly pulled her hand away. 'Damn!' She peered sharply ahead as a young boy approached them. 'Mrs Gloyne's son, and he's staring straight at us. Trust him to be up here. It'll go back to her! And next, on to Mummy.'

'I don't see why that's a problem. I'm respectable enough, aren't I?'

'It's not that. I've got to finish my exams first.'

And I haven't even told them about you, she thought. Mawgan led them to their secret hollow on the cliff-top. 'I think we've earned a rest,' he said as he dropped into it. He stretched out a hand for Reenie.

Soon, she lay enfolded in Mawgan's arms, their bodies wrapped together. Sunlight glinted on the water and warmed their faces, while the chill of sea breezes didn't quite reach them.

And neither did prying eyes reach to spy upon their passion.

'If you asked me to drop down this precipice to pick up one black pebble, I think I'd do it – for you!' said Mawgan.

'But I don't need a pebble.' Her hands encircled his face as she drew him back for another illicit kiss, while his fumbled at her dress until they rested in heaven.

Like the gull soaring effortlessly above, euphoria took her to similar heights. With her cheek resting against Mawgan's chin, they both paused, soaking up their rapture in harmony with the rhythm of surf breaking on the shore. Salt spray traced their lips. So close to ultimate sublimity.

She eased her shoulders and looked into Mawgan's dark

Cornish eyes. His mother's words rang through her head: *'Don't you let that son of mine beguile you. Him an' his chestnut eyes.'*

'Oh, but I want to be,' she murmured.

'Want to be what?'

'Like this for ever.'

Mawgan snuggled in.

Maybe it was bliss, she thought, that made him close his eyes, although she appreciated his day started several hours before hers. The arm lying across her was swarthy – from his inheritance? Or from toiling on the farm, out in all weathers? She could feel the roughness of his callused fingers.

She loved him.

Even if she was only sixteen, she *knew* she loved him. Being three years older than her somehow made him all the more exciting. *If Jenny could see me now—* "My God, what a find!" she imagined her closest friend saying. A deep-drawn breath from Mawgan interrupted her daydream – he was asleep, head now resting in the curve of her neck. She sighed. They had so little time together. How her parents would disapprove if their courtship came to light. *You're too young,* they'd say, but more to the point, *he's just a labourer.* When she thought of his parent's humble tied cottage with its single room, she conjured up her mother's pinched face and humourless lips should she ever see it.

Mawgan puffed once or twice as he dozed and the sound took her back to watching old Mrs Gloyne dozing in the stifling boredom of a chapel service. How old had Reenie been then? About five? She remembered wriggling on a hard pew, feet swinging as they didn't quite reach the floorboards. But she loved her "Sunday Best" skirt and ran her fingers over the silk, watching the folds ripple. It had felt *so* smooth. And it was *hers.*

Reenie snorted and Mawgan stirred. She stroked his chin. Not quite as coarse as the thistle on the rise. There was nothing coarse about the Penrose family, sitting in a more elaborate pew, distinctively separate from the riff-raff.

But when Reenie walked past their pew she heard the click of the latch on the waist high door as Morwenna Penrose stepped out beside her, snickering. 'I see you're wearing my old skirt. I suppose you're used to hand-me-downs coming from Tyler's Row.' Reenie's cheeks burned. She hadn't realised it was Charity from the Big House.

I'm as good as them, she said to herself. *At least Mawgan thinks so.* As if mocking her, the gulls returned with their false laughter.

Reenie wanted to toss her head, but that would disturb Mawgan and the tranquillity of her surroundings. It was a pity her mind was anything but peaceful. She gazed at the vastness of sea meeting sky. Two loves in her life: Mawgan and Cornwall. So why did her mind keep slipping back to annoying recollections?

Well, they no longer lived in the Row. Reenie could understand how her mother had wanted better things for them and now didn't she as well. Yet ... was she becoming like her mother? A worrying thought. Even a posh accent, she noticed, was being cultivated. No, she couldn't be the same. It was simply natural to want a few nice things. And *never* be poor again. She wanted to shout at the Penroses: *One day I'll show you. Mawgan and me together.*

But how was she to tell her parents?

'Bloody-hell!' Mawgan's sleepy voice broke her reverie.

'How long have I been asleep for? Why didn't you wake me up?'

'You've only been asleep for a while. It felt … right.'

'Never thought I'd be able to say I'd slept with Reenie Meadows. Well, not yet!' Mawgan winked at her as they scrambled out of the dip, dusting off the evidence of their passion.

'Oh – mustn't forget "Algebra made Easy",' giggled Reenie as she picked up the book that was to be her alibi when she got home.

'Sleepin' away our precious time! We can take the longer way back. I got a few ideas to share with my sweetheart. We could do something with those old outhouses next to us. Make some money for the future.'

"We?" Her pulse quickened. Was she part of Mawgan's future?

'You could help when you've finished school. You got an eye for fashions and colour.'

'I, I don't know what Mummy … Oh Mawgan!' she chewed at her fingernail.

'It's your parents, isn't it? I'm not good enough for them.'

Reenie stared at her feet, unable to meet his gaze. All too soon they reached the fork in the road that took her away from him for another week.

'Are you ashamed of me, Reenie?'

'Course not.' With a hasty kiss, she hoped she reassured him.

*

'Where have you been all afternoon?' her mother demanded as soon as Reenie attempted to sneak up to her room.

'Revising. With Jenny.'

'We've been worried sick.'

Ignoring the chastisement, Reenie swung her algebra book defiantly on to the table. 'Where's Lizzie?'

'In her room, which is where you should be.'

'All right, Avril,' said her father. 'Give the girl a break. She's got to have a little time to herself, especially now that … I think you should tell—'

'Tell me what?'

'Your father's being appreciated at long last.' Her mother paused to straighten her blouse. 'Everything's working out just right. When you've finished school, we're … we're moving.'

'Moving! Where to? Why?'

'London – well, Tilbury, not far from London. Can't quite believe the promotion your father's got. We're really going up in the world now.'

'But what about my friends – Jenny and … and—'

'That Mawgan boy? Don't think we're completely blind, Irene. We know you've been out with that *farmhand* yet again. It's written all over you!'

Reenie gasped. Tears brimmed. Her father slipped his arm round her shoulders.

'It'll work out for the best, my dear. You'll see.'

The "best"! How could anything or anyone be better than the lover she had found in the sand dunes? Leave him behind, hundreds of miles away. For what? All Reenie could think of was losing the hollow in the cliff-top and never again seeing those chestnut eyes gazing into hers.

Chapter 3

Reenie darted into the hall and upstairs to her room. She slammed the door with such force that the neighbours must have felt the judder as well. Distraught, she paced round and round, up and down until she toppled on to her bed. Her head hummed, incapable of coherent thought.

The next thing she knew was Lizzie sitting beside her, taking hold of her hand.

'Just leave her be.' Their father's voice drifted up to them from the hall.

She rested her head on Lizzie's shoulder and sobbed.

'I wanted to get to you first,' said Lizzie. 'Knew Mother would never manage to break the news gently.'

Reenie searched for a hanky under her pillow and attempted to stem the tears. 'So, it's really happening. No changing their minds, then?'

Lizzie shook her head.

'Just when I couldn't be happier! They're doing it to separate us – Mawgan and me.'

'No, it's been on the cards for some time. Just hoped—'

'Well, I'm staying here. I can get a job in the bank.'

'We've a few weeks to think—'

'There's no thinking. I'm not going!' Reenie started to pace again. 'I shall work in the bank or that new dress shop.'

'But where will you live?'

Reenie chewed on her thumb nail. 'There'll be somewhere.'

'At sixteen? Mother would never let you be on your own

down here. Besides, I don't think they mentioned the college to you – they've approached a secretarial college. Near London.'

Reenie's eyes blazed. 'Without even asking me?'

Lizzie's pressed her lips together and Reenie guessed she didn't know how to answer.

'Oh God, I'll have to tell Mawgan. He won't believe it.' Reenie clutched her head and moaned. 'Do you think he'll still love me from hundreds of miles away?'

'If it's meant to be—'

'Oh Lizzie, we're meant to be *here*. Together.'

*

'Hells bells, Reene, nobody moves from Cornwall. Your parents are breaking the rules!' said Jenny as they set out for home after school. 'Have you told them how you're thinking of staying on in Falmouth?'

Reenie shook her head and sighed. 'I'm working up to it. You know what mum's like!'

'I can imagine. Anyway, what about Mawgan? Just as you're getting serious – are you? It's been pretty quick!'

Reenie smiled. 'Can't believe how lucky I am. Oh Jen, he's more than ... he's a dreamboat!'

'Crickey, that's a bit—'

'Go on, say it – "slushy". That's what you were about to say, wasn't it? But it isn't. I mean it. We're walking out good and proper now.' Her voice started to wobble. 'And then my family has to change everything.' She squeezed Jenny's arm. 'If only Mawgan had a brother, I'd introduce you to him.'

'Jenny laughed. 'As handsome as Mawgan?'

'*Handsome is as handsome does*, my lovely Granny always used to say. He's as kind as … as—'

'Lizzie?'

'Yup. That's it. And you, of course.'

'Guess our Saturday tennis is off now,' Jenny sighed. 'You'll be out with your beau.'

'Jenny! Just because I've got Mawgan it doesn't mean I'm ditching you. Of course I'm keeping to the contest – can't have you winning second time around.' Reenie linked arms with her. 'You'll always be my closest friend.' She stopped in her tracks. 'Just thought – could you do me a favour – slip a note to Mawgan for me on Friday eve? You'll pass his house on the way to your Grandpa's. I'd like to warn him of my bombshell before I actually drop it.'

'Course I can.'

By now they had reached the junction where their ways parted. Reenie flung her arms round Jenny, then wiped the corners of her eyes as she headed home. *Dear faithful Jenny.* Always reliable. She hoped she was as true a friend to her.

*

Reenie couldn't bear to see the sadness in Mawgan's eyes as they sat on a bench in the churchyard. He drew breath. 'I'll ask Ma if you can have my room. I used to sleep downstairs when my sisters had the second bedroom.' She shivered as he slipped his arm round her waist. A fox barked, a cruel sound. It seemed to reinforce the sudden bleakness seeping into her life. Tears blurred her vision.

'It don't seem fair to put myself on your family like that.'

'Ma likes you, that I do know.'

'I've had a week of rows with Mummy and Daddy. They won't budge. If I … I do go, will you write to me? I could come down in the holidays and you could …' Her voice cracked.

Mawgan took both her hands in his. 'You and me, we'll stay together. Just over a year and you'll be eighteen. 'Tis natural for your parents to think you're too young. I'll wait for you. There's no-one else I want. No one else to match up to Reenie Meadows.' Tenderly, he wiped her cheeks with his fingers. 'We got the summer ahead of us. A little time. An' I shall save up for that train journey. We'll manage.'

Beyond words, she gazed at Mawgan. In the twilight, his steadfastness outshone any doubts she might have harboured. 'So—'

'I do love you, Reenie. You know that, don't you?'

She buried her head in his chest and wept.

'That's not meant to make you cry! Besides, I shall need a dry shirt soon.' He lifted her face and kissed her. And kissed her.

She smoothed his damp shirt and tried to laugh. 'I love you, too,' she whispered.

A heightened scent of honeysuckle on a summer's evening enveloped her, as if to say, 'It's true, he loves you.'

Chapter 4

Tilbury Saturday Sept 28th '38

Dearest Mawgan,

How I miss you! There's enough room in this house to swallow up your whole family and hardly notice. But I would notice you! Keep saving your pennies and come here soon. I want to feel your arms tight round me, like we were in that hollow. All I can do is hug myself at night and pretend it's you. How can that compare?!!

It's nothing like Cornwall here – you'd hate it (but don't let that put you off). Apart from the docks and the cement works leaving layers of dust over everything, it's a mass of railway lines. Then there's nothing but houses, rows and rows of them, and the closer you get to London the factories sprout up like mole hills. And it's so FLAT. I shall miss the daffodil fields in the spring when it's so grey and lifeless round Tilbury.

I've just started at college – that could be more inspiring. Lizzy would come over as feisty in comparison with some of the girls, but one of them is quite friendly. Mummy seems to have high hopes for me, already eyeing up potential for a PA's job. I can hear her calling now, just when I've settled down to pour my heart out to you. We've a visitor to entertain tonight. Just my luck! Daddy's quite important in the docks here.

Oh Mawgan, couldn't you find a farm nearby? Somebody said there's a soap factory coming here where there's a bit of space – couldn't you bring your farm over, one smell might counteract the other! Oh, forgot to say, there's a highlight, after all – the State Cinema. Just been opened and it's as impressive as Buckingham Palace (well, almost. It's like a palace inside). I do love you with all my heart, dearest Mawgan. Say you feel the same for me. I'm working on Mummy and Daddy to spend Christmas back home (Falmouth still feels like home to me) but maybe you could visit before then? Give my love to your Ma and Pa and to dear old Cornwall.

All my love to the handsomest of all (but don't let that go to your head, Mr Pedrick).

Reenie xxxxxxx

PS I'm finding an envelope and sealing it double quick, with several kisses, of course. Mummy would have a fit if her eyes so much as glanced over this. Love you xx

PPS Lizzie's got a job in a dress shop, lucky thing, AND is walking out with someone. He's quite nice, as he should be for Lizzie. She sends her love (but not as much as me) xxxx

PPS Oh my God, I've just heard that a peace treaty has been signed. I know I should be glad, but why didn't Mr C. do that a bit earlier? We moved here so Daddy could build up the docks for the war effort and now it isn't happening. You might see me back in Falmouth yet! Xxxxx

*

Reenie sat passively in the lounge of their new home – the short-stay until they found their own place, close to the activity of the busiest port in England preparing for war. It was a grander house than anything she could have imagined but cold and alien, like their surroundings. She understood her mother's excitement and her father's pride in his promotion. But she missed everything from the only existence she'd ever known: the street where she'd played with her friends, Jenny her closest ally, ever faithful, even the harbour – the salt tang and pilchard harvest. When a gull screamed it took her back to the beach, the pools and the surf. But most of all, she yearned for Mawgan. As soon as she opened her eyes every morning a raw ache squeezed her heart.

'I'll post your letter on my way to work,' said Lizzie.

Reenie thanked her and hoped the letter hadn't sounded as miserable as she felt. She wondered how long it would take for him to reply – perhaps a week? Too long.

*

On a dank November morning Reenie listened for the clunk of the letterbox. It was Saturday, the one day when she was home before the postman called. There it was – a double clunk. Dashing to the hall, she lifted the pile of envelopes, scanning each one in turn. Nothing. Two months had passed now since her first letter. What was Mawgan thinking of?

She passed listlessly through to the dining room where breakfast was set, placing the post on the table.

'Anything from the Agent?' asked her mother. 'We don't want that house to slip through our fingers.' She peered at her again. 'You weren't expecting to hear from Mawgan, were you?'

Reenie shook her head. Her eyes misted as she buttered her toast with the concentration of Leonardo perfecting a fresco. Her mother sighed. 'I did warn you. It's time you moved on. Clearly, Mawgan *has*, thank goodness.'

25

Reenie pursed her lips and left the breakfast table without a word. From the hallstand she took her coat and slipped out to the street. Her feet scuffed the leaves falling from the stunted plane trees lining the avenue. Roof-tops and rainclouds covered the last shred of sunshine, as if determined to smother any flicker of hope from her mind. She marched round the predictable block. And the next one, until she felt able to return home. One more letter, she decided and then …

What had gone wrong? Surely, he hadn't stopped loving her. Had he?

Saturday 4th November

Dearest Mawgan,

I can't believe you wouldn't write to me. What's happening? You promised to write. Remember how we curled up together near Swan Pool? You told me you loved me! Every day I get back from college and there's nothing here. Mummy has said she'd always thought you weren't interested in me. She knew you wouldn't bother writing once we'd left. For pity's sake, prove her wrong! Please let me hear from you.

I still love you from here to Cornwall and back again,

Reenie xxxx

*

The week dragged. So did the next, and the next. Reenie waited and waited for the elusive letter from the most important person in her life. Should she write to Jenny? Ask her to find out what Mawgan was up to? But Jenny was away at college and somehow she couldn't bring herself to mention that Mawgan had deserted her. 'MAWGAN!' she screamed when her mother was out. 'How could you?' Telling her there was no-one else dearer to him, swearing to wait for her, promising to visit … all lies! Contemptible, worthless LIES. She would never, *never* trust a man again.

She flung herself on to her bed where sobs raked through her as if her lungs would tear to pieces. But it was her heart that tore. She couldn't imagine how it would ever mend.

*

One ray of light shone, however, for Reenie in the shadows of wartime: Jenny renewed their friendship with an unexpected letter. Reenie mentioned Mawgan once to tell Jenny he had abandoned her.

The Lodge,
Bradleigh Ave, Grays
3rd July '44
Dear Jenny,

Lovely to hear from you again. Belmont always looked beautiful– it's hard to picture the gardens turned into trenches, though I can just see you hurrying the children over there. You almost get used to the sirens wailing, yet, you don't, do you? They still chill my bones to the marrow. I guessed Falmouth Docks would be a target, much the same as here, though Hitler would probably love to annihilate our docks more than anywhere else. No wonder Daddy's so busy. How terrible – that whole family killed near where we used to live and those smart hotels on the seafront up in flames. So many people have lost their lives here, houses flattened. It's not just the bombing raids

– a friend was almost killed last week when a car ran into her in the blackout.

At least you're spared the dreaded doodlebugs, Hitler's latest pleasure. We had such a scare last week. Oh my God, the noise they make. The awful thing is, when they go silent you know they're about to drop – on you! We could hear one coming, hear the wind in its fins right overhead. Daddy put his arms round us. 'Oh, my loves,' he said. I closed my eyes for my last second on earth. Then it glided on to hit the railway. We were all shaking as it exploded. Then we saw the flames as high as the cinema. Can't tell you how much I appreciated being alive after that, even if it does mean trying to sleep the next night in a fusty air-raid shelter with Mr Peters' smelly feet inches away from me! Will our lives ever be the same again?

On a lighter note, it's good to hear you've greater opportunities to meet the opposite sex – all those American soldiers round Falmouth. Don't get stuck on chewing gum (sorry – couldn't resist that one!) and if you do stick to a soldier please persuade him to settle here. But I am coming back to see you once the war is over.

Nothing to report on my non-existent love-life, I'm afraid. Mummy's still desperate to push the right man in my direction – all rich and BORING! There's no-one eligible round Grays. If there was, they're probably fighting in France now, or worse, getting killed. So many local casualties. It's awful. Besides, you know I've sworn never to fall in love again. It might work for others, but not for me – too much hurt involved.

Can't finish on that note, Jenny. At least I enjoy my work and Lizzie's much happier as a nurse. She and George are perfect for each other, but we're on tenterhooks every time the post-boy knocks on our door – George is back in France again. It would finish Lizzie if anything happened to him.

When will this wretched war end?

Let me know more about your GI – you're bound to find a suitable admirer.

Much love,

Reenie xx

Chapter 5

September 1945

'All that way to Cornwall! Just to see Jenny?' Reenie's mother snorted.

'Oh, Mummy, don't go on! You know how much I'd love to see her again. We've got some catching up to do. And I can't wait to breathe in Cornish air.' Reenie hugged her. 'Only away for a week. I've given you the number for the B and B. And before you can sneeze ...'

Reenie was outside, clambering into her father's car as he waited to take her to the station. Excitement at being re-united with her beloved Cornwall and closest friend filled every pore of her being. But she could barely admit to the one ache in her heart, which she pushed to the darkest recess in her mind. When the train lurched, so did her stomach at the thought of possibly bumping into Mawgan.

Eventually, the train whistled and chugged into Falmouth Station. As Reenie closed the window before the inevitable black smuts flew in to cover her face, she spotted Jenny waving furiously from the platform. She leapt from the carriage, clutching her small leather case, and raced towards her.

'Reenie! My God, I can't believe it's you!' said Jenny, flinging her arms round her.

Reenie pulled back from their embrace for a second or two to soak up the image of her friend smiling at her. She squeezed her hand and blinked at her tears. 'Waited a long time for this. You haven't changed a bit.'

'No grey hairs yet,' Jenny laughed. But a tiny flicker of … something? … crossed Jenny's face. Was Reenie imagining it? They linked arms as Jenny steered Reenie past the noisy repairs to the harbour and reduced warehouses. 'You must be starving, so I thought we'd stop for a bite to eat first before …' Jenny hesitated.

'Before?'

'Let's get to the café and then I'll explain.'

Reenie chewed her bottom lip. What was it? She wanted nothing to cloud this most special of days. 'Oh, the cafe with the best scones in town,' she chuckled as they settled at a table in the bay-window. 'Always jam first,' she pointed out when the cream tea arrived and they chattered about old times. Until Jenny cleared her throat. 'There is something I need to tell you.' She brushed her hair behind her ears. 'It's difficult.'

'So—?'

At this, Jenny pulled a small box from her handbag and took out an emerald ring. 'I've just got engaged.'

'Oh Jen, that's wonderful! What a dark horse – why hadn't you told me?' She stood up to hug her congratulations.

'No, wait. Let me—'

Jenny's gaze flickered past her. Reenie turned to the window. Mawgan stared back from outside, then quickly jumped to one side. 'What …?' Reenie gasped. 'You don't mean … not … Jen?'

'I'm sorry, really sorry. I … I didn't know how to tell you. It was all finished between you and—'

'But he was mine. He loved *me*. How could you?'

Jenny's eyes brimmed now. 'I never wanted to hurt you.'

'Well you bloody well have!'

Reenie threw her serviette over the scones, grabbed her case and stormed to the door.

'Wait!'

She heard Jenny calling to her as the door slammed with the loudest jangle of the bell.

'Reenie!' said an oh-so-familiar voice. Mawgan stepped towards her and the wound in her heart burst open.

'Don't even try to speak to me! All that time I waited for you. All those letters.' She wanted to slap him. She pushed through a huddle of shoppers. She had to get away ... away from the person shredding her into pieces.

'Reene, don't. What ...?'

By now she was running, hot tears coursing down her cheeks, anything to avoid her betrayers. She thought she could hear Jenny again but if she did, nothing would stop her flight. When she reached Killigrew Street, she wiped her face sufficiently to check into the Bed and Breakfast. Then flung herself on her bed and sobbed until she felt rung dry.

My best friend and the person who swore undying love to me! All lies. Traitors. She had to get away from Cornwall. It would never mean the same to her again. And she knew she would never trust a man again. Ever. She would have to catch the train back to London the next day.

Chapter 6

May 1950

'Ah, Miss Meadows.' The founder of *Hartley Homes* ushered her into his office for the new Personal Assistant interview. He shook her hand. It was a firm, warm grip, giving Reenie some confidence as she took the seat offered to her. She wove her fingers together in her lap and Mr Hartley smiled at her from the other side of his desk. 'I feel I already know you a little after your father's introduction.' He glanced down at her application form. 'Let me see, tell me about your present employment.'

Reenie took a deep breath and attempted to describe everything in the best possible light.

'And how do you feel *Hartley Homes* might benefit from your expertise?'

She looked at Mr Hartley. Despite his prestige, his sharp, intelligent eyes suggested humanity, possibly even humour? Reenie took courage and launched into what she hoped would secure the job with *the* building magnate of Essex.

'Is there anything else you would like to add, Miss Meadows?'

'Well, I know the specification is for a PA but,' she hesitated, 'I've always had a love for interior design. I helped re-design my parents' new home—'

'Oh yes, my dear ...'

My dear!

'Your father has told me about that. A proud parent, indeed.'

Reenie blushed. 'So, I feel a sort of, um, affinity with a business where design is so crucial.'

More questions followed and then the interview drew to a close. Miss Cray, the receptionist, bustled in to thank her for her attendance. 'You will receive a call soon to let you know if you have been successful.' She beamed at her. Then glanced back in Mr Hartley's direction. 'Remarkable person, you know. Started the business from nothing and now look at it.'

Well, that seemed to go quite well, Reenie thought as she sauntered down the road to the bus stop. She decided to call on Lizzie on her way home to tell her all about it. She smiled to herself as she thought of Lizzie and George on their wedding day, and then Graham, born soon after VE celebrations. Dear Graham – she did love him.

A picture of Elizabeth Taylor's marriage to Conrad Hilton caught Reenie's eye outside the newsagent's, *The Daily Herald* promoting sales with a photo of the glamorous couple. But it took Reenie to Jenny and Mawgan and that wedding ceremony she couldn't bear to attend. She had managed to send a card and congratulations when Abigail arrived, quickly followed by Daniel. Lizzie would no doubt be saying, 'Are you going to tell Jen about the job?' if she did get it. Dear Lizzie, always trying to patch things up. Reenie sighed. She supposed Jenny should know.

Reenie got home later than she had thought. Her mother greeted her with the phone outstretched, mouthing, 'It's for you.'

Reenie rushed over.

'Miss Meadows?'

'Yes. Speaking.'

She held her breath.

'Harold Hartley here. Well, Miss Meadows, you have the job! I am delighted to welcome you to *Hartley Homes* as my personal secretary.'

Reenie puffed out her cheeks and sank to the stool by the telephone. 'Thank you so much. I shall be *delighted* to work for you.'

The victory whoop in *The Lodge*, once the receiver had been replaced, almost echoed a similar one five years ago at the end of the war.

*

Reenie tidied her desk ready to leave after her second week in her new job. Mr Hartley's door suddenly opened. 'Ah, Miss Meadows,' he said. He glanced at his gold watch. 'Six o'clock! I'm sure you've covered more than was expected today.' His smile softened his business-like features: that keen concentration, with an eye sharp enough to pierce any hidden information. 'But if you've a minute to spare ... I've not forgotten your interest in interior design. Might you like to cast your eye over our new upmarket four bedroom house?'

Reenie beamed. 'Oh yes!'

'None of those penny-pinching make-do's going up terrace by terrace, especially since Mr Attlee took the reins from Churchill. 'Hartley Homes – Houses with a Difference.' He chuckled at the jingle. She remembered it from the advertisements the last time she was in the cinema. He beckoned her to his side and she slipped on to the seat he'd pulled over for her, gazing at a ray of drawings across the desk.

'Firstly, the front entrance – always impressive, and once inside—'

'Oh, the staircase – I love the curve and the banister,' said Reenie, forgetting her nervousness.

'Heavy oak, carved spindles. Now, follow me through to the lounge. What works well here?'

'The bay window is a lovely feature and those alcoves, but the fireplace is magnificent. Love the wooden surround and the tiled panels – ancient Egyptian designs?'

'Ah, the devil's in the detail, my dear. It's what makes a *Hartley Home* stand out from the crowd. But I do think the finishing touches aren't quite there. What d'you reckon?'

Reenie scanned the careful artist's impression. 'I wonder if … that sculpted edge to the fireplace could be mirrored with something like it just below the ceiling. Oh, and the little windows at the far end – could they be stained glass, matching the design in those beautiful tiles?'

Harold stared inscrutably at the drawings and then Reenie. What had overcome her, talking so boldly to her boss?

'You might just be on to something there!' His fingers drummed on the desk. That was when she noticed his disfigured left hand and wondered how he'd come to lose the tops of three fingers. It hadn't hindered his success. 'More hidden talents, Miss Meadows! Right, give these the once over.'

Design after design opened up before her. Together they pored over them. Reenie totally absorbed with images and ideas, glowed under Harold's encouragement. Until a cheerful whistle from the landing outside startled her.

'Good grief, what've I been thinking of? I've kept you here way beyond office hours. That's the caretaker's favourite tune.'

Harold's eyes twinkled. 'Think he's got a soft spot for you, Miss Meadows, or might I say *Irene*?'

'Sorry?' Reenie blushed as the lyrics for the song came to mind.

'Oh – *Goodnight, Irene!* Doesn't that mean …?'

Her hand flew to her lips as she remembered the next line, *I'll see you in my dreams.*

Her boss laughed again. 'Come on, I'll take you home. 'Second thoughts, if we stop off at *The Queen's* for a bite to eat, we can share a few more ideas.'

Reenie's head whirred in amazement. *The Queen's Hotel!* 'Really? You mean—?'

'I mean you have a real gift for design. And for planning. Don't you think this should be explored a little further?'

*

Once settled over a light meal, a rich Bordeaux wine fortified Reenie sufficiently to ask questions she would never have imagined allowing herself. 'Do tell me how you came to have such a flourishing company. Everyone knows about *Hartley Homes*. Did *you* start the business and if so, how?'

Harold smiled. 'It's a long time since I've shared my story with anyone.' He rested his disfigured hand beside his place-setting. 'Used to be a carpenter, working partly at the sawmills in my youth. Losing three fingers actually started the whole venture. Gave me a small compensation, followed by a successful flutter on the horses. With this I bought the tools and a ramshackle house to improve. A friend, who was a builder, came in on the project – he taught me a thing or two about building and it went on from there.'

'But in such a big way!'

'We-ll, I have to admit that my wife's family had connections.'

'Your wife?'

Why hadn't she thought of it – Mr Hartley and his young PA out dining together … what on earth would that look like? As if reading her thoughts, Harold briefly raised his hands. 'My marriage finished years ago. But in those early days, Cynthia's father, a retired colonel, introduced me to the local alderman. He loved the refurbished house and one introduction led to another … and another. Connections, you see. Connections make money.'

'But, doesn't that sort of thing need, um, a lot of investment?'

'Of course. The Colonel helped out and don't forget this all started a long time ago. Cigarette, Miss Meadows?'

Reenie nodded and Harold snapped open a silver case. 'The best – *du Maurier*.' He cut and lit a premium cigar for himself, turning from her for a moment to recede behind a haze of smoke. 'I do believe our style, a more individual approach, helped to launch us. Something a cut above the rest. And now of course there's great demand since the war.'

He tapped his cigar on the ashtray. 'And I *do believe* we've made quite a scoop in finding you, Reenie, if I may call you by your first name, with not only perfect PA skills but other talents as well!'

Reenie felt her face flush. She glanced across the table at her effusive boss. Twice her age, with a shiny dome to his head, Mr Hartley was nevertheless interesting and certainly very clever. She imagined he was once quite handsome – a catch for a girl several decades ago. His most attractive feature was his eyes, or at least the enthusiasm shining from them, she had to admit, in her direction. *Calling me Reenie now!* She stifled a sigh. It was a pity he was so much older than her. And what about this wife he'd mentioned?

*

Reenie couldn't help inhaling the rich smell of new leather as she slid on to the passenger seat beside Harold. A Rolls-Royce! What would Lizzie think of her now? Was someone twitching the curtains at the window as the pinnacle of the motor industry dropped her home?

'What time is this?' said her mother as Reenie stepped inside.

'Oh, Mummy – time for a twenty-eight-year-old to be returning from … from an extension to office hours!'

'Well you didn't tell me you were going to be late.'

Reenie kissed her mother, pre-empting the next flow of questions. 'Sorry. I didn't have time to let you know. But it was too good to miss.' She leapt upstairs. If it had been possible to float, she was sure she would have managed it.

Chapter 7

Reenie loved her job, but was it also because her relationship with her boss had changed? Whatever it was, life had a sparkle to it now, in more ways than one. She fingered the pendant round her neck. Some extravagant spoiling was lifting the greyness that had settled over her. Apart from one aspect.

'But you told me your marriage was over. I believed you!' she said on their most recent date.

Harold took hold of her hand and squeezed it. 'Don't think badly of me. My marriage to Cynthia—'

'But you're … you're still living under the same roof?'

He nodded, remorse covering his normally well-controlled face.

Reenie lowered her eyelids and sipped her martini. 'I … I think this might have to be our last evening out together.' She hoped Harold hadn't noticed a tear trickling down.

'Darling—' he pleaded.

Darling? He's treated me like a hussy!

'You must know I don't want anyone else. It's just that for the moment, I'd rather we didn't tell anyone. You know what office staff are like!' He lifted her hand and kissed it.

Oh yes, no wonder he had asked for discretion! What should she think? A wife of sorts, still in the background. She shouldn't really … but she was enjoying herself! For the first time in too many years to count.

*

Home slightly earlier than usual, Reenie heaved a sigh of relief that for once she was on her own. Like the heavy July weather, her mother seemed particularly overbearing at the moment. She called to check that her mother was out. Instead, the new telephone answered. It gleamed in pride of place on the hall table. She reached out to pick it up.

'Reene, it's me. I'll have to be quick. I need to see you. It's urgent,' said Lizzie.

'Why?'

'Can't say now. But it's Harold.'

'Harold!'

The phone crackled and clicked. Somebody else was listening. Was it the party line or was someone …? She slammed the phone back on the receiver. A faded poster from the war, "Walls have ears", still clung to the side of the cinema in town. Her parents' home definitely had an extra pair of ears.

Footsteps clipped over the landing.

'That was brief,' said her mother, coming downstairs.

'Oh, you made me jump! You're in. I did shout.' Reenie smiled as if nothing in particular had happened. She gazed at the immaculate, pale grey suit her mother wore, with the pleated skirt swishing round her silk stockings. A cloying but expensive perfume enveloped Reenie as the usual obligatory kiss was offered.

'I was busy getting ready, dear. What was that all about?'

'Oh – just catching up with Lizzie.'

'Word of advice, darling,' her mother tipped her head knowingly. 'When you get a bite, don't ignore it.'

'Mummy!'

'We're out tonight. One of your father's dos again,' she smiled. 'Oh, there's the car. Got to dash!'

With a brief draught, the door opened, then slammed shut equally quickly behind the small, slight figure dressed for an evening out. A car engine revved, tyres rasped on the drive. Reenie heaved a sigh of relief. Had Lizzie been phoning from the dress shop where she worked? Should she try to call her back? No – couldn't risk busy-body Mrs Fosdyke homing in on their conversation. Damn that woman – Reenie so wanted to see Lizzie to find out what was wrong.

The grandfather clock chimed six times, full of self-importance and echoing round the substantial entrance. 'Sorry you're out, though, Daddy,' she murmured to the clock, as if it deputized for him. He was still the parent she, and especially Lizzie, could fling her arms round, chat about this and that – things that didn't matter but which, like mortar between bricks, cemented their relationship.

Reenie slipped into the lounge, picking up a letter or two – all bills, nothing interesting to read. She tweaked the flowers and plumped up the cushions. Then stared into nothingness. Her thoughts returned to the evening ahead. Was she encouraging her liaison and ... did it mean there was no need to feel guilty about it? *Guilty?* Was she?

Needing a drink, she slipped into the kitchen where a sudden rap on the backdoor startled her. 'Lizzie?'

'We need to talk,' said Lizzie, marching inside.

Reenie hugged her. 'I was hoping you'd drop in. Come up to my room,'

'What's the rush?'

'I'm meeting Harold.'

'*That's* what I wanted to talk to you about.'

Leaping two steps at a time up the stairs, Reenie took the lead. Her latest dress, emphasizing her tiny waist, was halfway over her head as Lizzie entered the bedroom.

'Reenie – listen. People are talking about you?'

'What do you mean?'

'They know. It's out. You're a scarlet woman.'

Reenie's cheeks burned. 'I don't care. Make yourself at home. I'll tell you about it while I smarten up.' With confidant, sweeping strokes as she sat at her dressing table, Reenie brushed her wavy, auburn hair. She glanced at Lizzie.

'He gave me this the other day, an early birthday present.' Eagerly, she pulled at the necklace hiding in her cleavage. She turned to show Lizzie, as if the reflection might not display it to its full advantage. The gold chain and a heart shaped pendant embellished with a ruby certainly took the gleam off the gilt-edged looking-glass. 'Worth a fortune, he said.' Reenie dropped the present back to its retreat. She returned her gaze to the mirror and dusted her cheekbones with rouge.

Lizzie's eyes widened.

'Aren't I lucky?'

'Oh,' murmured Lizzie.

'Apparently, rubies stand for wealth, but I like its other attribute, too – the wearer makes *wise* decisions.'

With a well-trained hand, Reenie applied an exact red bow to her lips, a "Hedy Lamarr" she liked to think. Briefly, she sucked in her cheeks for the sultry look, slender eyebrows arched, hair flowing in Hollywood fashion. She stared at the result with satisfaction. 'It's going to be a ring soon, he's told me.'

'But, what about his wife?'

One of Reenie's eyebrows soared even higher for a second. With a final patting of powder to eliminate a sneaky gleam to the tip of her nose, she swivelled round and took Lizzie's hands into her own. 'Oh Lizzie, I've told you, Harold's as good as *was* married. He can't stand her! It's *me* he loves. A divorce is imminent.'

'But what about *you? How do you* feel?' Lizzie gazed at Reenie: 'You're by far the prettiest in the family. You could have anyone. And he's … he's a lot older than you. Too old.'

'I've told you – age doesn't matter!'

'And how do you feel about people muttering under their breath? I started to tell you when I phoned.'

'They'll be laughing on the other side of their faces when I'm flashing a diamond on this finger!'

'Reene! Do you *love* him, that's what matters?'

Reenie smudged a little eye-liner on to her natural beauty spot, enough to enhance it. 'Elizabeth Simmonds, at least I *love* being with him. Harold and I have lots in common. He's more exciting than you think – got imagination, a sense of humour … and maybe a bit of spoiling makes the age difference not so bad after all.'

'But if Mother and Father were to hear—'

'I'm working on that, so don't say anything yet. I'm pretty certain Mummy's in the picture *and* approves. For the last time, Harold's assured me his marriage folded years ago.'

'You've never got over Mawgan, have you?'

'For pity's sake, that was years ago. Lizzie! I don't want us to fall out – I hoped you'd be glad for me. At last, something *good* is happening in my life. My God, we can both remember what it was like to be poor.' Reenie stared into the mirror. She guessed Lizzie hadn't finished.

'But *divorce* – Oh my word, think of the gossip!'

By now Reenie raised both eyebrows, while the flush to her cheeks wasn't totally artificial. Lizzie had overstepped her patience.

'I'm not going into details, but there won't be a problem.' Reenie stood to slide her feet into a pair of glossy red high-heels. 'I'm ready! Come again soon.' Then she added, 'I *will* be married, you'll see. If Edward and Mrs Simpson can manage it, so can I!'

An image of the Windsor's exile flashed into her mind. She wasn't going to mention *that*.

"But do you love him?" persisted in her ears as she made for the rendezvous. Well, she liked him … a lot. What was wrong with desiring a life of luxury, too, especially as this could be her one and only chance. Wasn't she running out of time?

Chapter 8

Harold paused at the mirror on his way out of the office cloakroom. He would be meeting Reenie soon. Running his fingers over his tailor-made jacket, he appreciated its quality. He stared at his missing fingers on his right hand. That happened so long ago.

'Darling, it's you I'm interested in, not the tops of three fingers,' Reenie had protested when he implied that his disfigurement might discourage her. He turned to study his profile. Stomach needed sucking in. He breathed out. The constraint on the last notch of his trouser belt reasserted itself and he sighed. *Face the facts, Harold Hartley, fifty-nine, going on sixty – what've you've got to entice a pretty twenty-eight-year-old?*

Everything's still functioning – certainly felt like it last week! God, how did I stop myself?

An image of Reenie danced before him – long, wavy hair framing a heart shaped face from which blue-grey eyes sparkled. Curling luxuriously, her dark eye lashes fluttered. In his direction, of course. The sunlight glanced off her ruby lips. *That mouth!* Always teasing, tempting him to meet them with his. No wonder the bejewelled pendant was so appropriate.

Adjusting his silk tie already in perfect order, he peered sideways once more, this time at his chin. Well, the two of them. *Overweight and sagging! What'll she think when we peel off ...?* For a moment Harold felt Reenie's fingertips working their way under his shirt. It would have to be dark.

46

Reenie was different from his other dalliances. They were nothing but frivolous flirtations. Even Cynthia had dismissed them as part of the package when she married him. Like a mere dusting of icing sugar on the cake, with the lightest of touches, each liaison was soon brushed out of his life.

Harold mopped his forehead with his handkerchief. Reenie had captured his imagination at first glance: lively and intelligent, she shared a similar personality and interests, with a sense of fun and humour. Not only vivacious, in his eyes, his paramour's petite and pretty features competed with film stars. So, was she genuinely attracted to him? He was no Clark Gable, but then he had other assets. Thinking of assets, he pondered over Reenie's sharp business acumen. Even that appealed to him; he quashed a distant alarm bell into the corner of his mind.

It wasn't infatuation, he *was* in love. But, thinking of the ring, why did he act so impulsively? Cynthia would never give him a divorce. He shook his head. He couldn't let Reenie go.

His diminished hand caught his attention again. When was it – 1908? Just eighteen when the accident took place in the saw mill. 'Watch out!' a voice from the past had yelled.

A sudden violent thud from behind catapulted him across the workshop.

'Grab him,' someone shouted as the machinery screamed. But it was too late. In a split second he was staring in disbelief at three of his fingers, the top halves, lying in the shavings. Still the saw shrieked, yet now it was more distant as the thrum in his head took over. Toppling backwards, the room darkened, then spun round. He slumped on to the floorboards, blood pumping from his injury. Equipment silenced. Voices shouted; people lifted him. Fighting the blackness blotting out his life, his eyes fastened on one tiny pin-prick of light. Then … blackout.

'Poor bugger, he won't know what's hit him,' Harold heard his father's friend say as he came round. 'Is he right-handed?'

'He won't be any more!' said someone else. 'Everyone saw that timber in the wrong place. It was asking for trouble. I saw him falling on his back.'

He remembered keeping his eyes closed, realising what they were talking about. The agony burning through him spoke for itself, but somehow, he couldn't unlock his eyelids.

'The boss should pay for it – it was *his* fault. Everyone knows it. Pull on this bandage – it's got to be tighter.'

A picture of his fingers in the sawdust flashed before him once more.

'Harry, you're with us, lad,' a colleague said. 'Come on, let's help you sit up. Need a little nip from Jack's flask?'

Something fiery scorched a passageway down his throat.

'What happened?' he murmured when no-one needed to tell him.

'Had a tussle with the saw, mate,' said the other friend. 'Mr. Mitchell's called the doc 'n' he'll soon sort you out.'

Startling Harold back to the present, the door to the cloakroom opened and one of his colleagues stepped in for his coat.

'Oh, Harold – a pleasant evening to you. Glad that deal's signed and sealed now.'

Harold smiled a little smugly. 'Another boost to *Hartley Homes*.' He dropped his hat on to his head and smiled again, this time to himself. Who would have thought the trauma at the saw mill would have brought him so much? And now – Reenie Meadows!

As he reached the stairs, a figure took him by surprise. 'Oh, Mr Hartley, there's a call for you,' said Miss Cray.

'Still here, Miss Cray! Who is it?'

'I … I think it must be Miss Meadows. Shall I tell her to call back tomorrow?' she said, a little coyly.

'No, I'll take it.' He drew breath and turned back. 'Feel free to go, Miss Cray.'

'Harold Hartley speaking. How can I help?'

How long did it take for Miss Cray to put a coat on? Eventually, the door clicked behind her. Convinced her ear was pressed to the key hole, Harold swallowed his exasperation and continued, business-like, 'More ideas on the new shopping mall from our old acquaintance? That's excellent.'

'Sorry?' said Reenie softly. 'It's about this evening.'

'That's right the meeting has been arranged … as noted. The meal should confirm the arrangement nicely.' He dropped the phone on to the cradle before Reenie could reply and listened. Was that the squeak of a shoe at the top of the stairs? For the second time he mopped his brow. His imagination was running riot: no one knew about their friendship. Did they? Pushing the interfering thought to a distant cloud, he neatly stacked his papers on the desk. There was so much to look forward to. Knowing all his energy was needed for the evening, he took the lift to the ground floor.

*

Harold reached across the table in the hotel dining room to pick up the receipt. Reenie placed her hand over his. 'Thank you, darling. It's been a perfect evening.'

With the lobster thermidor sitting a little heavily, Harold's trouser belt protested. Nevertheless, his eyes travelled hungrily from the red painted finger nails up the slender porcelain arm to the curves that beguiled him. Sensations which had recently come to life stirred within. He smoothed the creases in his trousers and welcomed the discrete lighting in their corner. 'I've booked a suite for the night – Mr and Mrs Chapman,' he whispered. He seemed to have persuaded Reenie that, though his marriage was a charade, discretion was still necessary. But he wished she hadn't bitten her lip when he'd mentioned the rooms.

'What did you say to Cynthia?' said Reenie as smoke curled from a cigarette holder poised in her other hand. He gazed at her. Whatever she did, Reenie was the essence of elegance.

'She thinks it's a big pow-wow over the new apartments. I'm stopping overnight after the late meeting.'

'But might she check up on you? There's nothing to prevent her phoning someone.' She swirled a cherry cocktail in her glass before taking her next sip.

The chink of ice on crystal generally had a soothing effect on him, especially after a fraught day at work.

'I've told you; she's not interested. Anyway, she's with her mother, who's far too ancient to have a new-fangled thing like a telephone. So, Mrs *Chapman,* here's to us, and the next twelve hours.' He raised his glass and drained the last drop of port.

'Darling, I can't think of anything else I'd prefer, but it's not possible tonight.'

'Come on. Just one night. Perfect opportunity.'

'I know. I thought it would be all right. But Mummy has a friend staying – she's asked me to pick her up tomorrow morning – early. She'll think it odd if I don't come home. That's why I rang you tonight.'

'Phone them. You can make something up.'

Reenie shook her head. 'Believe me, I would if I could.'

His heart sank. 'Well, the room is ours for the night. We might at least make use of it for the first couple of hours.' He peered at his watch. 'Ten o'clock. They won't worry if you creep back in the small hours, knowing you're in safe hands.'

'Well—'

'On the tab, young man,' he said, waving the bill at the approaching waiter and slipping him a generous tip. Harold basked in the pleasure he took from fellow diners watching enviously as the prettiest woman amongst them was escorted by him to the lift. He smiled. 'Let's just enjoy the precious little time we have together.' Reenie swayed into him with the rhythm of the music drifting across from a live band.

As he opened the door to *The Gainsborough Suite* she gasped. He could tell the gold drapes at the window were enough to snatch her breath away, gleaming in the light from the chandelier. He watched her drop, as if stunned, on to a similarly opulent satin bedspread, then she shook off her shoes and wriggled her stockinged feet in deep-piled carpet. Laughing like a school boy, Harold copied her. His fingers would soon be exploring … he'd chosen well for the love of his life. If only they had longer.

Stretching out, Reenie's dress rustled against the cover as she melted into the eiderdown.

Was this *really* happening?

He recalled his constant distraction through the day when the deal for the hotel had almost collapsed. *So out of practice and twice her age – am I up to it? Should have gone on that diet Cynthia referred to.* Satin rustled seductively as he stepped towards the door.

'What are you doing, Harold?'

'Turning the light off.'

A street lamp glimmered through the curtains: sufficient to find his way back to Reenie, but weak enough, he hoped, to hide his imperfections. Undoing his belt and top trouser button, he groaned with relief and longing. Ready to slip the silk hosiery down her equally sleek legs, Harold lowered himself beside her. Desire was as fresh and mouth-watering as the truffle trickling down his throat moments previously.

Reenie turned to spoon into his embrace. For one moment he wondered if she couldn't face him. Kissing the nape of her neck, his hands glided from her tiny waist. He felt closer to his goal, groping for her thighs with suspenders to release.

Reenie turned and grasped his hands. 'Lips,' she said as she manoeuvred to plant hers firmly on to his. His pulse quickened – when had he last tasted such lips, if ever? She paused to whisper, 'Lips and legs, darling,' and the stockings slithered off effortlessly. Now the dress. 'Help me, Harold. It's a bit tight.'

'How could I refuse?'

Reenie giggled as he fumbled and tugged at the fabric.

'Buttons first.' She guided his left hand to the dip at the top of her heart shaped dress. 'It's all right, I'll help – I know buttons are fiddly for you.' As if by magic, the dress opened. Brushing his palms over the petticoat, Harold slid them inside, then buried his head into her softness. *Delectable!* He soaked up the perfume, remembering how he'd chosen it for her on their first evening together. Its sweet scent mingled with the slight dampness of her flesh. Perspiration? Was she as excited as he was?

'Now for the next layer.' *I can manage this one,* he thought as he eased the first strap over her shoulder.

But Reenie struggled to raise herself, pulling the ribbon back into place. 'Not the whole way, Harold.'

'What d' you mean?'

'I mean this is as far as it goes. I can't bring myself ... When we're married. We can't take any risks.'

'I ... I thought you might have come prepared.'

'Oh, how would I manage that?' She wrapped her arms round him. Every exquisite contour pressed into him and he guessed his excitement was as obvious to her as their state of undress. 'We can still enjoy each other, like then last time, but, go no further,' she said as her lips stroked his cheek and briefly silenced him with another kiss.

'My God, you've turned my bones to water!' His hands smoothed over the lingerie once more. 'Let me! You're irresistible. I promise—'

'One day, Harold Hartley! But not now. Think of this as a taster – things to come. It'll be even better when we're married.'

Chapter 9

Cynthia Hartley had a feeling Pamela had called with an agenda that afternoon. She looked across her best marble-topped coffee table at her closest friend who stirred her tea studiously, teaspoon clinking the edge of bone-china.

'I don't think,' Pamela hesitated, 'I'm supposed to tell you this, but—'

'It's all right, I know what you're going to say. It's Harold, isn't it?' Cynthia sipped her tea.

'Well, yes. Oh, damn it, you know that secretary—'

'She's just another toy of the moment. They never last,' Cynthia huffed. 'Besides, his paunch must be a deterrent for anyone younger than him.'

'You're too good for him. If he was mine—'

Cynthia laughed. She was tired of his silly flirtations, especially at his age. 'I think we need something a little stronger than earl grey.' Taking the scotch from the drinks' cabinet, she poured them both a healthy measure. 'Cheers! He's not really interested in that former PA, darling.'

'No, he's not! He's moved on to his *new* secretary, Irene Meadows. Have you met her?'

'No, but I've heard about her. The younger the better – for Harold, I mean. It'll fizzle out. Once she starts getting pushy.'

'Well, I listened in to her the other day – in the coffee shop. Said she was going to the book signing from that local writer. At Joliffe's. Sometime after four on Thursday.' Pamela described Irene down to the painted nails. 'Why don't you

54

happen to be there at the same time? You could look out for her.'

'Hmm, I might just take you up on that idea!'

*

Cynthia's spectacles pinched her nose as she peered over the top of them in the book shop that Thursday afternoon. She pored over a Raymond Chandler. – a murder suited her mood.

'Guide to Wiltshire? Yes, Madam,' she vaguely heard an assistant affirm to a young girl. Wasn't Harold visiting somewhere in Wiltshire soon? Something about checking his new hotel there?

Back to the book: "Farewell, My Lovely".

'Made a film of that one. It's a good read,' said a gentleman nearby as she glanced across. "Murder, My Sweet," that's what the film was called.'

'Perhaps I *will* get it, then. I could do with taking a leaf out of this book,' Cynthia muttered. She rubbed her forehead wearily. *How much longer.* It was five o'clock and the writer had left. Clearly, the shop was quietening – enough to hear the assistant talking to his customer: 'So sorry you missed our author. Taking a pleasant spring break, I hope?'

'Planning to this weekend. This'll help,' said a young female voice.

Cynthia gazed towards the till and "Farewell my Lovely" dropped to the floor. She must be the mistress. Surely it's *her* – Irene Meadows! The hum in Cynthia's ears increased. So, the minx had come after all. *My God, how come I didn't recognise her?* She had to get closer. But the girl was already

55

tugging the door handle. Devoid of any plan, Cynthia rushed at the disappearing figure. 'Oh! I'm so sorry,' she said as they collided. Her spectacles clattered to the lino, while the suspect fell to her knees, the newly purchased book flying out of its bag.

Cynthia quickly replaced her glasses. 'So very sorry. Let me help you up.'

As she did so, something caught her eye: an exquisite gold pendant swung from the girl's neck.

'Don't worry,' the casualty said as she rubbed herself down. 'Accidents happen. Where did my book go?'

And where did that necklace come from? Secretaries didn't normally take home that much pay. 'There, I've popped it back for you,' said Cynthia. *My God, she is pretty and can't be more than mid-twenties.* 'Is it Wiltshire you're making for, my dear?'

'Yes. Fancy you noticing the title of my book!' she laughed and brushed her fingers through her auburn hair.

Suddenly conscious of her own unrelenting perm, Cynthia satisfied herself with the fact that she rarely forgot a face. She would find out about the Wiltshire trip.

*

As the chauffeur swept up the avenue to drop her home, Cynthia's head tingled like the lemon sherbet she once shared with her daughter, exploding in her mouth. Only this sherbet was starkly acidic – no sugar to sweeten the affront. Even her tongue tasted bitter. *It's not just a box of chocolates and a giggle at the office party. Gold and a shared bed at a furtive destination!*

'Thank you, Hobbs,' she said to the driver, slamming the car door vindictively. Harold wouldn't be back that night and anyway it would be useless plying him with questions. A pile of *Gazettes* filled her vision. That was it, the picture was there. As always, the maid had stacked them neatly in the pantry. Taking the hoard into the lounge, she first poured herself a dry wine and settled on the settee. She noted the date and turned the pages of the journals assiduously. *Damn! The one copy I need, it's always the one that's missing.* Then she poured a second glass, gazing at the photo on the cabinet of the family trio. Diana, their daughter aged ten, stood between her parents, snapped about twenty years ago in Monte-Carlo, outside the Hotel de Paris.

She had been quite elegant back then, no sagging chin, no need for the loose-fitting shirt or jacket. A figure-hugging bodice like the one that trollop was wearing was simply out of the question for her today. And certainly not the latest pencil-slim fashion! Harold, who used to be the life and soul of the party, had also been almost handsome all that time ago. She had to watch him even then. Her father never had been keen on their match: 'He's *Trade*,' he would say. *Should have listened to him.*

With one final gulp, Cynthia drained her second glass. The sherbet sting settled into a sludge of depression at the thought of the necklace and the slender neck it embraced. So young! Much the same age as Diana. If only her daughter hadn't moved to Edinburgh, so far away. She missed her.

Should she phone Pamela? No, it was all too demeaning.

She wasn't going to let a common tart defeat her. She returned to the photo. Though the casino wasn't in the frame, she remembered how successful Harold had been that summer; And it wasn't all due to good fortune – he could make a business tick. But Papa's money had helped. And *her* support. She twisted her wedding ring, contemplating on how little it meant to her now, other than maintaining her status.

But that slut's not getting it!

Coals of humiliation burnt in Cynthia's cheeks. With a final effort, she turned to *Village Gossip* in the last newspaper … and Irene Meadows stared up at her, still smiling. For a moment Cynthia froze, her eyes fastened on the image as if watching a scorpion at arm's length. Before she could move, the telephone rang again.

'Hello, darling, it's Pam.'

'Pamela – heaven sent! You're right. I've just seen her.'

'Seen who?'

'Irene Meadows. I'm sure they're going away together. This weekend.'

'What are you going to do?'

'Find out where they're staying. I'm going to follow them.'

'How the Dickens—?'

'I don't know, but I'm determined to ruin her reputation.'

'You'll certainly prove your case for a divorce, if that's what you want. Would you like me to come round?'

'So sweet of you. No, it's all right. I've got things to do. I'll ring back later.'

Cynthia seethed, reaching for the road atlas. There wouldn't be a divorce. Just what Irene Meadows wanted. Oh no, that was the last thing she'd let happen.

*

'So sorry, Madam. That would be breaking client confidentiality. We cannot disclose any names of our guests.'

Cynthia took the telephone from her ear, glowered at it and then continued. She'd been on that phone all evening. 'Well, could you leave a message for my husband, if this happens to be his hotel? So silly of me to mislay his address. It's for Mr Hartley. Could—'

'Oh, there's no reservation for Mr Hartley.'

'Are you sure?'

'Quite sure, madam.'

Cynthia sighed. 'Thank you.' Her gratitude was as clipped as the speed at which she slammed the receiver down. 'Damn every one of those smug hotels. He must be staying somewhere!' She wound the telephone cord round a finger. 'How stupid – I wouldn't put it beyond him to harp back to the past.' An image of a timbered, thatched hostelry greeting them on their honeymoon wavered before her.

'That's it. Last try.'

Realisation suddenly flooded her frazzled mind – a secret assignation with a trollop young enough to be his daughter? He'd have to change their names. How could she be so slow?

She poured herself a large scotch and slumped back on to the sofa. Two road maps sprawled across the coffee table, together with her jottings on the route to be taken. She *would* find a solution; her heart was set on greeting the happy couple as she joined them in the dining room. But how could she manage it?

A second persistent ring-tone took a few moments to register. She lifted the receiver.

'Thatcher's End Hotel speaking. Is a Mr Chapman available please?'

'I'm afraid you have the wrong number – wait! Did you say "Hotel – Thatcher's …?'

'End. That's right.'

Cynthia's pulse quickened. 'Might I ask what number you dialled?'

'Grays Thurrock 2895.'

That *is* my phone number. I'm afraid I didn't quite catch what you said.'

'A Mr Chapman left a note with his work's number but there appears to have been a mistake there as well. We spotted 2895 scribbled on the other side so thought it worth a try. I do apologise for wasting your time.'

'It's not a problem. In fact, I think I remember staying with you.' Cynthia drew a quick breath, 'Oh, a long time ago now. Is the wisteria still there?'

'It is, madam, though not quite at its best now.'

'Um … look, I know this is going to sound extraordinary, but you've brought back such lovely memories of my honeymoon. Is there … er … any chance of you booking me in for one night, say, tomorrow evening?'

'Let me see … yes, room 15, a single, overlooking the lake, Mrs …?'

'Hartley. Mrs Cynthia Hartley. Thank you so much. Oh, and reserve me a table for dinner, would you? That's excellent. I shall *so* look forward to my visit.' Perspiration pricked the nape of her neck. Her face flushed with anticipation.

*

Sleep didn't come easily to Cynthia that night. How fortuitous was that – the hotel mistake? She comforted herself with a whisky or two before going to bed. The next morning she checked her hair and make-up as she rose. 'The bastard! He *is* staying in our honeymoon hotel!' She smoothed her Jaeger skirt, which unfortunately clung to her contours, but was, nevertheless, quality, a little warm for this time of the year, but the evenings could be chilly. Particularly this one. She smiled as a picture of the two startled faces took shape in her imagination, then she ran downstairs. Coat, case, driving shoes, money; and camera. She shouldn't have tipped quite so much Cointreau into her coffee that morning, but it was needed. Her check list complete, she swept up the maps and her notes in the lounge, dropping them into her designer handbag. It snapped shut with a resonance reflecting her resolve.

No time to tell Pam. She had to allow for wrong turns and simply couldn't be late for supper. Cynthia revved the Rover into action. 'Come on, my beauty. Never mind about the rain, we're on an urgent mission today.' It didn't need telling twice.

Chapter 10

With Saturday's local paper fresh off the press and tucked under her arm, Lizzie panted as she hurried towards her parents' house. She could hardly wait for the telephone, her father's generous present to her, to be installed. She paused briefly to draw breath as a stitch clutched her side. *Please let Reenie be home – maybe she didn't go to Marlborough last night after all.* She reached to press the bell on *The Lodge's* gleaming front door.

'Lizzie, you're an angel. Can't tell you how pleased I am to see you.' Her father embraced her, sweeping her into the hall, where the newspaper fell to the floor. A bold, glaring headline stared at them: "Hartley Horror Crash". She stared back, as if her gaze could somehow eliminate it.

'All I know is what I've read this morning. When I first saw it, I thought it was Harold,' Lizzie said, avoiding mention of Reenie. How much her parents knew of her relationship with Harold was not for her to explore. She knew her father was on both friendly and business terms with Harold.

Her father wrinkled his brow. 'Reenie would be upset if she knew. She's away for the weekend – staying with a friend, I think. The awful thing is, I don't think Harold's aware of his wife's accident yet.'

'How do you—?'

'I phoned *Cedars* – spoke to the maid. She said Harold wasn't home. Something to do with overseeing his new hotel in Wiltshire. It's most unlike Harold, but he hasn't left an address or phone number. The police are trying to contact him.'

Lizzie hoped her voice sounded steadier than her nerves 'But Harold's bound to be at his latest venture today.'

'The police realise that. They'll be at his hotel now. What a terrible shock for him!'

Lizzie's mother, joined them. 'I understand there's little chance of survival. She must have hit the tree at something like fifty miles an hour. Whatever possessed her to drive like a demon when the roads were wet, *and* so far from home?'

'She was probably late meeting up with Harold,' Lizzie's father said. 'Heading for Wiltshire.'

Lizzie's heart missed a beat. So did Cynthia know about Reenie? 'I wonder which hospital they took her to?'

'It doesn't bear thinking about – two hours to get her out of the wreck!' Her mother shuddered.

Her father steered Lizzie towards the kitchen. 'Come on. There's still tea in the pot. There's nothing we can do except hope Cynthia pulls through. Harold will appreciate that we're here to help, if we can, when he gets back.'

'I can't stay too long, I'm afraid.'

Her mother fussed round the sink, stacking a few plates and saucers. The house could never be too tidy for her. Lizzie sipped her tea. Her cheeks flushed, but not with the heat from the tea – Harold's wife was fighting for her life and she was thinking …

'Irene will be concerned when she gets back,' her mother continued, 'working for Harold now.'

By now her father had pulled out his favourite pipe and picked up the News Chronicle. Lizzie wandered over to the open backdoor and gazed at a garden that was as orderly and immaculate as the interior of the house. Nothing else seemed orderly, though, at least, not in her sister's life. How would she get home? What if the press found out about their tryst? *Oh, Reenie, why have you got yourself into this mess?*

She could hear Reenie laughing. 'Stop being a goose. You know I can take care of myself.'

Chapter 11

Reenie turned to look at Harold, the Egyptian cotton pillowcase still crisp and cool to her cheek. It was six-thirty on Saturday morning in *Thatcher's End's* luxury suite. Despite the indulgence enveloping her, she knew there could be no luxurious lie-in – Harold was busy that day, but later they had the rest of the weekend together. She eyed her lover: still fast asleep, his mouth drooped open to allow a rumbling snore.

Fingering the pendant round her neck, Reenie found it impossible to sleep. Deliberately, she had reserved a room with twin beds and Harold had promised not to force himself on her. It was still possible to enjoy themselves without ... then she'd let him go the whole way. Not as planned.

Lizzie's question, "Do you *love* him?" refused to fade. She did *like* Harold. She had to admit that the urge to make love had been his, though she hadn't resisted. It wasn't what she'd imagined it to be. Momentarily, she recalled schoolgirl giggles over what it must feel like. Someone had said it was as exhilarating as leaping from a summit. Rushes of adrenalin? Unbidden, memories of Mawgan's passionate kisses pushed into her mind, his caresses under her blouse, the throb of stirrings sweeping down to the most private of places. No, she hadn't forgotten.

She pursed her lips. Maybe next time with Harold might be more exciting? Next time would definitely have to be when they were married.

Disappointed with herself for giving in, Reenie wriggled her silk nightie, another present from Harold, down below her knees. Silently, she lifted the covers and tiptoed to the bathroom. She ran the water in the bath until it almost reached the rim, then sank into exotic, scented bubbles. Had she similarly just sunk all her plans? *Lady Hartley* of Grays Thurrock fame, she'd pictured herself. One day. She popped the largest bubble with a painted toe.

'Reenie, let me in,' Harold called softly. Apart from the distant rattle of breakfast, the rest of the hotel slumbered on. The door handle creaked and Reenie was glad it was locked. Harold needed to need her, but not as a mistress, as his wife. Hadn't he told her over and over again that Cynthia meant nothing to him?

'I won't be long, darling.' She slid further below the foam. He can wait.

When she emerged, not too late, her sulk was well behind her. A sullen seductress was no seductress at all.

'Darling,' Harold murmured as they sat at their breakfast table, 'I've never had a night like it before! My God ...' Slowly, he shook his head.

Reenie twisted her false gold band around her wedding finger.

Pressing a bundle of crisp new notes into her hand, he continued. 'A little something for you, the love of my life.'

'Harold! You're not paying me for last night?'

'Of course not! You're far too precious. Choose a new dress for yourself. Not that you don't always look stunning, but I'll be out till early afternoon and you'll need a spot of lunch as well. Besides, had a lucky break on a horse last week.' He winked at her, as if to say his luck was in, definitely in more than simply horses. They arranged to meet again in the lounge at three-ish.

*

With two huge carrier bags, Reenie sauntered into the hotel foyer, her faith in sterling reassured. Three o'clock had arrived unbelievably quickly.

'Oh, Mrs Chapman, there's a message for you,' said the receptionist waving an envelope at her from his desk.

Reenie walked past.

'Mrs. Chapman!' the receptionist raised her voice. Reenie stopped dead.

'Oh so sorry, I … I was in a dream,' said Reenie. *She*, Reenie Meadows, was Mrs Chapman, wasn't she?

'Thank you so much,' Reenie said as she backtracked for the message. Imagining the missive would tell her Harold wouldn't be back for another two hours, she visualised trying out her new clothes and re-applying her make-up. She dropped the bags and opened the envelope, a five-pound note sliding out with blue vellum writing paper.

Darling,

So sorry to let you down – am at the local hospital. Cynthia in bad car crash – in intensive care. Please use enclosed to help you get home. Thank you a million times for such a special night.

All my love – always!

H x

Reenie glanced back at the impassive face of the receptionist. 'Has my … husband just left?'

'Oh no, Mr Chapman checked out some hours ago – earlier this morning, Madam.'

An uncontrollable flicker in her left eye sapped Reenie's

confidence and she hoped it wasn't obvious. 'There's been an unfortunate accident. I wonder if you could order me a taxi, please. I'll just put my things together.'

Intensive care. Local hospital? Had Cynthia been ... Life threatening. What if? Reenie's heart missed a beat. No, I shouldn't! That's dreadful. But she was only human. She couldn't help thinking the worst or was it the best?

She glanced at the huge gilded mirror as she entered their bedroom. 'That only happens in novels!' she whispered to her reflection.

Chapter 12

Lizzie slipped out in her lunch hour from *Cole Creations* to phone Reenie at work. They had not had a chance to chat properly for several weeks since the Wiltshire disaster, so she was eager to see her again. 'Reene?' she said once the money had clattered through the telephone box.

'Lizzie! Can I come round? I need to talk to you.'

'You know you can. That's why I was phoning.'

'Wonderful! Look, why don't I pick Graham up from school today? He won't have to stay on late then. I'll put the kettle on for when you get back.'

'Perfect. See you then.'

Lizzie didn't find Reenie's breezy tone convincing.

She continued to straighten the dresses on their hangers in the shop where she had worked part-time for the last year. Once Graham arrived, being a nurse had no longer been possible. At least this job was a pleasant distraction and it boosted their meagre income. She enjoyed meeting customers, helping them to make suitable choices, arranging the merchandise, even selecting some of the clothes from the warehouse now she had proved her worth. What joy it was to have such a selection since clothes rationing had come to an end! She picked out a blue outfit with tiny waist, full skirt and short sleeved jacket. As she smoothed her fingers over the glazed cotton, Reenie came to mind. *But Reenie wouldn't give it a second glance* – haute couture *only from now on!* Lizzie sighed. Still half an hour before closing time. Surely there wouldn't be many customers now.

To her surprise the doorbell jangled as two middle-aged women walked in, making straight for the knitwear.

Damn, now I'll have to fold it all up again.

'They say she's paralysed. Helpless,' the lady with the most rouge on her cheeks said to her friend.

'Poor thing. Money isn't everything.'

'What do you think of this colour?' she said, holding a soft fawn cardigan against the brightness of her face.'

'A bit pale. Did you hear her husband was messing around with someone else's wife?'

'Yes, but she's not married. Think she's his secre—'

'Can I help you?' asked Lizzie. Anything to halt the conversation. She blushed, as if she were the guilty party.

'It's a bit late, thank you. I'm not sure about choosing in such a hurry. But you've a nice variety,' said the friend.

'We can come back tomorrow morning, Janice.'

With her head buzzing, Lizzie watched them leave. *See – I told Reene people were gossiping!* It was obvious who they were talking about. The local paper had been full of Cynthia's injuries. The fact that she was still alive was a miracle.

'Have you secured the front door, dear?' asked Mrs *Cole*.

Lizzie slid the bolt across and then left by the side door. It was as if the gloomy nights of blackout, only five years previously, had descended upon her once more as she thought of her sister's tangled life. Her tired footsteps rang on the paving stones on her way home. Flowers shouted vibrancy in the early evening sunshine, neatly positioned in small suburban gardens, but they were no consolation to her. She passed into the street of terraced houses built straight on to the pavement, where only a few sagging window boxes stood for token gardens. She gazed at the potted geraniums by her own front door and turned the key in the lock. Laughter rang from the living room as she stepped inside. Graham was rolling on the rug, knees to his chest and giggling helplessly, while playing cards littered the floor. His Auntie Reenie sat on her heels next to him, head thrown back, her rich auburn hair rippling in sync with her mirth.

'Well fancy—'

'Mum,' yelled Graham. Lizzie scooped him up, burying her face into his hair. How similar it was to his aunt's. Even his eyes were the same blue-grey. 'Look, Auntie Reenie brought us some cakes!'

Reenie smiled at them both, nodding her head at a decorative box.

'Oh my word! I might just try one of those fancy gateaux.' Lizzie sank gratefully into an armchair, while Reenie passed the cakes round.

'I know what you're like, Dan Dare. Super Heroes still like their treats,' Reenie chuckled in Graham's direction.

'Guess what, Mum, we were playing "Cheat" and Auntie Reenie nearly beat me!'

Lizzie sank her teeth into the lightest of sponges, closing her eyes for a moment. After the years of deprivation, such luxuries were heaven sent. When Graham raced upstairs to find his latest model aeroplane, she turned to Reenie. 'Graham does love his aunt! We've missed you.'

'Sorry – I've been preoccupied. Tell you later.'

Lizzie sighed. She knew Reenie only too well.

*

'Right. Dishes soaking, Graham's in bed – spill the beans,' said Lizzie.

Reenie swallowed. 'Harold says it's over – we're finished.'

Bathed in relief, Lizzie hid her sentiments, 'Don't stop,' she murmured.

'I knew what he'd say as soon as I heard Cynthia was paralysed. It's obvious, isn't it?'

'Probably.'

'Can't be witnessed marrying the mistress when your wife's so tragically disabled. We drove for miles away from Grays last week. Then we walked in the woods. Just the two of us. He said how much he loved me; told me I'd changed his life.'

Reenie turned her mouth down at the corners. 'After that night in Marlborough, no, even before then, he was set on asking Cynthia for a divorce. Couldn't live without me. Now, I'm wiped clean off the slate. Oh, he thought we might have an occasional tryst – *very* occasional – but I said I wasn't prepared to be his mistress for the rest of my days.'

Rest of? Ten to twenty years at the most – Harold's sixty. But I suppose that is a lifetime when you're young, Lizzie thought.

'Elizabeth Simmonds, are you listening to me?'

'Most definitely! What did you say after that?'

'Nothing. I … just cried.' Reenie dabbed her fingers at the corner of her eyes. 'Not like me, is it. But once I start …' Her words wobbled; more tears trickled down her face. 'I've not said this to anyone else.' She fumbled for the handkerchief from her sleeve as she whispered, 'I even wish she'd died in the accident. How dreadful! Am I so wicked?'

'Shh! Don't say it. Look at Graham playing with you tonight – he doesn't think so. Neither do I.'

'Harold hugged and kissed me, even wept. I *know* Harold loves me. But Cynthia's in a wheelchair.'

Lizzie took Reenie's hands in hers. 'Do you love Harold as much as he loves you? Be honest with—'

'Of course I do!'

Muffled sounds from Graham of a low flying spitfire underscored the lull in their conversation. 'My son practising his World War Two special effects.' Lizzie ventured a chuckle.

Reenie managed to smile through her tears. 'I wanted to bawl at somebody, scream, slam doors, throw ... oh, I don't know – something at the wall! But I haven't been able to. That's the trouble with not having your own place.'

Lizzie gazed as sympathetically as possible. 'I'm probably going to say the wrong thing now, but—'

'I can guess.'

'Harold's not the only fish.'

'But he's the fish I want! You know I couldn't have Mawgan. Mummy saw to that. I've had boyfriends but they were just boys.' Then she added softly, 'And I've lost *Cedars*. I loved that house!'

'You're the prettiest girl in the district. You can have the pick—'

'Twenty-eight going on thirty. I've waited for Harold and now I'm on the shelf. Anyway, I've told you – I don't want "The Pick". I'll just have to plug away at my job.'

'At least it's a good job. Lots of girls your age would give their eye teeth to be a PA like you. And your room at home—'

'Don't mention that room!'

Lizzie realised she should have been more careful. She

scanned her living room: second-hand chairs, faded fabric, their arms burnished with years of family wear, linoleum chipped. She smiled when she remembered Reenie painting the melted hole in the lino after she'd dropped an illicit cigarette. Reenie had always been good with a paintbrush. Mother gave the stored flooring to her willingly when she and George bought their new house, a bald mat now covering the hole. Graham had pulled the cords on one side to form a runway for his aircraft. The latest in half-moon rugs covered the other melt by the fireplace.

Since drawing the curtains, at least the dingy street was hidden. Lizzie's eyes rested on the photograph on the mantelpiece: George proudly clasping Graham. Dear George. The war had interrupted his apprenticeship, but at least he'd survived and even kept his sense of humour after all he'd been through. Not particularly handsome by James Stewart standards, especially after a bullet grazed his cheek, but he would always be handsome to her. Kindness radiated from the picture.

'Riches don't necessarily bring happiness,' she whispered to Reenie.

'But they do help!'

Lizzie pushed her hair from her brow. She should have known better – preaching wasn't helpful. After all, she knew what it was like to yearn for the unattainable. Hadn't she always longed for a kinder mother?

Chapter 13

Lizzie hoped as Reenie left her that releasing the emotional straight jacket had helped. Now it was *her* turn to be in turmoil. Like the stirring of a murky pond, assertions and memories swirled to the surface.

It was a long time ago now.

Her mind reverted to her family. She knew her father cherished her. That had kept her going over the years, but then she dwelt on his absences from home, now more pronounced as time wore on, as with his consumption of alcohol. Did her mother's spite have something to do with it? In the stillness of her bedroom, Lizzie reconstructed a more pleasant recollection: an autumn evening in '39 when, despite the recent declaration of war, she had been happy. George told her she was amazing and he adored her. With her engagement ring newly on her finger that night, Lizzie had stretched out her hand to her parents, the stone glimmering under the hall light. Though the gold band was thin and the garnet small, it had taken months of saving for such a prize. Tangible evidence of her esteem in George's eyes and a happier future encircled her finger.

'Is this the office boy you mentioned?' said her mother.

'No, it's George Simmonds and he's apprenticed to a plumber. You know I've been going out with George for the last year,' she remembered saying.

'I hope you'll both be very happy together, my dear,' said her father, kissing her brow. 'Shouldn't we be opening something to celebrate?'

'Well, I think Elizabeth needs to be *absolutely* certain of her choice.'

'I *am* certain!'

Her mother folded her arms. 'What are his prospects – digging holes in the road?'

'He's hoping to run his own business – one day. But I have a …' Lizzie swallowed, 'a feeling the war might get in the way. He's talking about enlisting and I don't want him fighting battles without knowing I'm waiting for him. Anyway, you can hear more about it when you come for tea with his mother and sister. They've invited you next Saturday, a "Meet the family day". I need to tell them you can come.'

Her mother wrinkled her nose. 'Barton Terrace!'

'We can manage that. Tell Mrs Simmonds we'll be there,' said her father.

Lizzie smiled at him as she slipped away.

'You're marrying beneath you,' her mother hissed as Lizzie's feet met the stairs. 'And you're not quite twenty-one. You still need our permission.'

Lizzie recalled her dread, as when Saturday arrived, she'd been faced with the prospect of her parents scrutinizing her fiancé's widowed mother and Lucy, his sixteen-year-old sister.

'Lizzie, I'm not marrying your mother,' George had laughed the day before. 'Stop worrying. We'll cope.'

If only her family had been as easy going as George's.

'All aboard,' said her father as they piled into the Humber that afternoon. 'Don't forget it's a *Super Snipe*,' he liked to say. It turned out to be the only car parked in Barton Terrace, let alone one of such superiority.

The gate creaked as Lizzie led the family on to a patterned, tiled path to the Simmonds' front door. The tiles had been scrubbed and the red ones in the little porch gleamed like the gemstone on her finger.

'Come in, come in. It's lovely to see you all,' said Mrs Simmonds, whose hair had been set for this special event, crimped into linear waves and tied into a loose bun in the nape of her neck. Her blue-green eyes mirrored her son's, radiating kindness.

'Do follow me,' said Lizzie's future mother-in-law.

She ushered them into the parlour. Being preserved for special occasions, the small room had a slight smell of moth balls and years of polish. A looking glass, suspended on a chain over a tiled fireplace, confirmed Lizzie's anxiety. Each member of her family lowered themselves simultaneously into the armchairs, smiling at their host, while a gallery of youthful Simmonds beamed down on them from the opposite wall.

Lizzie's mother stared blankly ahead, a hanky dabbing her nose as if it might eliminate an unfavourable odour. With just enough space for the Meadows and the Simmonds, Lucy trundled in a tea trolley, offering sandwiches and homemade cakes. 'Is the kettle on, my lovely?' George's mother said to Lucy who sped out.

Keep smiling.

George reciprocated. 'We've been looking forward to this. I probably should have gone on bended knee and asked you first for Lizzie's hand, Mr Meadows, but I saw the ring and I … I can't *not* marry Lizzie! She's worth more than a thousand rings!'

With some embarrassment, Lizzie had blushed and attempted to relax into the cushions. The antimacassar slid round her shoulders and Reenie fidgeted, while her father chuckled and agreed with George's sentiments. Her mother's lips pinched at the corners.

Rattling crockery heralded refreshment ready to nurture the fragile bond between the two families. Lucy blinked nervously, placing the tray on the sideboard.

'Can't tell you how pleased we are to 'ave Lizzie as one of us,' said Mrs Simmonds. 'We weren't surprised by their announcement.'

'We'd be delighted if you could tell us more about your work, George,' said Lizzie's mother, sipping her tea. Her little finger, in perfect etiquette, extended beyond the porcelain.

'Mrs Simmonds—'

'Oh, please – call me Edith. Can I top you up? I'd 'ate your tea ter get cold.'

Lizzie nibbled her sandwich with caution.

'My favourite, Mrs ... er ... Edith,' said her father as he reached for egg and cucumber.

Undeterred, Lizzie's mother continued, 'So, you were about to tell us ... argh!' She screamed, leaping to her feet.

'Mummy!' yelled Reenie.

Lizzie stared in horror at her mother. Between her fingers she held a small bone-china handle, while the cup itself lay in pieces on the floor. Tea stains spattered her pale cream suit. Lizzie could see the infamous temper steamed as much as the ruined skirt. Even worse, was a sharp cut on the back of her left hand.

''ow terrible! I'm so sorry. Lucy, quick – pass that tea-towel.' In the commotion of mopping the outfit and gathering the debris, George and Edith apologised profusely. A plaster soon covered the wound.

Eventually, the visit drew to a close. After even more

apologies from Edith, the Meadows climbed into the car. With the choke pulled out, the engine sprang to life. Lizzie gazed at George who was blowing a kiss of concern in her direction.

Reenie whispered, 'Sorry, Lizzie. Knew Mummy would be like that.'

'The poor woman wanted to serve up her Royal Doulton for us. You happened to be the unlucky one who got the repair job,' said her father glancing sideways at his wife.

'Glued! The handle *glued* to the cup,' Lizzie's mother rasped. She swivelled round, 'I told you, Elizabeth – you're marrying beneath you.'

Lizzie had stared out of the window. She knew George would never be accepted by the Meadows family now.

*

Jolting Lizzie back to present time, the clock in the hall whirred and struck the hour.

'Lizzie, where are you?' George called from the hall.

'In the bedroom, my love. Coming down.' With George's arms soon round her, Lizzie's recollections faded.

'Had a good evening?'

'W-ell, sorting things out with Reenie. Unlike me, she can't seem to find Mr Right.' She kissed him and drew him into the lounge, where they nestled into the sagging settee. She turned to kiss him again, this time as if he'd been absent for at least a month.

'Phew! I might just take up more evening classes,' he laughed. 'Coming up for air.' Then he planted his lips firmly on to hers once more.

Worth more than a thousand rings! Her fingertips smoothed George's wedding band. Well that goes for you, too, George Simmonds.

If only Reenie could make as good a choice as she had.

Chapter 14

'Another day's work,' Lizzie said to herself as she stepped into *Cole's Creations*.

'There you are, my dear. Before the customers roll in, I was hoping you'd change the window display. We've some stunning dresses arrived only yesterday and some new handbags. You've got quite a talent for dressing up the double bay.'

Lizzie smiled. It made a change from the more hum-drum aspects of her job.

'And Gillian could do with watching you,' continued Mrs Cole. 'You could teach her a thing or two at the same time.'

Gillian! Cole's new assistant was such a chatterbox. Normally, it wasn't too much of a problem, but arranging the merchandise at its best needed Lizzie's full concentration. Besides, her head was buzzing with the prospect of promotion for George. *Hartley Homes* was possibly offering a crucial contract to George's firm, which in turn would boost his work experience. *And* his employment security. But an undercurrent of concern still tugged at her mind. Were they all becoming embroiled in the Hartley connection?

'If you take down what's already there, I'll start selecting the clothes,' Lizzie said to Gillian.

With dresses, cardigans and a clutch of bags over her arms, Lizzie set to work.

'Shall I put the manikin back where it was? said Gillian.'

'Yes please.'

'Mrs Cole is lovely, in't she?'

Here she goes! 'She is. Can you pass me the cream bag?'

'Never thought I'd get this job. Lost me last one – two months ago!'

'Oh dear.'

'Weren't my fault. Bitch of a boss. Do you want the black 'andbag, too?'

'Please.'

'What a cow! Such a snob, too. Told me m'bloody language was too rich. "Oh, Mrs Baker I really can't abide your manner of speech. One of my guests 'appened to overhear you in the kitchen yesterday," she says to me, so 'oity-toity. Shouldn' have been bloody listenin'."

'Well—'

Gillian laughed. 'Don't worry, I know when to 'old me tongue – just lettin' it all out now. 'onest to God, I never swore in front of her. Shall I pass you the pink dress?' Lizzie nodded, her mouth full of pins. 'So, there I was – dismissed. Two kids to feed, 'usband buried in Dunkirk, an' no work.'

Lizzie pulled out the pins. 'How terrible!'

'Told you she was a snob – wanted a French maid instead. Used *my* French ter get rid of me. Cross-channel staff much more *lah-di-dah* than an Eastender like meself. Heard she got some French bird in the next day. But—'

'Pass me the scarf, Gillian.'

'*But* ... I could get me own back now.'

'Own—'

'Yup. She might have been listenin' to *me* in the kitchen, but I listened into *her* in that super-posh lounge.'

Lizzie glanced at Gillian's face. Mischief covered it as boldly as the price tag in her hand.

'Thought what she had to say was only for 'er equally jumped-up friend payin' a visit. "Huh, that philanderin' 'usband of mine," she says, "he's still got no idea about Dee-dee."

"That's probably just as well, d-ar-ling," says the other one. "You don't want 'im to know he's not the father." Hells' bells – I nearly passed out! Dee-dee's their daugh'er. What d'you think of that?'

'I imagine you'd—'

'Then she went on, laughin' "Thank the Lord she was small. If she'd been one of those big and bonny babies I could never have feigned the premature infant." *Infant*, my foot. Told you she couldn't speak proper. Who calls a new-born babe an "infant"?'

Lizzie drew breath. 'Well—'

Gillian cut Lizzie short, '"How tall is she?" asked her friend.'

"Too tall, but then *my* father used to be a string bean, so *he* still hasn't twigged. Should have listened to Daddy. He never wanted this *ghastly* marriage. But what was I to do? Damned bad luck! Darling, you do realise you are the *only* person who knows this."

'"Not now," I says to meself. "Gillian Baker knows too. Knowledge is Power."'

'The flowers by the till, they would be perfect next to the shoes,' said Lizzie. 'Phew, quite a story.' Some interest needed to be shown, she supposed. Perhaps it might bring closure to the conversation. Her head was beginning to buzz.

''Course you know who I'm talking about?'

'No idea.'

Mrs Cole reappeared, smiling as she gazed at the window. 'I'm just going outside to appreciate your handiwork properly.'

'We'll come with you,' said Lizzie, who then had to admit to herself that she, too, was pleased with the results so far, despite Gillian's revelations.

Mrs Cole turned to Gillian. 'Well, I do hope you're learning a bit more from Lizzie,' and returned to the shop.

Instantly, Gillian added, 'But you, Lizzie, 'aven't learnt who she was.'

'She?'

'My old boss – Queen Bitch. They're stacked out – richest in Grays– he owns 'alf the bloody town – at least, 'e built it.'

Lizzie's stomach lurched. Surely, she wasn't talking about Harold and Cynthia? The doorbell jangled and three customers walked in.

'The pink dress in the window – I love it,' said a young, blond girl. 'Is it my size?'

'No, but I think we have more in stock if you'd like to try one on.' Lizzie raised her cool fingertips to her cheeks in an effort to reduce her temperature. 'I'll just go and see.'

*

'I still 'aven't told you who the Bitch of Grays is,' Gillian said to Lizzie as they tidied the last pile of blouses at the end of a successful day.

Lizzie flushed with irritation. 'Might you need to be a little careful over telling too many people?'

'Hell's bells, not after what she did to me! 'Spec you've guessed anyway.'

'Well, if she's as rich and famous as you suggest, I'd be extra cautious. People like that usually have influence. You don't want to find yourself looking for work again.'

'Blimey – never thought of that. Do you think she really could?'

'I don't know, but if she *is* the Witch of Thurrock—'

'Nah, not "Witch". I said "Bitch". Same difference though. I was thinkin' I … might be able to benefit – you know – financially from my little "gem".' Gillian winked.

'Are you suggesting … blackmail? If you are, have you thought through all the implications – like your two children managing on their own while their mother's behind bars?'

'Five-thirty, girls,' Mrs Cole called out. 'I'm staying on – taking me a bit longer to tot up the takings, but I'm not complaining. Can you leave by the back way? Oh, and well done, Gillian. You're shaping up nicely now.'

'Glad somebody appreciates me,' Gillian muttered to Lizzie as the door swung behind them. 'It's so temptin', though. But you're probably right. Hey – you've guessed it's Mrs Bloody 'artley – you know – *Hartley Homes* an' all that. Well, ain't you going to say something?'

Lizzie cleared her throat. 'You had heard that Cyn – Mrs Hartley was seriously injured recently in a road accident?'

'Yeh, she got her come-uppance after all.'

'I don't think you can push that on to her, not when someone's so badly hurt. It's best if you just keep your tale to yourself. You've told *me* today, so maybe that should be enough.'

Gillian grimaced. 'Trouble with you is that you're too nice. But you're probably right. Too bloody right.' She sighed, deeper than the hubbub of traffic wending its way home. 'And now I've even got to watch me language – can't 'ave the kids pickin' up anything bad!' she exclaimed. 'Oh, there's me bus – cheerio.'

Now it was Lizzie's turn to breathe out. She was going to meet Reenie tomorrow. They were both taking Graham to the zoo. She might have to practice an innocent face beforehand, Lizzie mused. She could just imagine Reenie peering into her eyes. 'You're hiding something. You're as transparent as mother's lounge window and that's after she's polished it fifty times!'

Shall I tell her?

Better not. Could be dynamite.

It sounded like the picture Reenie painted of Cynthia wasn't so far from the truth after all. But best to leave gossip alone.

Best, yes, but would she manage it?

Chapter 15

'Quite a project that one, but I never doubted it,' replied Harold, attempting to concentrate in his office. He stubbed out his second cigar of the morning. *I doubt everything else in my life. Four months now since Cynthia's bloody accident. Feels like four years.* The cigars were usually saved for the pending executives' lunch. A final coil of nicotine fogged his vision as if symbolising the confusion in his head. Even the dismal November weather didn't help. He drummed his fingers on his blotter in front of him. Normally steeped in confidence, Harold's uncertainty was a new experience.

'The opening of *Hinton Heights* exceeded my expectations,' said Roger, Harold's business colleague. He hesitated. 'Look, I'm so sorry about Cynthia. If there's anything I can do? Are you up to chairing the meeting today?'

'Such faith in my abilities, Roger!'

'I didn't mean—'

'Course you didn't. No, I'll be fine. Got to keep my finger on the pulse – especially when it's mine! Might have a dash of whisky and soda before it all starts, though. Pour us one, and one for yourself, of course.'

'Just for you, thanks Harold.'

Smoking more, drinking more, snapping at friends, who are noticing my befuddled brain. And they think it's all because of Cynthia! Well, it is really, except it's Reenie I can't forget. Little do they know – well, hope they don't. Tried my damnedest to keep it secret. Harold tipped the whisky down.

'I'll be back with the statistics you need in a jiffy,' said Roger, closing the door behind him.

Now alone, Harold considered how he'd changed over the years – an epoch of building up, quite literally, his empire, including the latest hotel. He found it hard to believe he'd once been so vigorous, even athletic, but it was true, he had been strong in mind and body, determined to overcome his disability after the saw had struck and make the most of his life.

Briefly, his companions from the mill stole into his mind's eye, most of them covered in blood-soaked soil at Ypres – Wipers, they called it – and finally, Paschendale. Few returned to Grays. Losing three fingers was nothing in comparison to their loss. In fact, it saved his life and then gave him the opportunity to develop the Hartley venture. He smiled again, recalling his trip to Newmarket and his mother's face when he told her how much money he'd placed on *Golden Girl*.

Harold!' she'd gasped. 'Your damages!'

He gave her a convincingly rueful face.

'I can't believe you. Thought you had more sense.'

'Uncle Soames—'

'You haven't listened to him! You could bang the heads of our chickens together and get more sense out of them than your Uncle.'

'Uncle Soames placed my tip on an outsider!'

'Oh no!'

'Yep. And she won!'

He lifted his mother and twirled her round the parlour in a victory caper.

'Harold Hartley, put me down now and listen to a word of advice.'

Keeping a sober face, he obeyed.

'Luck might have been on your side *this* time, Harold, but think of the consequences if you'd lost. It doesn't bear thinking about.'

'I was winding you up. It wasn't *all* my money – just a bit, but it'll help. I can buy extra tools now.'

'Promise me you won't become a gambler – that's the road to ruin.'

He promised.

But he'd always liked a little flutter, every so often. Seeking reliable sources of information, with a pinch of caution, never vast sums, he frequently left the races, or the casino, with a wallet far plumper than when he'd set out. Generally, he funnelled it into the business.

He pondered over his pastime. Then returned to the present – in the office, then back to Reenie. Was he gambling with different stakes when it came to her? An affair? A Divorce? He'd had enough nous with the horses to avoid the destination his mother referred to. Was he risking the coveted OBE waiting on the threshold?

Cynthia's father, Colonel Peter Smythe-Fisher, elbowed into his reminiscences. He was such a snob and Cynthia his only child. It was quite a party when Harold and Cynthia met, followed by a jaunt into the countryside – Harold's first car, first fumble. First mistake. God, was her father mad when she told him she was pregnant! Harold could still imagine him roaring at the ranks. All Peter's guns certainly blazed at him. Apart from precipitating a hasty marriage, Harold recognised that in Peter's eyes he had fallen short of the husband expected for a Smythe-Fisher. In his metaphorical apartment block he, Harold Hartley, was definitely in the basement, while Cynthia occupied the penthouse.

At their wedding Cynthia appeared deceptively docile in comparison, and not particularly plump – no mention of shotguns. The only indemnity then was the dowry her father gave them. Another boost to *Hartley Homes,* oh, and of course, Diana who arrived a little prematurely.

Cynthia and Harold Hartley. They had held their marriage together in parallel grooves, Diana, like so many daughters, being the bridge between them. He never had been that close to Diana. She was her mother's daughter, more often than not on the maternal side of the chasm. And now the mother of their grandson. He couldn't imagine what Diana would think of him if he ditched Mama.

Somehow Reenie still managed to manoeuvre herself into his reflections, looping her arm through his, drawing him in.

'Here they are, Harold.' Roger burst through the door, bounding up to his desk.

'For God's sake knock before you open that bloody door!'

Roger stared at him, open mouthed. Then slammed the paper work down and left.

*

With the board meeting over, despite it being a Thursday, Harold made his way to the club. Friday was normally his day, but he couldn't wait that long this week. He made for the corner furthest from activity, and furthest from the general purpose of the fraternity, nursing a double malt whisky. His mind slid back to an image of his wife in the wheelchair, her head lolling to one side with the effort of having existed for another day. But her eyes still flashed at him. Her tongue, the one fully functioning part of her now wasted body, bit as sharply as the new cutter in the workshop.

How could he forget the day she came home from hospital? 'You and the Trollop. If it weren't for her … I hope you're satisfied with the result,' she spat as the nurse left them together.

If it weren't for the alcohol and your driving … He held his tongue. Another new experience, yet short-lived. 'I've told you—'

'No, I'll tell *you*. Try any more of your philandering, just once more and the world will hear what the two of you did to me!'

He ground his teeth and tucked the blanket into the sides of the chair sharper than necessary as the nurse returned with Cynthia's drink: an orange juice with a straw. The irony mocked. Slipping away to his study, he'd needed something stronger than orange juice.

At least others managed the situation – a maid through the day, nurse calling am and pm. He didn't have to suffer Cynthia's ill humour too often, nor respond to that blasted bell she kept ringing. He sighed. It wasn't possible to visit his most popular haunts too frequently, otherwise the impression of an attentive husband might dissipate. But some means of distraction was needed if he couldn't have the love of his life. Tonight, he was too exhausted to do anything other than sip whisky and reminisce.

For the umpteenth time he halted his rewind at the point where he told Reenie their liaison had to finish. He had picked her up in the Talbot, the Rover being in several pieces in a Wiltshire scrap yard. Reenie, so elegant in her full skirt and heart-shaped top, waited near the park, well outside Grays. She had poise – petite, head held high, shapely legs balanced with self-assurance on high heels. So desirable! And *so* vulnerable. The sunlight danced off the pendant he'd given her.

As she climbed into the car, her apprehension was palpable. She clutched her hands in those neat white gloves as if the car was about to meet a tree like Cynthia's. The strange thing was that when their flirtation just boosted his ego, he hadn't predicted Reenie working her way so securely into the centre of his being.

Younger than Diana. You thought Reenie would be a mere distraction. Just a dabbling. Then, when all seemed hopeless without Reenie, you reckoned the love-of-your-life could be persuaded to – go on, admit it – be your mistress.

Someone had told him she was feisty, but he had underestimated her.

But after that night at Thatcher's End ... my God, I can still feel us locked together. And then my stupid wife – I never meant anything to her – has to ruin everything!

'We could take a holiday, say twice a year, somewhere remote,' he remembered saying to Reenie, though he guessed she wouldn't find the bait tempting. With his hand clasping hers, they had walked through the wood, tears coursing down her face. He pictured Reenie as his wife, her arm resting on his as he showed her off to his colleagues.

Recalling how out of control he had felt, Harold experienced the same sensation washing over him again. Alien. Unsettling. *Hell's teeth, I can't stop thinking about you, Reenie Meadows. I've never been like this before.*

He reconstructed their Marlborough tryst, smelling

Reenie's hair, the heady perfume, and feeling the softness of her cheek. If only he could hold this memory for all time, so that, somehow, she remained with him: her laughter, arms embracing him, loosening his tie, teasing …

'Harold! Good to see you. Can I get you another drink, old boy?' Brian, an old Masonic friend from the club, cut into his nostalgia, just as Roger had done at work, and now Brian was joining him in the corner.

Irritation prickled. Harold swallowed. 'Better not – got to get home vertical tonight.'

'Oh, there's always a taxi. Got to have some freedom.'

'Don't wish to be rude, but I think I'm going to call one now. Past my bedtime you know.'

With a smile and a nod, Harold lifted his overcoat and extricated himself. He wasn't in the mood for conversation. He wasn't in the mood for facing Cynthia either, but at least he wouldn't have to – she'd be asleep in her ground floor bedroom.

As the taxi took him home, Harold mapped out the next day. He would steal out early, avoiding any contact with Cynthia. Her day always started late, by the time the maid managed to clothe her in the outfit she wanted and then given her breakfast. He pondered again over the deal calculated to take place tomorrow. Life was still hectic. What a contrast to Cynthia's. He almost sympathised with her until he recollected her recent threat: wheelchair or not, Cynthia could still strike. For a fleeting moment he pictured himself skewered to a bull's eye by a victorious wife. Would she?

Chapter 16

Cynthia bristled as she thought of Harold ignoring her each morning before leaving for the office. Though she could move her fingers on her right hand with some difficulty, her hearing and vision were fully operational.

Tomorrow would be Saturday. All the days blurred into one unidentifiable fog, but Pam had sorted her when she phoned. Maybe the weekend would be a little different?

'I 'elp you,' said Adele, her French maid, brushing at the crumbs on her cardigan. Cynthia huffed loudly. She'd eaten as much lunch as she could manage and now she had someone fussing round her.

'My pillow doesn't require plumping every five seconds,' she snarled. 'I'll ring when I need you.' Her head jerked, indicating that Adele should leave instantly. Despite the paralysis, Cynthia's feet still burnt as if walking over hot coals. *God in heaven, why is everyone so exasperating. Why don't they understand I just want to be left alone?*

Finding that she could let her mind drift into a semi-awareness of her surroundings, in fact of her very existence, released her from crushing reality. A twilight zone. She was working on a technique reminiscent of a childhood foible when she let sounds, images and colours meld together like a Turner sunset. She listened to the clock ticking, becoming louder, more insistent by the minute. That had to fade, together with the birdsong wafting from the window.

Plates clattered in the distance, jarring her concentration.

With her eyes half closed, she breathed in as deeply as her rib cage permitted and then let her breath out slowly. The outline of the three-piece seating misted, merging with the fading stripes on the wallpaper, now tilting, head buzzing. A gentle surge of warmth cocooned her, took her away, relaxing, floating ... away ... away ...

Snap out of it! You said you'd work out what to do with The Trollope!

Returning to reality, the pain of consciousness washed over her yet again. *She brought me to this. I'm not letting her get away with it. Think, Cynthia Hartley, think.* She closed her eyes but this time remained alert. She should ring her bell.

Adele was beside her in an instant, wiping her hands on a tea towel. ''ow can I 'elp, ma'am?'

'Take me to the telephone.'

Adele wheeled her to the far side of the lounge.

'Would you like me to, erm, make the numbers like yesterday for you, ma'am?'

'I certainly would. Just a moment.' Cynthia dug into the side of her wheelchair, hands like feeble claws but still capable of taking out a small slip of paper from Pam. 'Here it is – the number I need.' 'There's something you must do for me – when you've dialled my friend and passed me the phone, I want you to go straight to the kitchen. Take my bell with you and ring it, so I can tell when you're there. Then, I want to hear you tidying the pans.'

'I think they are tidy, ma'am.'

'Make sure you tidy them again, then! I'll be listening out for you.'

'Yes, ma'am. Shall I ... return with the bell—'

'In fifteen minutes. No – I'll call when I'm ready. Listen out for me. I do *not* wish to be disturbed until then. Do – you – hear – me?' *Only* one *other person will do that – on the end of this line. And by the time I've finished with her —*

'Yes ma'am. The telephone – it rings.'

'Leave me. Now!'

'Oh, the bell – I 'ave it.'

As the door swung behind Adele, Cynthia listened to the dring-dring of the phone. Come on, pick it up can't you? What's the matter with you? It's your friend Mrs Hartley calling.

Click! 'Hello. Grays Thurrock 2540,' said a young female voice.

'Good afternoon. Might I be speaking to Irene Meadows?'

'That's right. To whom have I the pleasure?'

Ting–a–ling-ling. Ah, that's better. Adele is in the kitchen now.

'The pleasure's all mine, my dear.'

Chapter 17

'Harold, what are you doing calling me – *and* at home?' Reenie hissed into the receiver.

'Your voice – have you been crying?'

'No!' A rebellious tear trickled on to her hand and down her sleeve. 'But I've had enough of Hartleys phoning me for one day. Have you forgotten that I'm no longer your secretary?'

'What do you mean, "Hartleys"?'

'You promised not to—'

'I know, but something—'

'Hellowee!' Reenie's mother breezed in, turning to shake the drips off her umbrella. How was it that her mother could always arrive at the worst possible moment?

'Got to go,' Reenie whispered.

'Stop. Ring me back – soon. It's urgent.'

'Visiting Lizzie tonight, Harold, so maybe—?'

'Please! Just for me. It's something you need to know.'

'Bye,' she said as brightly as possible.

'Phew, what a day I've had! Who was that?' said her mother. 'You look terrible. Have you been a bit teary?'

'No, I have *not*! But I'm having a rest before going to Lizzie's tonight.'

'Darling, do you think that's wise – you don't look at all well. I'd no idea you were going there this evening.'

'I'll be fine after a snooze. I need to be well for that interview next week.'

Her mother snorted her exasperation yet again over Reenie's resignation from *Hartley Homes*.

Reenie chose to ignore her. 'Don't include me for supper – couldn't eat a thing tonight.' She trailed upstairs, secretly stemming the tears.

*

A sense of relief caught hold of Reenie as Lizzie pulled her inside, hugging her tightly.

'Auntie Reenie!' yelled Graham who burst into the front room and leapt into her arms.

'Graham – you're supposed to be getting ready for bed. It's gone seven o'clock,' said George, coming up behind them. 'Hello, Reene. Good to see you – just in time to read Graham a bedtime story!'

'Oh, I'm ...'

'It's your turn tonight,' Lizzie said to George, with her all-knowing look.

'Oh pl-ea-se, can't Auntie Reenie come up? Pl-ea-se!'

'I ... I think I must talk to Mummy first, if she doesn't mind,' said Reenie.

Despite the protests, George steered Graham towards his bedroom.

Hoping that the next chapter in *Peter Pan* would be especially long, Reenie followed Lizzie into the kitchen.

Lizzie wrinkled her brow. 'Out with it, then, Reene.'

'Hartley phone calls – Cynthia first, then Harold.'

'Have you gone back on your decision – no further contact with Harold?'

Reenie squeezed her fingers together. 'Not me, it's Harold. *He's* doing the contacting.'

'You're as white as Mother's laundry, and that's saying something!' Sweeping the debris from supper to one side, Lizzie pulled out a chair at the table. 'Wait a moment, I'm putting the kettle on – Cornish tea, that'll perk us up. You have eaten, haven't you?'

Reenie shook her head. 'Harold wants me to phone him. Tonight.'

'You don't have to—'

'It's not Harold I mind so much. It's Cynthia!'

Lizzie breathed in sharply. 'How did she have your number? Oh, I guess she ... what did she say? You're shaking! Just a minute – kettle's boiling over.' She turned off the gas.

'It was awful. But I stood up for myself. I probably shouldn't have said this, but ... you know, I think I'd better get it over with – phone Harold, I mean. He said it was urgent.'

She stalked into Lizzie's tiny hall, took a deep breath and dialled *Cedars*. Something about Harold's voice sounded different as he answered her call.

'Harold, it's me, Reenie. Whatever it is, you'd better say it now and then make an end of it.'

'It's Cynthia.'

'She's told you then. '

'Told me?'

'The abuse she hurled at me today.'

'What? I don't understand. When—?'

'After lunch. How did she—?'

'But that's when Cynthia ... she's dead, Reenie!'

'Dead! What d'you mean? She can't be – I was talking to her. This afternoon.'

'Well, she must have died straight afterwards. The doctor thinks it was a heart attack. Not sure what caused it.'

Silence filled the room. The stove crackled. The clock ticked.

'Reenie? Are you there? *What* did you say to Cynthia?'

'I … I can't really—'

'Does anyone *know* you were on the line to her?'

'I … I don't think so.'

'Might be best to keep quiet, then. She had a bell to ring when she needed something but for some reason, she'd *insisted* Adele took it away with her. Otherwise she could have been there in time to help. Doctor said she'd been dead for at least half an hour before she was found.'

'Oh no! Oh Harold, that's terrible!'

'Look, I've snatched a minute to myself in the study. Diana is on her way with her husband and Alastair, my grandson. The police have been here.'

'Police!'

'Apparently they always call with a sudden death. Adele's upstairs in tears, blaming herself for following Cynthia's instructions. I wanted you to know before you heard from anyone else.'

'I'm so sorry. I don't—'

'Just a moment.'

An unfamiliar, muffled voice in the background interrupted. 'Can we speak? Oh, beg your pardon.' Someone had entered his study.

'I must go. Will contact you again, Mrs … Mrs Chapman.'

Reenie dropped the phone on the table and slumped on to the stool beside it. Lizzie came out and replaced the buzzing telephone.

'Oh my God, oh my God, what have I done?' At that moment, George came downstairs.

'Blimey – looks like you've both bumped into the Tilbury Bogey Man. Are you up to reading the last page with Graham, Reene?'

'I don't know if I ... can.'

Lizzie glanced at George. 'She's not up to it. Pop back up to Graham, my love.'

Oh my God – a heart attack! Have I just killed Harold's wife?

Reenie's head buzzed as much as the phone had a minute or two ago.

Chapter 18

It was a dank morning, typically December at its worst; so drab that Reenie wondered for a moment if time had reversed – had she stepped straight into late afternoon as her heels tapped over the pavement? Cars passed by with headlights peering through the gloom. The moisture in the air, laden with an odour of soap factory, settled on her face, chilling her like the few stark leaves struggling to cling to mutilated plane trees.

Reenie shuddered. 'Won't be long before I leave all this behind,' she thought as she turned into the cafe. *Kelly's* wasn't her idea of the perfect restaurant, not now, but it suited Lizzie and, more importantly, it gave them time together to finalise her plans. She knew Lizzie would find it difficult to approve, but her help was vital.

The bell jangled. Reenie winced at the discordant sound and her surroundings. She spotted Lizzie at the far end of the room. A plate of buttered scones sat heavily on the chipped Formica top and a utility teapot was on its way. Reenie took off her damp coat and sat down. 'Thanks for coming.' She smiled at Lizzie across the refreshments.

'Tuck in. I'll pour the tea,' said Lizzie. Tempting scones beckoned, but Reenie picked up a half piece – she couldn't afford to relax the rules for keeping her sculpted waistline.

'Have you come to a decision?' asked Lizzie.

'You do like to cut to the chase!' Reenie hesitated. How would Lizzie react, especially so soon after Cynthia's death? 'I've decided – Harold has proposed and I've accepted.'

'Oh … I guessed you were going to say that.'

'You could sound more enthusiastic!'

'Reene! I'm pleased for you if it's what makes you happy. But—'

'But he's twice as old. I know, we've travelled down this road before.' Reenie knew the bite was back in her voice. 'Age doesn't feature. He *does* love me! We still have to meet discretely, though. It wouldn't look too good if people saw us together … yet.'

'But Harold *has* asked you?'

'He has.' Reenie slipped her hand into a Chanel shoulder bag, one more present from Harold, and brought out a small box. 'See!' Glancing at Lizzie, she slid a gold band on to her finger. Even in the dim light of Kelly's, the diamond sparkled like a miniature chandelier, a splinter of Versailles glinting in the twilight of a Grays' café.

Lizzie gasped.

'Thought you'd like it!' Reenie pushed her fingers through her hair in an effort to by-pass the guilt still shadowing her. *Was she the cause of Cynthia's death?* Gazing at the ring, she noticed it not only caught the mean fluorescent lighting but also the eyes of several customers, even if they were a few tables apart.

'It is truly beautiful,' murmured Lizzie. 'How long do you have to keep it a secret?'

'Only a few months. I … I think it could be a summer wedding.'

'Have you told Mother and Father?' Lizzie said a little awkwardly as she broke the lull in their conversation.

'Hinted at it.'

The room hummed with the chatter of other diners,

blending with a Perry Como croon in the background. Reenie was grateful for the cover it provided. 'I've something else to ask you.' She lowered her voice. 'When it's your half-day at the shop, would you do me a favour? I've an appointment – at the clinic – in two weeks. Do you think you could come with me? Make it a full day and I'll pay your wages. We'll take a taxi.'

'What's the matter? Are you all right?'

'Couldn't feel better!' It took an effort maintaining a light-hearted tone. If she wasn't careful it would topple the choice about to change her life. No, Harold's choice. And everything rested on it. She wanted nothing to stand in the way.

'It's a clinic. In London.' She paused. 'I'm going to have a minor op, but don't tell anyone. Harold and I have agreed not to have children. He doesn't want to start a family all over again, so … we're going to make sure it can't happen.'

Lizzie gasped for a second time. 'You mean … that's so final! I can't even say it.'

'But it's what we want.'

'Are you certain it's what *you* want?'

'Absolutely.' Reenie had practised her certainty until she was able to announce it without a single waver.

'There are other ways, without making it irreversible.'

'I told you, it's what we want. There can't be the slightest risk of things going wrong. Harold insists, otherwise, the nuptials are off.'

'So, it's really Harold's—'

Reenie arched her eyebrows. 'Lizzie! I'm beginning to wish I hadn't told you. How long have I been waiting for this?'

'But you might change your mind. What if Harold … died? He is—'

'Lizzie! Don't!'

'Look how well you get on with Graham. He adores you. Might you feel one day that you've missed out?' 'As you've said, I've always got Graham. I've made up my mind. Are you coming or do I go on my own?' Lizzie sighed again. 'I suppose— all right. I'll come. But I think you're making a big mistake. And—' 'Dearest Lizzie, I didn't ask for a sermon. I can't afford to let another mishap take place. Not now.'

Reenie rested her left hand on the table and gazed once more at the ring. She could hardly believe it was real. Reluctantly, she slid it off her finger and slipped it into the box. 'There is something else, a couple of things. Jen and I have made up. We used to be such good friends and I'd like her to come to our wedding. BUT my next best news is – wait for it – Harold has been awarded an OBE! He's over the moon and I'm so pleased for him.'

Lizzie smiled genuinely this time. 'That's amazing! Do give him my congratulations.'

'Certainly will. Right – time to go. I think I'll find some flowers for Mummy on the way back – she had a migraine yesterday.'

'Oh, I might just pop in on the old folk for half an hour on the way back,' Lizzie said as she rose to leave. 'Really pleased about you and Jen, too. Thanks for the tea and … I'll see you very soon.' She kissed Reenie goodbye.

With the bill paid, Reenie set out first for the newsagent's, carefully selecting a *Vogue* with an extra on wedding dresses and then diverted to the florist to choose a large posy of chrysanthemums. Eventually, she reached home, stepping quietly through the backdoor. Voices murmured from the lounge. 'Well, Reenie …'

Her ears stretched.

'Influence? What, to change her mind about Harold? We certainly wouldn't want to do that,' her mother was saying. 'Reenie's almost twenty-nine and she knows her own mind.'

Her father joined in: 'He's not a bad chap, my love. I'm sure he'll look after his new wife perfectly. She'll want for *nothing* for the rest of her life.'

'But life isn't solely about money, money and more money!' Lizzie's voice rose with each word. 'He's too old!'

Reenie burst into the lounge. 'How dare you talk about me like that. Behind my back!'

Her startled family stared back at her. She guessed her eyes must be flashing as much as the hidden ring. 'You're right – I do know my own mind. Plenty of people have age-gaps in perfectly happy marriages. I *am* going to marry Harold! How could you betray me, Lizzie?'

She flounced out of the room, slamming the door behind her.

*

When the time came for her to comply with Harold's ultimatum, Reenie repeated to Lizzie, 'You're only coming if you don't try to persuade me to change my mind. Agreed?'

'Agreed – reluctantly.'

Like drawing the curtains back in the morning to reveal a startling blanket of snow, Reenie faced her decision in equal surprise and clarity. Did she want to ensure she remained childless? Forever? She didn't. But neither could she bear the possibility of her happiness being snatched from her grasp. She shivered. It wasn't feasible for her to share her realisation even with Lizzie. That could have consequences.

'This is it,' said Reenie when the taxi pulled into the clinic. She glanced at Lizzie shrinking into the leather upholstery. 'No need to follow me in. I've got to do this part on my own.'

'Don't you want me to come with you?'

'No, I just needed some friendly support to the clinic and when I come out again. I've arranged for our driver to take you into town – a shopping spree will do you a power of good.' She slipped two five-pound notes into her sister's hand. 'Spend it on something for *you*. And a little something for Graham from his Auntie.'

'But?'

'No "buts". Just be back here at five. The driver will pick you up from Harrods at four-thirty. It's all arranged.'

As the cab took Lizzie away, Reenie's legs trembled. Even the exterior of the building was as clinical as she had imagined the doctor's surgery to be. And as clinical as her decision in every sense.

Was Harold changing her personality as much as her physiology?

*

'Why didn't you wait inside? You shouldn't be standing out here on the steps,' said Lizzie when the taxi returned her at five. She hurried over, her face filled with concern as she took Reenie's arm.

'I'm not an invalid,' Reenie said as they climbed into the London cab. 'Did you think I'd leave with two noses, just to put Harold off!'

'So, it's done. That's settled then.' Lizzie's eyes blurred.

'Settled. One last thing, Will you tell Harold you took me here? He'd like it confirmed.'

'Confirmed! Is that why you needed me? What sort of man is he? Don't you *trust* each other?'

'Show me what you bought. And I'd like to see what you chose for Graham.' Reenie pinched her lips together. 'This is the *only* thing he's asked me to do. I'll have everything else that anyone could possibly dream of!'

PART 2

Chapter 19

After the interminable wait, Saturday 5th of January 1952 arrived. The wedding day. 'Harold and Irene Hartley,' Reenie practised as she slipped on a Dior-styled skirt, royal blue, billowing but clinched into her waist, emphasizing her hourglass figure and the colour of her eyes. 'That'll do v-e-ry nicely, Mrs Hartley.' Being an older bride, and Harold a widower, Reenie had dismissed the idea of a white dress, after all. No-one mentioned the clandestine trysts two years previously.

Who would have believed it of little Reenie Meadows – marrying the business magnate of Grays? Mr Hartley, OBE. Almost a "Sir".

Sliding her arms into a well-fitted jacket, she then stepped into a pair of sleek stilettos, the heels of which would raise her to Harold's height. He wasn't tall, in fact, his daughter had pointed out that he was shrinking with age. 'Diana *would*,' she said to her reflection in the mirror as she carefully positioned her hat. The feathers embellishing it curled round her matchless hair-do, while the light birdcage net covering her eyes enhanced the arch of her eyebrows and the bow of her painted lips. She gave her lipstick one final lick, with Audrey Hepburn in mind, then glowed confidently at her image. Glancing across her bedroom, she checked the silver fox stole was ready for their departure, together with her suitcase containing all she needed for a glamorous honeymoon. And a new status.

'Last time bedroom number four, *The Lodge*,' she murmured, picturing *Cedars* and then their post-wedding destination. Monte Carlo was difficult to conjure up as she'd never been there before, though she had viewed the photos.

'Why Monte Carlo?' Lizzie had asked.

'Harold's favourite place.'

'Then, he probably took Cynthia there. Are you okay with that?'

'Oh, I can't wait to go abroad. You should see the hotel!'

But first – the ceremony. Someone was running up the stairs, quickly rapping on the door.

'Are you ready?' Lizzie called.

'I'm just coming.' Reenie fingered the pendant Harold had given her, her first token of his admiration.

'Oh my … Reene! You are stunning! Give us a twirl,' said Lizzie as Reenie came out to the landing.

Laughing, Reenie obliged. 'So, I'll pass muster.' Then she inspected Lizzie. 'You look pretty good yourself, the best matron-of-honour anyone could have.'

'Not too much of the "matron",' Lizzie chuckled, hugging the dazzling bride.

'Careful! Mind the hat. It's taken hours to get ready.'

A car horn honked in the drive – the *Rolls Royce* awaited, with the *Supersnipe Mark 3* taking a neighbourly second place, beckoning to the rest of the family. It was a simple affair, out of respect for Cynthia, Harold had said, at the local Registry Office. Neither of them wished for a pageant. Reenie supposed Lizzie squeezed her arm to give her courage, but she didn't need it, not when her greatest desire was at last being fulfilled. She floated, or so it felt, on her father's arm to the registrar, turning to smile at her groom. Harold was, as ever, immaculate and beaming, his face and the top of his head glowing under a shaft of light from the window. With the gold band on her finger, Reenie's dream simultaneously slid into her life.

The small party made their way into the dining hall of Langley Manor, where the reception was more elaborate than the ceremony. With a hug for Lizzie, George and her parents, Reenie eyed their guests: Roger, best man, was in his element, sipping champagne and soon engaged in conversation with Harold's daughter. "The Ice Queen" Lizzie called Diana, as frosty as the patterns on the inside of their childhood bedroom window panes. Fortunately, there was nothing about Diana which reminded her of Harold. And why should she let Diana's disdain spoil their wedlock?

'Jenny!' Reenie said when her friend embraced her. 'Harold – my old friend from our school days.' No mention was made of their once fractured relationship.

'Wouldn't have missed this for the world.' Jenny turned to shake Harold's hand. 'So glad to be here for such a special milestone.' No reference was made to Mawgan staying back to look after the children and farm. 'You look as beautiful as ever, Reenie!'

Reenie continued to the next guest, 'So pleased you could come.' But her mind was elsewhere. With such a nod from her past, nostalgia surged through her, taking her by surprise as she returned to a Cornish cliff top. She could still see the amber specks in Mawgan's eyes, hear the laughter in his voice. The hand round her waist ... It was Harold's. She squared her shoulders. She'd got over Mawgan long ago.

'Sweetheart,' said Harold, nudging her arm. 'That gleam in your eye – we haven't started the honeymoon! Yet!'

Reenie blushed. The last thing she could do was explain its source, memories of her first kiss wistfully tingling her spine.

'This is Andrew, my love, a colleague from Rotary.'

'Delighted,' she said.

Andrew kissed the back of her hand as she stretched it towards him. She would more than manage the "lady of the manor" role.

'The pleasure's all mine. Hope Harold appreciates his good fortune.' Andrew winked at the bridegroom.

If thoughts were transparent ... old flames, fortunes ... thank heavens they weren't!

Chapter 20

Reenie glanced at her new gold wrist watch: six o'clock in the morning. She couldn't sleep, but what was there to get up for? Everything was taken care of. She stared at her husband. *Have we really been married for over a month? Harold Hartley, your mouth has sagged yet again and I don't think I can take any more snoring.* Wrapping a silk dressing gown round her negligée, she crept out of bed and padded downstairs to the kitchen. She sank her toes into the deep, soft pile of the carpet, still revelling in the luxury.

Since leaving her job, with so few demands being made on her now, Reenie needed less sleep, so perhaps it didn't matter if Harold kept her awake. On reaching the kitchen, she made a strong cup of tea and wandered down the hall to the lounge, where she stirred up the fire. She watched the coals lick into life and fed them a few more nuggets to keep the room warm.

Then she curled up on the sofa and gazed around, feasting on the light glinting from the cut-glass pendants on the chandelier, the chintz floor-to-ceiling curtains in the bay window with matching chaise longue opposite and the antique vases in the two alcoves, always filled with fresh flowers no matter what the season. A highly polished walnut cabinet near the door contained more alcoholic beverages than she could imagine, but she was learning. Little by little.

Harold's portrait hung over the marble fireplace. It must have been commissioned at least twenty years ago when he was almost handsome. A rectangle of slightly bolder wallpaper where another portrait had hung shouted at her. The reminder of the former obstacle to their union had been consigned to the cellar and Harold temporarily moved centre stage. Reenie's picture, the new lady of the manor, would soon be hanging next to his.

'One thing's for sure,' she whispered to the dancing flames, 'I shall change the décor to my own. It can't be Cynthia's for much longer, even if it's more extravagant than anything I've ever known.'

If her parents' house was a testament to tidiness, this one, *Cedars*, was to affluence – late Georgian, red brick and three storeys high, with Victorian tendencies creeping in. Wrought-iron details embellished the otherwise simple triangular porch and the ground floor windows, of which there were so many. In perfect symmetry, they heightened the imposing air. Was there a hint of Ten Downing Street about it? Wisteria's naked branches embraced the first two floors, detracting from such a consideration. A long drive swept from the side of the house to the old stables, while a gravel path led directly to the white front door. Beyond this, a high box hedge surrounded a swimming pool.

With a wintry dawn filtering through the window, Reenie contemplated the front garden with satisfaction. A magnificent cedar from bygone days spread its boughs over a weed-free lawn. It partially hid the entrance to the newly laid tennis court she'd persuaded Harold to construct.

'Darling, Diana and Alastair *love* playing tennis. When they come to stay—'

'I'm not sure how often that will be, sweetheart.'

'*I* love playing. We can still have tennis parties with our friends – think how wonderful that will be in the summer.'

She had curled into him, picturing herself in her waist-hugging, tennis dress, revealing the slight tan she would acquire with a season to sun bathe, cocktail in hand, smiling as a hostess should do.

'Hmm.' But Harold came round to the idea and the court was almost complete.

She reached out for a cigarette, her magazine abandoned on the coffee table. Somehow Cynthia's shadow still haunted her. Like a fledgling snuggling into the soft down of its nest, Reenie retreated into the sateen cushions, a wisp of smoke curling upwards from her cigarette. Her diamond ring reflected the mesmerising patterns of flames in tiny flickers across the hearth.

Footsteps squeaked across the hall floor. 'There you are.' Harold bent over her and kissed her forehead. 'Penny for them.'

'You don't need any more pennies, Harold Hartley.'

'Not when I've got you. Long day at the office, I'm afraid. What have *you* got planned 'til then?'

'Interviewing the new maid this morning. Then ... I'm not sure really.'

She left the lounge to set the breakfast table, turning the wireless on to listen to the news. A young Queen was adjusting to her new role, though the Princess had always been used to a life of luxury. But Reenie still found it strange to be staying at home.

'You don't miss the hurly-burly of former times, do you?' Harold asked, gazing at her from the hall.

'Of course not! How could I?'

But a furtive worm of doubt wriggled in her mind.

Chapter 21

Cedars July 1955

Reenie trailed round the house, looking for alternatives since her alterations to the decor. But after three and a half years of adjustments what else was there to do? Her diary was blank, the maid had polished the silver and prepared the meal for later. Harold would be staying on at his club. *Yet another endless evening.* She sighed as she reached the hall. A pile of letters on the doormat caught her eye, an interesting one peeping out from the brown "officials".

She pounced on familiar handwriting and tore open the envelope.

Dear Reenie,

Surprise! We've an unexpected week in London so please can we come over and stay with you – just a couple of nights? Hope that doesn't sound a bit cheeky but I would so like to see you again – it's been a long time since I gave you that hug at your magnificent wedding ...

A week later, on a warm summer's morning, Reenie waited for the London train to pull into Grays station. A mixture of excitement and trepidation filled her. Mawgan was coming, too. She couldn't really refuse. Anyway, the Mawgan "thing" happened all so long ago. And hadn't she done well for herself since then?

'Hello-ooo,' she yelled, waving to the face leaning out of the carriage window. The train puffed to a slow halt. In a cloud of smoke and steam Jenny emerged with her two children jumping out next to her.

'Reenie!' said Jenny as she hugged her. 'This is Abigail, Abi for short, our eldest at eight years old. She likes to be noticed! And here's Dan the man, who's just six.'

Reenie beamed at them. 'How lovely to see you!' Abigail jiggled, her plaits in sync with what Reenie could see was excitement.

'Hello, Reene,' said Mawgan, suddenly appearing with suitcases from amongst a crowd of travellers.

Reenie's heart skipped. The amber flecks still added sparkle to his chestnut eyes.

'Long time no see.' He embraced her like a long-lost friend. For a split second she thought the clasp lingered.

'Just look at us all,' Jenny laughed. 'I hope we're not too much for you.'

'Of course not. Rosemary has all the beds made up.'

'Who's Rosemary?'

'The maid.'

'Maid! For one moment I thought you had a secret love-child!'

Reenie waved her hand in a mock slap. 'Jenifer P!' Somehow, she couldn't bring herself to say "Pedrick". Her legs were still wobbling. 'You haven't changed one bit. Come on, the car's parked round the corner.'

The Pedrick clan piled on to the back seat. Hobbs, the chauffeur, slammed the last door and slid behind the wheel. A sense of awe filled the *Rover* until Jenny broke the silence. 'Not a flick of cow dung across the doors. And not a speck of straw in the creases.'

Reenie managed to laugh. Hadn't she once suggested Mawgan settle close to the soap factory? She brushed away her thoughts like unseen cobwebs snatching at her face. But cobwebs had a habit of clinging on.

'Don't it smell good,' said Abi, while Dan wriggled to listen to the squeak of polished leather.

A hush fell again when the car glided up the driveway until Abi whispered, 'Just look at that house!'

They rounded the bend; window after window in their three neat rows sparkled, with the huge cedar on the lawn doubled in reflections.

'Welcome to *Cedars*.' Reenie said as they spilled out of their first taste of sumptuousness.

Jenny stared. 'My God, you've married into money all right.'

'Hobbs will put the car away.' Reenie beamed. 'Now, coffee. Let's go in and make ourselves at home.' She gestured to Mawgan. 'Leave the cases – Hobbs'll see to them.'

'Can't be doin' with that, not while I got a good pair of hands.' He picked up the luggage and put it down in the hall.

'Can you bring the children's bag in, Mawg,' Jenny called, eyeing the vases on their pedestals.

It didn't take long for Reenie to wheel in the trolley, all prepared by Rosemary during her morning shift. Best Spode was passed round.

'Sorry, got a job to hold this small one. We're used to half-pint mugs with "Daisy's Dairy" stamped on the side,' Mawgan chuckled.

Jenny rolled her eyes. 'Can't take him anywhere! If it's all right with you, Mawgan's taking the children out this afternoon. We've promised them a treat. He said you and I needed to be together *without* all the Pedricks crowding in.'

'Quite right!' Reenie crossed her legs and sipped her coffee, while Jenny took a playful swipe at Mawgan trying to extricate his fingers from the handle on his cup. 'You're like Clarabelle at a cocktail party!'

*

'How about me taking you round the house, so you can see what's what for your stay?' Reenie ventured after the coffee. Abi and Dan leapt at the suggestion, sizing up the banister and catching their mother's eye. Reenie could tell the tour would have to be swift.

It didn't take long to impress her visitors. Jenny's eyes snookered with the cues across the billiards table as she ushered them into the attic.

'Can we try it out?' said Abi.

'Perhaps when Uncle Harold gets home,' Reenie replied. 'It's really *his* special room. But you can have a go on the tennis court if you like.' Before Abi and Dan could whoop out *tennis court*, she added, 'and there's somewhere else you might like even better.'

'*Better!*' the echo reverberated.

Reenie led them down the three flights of stairs, out the backdoor and through more gardens. 'Oh!' said Abi, scooping up petals from the path snaking under rose arches. 'Can I keep them?' Reenie nodded. By now they had reached the hedge with the door at the near end, like the *Secret Garden* Reenie had lapped up in her childhood.

'Go on, open it,' she smiled at Abi.

She watched their faces as they burst through to the swimming pool.

119

'WOW!' yelled Dan.

'Hell's bells!' said Jenny. Mawgan gaped a perfect ellipse. Ripping off their clothes to their underpants, Abi and Dan leaped into the water, screaming. Reenie screeched in turn as a fountain of water splashed over her and she stumbled on her stilettoes into … Mawgan's arms.

'Not too gallant, Mawgan Pedrick,' Jenny said. 'Didn't realise you meant your *own* pool when you told me to bring my costume. Afraid I forgot to pack it.'

Slightly embarrassed, Reenie unhitched herself. Did she imagine that Mawgan looked equally uncomfortable?

'Why don't you two go back to the house to start gossipin' while I'd join the kids?' he said. 'My underpants aren't meant for public display. If you could bring some towels, Jenny, I won't be an embarrassment to Reene.'

Reenie breathed out. 'Come on – we can start with a martini.'

'Martinis! In the morning?'

Reene giggled. Once back in the house, she poured her favourite refreshment. 'Almost mid-day and it's a memorable occasion.'

After hearing all about Jenny's teaching, the farm and what the children were into, Reenie felt an unexpected dullness creeping over her. She poured two more glasses.

'My news can't be as interesting as yours,' said Jenny. 'Tell all, Reenie – bodies under the billiards table? *Cedars* is something to talk about. By the way, where's Harold?'

'At his club. Either that or the Races. He'll be back tonight.'

Jenny screwed up her eyes. 'How do *you* fill each and every day?'

'Um, various committees, important ones, of course.'

'You didn't used to be a committee person.'

'Well, I am now.' She could see Jenny stifling a yawn. Reenie tweaked her hair, as if to reassure herself that yesterday's appointment had been worthwhile. 'You'd never believe it, but I opened the church fete last week.'

Jenny puffed out her cheeks. 'But what do you do for yourself?'

'Cocktail parties, socials with Harold. He's into Rotary, Town Council, the Masons, just to name a few.'

'My God, doesn't it bore you stiff?'

'At least I've some recognition! I'm quite an important person in Grays Thurrock,' Reenie snapped.

'Sorry. I didn't mean …'

Silence fell between them until Jenny reached for the towels. 'I'll take these down to the trio.'

They'd only had a martini and a few cocktails, but Reenie wondered if Jenny was a little unsteady on her feet.

*

At last, Mawgan disappeared with the children for the afternoon. Reenie guessed Jenny would have a few questions to ask as they leant back into the swing-sofa under the shade on the lawn.

'What about your sister, Lizzie? What's her husband doing now?' said Jenny.

'Oh, he's a plumber. I think Harold's going to offer him a job he won't be able to resist.'

'That's good. Children?'

'Just the one – Graham. I'm rather fond of him.'

'Might you and Harold start a family?'

Reenie shook her head. 'Not now. They'd spoil our lifestyle.' She swallowed. Had she sounded wistful? Somehow, Jenny's questions unsettled her for the rest of the afternoon.

*

Later that day, when Jenny and Mawgan gave her a little respite, Reenie checked on the dining room. Rosemary had polished the silver, including the candelabras, till they gleamed, while the cut-glass shimmered. The cutlery had been laid in perfect symmetry, while several glasses stood to attention by each place-setting. It couldn't fail to amaze.

Reenie had time to slip into her new dress. Letting the full skirt from a neat waist band flare like a ballerina's, she twirled round by the mirror in the dress not so unlike one she remembered from Cornish days. She smiled at her reflection and went out on to the landing.

'Anyone at home?' Harold called from the front door.

'Yes,' chimed several voices in unison. He hung his hat and brolly on the stand in the hall and looked upwards.

'Darling, meet my favourite people,' said Reenie as she came down and kissed him. Then the Pedricks descended the stairs. The children looked nervous, but Jenny confidently embraced Harold, while Mawgan reached out to shake hands. Instantly, the shock of reality hit Reenie: Mawgan's youth, his dark wavy hair and the handsome eyes that once danced in her direction contrasted with Harold's spreading physique, his creased and rounding face with shiny dome topping it. As he shuffled to the dining room, his entire posture shouted the years between them. He wasn't even a young sixty-four.

Starting with an aperitif, the foursome moved to the table

and Rosemary entered with the consommé. Reenie noticed Mawgan raising his eyebrows.

'Cold soup,' whispered Jenny.

Reenie pretended she hadn't heard.

'Tell me about your farm,' said Harold, at which Reenie breathed out.

Wine flowed, with steak to follow the soup and then the pièce de résistance – a pavlova with strawberries toppling from Cornish cream.

'Gordon who?' she heard Mawgan saying.

Jenny nudged again, 'It's Cor*don Bleu,* the recipe.'

'Now this is the best Merlot from the cellar,' Harold announced as a rich red liquid filled their glasses. Jenny snapped her hand over hers and glanced a warning in Mawgan's direction,

'No more, thank you, or we'll be under the table.'

Even Reenie felt a gentle swaying as she brewed the coffee, Rosemary having left once the main course was on the table.

Eventually, chairs scraped on floorboards. Harold tottered out and up to bed. 'Time to rest those pickled brain cells.' Jenny looped arms with Mawgan. 'Shall we clear in the morning?'

Reenie nodded. Had the evening gone well – Harold's gruff prattling, Mawgan's awkward responses, Jenny's remedial laughter? Reenie's thoughts swirled as much as her head. The door squeaked and she turned to see Mawgan coming back. 'Reene! Didn't know you were still here. Came down for my jumper.'

'Was it all right? The meal, I mean.'

'Course it was.'

Oh, Mawgan, so kind and gentle! Was that what made her

123

impulsively ask the next question? 'There's something I …
I've been meaning to ask you. Why didn't you answer my
letters all that time ago?'

'I did. Every one!'

'What?'

'But I could tell you weren't gettin' them.' Moving to her
side, Mawgan took hold of her hand. 'Then you stopped
writin'. So, I came to London—'

The floor slanted under Reenie. 'You came—'

'Careful,' said Mawgan, slipping his arm round to steady
her. 'I came to the address you gave me—'

'No!'

'Nobody could say where you'd moved to. I couldn't find
you. And I tried bloody hard, too.'

'Oh God, how … my mother – she must have taken them!'
Reenie's tears spilled over.

'Don't!' said Mawgan. The same hands that used to caress
hers so tenderly tilted her face up to his.

Then it happened.

His lips met hers in a kiss surging buried emotions from
the depths of her being. She melted into the arms enveloping
her like the young girl once saved from a rogue wave. Surf
tumbled, sand skittered, calloused fingers stroked her
shoulder …

'How could you!' With the squeak of the door, Jenny burst
into the room, eyes blazing.

'I'm sorry, I'm so sorry,' Reenie said, springing back from
Mawgan. Her fingers fumbled at a strap slipping from her
shoulder. 'Believe me—'

'Believe you! Oh yes, I believe what my eyes have just
witnessed. Perfidy on the menu – the last course I happened

to miss? You've got *every*thing, *Lady-bloody-Hartley*, but you've still got to steal my husband!'

'Jenny—' Mawgan pleaded.

'Up you go, Lover-boy.' Jenny shoved him towards the stairs. 'It's *our* bedtime now, husband and wife time. *You'd* better find Grandpa,' she snarled at Reenie.

'Hush, Harold might hear us,' said Mawgan.

'You must be joking. He's too old to hear De Haviland's Comet flying overhead.'

'No excuses. I've been a—'

Their voices trailed upwards and behind closed doors. Reenie sank on to the nearest chair, trembling. What had she done? Tears trickled down her cheeks. She pictured Harold, head on pillow, mouth open, snoring loud enough to rattle a snooker red above him. Her stomach churned. Mawgan's jumper, the source of their disaster, lay on the floor. She picked it up, curled on to the settee and wrapped it round her. It smelt of Mawgan, with a hint of salt and clifftop hollow.

Sleep was impossible. She had to find pen and paper:

Dearest Jenny,

I've tried writing this letter over and over again but the right words just won't seem to come – probably because I feel so bad about last night. Please forgive me. Even as I write, I can't explain or understand what happened. Except that we'd had too much to drink and Mawgan found me crying.

I think I can hear you saying, "Why should you be upset? You've got everything anyone could possibly wish for." Well, perhaps watching you and Mawgan, the children and your happiness, has highlighted what might have been for me. Please don't blame Mawgan. He always cared about everyone and I think when he saw me in distress – 'nuff said.

You have always been a dear friend. Listening to you talking about all your colleagues in school and in the village, I realised more than ever how much your friendship means to me. I don't have another friend like you. So – please forgive the unforgive-able.

I know it's going to be too difficult to talk properly when we see each other in the morning, but please, please write to me when you get back. I shall miss you.

With all my love,

Reenie x

*

Sunlight streamed through a gap in the lounge curtains. Morning had arrived. Reenie crept up to the guest bedroom and slid her apology under the door. Then she set out the breakfast that had to be faced, praying Harold would get up too late to join them. Stirrings upstairs suggested the Pedricks had woken early, too.

'Eat your breakfast fast, we're leaving straight afterwards,' Jenny said to the children as they trooped into the kitchen.

'Don't feel you have to go yet,' Reenie said, attempting cheeriness.

'I think we do.'

Mawgan stared at his feet. 'I'll phone for a taxi?'

'No, I must be the one to take you to the station. The least I can do,' murmured Reenie.

Abi looked upset, 'Mummy do we *have* to go now? We wanted to go swimming.'

''Fraid so. Make sure you don't leave anything behind – not sure when we'll be back.'

After what seemed to be half a day, but in less than an hour, the family that had breathed life into *Cedars* piled on to the ten-thirty train.

'Bye, Auntie Reenie,' said Abi. 'Thank you for a lovely time.'

'Thank the Lord someone hasn't forgotten their manners,' said Jenny.

Reenie blinked.

'Bye, everyone.' Mawgan glanced briefly at Reenie, his eyes expressing more anguish than any words. Doors slammed, steam shrilled and the guard blew his whistle. The children waved from the window, unaware of all that had transpired during their trip to a palace.

Reenie's tears could flow freely now. She wished she hadn't heard Jenny's reply when Mawgan asked if she'd read the letter.

'Yes, but I won't be answering it.'

Chapter 22

Late Summer '56

The leather chesterfield squeaked in Harold's London club as he slid back, whisky in one hand and a freshly lit cigar in the other. He'd had enough of his discussion over the Suez Crisis – his own domestic problems were encroaching in a more immediate manner. The combination of alcohol, post-supper contentment and general comfort lulled him into sharing his disquiet with Roger.

Roger winked. 'You're looking tired. Life's not too demanding back home is it?'

'Got to take a break occasionally,' Harold sighed, while his friend settled in the opposite armchair. 'I'm a lucky bastard, you know. Been married four years now.'

'Must admit you look ten years younger – even if tonight's the exception!'

'Flattery'll get you everywhere.' Harold drew on his cigar. 'You know, Reenie seems different.'

'What d'you mean?'

'She's not as bubbly as she used to be. Quite moody.'

'Time of the month and all that?'

'No, it isn't.' Harold shook his head. 'It's been building up for a while. Do you think the age gap widens as I get older, I mean I'm close to retirement and Reenie's early thirties?' It was strange – he wasn't normally the sort of person to reveal his innermost thoughts.

Roger sipped his whisky thoughtfully. 'Nothing's changed there. You must have worked all that out before you got married, unless, satisfying a young woman's demands, well—'

'She's completely satisfied in that department,' Harold snapped. 'And so am I!' Now he was getting like Reenie. For a moment he had to admit to himself that at times he was the one making the advances, which weren't always returned. 'I've given her everything, but I can tell, she's not right. Lost her sparkle.'

'Invite a friend round, someone she can confide in. Women are like that – need someone else to talk to, a soulmate. It lets the steam out of the pressure cooker.'

'Easier said than done. It's not only me she's sniping at – seems to be having a go at everyone. The tennis party had a few tense moments. Oh, that's the end of another friendship I said to myself when I heard a door slam.'

'Well, I wouldn't have thought that of Reenie. She's always been sweet to me. Probably not meant to say this, but do you think that some of her so-called friends are ... hanging on to the Hartley name, and all that goes with it?'

'Possibly. Still, they've not all quite vanished into the Thurrock smog. A Conservative Party Social is on the agenda soon. All helps to promote *Hartley Homes*.' Harold swirled his whisky round the glass and sipped it. *It was about this time last year when that nice family came to stay. What was her name? Jenny, that's right, Jenny and Mawgan. Cornish folk. She was that soulmate Reenie lacks now. Thought they were staying longer, but they were gone in a jiffy.*

'A holiday, that's what you need, old boy. Both of you. Take some time off. *Hartley Homes* won't fold if you have a couple of weeks away.'

'P'raps I will. A few days in Monte Carlo could be just the ticket.'

Harold dug his hand into his pocket for a final bet, then changed his mind. 'Maybe not. A: my winning streak this evening might not last and B: I ought to start saving for that second honeymoon.'

It was Roger's turn to chuckle. 'What would I give to step into your shoes – with another model,' he added hastily.

But would you? Harold contemplated, shocked that such a thought should enter his head. A picture of the swimming pool revamped, the tennis court and the latest summer fashions filling a new wardrobe suddenly replaced Reenie. She was certainly dipping into the Hartley purse. Then, there was that social she was planning, ordering a marquee for the back lawn. *I heard her muttering about some bloody jazz band being hired to play. I wouldn't even put it past her to take on that latest hideous craze – what was it: Bill Hayley and the ... ?* He shuddered. *Vera Lynn, yes, but jazz, pl-ea-se spare me!* He hummed "I'm in the mood for love" as a vision of his wife with pen and notepad in hand came into focus.

His consciousness slid into a late Friday night torpor, matching the dimmed lighting of his particular corner. But it was Thursday. He'd visited the club a day earlier again.

'Come on, old chap,' said Roger, putting a slightly unsteady hand on his shoulder. 'Better call that taxi to get you home. Reenie'll be waiting.'

'Doubt it. Had a stomach upset this morning – she s'prob'ly cuddling the hot water bottle now.'

'Don't sound so glum – won't take you long to jettison the substitute.'

'Dead right – got to keep the home fires burning.'

Chapter 23

Despite her growing queasiness, Reenie forged ahead with the tennis party. Harold had invited the usual crowd. 'Not just tennis, is it?' she felt like saying. The agenda of promoting his business simultaneously was hardly hidden.

When the final preparations were in full swing, the doorbell rang. Rosemary answered it.

'It's Mrs Simmonds, ma'am. Should I ask her in?'

'Lizzie! Whatever is she doing calling on me so late? You finish the profiteroles ...' Reenie skated through the hall to the entrance. The interruption would delay her.

'Any chance of stepping over the threshold?' said Lizzie.

'Oh, Lizzie! Not good timing. We've a party starting any minute now.'

'Sorry. Just happened to be passing. Though ...' Lizzie's voice trailed.

Reenie gazed at her: slacks and a faded shirt? Not party material.

'So, I'm the wrong person in the wrong place for now. It's all over your face, Reene. Don't worry, I'll go.'

'Well ...' Why did Reenie's tongue freeze? She watched Lizzie turn and walk briskly down the drive without looking back.

When Reenie returned to the marquee, a heavy depression settled over her. She reached for a canapé in the deadliest of parties and her stomach flipped. Remorse seeped into her appetite.

*

The stomach upset persisted. Reenie leaned over the toilet bowl and retched for the third successive morning, spitting out bile refusing to be quelled. When the last wave of nausea passed, she put the lid on the toilet and collapsed on to it.

'Are you all right?' called Harold, rattling the door handle. Why was he always trying to invade every facet of her life? 'Will be in a moment. You go downstairs. I'll join you when I've showered.' After swilling out her mouth, Reenie splashed cold water on to her face. She rubbed her cheeks briskly with the linen hand towel, hoping to bring some colour back to them. Then she slipped out of the stained nightie and stepped into the shower, turning her face into a warm stream of water. Was something seriously wrong with her? She dressed slowly. With legs still wobbling, she clung to the banister on her way to the breakfast room, hoping Harold wouldn't fuss over her.

'Darling, you look like you need whisky in your milk this morning. Have you still got that bug?'

'It's on its way out. I'll just have toast this morning and maybe a black tea.' But one mouthful of toast was sufficient. 'Can't eat it,' she said, pushing the plate away.

'Reene?'

'I'll have it later.'

'Got to go!' Harold blew her a kiss. 'Better not get too close, could be catching. I've a board meeting this morning but I'll ring midday to see how you are.'

'No need. Feeling fine already. I'm out this afternoon – meeting at the church about the new school.'

'Oh, forgotten about your recent link with religion.' Harold glanced at his watch as he reached the hall.

How irritating and patronising he'd become. 'It isn't recent and they just need my expertise.'

The front door slammed and Reenie, with a sigh of relief, heard their latest *Rover* glide down the drive. A magpie chattered. Was it laughing at her? What did her mother say? "One for sorrow, two for joy ..."? She gazed out of the window. *Damn* –why wasn't there a second one on the lawn?

Reenie drifted back to the bedroom, wondering what to do with the morning. It was difficult to find less than nothing to occupy her time, apart from a few meetings. Like a finger tapping her shoulder, Jenny's exclamation still troubled her: "My God, doesn't it bore you stiff?"

She glanced at the calendar at her bedside. This stomach complaint had been rumbling on far too long. Vague memories of an aunt suffering with cancer haunted her. Could it be a family inheritance? That would be typical wouldn't it – get to just where she wanted to be and then ... snuff it. She picked up the phone and made an appointment with her doctor.

*

The following week, despite the sunshine, Reenie shivered as she left the doctor's surgery. A baby. Expecting a baby! She needed time to let the news sink in, time to work out what she should do. How was she to tell Harold and her family? With one word her entire world had imploded.

'Mrs Hartley, would you like my receptionist to call a taxi for you? You've had quite a shock,' the doctor said. 'Is there anyone at home to look after you today?'

'No, I'm all right.' She ran her clammy hands over her brow

and then her skirt after fastening it. 'I think ... I think I'd rather walk a bit. Get some fresh air.' A restaurant nearby might revive her with a cup of tea while she also drank in the diagnosis.

'Damn these shoes,' she muttered to herself as her faltering steps took her to the tea rooms. Stilettos had been the wrong choice of footwear when coping with a bombshell but, nevertheless, she managed to reach her destination. The far corner of the restaurant beckoned to her, as if it could give her some anonymity. Might her secret be obvious to any onlooker?

'Would madam like to view the cake selection?' asked the waiter.

'No thank you, just a pot of Earl Grey. That'll do nicely,' said Reenie. How distant her voice sounded, as if she was listening to a stranger. She sipped her tea, wishing she hadn't been so unkind to Lizzie the other day. How she longed for her now!

'Scones are freshly baked, ma'am,' said the waiter, interrupting Reenie's thoughts.

'Thank you, but I'm really not hungry.'

She poured herself a second cup and lit a cigarette, then blew out a circle of smoke and watched it ascending, contemplating how she'd distanced Lizzie on the doorstep. She would never have fitted in with her pretentious guests, wasn't dressed for it, either, but ... she had treated her badly. Was Irene Hartley becoming as much a snob as the rest? And now she wanted Lizzie more than anyone else, certainly more than any of the hangers-on at that ridiculous party.

The doctor's disclosure buzzed round and round in her mind, an angry wasp in a jar. The ash curled off the end of her cigarette until the obvious stared at her. Reenie stubbed out the embers, paid the bill and left the restaurant. Hailing a taxi, she was soon on her way to *Cole's Creations*, despite it being on the wrong side of town.

To her surprise, the window display first caught her eye – how attractive it was. But she hadn't time to gaze at clothes. She stepped inside, scanning the premises.

'Can I help you, dear?' asked an elderly lady. Reenie winced at the "dear".

'Actually, I was looking for Mrs Simmonds. Is she—?'

'Oh, that's a shame, she's on holiday at the moment. Off for a week.'

Reenie's heart dipped.

'Are you all right, madam?' asked an assistant.

'Yes, I'm fine, thank you.' But her head reeled.

'Sit down, love,' said the same assistant, guiding her to a chair. Reenie sank on to it, with head bowed until the faintness passed.

Now what was she to do? Lizzie was the only person she could confide in, the only one to trust. How could she hang-fire for another week with such earth-shattering news?

Chapter 24

Lizzie pressed onwards to *Cedars,* hoping her reception would be better than the last time. She was certain Reenie was in some kind of trouble – it had to be fairly extreme for her to plead a visit over the phone. If only Reenie didn't drink so much. She was sure it was changing her personality.

Pondering over Reenie's possible difficulties, Lizzie found herself advancing up the long, curved drive to Grays' *Manor House.* The pines were maturing, their scent mingling in the evening with the ever-profuse rose trees. The closer the house loomed, the more Lizzie's pulse quickened. She pushed her hair from her forehead, then raised her eyes to Reenie framed in the doorway.

'Lizzie, you're an angel, coming out on a Friday after a week's work,' Reenie smiled. 'It's Harold's night at the club, so we can suit ourselves tonight. Hope George didn't mind.'

Lizzie smiled back. 'He's quite happy to have a little time to himself – Graham's at scout camp for the weekend.'

Neither of them mentioned the party and Lizzie stepped into the hall. 'You're so pale, Reene. Do you want to tell me now what's bothering you?'

'Meal first, a light wine and then I'll begin.' Reenie's brightness was an obvious cover-up.

Before long, Lizzie slid on to the sofa in the lounge, next to Reenie, who, she'd noticed had pushed her food round her plate and then left most of it. Reenie was definitely "not herself", as their mother would have said. The opulence and formality of the room was still alien to Lizzie, who couldn't help gazing at the lavish surroundings. A few toys strewn over the carpet and a jacket crumpled on a seat would have made her more relaxed. 'Take a deep breath. Are you ready?' said Reenie.

Lizzie nodded. 'Fire away.'

'I visited my doctor two weeks ago and he confirmed,' Reenie's voice faltered. 'I'm pregnant!'

'What? That's impossible!'

'That's what I thought. Doctor Hayley said that coils rarely let you down, but this one—'

'Coil? You were sterilised.'

Reenie dropped her gaze. 'I backed out. Couldn't go through with it. I think *you* persuaded me after emphasizing how final it would be. Had a coil fitted instead.'

'Did you tell Harold?'

'No, of course I didn't. Would he have married me if he'd known? I didn't imagine this could happen, though. Was just keeping my options open.'

'How far gone are you?'

Reenie grimaced. 'About ten weeks, maybe slightly less.'

'Does Harold—?'

'No. He thinks it's a stomach bug plaguing me. I do get awful pains. I … can't bring myself to tell him, not yet.'

'So, what are you going to do?'

Reenie lifted her gaze to Lizzie. 'I've been considering a termination.'

'Abortion! That's illegal. I don't want to be visiting you behind bars.'

'I know, but I thought I might be able to find someone – if I paid enough. The trouble is they're … Harold's contacts. I've even tried the old remedy of a hot bath and whisky.'

'No!' Lizzie clamped her hand to her mouth in horror, while Reenie shook her head.

'Failed miserably yet again.'

'You mustn't! It could harm the baby. What about the coil – did the doctor say if it would affect—'

'No, he said the infant just pushes it to one side.' Lizzie curled her fingers through Reenie's. 'This baby is meant to be. Harold's going to guess there are changes taking place in his wife soon enough. But it would be better to broach the subject before that happens.'

'Can't imagine him noticing till it's more than obvious, nor how he'd take it. Yes, I can – he'll explode! I'll have to get rid of it.' Reenie's eyes brimmed. 'Besides, I don't think I could handle all those awful changes to my body.'

'It's not for long. Stop panicking. I'm sure your figure will be restored before the baby cards arrive. And Harold? He'll come round to the idea. You've enough money to spend on child care to relieve him of any changes to his life, fatherhood or not.'

'There is something else, if Harold knew … oh, I can't reveal it.' Reenie's eyes welled again. 'You'll find this hard to believe, but I've started to *want* this baby.'

'That's how it should be. It will be all right. It'll be wonderful! Look at how you are with Graham – best Auntie he could have.'

Clasping her head, Reenie rocked to and fro, like a child in fear of imminent retribution. Her tears spilled between her fingers. 'Oh God, what a mess I've got myself into. What shall I do, what shall I do?'

'I'll help in any possible way,' Lizzie threw her arms round Reenie, swaying in time with her, like the mother neither of them had experienced. 'All things work out for the best.'

Reenie suddenly sat bolt upright. "What's that? Was it the back door?'

They listened, Reenie wiping her tear-streaked face with her sleeve.

'You're overwrought,' said Lizzie, 'imagining things now.'

Reenie drew breath. 'So, you think I'll have to go through with it?'

'Go through with what?' said Harold as he shuffled into the lounge.

Chapter 25

'You're back early! What's happened?' She sprang up with an air of guilt, while Lizzie stayed put, her eyes fixed on her feet.

'What's happened? Nothing more than needing an earlier night with my wife because I'm concerned about her health. And I can see that I was right. Hello Lizzie. Didn't mean to ignore you, but I can tell Reene is in a state. Now, explain what you mean by "Going through with it". Going through with what?'

'Oh, it's nothing.'

'With eyes as red as yours? What's it all about?'

'That stomach upset. I'm still not over it.'

Harold eased on to the sofa opposite her. 'Come on, that's not the only trouble. A stomach bug doesn't mean it has to be "gone through with".'

'I've been asked to take on the chair of *The Ladies' Circle*, that's all. I'm not really keen.'

'Well, I'm ringing Andrew Hayley tomorrow morning. We'll sort the germs out first. Something's been troubling you for a while now.'

'It's Saturday tomorrow – Dr Hayley won't be working.'

'He won't mind. That's what old friends are for.'

'Harold! Don't keep interfering. I can sort my own problems, thank you.'

By now Harold's eyebrows had reached their summit. Lizzie stood and straightened her shoulders. 'I think it's time I left. This is your time together and I shouldn't be here. Ring whenever you need me, Reenie.'

'Let me phone for a taxi,' said Harold, politely urging Lizzie to leave. He left Reenie searching for her sister's jacket, fighting back more tears.

All too soon, Harold returned. 'Good old Hobbs – he's on his way.'

Reenie could feel the tension crackling. After a hasty farewell at the door, she returned to the lounge.

'Whisky?' she asked.

'I wasn't born yesterday. Sit down – next to me. You're hiding something. Come on, spill the beans. Why don't you want me to call Andrew Hayley?'

She dropped on to the seat, crossing her leg to control the trembling. 'You're going to find what I have to say difficult. That's why I wondered if you might like a drink first.'

'I've come from the club! I'm a hard-nosed business man, lived through two World Wars, so I can probably cope. I'm listening.'

She closed her eyes for a moment, then twisted her cardigan between her fingers. 'What I did, I mean I haven't been altogether honest – in the past, not now. I'm trying to—'

'Reene! Get on with it!'

Had someone else seized her voice? 'When I went for that op, the sterilization, before our marriage, I didn't ... go through with it. I couldn't! So, I had a coil fitted.'

'Bloody-hell!' It was Harold's turn to pause. Reenie couldn't bear to look at him. 'You're not pregnant, are you?'

'I was so worried you wouldn't marry me.'

'Are you pregnant?'

'Yes, but we can work round it.'

'Work round it!'

'We can afford a nanny. It won't spoil anything for you.'

Harold raised his hands to the ceiling. 'You're talking about nannies when all I can think of is your deceit!'

'Don't say it like that. You should have loved me enough—'

'I *did* love you. I've given you everything. You were *nothing* when I married you.' Harold's voice rose in fury. 'Lizzie was in cahoots with you, too. I remember her confirming she'd been with you to the clinic. Never doubted either of you.'

'Don't drag Lizzie into this – she thought I'd had the op.'

'So, you lied to her as well. Someone told me I shouldn't be marrying a *Meadows*,' Harold snarled.

'How dare you malign my family?' Anger welled, competing with her tears. 'If you'd truly loved me you wouldn't have demanded I go childless through my life.'

'Demanded! You were totally acquiescent. I seem to recall you saying that children would get in the way. It was a mutual agreement, might I remind you.'

'Well, it was a cover for the real way I felt. I told you, I didn't want to lose you.'

'You bet you didn't – laughing all the way to the bank, as they say!'

'How could you!'

He swung away from Reenie, making for the cabinet. 'Nothing for you, darling – you need to take care at the moment – "tummy bugs" don't thrive on alcohol.'

Reenie wept into a hankie pulled from her sleeve, while he lifted the stopper on a decanter. Glowering, he continued, 'I thought the last board meeting was heated, but this! It needs to be resolved.'

'What do you mean?'

'You'll have to get rid of it.'

'IT? *It's* a baby!'

'I *will* make that phone call tomorrow – Andrew probably knows someone.'

'There you go, just thinking of yourself. What about me? Dr Hayley can't terminate a pregnancy – it's … it's illegal.'

'Haven't you heard of the expression "Money talks"?'

Reenie's head thrummed. *Tell him!*

'But I want this baby now,' she whispered.

'My God, our lives would never be the same again. I'm done with child rearing. At sixty-seven the last thing I want is a baby howling through the night.'

'It's all you, you, you! What about *me*? Yes, you've given me everything money can buy.' Her ring flashed under the chandelier as she fingered the ruby pendant. 'But I'm just another Hartley trophy – glamorous Irene, to be admired by all your friends, trotted out for all the socials to be the perfect hostess. I've probably helped to promote *Hartley Homes* far more than Cynthia ever did.'

'Well, at least Cynthia never lived a lie like my second wife.'

'Is that what you think? I can soon dispatch that myth!' she snapped.

Harold glared at her. A momentary lull gave them time to re-arm.

'Don't imagine I haven't agonized over our problem, dear husband.'

'Our problem? Our myth!'

'Yes, *our* problem. I meant it when I said I wanted this baby. I've only just recognised how I feel, but it's true.'

Harold leant forwards, about to interrupt.

'No, don't start arguing. Let me finish.' Reenie breathed in. 'Try to think differently. Picture what it might be like to have a son. Someone else to love you as … as you get older. And –

the laws of nature being such as they are – I shall have someone to love after you've gone. Is that such a huge ask? What's more, the Hartley name might be continued. Harold, pl-ea-se.'

'I don't—'

'I said, let me finish!' She took hold of his hand, but he snatched it from her. 'We've sufficient funds to pay for child care. You wouldn't be bothered by him. You're hardly ever home, anyway. You'd just reap all the benefits of fatherhood.'

'Oh, you mean something like the Royal Family?'

'Since you mention it … But, truthfully—'

'There's been little of that recently.'

Reenie folded her hands over her stomach. 'This will be *our* child. Try to think how special that could be. Your only son, or daughter, and heir.'

'Don't be ridiculous. Have you forgotten Diana and my grandson?'

'That's the point I'm making – I haven't.' She swallowed. 'This is going to be even more difficult for you, but I've got to say it now. You've forced me to.'

'Forced?'

'Diana isn't your daughter.'

Harold rolled his eyes heavenwards. 'Now who's being ridiculous?'

'Obviously she's Cynthia's, but *you* weren't the father. This isn't gossip, it's fact.'

A stinging slap across Reenie's cheek stunned her. She gasped, raising her fingers to her scorched face. 'Harold!' She stared at him in disbelief, watching the colour drain from his face as much as hers inflamed.

'What have you reduced me to?' he said. His fingers

trembled and the tumbler slipped to the floor. Whisky splashed his suit. He cleared his throat. 'Explain yourself.'

'Give me a moment. I'm not used to being abused.' She ran her fingers over the insult. 'Have you never noticed that Diana towers over you, that she bears no resemblance whatsoever to her supposed father? There is a touch of Cynthia about her, but not much. The rest is someone else, as told by Cynthia herself.'

'I can't believe you have the gall to even hint—'

'It's not a hint. It's straight from the witch's mouth.'

'So now you dare to speak ill of the dead!'

'How's that different from the diatribe I used to hear from you? And Cynthia barely had a good word to say about you, which included her hoodwinking you to her dying day! Think about your hasty wedding and then Diana's premature birth. Wasn't she quite a *big* baby for one born prematurely? But that passed you by, didn't it? Well, it didn't pass me by. I just had the consideration to leave you blissfully unaware. Till now.'

Harold gaped at her as if she had struck him. His face greyed, apart from one angry red spot burning his cheek. Losing his temper was unusual. He bent over to pick up the glass and she shrank into the corner of the settee.

'All I need to know is how you came by this information. It appears that both my wives have had a talent for deceit.' He stood the empty tumbler on the side-table.

'It was the maid Cynthia sacked – do you remember her? Gillian—'

'Baker. A loud mouth. Cynthia couldn't understand her poor judgement in employing the woman. I can guess – she slandered Cynthia after her dismissal, and you believed her, though God only knows how the two of you coincided.'

'Gillian, working with Lizzie in her shop, had no idea that my sister had a Hartley connection and her story rang true. She, Gillian, eavesdropped when Cynthia was talking to Pamela. Oh!' Reenie clutched her side with a sudden stab of pain.

'More dramatics?'

'Damn and blast you. I'm wracked with pain and that's all you can say! These are the cramps I keep … getting … the bug you thought I had.' She rubbed her stomach until the pains eased, sweat beading on her forehead.

'Yes, I remember Mrs Baker, and Pamela,' he said icily.

Reenie repeated word for word the story she'd memorised from Lizzie. When she finished, Harold rubbed his chin thoughtfully. 'Pamela is within reach. A few direct questions should establish the facts. Then, true or not, I'll find that meddling Gillian and hang her out to dry!'

'I shouldn't —'

'After that, your sister needs taking to task for repeating gossip.'

'No! Leave Lizzie out of this. She persuaded the stupid girl to keep quiet and forget about blackmailing Cynthia. Lizzie told me when we'd split up, thinking it might help me in some way. I promised not to say anything unless some kind of uncompromising situation arose – and it has now.'

He moved from the sofa to the chaise-longue. She supposed sitting next to his wife was more than he could tolerate. In the silence, the clock ticked. Was time running out for her on this baby? On her marriage? 'I think it might be best to leave things as they are. Don't contact the maid. It'll just stir everything up. It could become public knowledge and that won't do your reputation any favours. Nor Diana's.'

'God, the frost between the two of you has always been enough to glaze Greenland, but you won't turn me against Diana. She'll always be my daughter, whatever the idle talk.'

'It wasn't idle, and I've nothing against her. The trouble is entirely on Diana's side.'

'I'll sleep in the blue room tonight. Phone calls,' he threatened, 'can wait till tomorrow morning.' He struggled from his seat. 'You never did meet Cynthia, did you?'

'I made a point of avoiding her.'

'Just checking that I'm the *first* member of the family to receive this news, apart from your sister, of course.'

Reenie's heart missed a beat. Had he put two and two together – the phone call preceding Cynthia's death? His limbs were faltering, but not his brain.

He slammed the door behind him.

Chapter 26

After a sleepless night and more pains in the morning, Reenie revived herself yet again in the shower. How could she avoid Harold through the day? It was Saturday – hopefully, he'd do his usual and slope off to the races. She needed to listen for any phone calls he might make. But obviously, she couldn't follow him once he'd left the house. Anxiety shivered through her when she thought of Harold's threat to Lizzie.

The telephone rang after she'd laid the cutlery for breakfast. Reenie stretched the cable to the furthest corner of the hall as she took the call.

'Lizzie, how are you?'

'I'm fine. More to the point, how are you? Are you able to speak, I mean safely?'

'I think so – but not for long. I've told him everything. And I told him about Diana – had to,' she whispered. 'Is it possible to meet again today?'

'I've promised to take Graham to the park this afternoon, but you can come over to me if that helps.'

'I'll see what I can do.' Reenie struggled to control her tears. Stirrings upstairs from Harold suggested he would be down soon. 'Got to go. Will call when I can. Bye.'

What should she do next? She thought of more arguments stretching over an entire weekend or even the Hartley cold-shoulder. Where was it all leading to? The metamorphosis in her body and her own change of heart were enough to cope with, never mind all that had happened the day before.

She returned to the kitchen. Harold's heavy tread on the stairs sent goosebumps surging as she braced herself for his entrance. She pictured him picking up the newspaper, then the front door slammed shut.

An empty silence filled the house.

One glance in the hall told her Harold's hat was missing from the coat stand. Had he left her for the day with no indication of when he would come back? Or was he meeting with the doctor? She poured herself a tea and the cup rattled in its saucer.

After two earl grey infusions and one cigarette, Reenie breathed more easily. She picked up the phone and dialled for Lizzie.

'It's me. Harold's gone.'

'Gone! He's left you?'

'No, out for the day. Probably lounging round that blasted club. Please, can I come and see you now?'

'Of course you can!'

Within minutes Reenie was behind the steering wheel, heading for Lizzie's house. So many transformations in her life – yesterday it would have taken her an hour to get ready and now … two dabs of rouge, a dash of lipstick and she was outside. No stilettos, just a pair of comfortable sandals.

As soon as Reenie arrived, it was decided: she would take Lizzie shopping, giving her time to tell her what she'd missed the previous evening. Except, of course, for Harold's threats towards Lizzie. A pang of guilt struck at Reenie's composure; somehow, she couldn't bring herself to mention this.

Lizzie beamed at Reenie as she picked up her bags. 'You've been so brave. I'm certain the baby will prove to be a blessing. See – you're thinking positively now.'

'I think deep down it's what I've always wanted, even though it's been a pitched battle inside my head. Otherwise I'd have gone along with the operation in the first place. All I've said and done has been … oh, it's called self-deception! Whatever's going on in the old grey matter, it's definitely all happening down here.' Briefly, she rubbed her stomach, but with approval, then puffed. 'I wish it didn't make me feel so ill.'

'You'll feel better soon – first three months and then, you'll both start to blossom. When are you going to tell Mother and Father?'

'Not yet – let the dust settle first.'

Reenie parked the car outside the supermarket. 'I never imagined I'd feel like this. I'm making another person, a whole, unique person, with a future ahead of them – with me! How could I have contemplated destroying it? I shall watch this individual growing up – perhaps he – I think it's going to be a boy, it's causing so much trouble – will be a bit like you or Graham. That'll be good. Better than like me!'

'Oh Reenie,' Lizzie rubbed Reenie's hand.

'You know, Harold's not such a bad person really. He's powerful here– contacts all over the place. He doesn't understand that I have needs beyond *Cedars* and *Hartley Homes*. Jenny planted that seed of discontent and now – I know there's more to life than committee meetings. But I'm still worrying about Harold. He can dig his heels in more than most.'

'It's all bluster. I'm sure he wouldn't force you to …' Lizzie couldn't finish her sentence. 'He wouldn't leave you.'

'No – too old to change now. Likes his routine and home comforts, which includes his glamorous wife!' Reenie wrinkled her nose. 'Come on, let's get the shopping done. Do you mind if I do my own thing?'

'Of course not!'

Reenie chose the best bouquet on display, together with a huge box of *milk tray* for Lizzie. Then she snatched up a set of Dinkie cars for Graham from the temptation stand near the check-out. She smiled for the first time in the last twenty-four hours.

*

'Auntie Reenie!' yelled Graham as they opened the back door to his home. 'Mum said you were coming.' He leapt into his aunt's arms, and she wrapped hers round him.

'Careful,' said Lizzie. 'Make the most of a sit down now, because Graham and I have plans for this afternoon. We're having a family outing in the sunshine, complete with picnic and, of course, afternoon nap by the Pitch and Putt.' Then she added, 'Think of all you've got to look forward to!'

Reenie toppled on to a chair in the kitchen. She clutched her stomach as the pains returned, trying not to make too much of her discomfort while Lizzie put the kettle on.

'Will you help me with my model?' asked Graham, planting another kit on the table. 'Daddy said he had to do the garden this morning.'

'I'll have a go, but I'm not sure … oh!' A searing pain shot through Reenie's stomach.

'Graham, tell Dad to come quickly,' Lizzie shouted. 'Take that box with you and stay in your room. You can finish it there.'

Graham froze. 'What's happening? Auntie—'

151

'Do as I say – now!' roared Lizzie as she steered Reenie to a kitchen chair.

Reenie watched in horror as a trickle of blood down her stockings became a flood. A crimson pool spattered the lino at her feet. 'No!'

The last thing she remembered was grabbing the table as if she could snap it between her fingers.

Chapter 27

'Where am I?' Reenie murmured.

'Hush, sweetheart, just rest. I'm here, right beside you.' Ever faithful Lizzie was at her side. Her bedside. White and misty. Quiet. Voices humming in the background, starched clothing rustling.

Something's happened!

'Mrs Hartley? Open your eyes. The doctor will be with you in a moment. You've just come out of theatre. You'll need to rest and I expect your husband will be with you soon.'

Husband? Rest? Who …? She was in hospital. That explained the strange smell, redolent of hygiene and medication, but the pain in the pit of her stomach was worse.

'My baby?' Reenie strained to form the words. If only her lips weren't made of rubber. The walls surrounding her buckled and swooned. A cool hand soothed her forehead, while something tightened on her arm. What was that thing in the back of her hand and … something swaying to the right, clicking like a clock?

'I'm here to make sure you're comfortable, Mrs Hartley.' A nurse smiled down, her mouth distorting for a moment as in a fairground mirror.

Reenie tried to shift her arm, to place it over her aching body.

'Don't try to move,' said Lizzie.' It's a drip in your hand, putting some life back into you after … after all that's happened.'

Were Lizzie's eyes misting over?

Life – what life? Did they think she couldn't tell? She closed her eyes again. Her head pounded. Why had she been to the theatre? Vague sounds merged and melded round her, the words "husband" and "contact" mingling amongst them.

*

'Reene? You awake?' It was Harold.

Reluctantly, she prised her eyelids apart. Her world was clearer now as she turned to Harold. But it wasn't the face she wanted peering at her.

'Reene? How you feeling?'

'Like a stuck pig,' she moaned. Strange. She never spoke like that. Mawgan did. It was one of his sayings. Fancy her remembering, after so many years.

'All works out for the best, my dear.'

My Dear! Harold never called her "my dear".

She wished it was Lizzie sitting next to her instead.

'Ah, here's the doctor. He'll tell you about your operation.'

Operation? She sensed Harold's discomfort overriding her physical pain, then looked at the man in the white coat with a clip board in his hand.

'Mrs Hartley, I'm Mr Arnott. How are you feeling?'

'Pretty sore at the moment.'

The consultant turned to Harold. 'Might I ask who you are?'

'Mrs Hartley's husband,' Harold growled, his chair scraping on the hospital floor as he attempted to stand. 'I'll wait outside.'

'It's important that I speak to you both. I'm pleased to say you were brought into the theatre just in time, Mrs Hartley. You've had what is termed an ectopic pregnancy.'

'Had?'

'I'm afraid so. This is when the embryo develops in a fallopian tube rather than the uterus. It's highly dangerous for the mother.'

'Have I lost ... the baby?'

'Sadly, it's never possible to save an embryo developing in this way.'

Desolation washed over Reenie as if her own life had been exterminated.

The doctor continued. 'I need you to focus on the fact that your life was saved because there were complications, requiring unavoidable surgery.' He hesitated with professional sympathy. 'A hysterectomy was necessary.'

Reenie closed her eyes. Harold would certainly prefer her body minus a womb.

'The good news is that you are making steady progress. This could have been fatal.'

Reenie's stomach churned. 'How long will I be in hospital?'

'Two weeks minimum, I would say. You lost a lot of blood. It'll take a while before your former strength returns. Meanwhile, keep taking the painkillers. Is there anything you would like to ask?'

'I don't think so,' Reenie whispered.

Painkillers? Would they anaesthetise the pain in her heart? How long would it take for that to be vanquished? Reenie stared at the ceiling as her physician moved on to the next patient. Her eyes focused on a small brown stain in the plaster.

Harold cleared his throat. 'I'm moving you soon to *Cherry Hill*, the private hospital. So much nicer. Got your own room, with a view on to the gardens. Couldn't refuse me – one of Hartley's builds a few years ago. You can stay as long as you like, I mean till you've recovered.'

Costs? No problem for the Hartleys. There are just problems if you should wish to raise a family. She stared ahead. What might she unleash if she opened her mouth?

'Oh, Hobbs cut you your favourite roses from the garden – said they were far better than anything you could buy. The nurse has put them here.' He pointed to her bedside.

'Thank you.'

'Look, forget about anything we said before this disaster. We can go back to where we were before.'

So, their existence would continue the same as ever: committees, cocktails and canapés, society commercials for a certain construction company. Reenie would, of course, be the ever obedient and dazzling young wife.

She blinked away her tears.

Harold teased a hair off his jacket,

As she wondered how she could cope with Harold's insensitivity for another moment, the door opened. 'Lizzie!' she cried, 'So glad you're back.'

'How's the invalid, then? Are you feeling more like your old self?'

Lizzie bent over and kissed her, 'Don't let me disturb you,' she said as she placed more flowers next to Hobbs' roses. 'Hello, Harold.'

'You never disturb,' murmured Reenie.

Abruptly, Harold turned from his sister-in-law. He lifted his hat and, for him, speedily found the door handle.

'You don't have to leave because Lizzie's arrived,' Reenie said.

'I do,' Harold muttered under his breath. The door closed behind him.

Lizzie frowned. 'What was that about? I thought Harold and I usually got on well together. Oh, p'raps I'm not being very understanding. We nearly lost you, you know!'

Reenie remembered how Harold on more than one occasion had annihilated the opposition. His recent threat exploded like a flashbulb in her mind: *Your sister needs taking to task.* What did he mean by that?

Chapter 28

'So nice to have you back, ma'am,' said Rosemary.

'Thank you. The feeling's mutual – two weeks away feels like four!' Grateful Harold wasn't there to greet her, Reenie smiled.

'I've set out a light tea for you, when you're ready. There's a pillow and blanket by the armchair in the lounge and your bed is made up, should you need it.'

With a steadying hand from Rosemary, Reenie reached the chair, sinking into it with a sigh. 'I'd no idea that a hysterectomy took the stuffing out of you like this.' No mention was made of pregnancy. That information, Harold said, had to be kept to themselves. Rosemary plumped Reenie's pillow and pulled the trolley closer, ready to swing it over her lap with the tea.

'Mr Hartley said he had an important meeting today but he'd be back as soon as possible, probably just after supper. Would you like me to stay on tonight? He said that would be all right if you wanted me to.'

'No, I'm fine now, thank you. You've thought of everything. Perhaps you could leave a note for my husband– I'll go to bed soon and would rather not be disturbed.'

*

The evening sunshine poured through a side window with that deceptively warm glow of early autumn, heightening the patterns on the bedroom curtains. It was a beautiful room, but, like the sunlight, had Reenie deceived herself into imagining this would satisfy all her cravings? In sharp contrast to the brightness, a gloom settled over her. She shivered, as if entering one of those forbidden tin mines from her childhood.

Eventually, she heard Harold's key in the lock, followed by his usual routine – hat and umbrella over to the stand, slippers on, check the post, tap breast pocket to ensure one more cigar. Next, his footsteps on the stairs, heavy and ponderous, slowing with age and his increasing girth. When the bedroom door creaked open, Reenie closed her eyes.

'Reene?' he whispered.

She responded with a long, deep breath, deeper than any from a genuine sleeper. Harold hobbled along the landing. It had worked.

*

The days stretched ahead of Reenie, each new dawn heralding tedium. To her relief, she and Harold managed to avoid each other and when their paths crossed, conversation was polite but guarded. Always kept to the minimum. Harold propped her cards on the mantelpiece, a particularly lavish one from himself in prominent position. The card with a drawing of a comet heading for the clouds, its trademark printed in wobbly capitals along the fuselage, took pride of place in Reenie's heart – inside was a less accurate drawing of herself eating, she guessed cream cake, signed with lots of love and a few fingerprints from Graham.

Depression thrust its roots deeper into Reenie. She

recognised there would be no "Grahams" for her. Ever. Distraction, that's what she had to find. She gazed at all the flowers: *The Ladies' Circle* bouquet graced the hearth, along with one from the firm and another from her parents in the alcove. A sweet perfume filled the room. Perhaps she wasn't so bereft of friendship after all. Yet, no-one visited, apart from her mother, always fussing, and her father had called twice, though he wasn't well either.

Something else bothered her. Lizzie hadn't made contact since she'd left the hospital. She tried phoning but there was no reply. 'Have I missed any calls from Lizzie?' she asked Harold at breakfast a week after her return.

'Were you expecting one?' Harold enquired from behind his paper.

'Not particularly, but—'

'The world doesn't revolve around your sister.'

Reenie smarted at his heartless jibe, while anxiety burrowed deeper. As soon as Harold disappeared, she lifted the phone and dialled her mother. 'Have you heard from Lizzie? I haven't been able to get hold of her.'

'I don't think we have, but we've been out quite a lot. I'm sure she'd tell us if there was anything untoward. How are you feeling today, dear?'

'Oh, not bad, but I think I'd better try Lizzie once more – it is her day off.'

The telephone rang and rang ... and rang. Three magpies strutted arrogantly over the lawn, tails wagging, feathers gleaming. *Three times something better.*

'One, four, nine, two, Lizzie Simmonds speaking.'

Reenie jumped. 'Lizzie! Oh, I'm so pleased to hear you. Where've you been all this time?'

She heard Lizzie swallow.

'What is it? Lizzie! I know something's happened.'

'I need to see you, but—'

'You can come here. I'll send Hobbs.'

Reenie heard Lizzie drawing breath. 'Is Harold around?'

'No. But surely that doesn't—'

'It *does* matter. I can't see you if Harold's at home.'

Reenie's heart missed a beat. 'He's out – all day. Otherwise I wouldn't sound quite so cheerful. I'll phone Hobbs now. He could be with you in half an hour.'

'All right. I'll get ready.'

The dullness in Lizzie's voice chilled her. 'I'll get the coffee ready,' Reenie said as brightly as possible. She re-dialled for Hobbs. 'You can go now? Excellent.'

Reenie paced the hall and then the lounge. Patience wasn't her virtue when under duress.

Eventually Hobbs returned and she was at the front door before Lizzie had time to ring the bell. 'Lizzie! Your face!' Without waiting for an answer, she grasped Lizzie's hand, drawing her into the house. 'Don't tell me you're the invalid now, just as I'm getting better! This time you're going to sit in the armchair while I make the coffee. Then you can tell me all about it.'

With a sense of foreboding, Reenie's fingers trembled as she spooned the coffee into the cups and took the tray into the lounge. A rush of anxiety flushed her face when she passed a coffee to Lizzie and sat down.

'It's George.' Lizzie frowned. 'He's lost his job.'

'What! He was doing so well.'

'He was until Harold contacted his boss.'

'No!'

'Your husband had persuaded George, who in turn persuaded Forbes, to take on the biggest contract beyond their wildest dreams. It was for that huge estate – almost a new town in its own right. George was so chuffed when they took his advice. We actually celebrated by dining out for the evening and Mother babysat.' Lizzie laughed bitterly. 'Little did we realise that our celebration augured unemployment. Forbes pushed all other work out of the way, declined everything, for the sake of such a scoop. I believe he even thought it worth scrapping one contract, paying a small compensatory sum as he did so.'

'Oh my God, how could he?'

'John Forbes had signed Harold's contract but there was something that had sneakily been left out, which was the get-out clause. So … Harold pulled the plug on him, cancelling that blasted contract and they're all spiralling down to the sewers. The first one to go was, of course, George. He'd instigated the whole operation.'

'I'm so, so sorry. No, "sorry" isn't enough.'

'Why? Why did he do it?'

Reenie scarcely knew how to look at Lizzie. 'You know the answer.' Reenie explained the Gillian Baker episode. 'I told him you persuaded Gillian Baker to keep quiet.'

'How could he be so spiteful?'

'Has George asked him why the contract has been withdrawn? How did Harold tell him?'

'A letter – it was a formal letter in the post, addressed to John Forbes. Can you imagine what Forbes said to George? I can't repeat it. George thought it was some kind of terrible mistake – rang the office to check with Harold.'

'What did he say?'

'He hasn't deigned to answer. One of his henchmen replied on his behalf. It's as if George is a complete stranger. Apparently, the terms of the letter were correct; *Hartley Homes* had changed its mind and would he kindly not bother them again.'

'But it's not legal; they could sue!'

Lizzie laughed bitterly. 'Do you think they can afford the lawyers? Harold's team would make mincemeat of lesser mortals!'

'Why didn't you phone me as soon as you knew?'

'George thought he could turn it around, speak to Harold. We couldn't quite believe it. I guessed he'd kept you in the dark. Is there anything you can do to help?'

'I'll go to his office now. I'll tell that bloody man what I think of him. How dare he treat my brother-in-law like this?'

Lizzie shook her head. 'You're not well enough to start marching into another affray. Besides, I don't think Harold's frame of mind is open to persuasion. George has been sacked and Forbes won't have him back.'

'He'll still hear exactly what I think about him when he gets home tonight.'

'If you can help, let me know. But I have my doubts.'

Reenie pushed her fingers through her hair. 'George is such a hard worker. He'll get another job easily in the area.'

'You'd think so, but he hasn't got a reference. He's made quite a few phone calls, but word gets around.' Lizzie burst into tears. 'Everyone knows about the contract. No-one will have him. It's worse than not having a reference!'

'He must be able to get one, even if I forge it myself.'

'But it won't work within a radius of twenty miles round Grays. We've a mortgage to pay and a part-time sales assistant's wages won't cover it.'

'I'll have to tackle Harold. He can't get away with—'

'No, no! It won't work. George wants *nothing* to do with Harold ever again. How could you imagine Harold would assist us after what he's done, and how do you think either of us would have any truck with him now?'

The lilies shivered in the breeze from the open window. Neither of them spoke, while Lizzie wiped her eyes and blew her nose.

'What will you do?' Reenie whispered.

'George will try a few more outlets, but if they aren't successful, we'll have to move.'

'No!'

'We'll have to let the house to pay the mortgage – George will stay with his mother, while Graham and I go down to our aunt in Cornwall. I'm sure I can find part-time work there.'

With a picture of the Simmonds' household fragmented, and all due to her problems and her husband's spite, the last bastion in Reenie's life crumbled.

'Don't leave me,' she whispered as the front door clicked behind Lizzie. A hush closed in on Reenie, her palace a prison with unbreachable walls.

*

All too quickly, the time had come for Reenie to drive Lizzie and the family to the station. There was no point in trying to dissuade Lizzie and Graham from heading for Cornwall. Reenie clutched her head at the thought of George staying back with his mother, looking for employment.

'He says there's a possibility of a job in the Cotswolds with a friend,' said Lizzie trying to see something positive in their shattered lives.

The inevitable train chugged into the station and Reenie hugged Graham. 'Right, young man, you take care of your Mum and as soon as I can, I'm coming to see you.'

'It's going to be by the sea!' said Graham, leaping on to the step into the carriage. Reenie still managed a smile for him. Determined not to cry, she turned to Lizzie and wrapped her arms round her. 'Dear, sweet, Lizzie ...' When would she see her again? She dared not say more or the dam inside her would burst.

Her fingers trembled as she opened her front door to return to a house now as desolate as a breaker's yard without Lizzie in her life.

'Reenie, is that you?' Harold called from the lounge.

Silently, she glided up the stairs to one of the many spare rooms. She locked the door and wept in isolation.

*

'It's your mother,' Harold passed the phone to Reenie. *What now?* Her mother hadn't stopped bothering her since Lizzie's help had disappeared.

'I'm afraid ... it's bad news, darling. Your father ... had a heart attack this afternoon. Oh, Irene – he ... he's passed away.'

Reenie dropped the phone to the sound of her mother sobbing. Blackness cut out the last pin-prick of daylight.

Chapter 29

Cedars

1st August '68

Dear Lizzie,

Almost twelve years since Daddy died. "Time flies" is probably what I'm meant to say, but it hasn't. I still miss him, don't you?

How are you all getting on? Sorry to hear George hasn't been feeling good – hope he gets better soon. Do wish the Cotswolds weren't quite so far away. I miss you terribly, but I know it's impossible for the Simmonds family to come here. You always made me so welcome at Stepping Stones. It's hopeless trying to leave Cedars now – the fuss from Harold when I return is unbearable and he's too ancient to leave on his own. Had to be satisfied with watching Wimbledon on TV. At least it's in colour now – another Billie-Jean win!

Wonderful news about Graham – well into his studies for architecture. I thought it would be in engineering or something to do with aeroplanes. I feel so sad I've missed watching Graham grow into a young man. I always knew he would do well, like his father. Probably shouldn't say it, but has it ever crossed your mind that Harold did George a favour all those years ago: your business is so successful, plus you live in a far more beautiful place than Grays. And all those lovely friends you have! If only – there's just Mummy and me here. She sends her love, but assures me the journey to see you would be too much for her at her age.

Mentioning Mummy, she's the same as ever. I generally have a job to get anything right! Remember the good old days? She's

166

round here most of the time, casting an eagle eye over the furniture after Lottie, our new maid, has finished dusting.

Harold is usually swilling whisky in his club or at the races. Anything to avoid too much contact with his wife. I don't mind – it gives me a free rein. Well, not quite free with Mummy in tow. At least it gives me plenty of time for writing to you. I don't do so many functions now– fourteen years is enough! Harold is too old for socialising, but I've still organised one or two get-togethers. Life would be unbearable without something to look forward to (though no-one bothers to call afterwards). Of course, there's always the annual Hartley promotion, when I appear as the ever doting and supportive wife. Hartley Homes go on for ever, even if Harold can hardly move – girth and arthritis can be challenging for him.

Oh, you'll never believe this – Diana, my dear step-daughter, has deigned to come and stay with us. (And it's just when we've invited a few of Harold's work colleagues round for drinks). I suppose it takes a bit of an effort to travel down from Edinburgh. I'll have to be on my best behaviour!

Damn, that's Harold in now. Will write again once the party's over (and once Diana, the dreaded Ice Queen, has returned home)!

Much love to you both and to Graham,
Reenie x

Chapter 30

Diana picked up the mail. One letter in particular caught her attention. It had been redirected and the telescopic handwriting intrigued her.

'Aren't you going to open it?' asked Edgar. 'I've been married to you long enough to know you like a touch of mystery, but you've been staring at it for at least ten minutes.'

'Hmmm, it's the "Personal" in the corner that's interesting.' She peered at the smudged postmark. 'I reckon it's from Stroud. Isn't that where Irene's sister moved to, somewhere near there? What was her name? Wasn't it Elizabeth? A mouse compared to Reenie. I heard their enterprise took off, though – probably since leaving Irene's clutches.'

Diana's shoulders shuddered for a second as she pictured the cuckoo who'd settled into her father's nest. *Papa might know someone who lived in that direction, but that wouldn't have anything to do with me.* She paused to consider her father who, though nearing his eighth decade, still managed to keep a finger on the *Hartley Homes'* pulse.

'Mmmm,' said Edgar, concentrating on getting ready to leave. 'There's only one way to find out who it's from.' A car horn beeped below their window. 'That's it – must go.' He bent over to kiss Diana and she heard the gate clang behind him before she'd finished her last bite of toast. The brown envelopes were in a neat pile, ready to take to her desk, but it was Saturday and Diana wasn't going to touch anything to do with work or household bills at the weekend. Even if Edgar couldn't forget the stock market, she wasn't going to let business impinge. She read the postcard from a colleague, enjoying a late summer holiday in the Alps. Then shivered; Edinburgh already felt the chill of an early autumn.

Carpe diem, she murmured. The silver paper knife sliced open the conspicuous envelope:

35 Barleymow,
Stroud,
Glouc
Tel 42175

17th July '68
Dear Diana,
    Please excuse a crusty old gentleman attempting to make contact with you. I have had to pluck up courage to do so, mainly because the last thing I want to do is hurt your feelings.

Who on earth … was it an ex-client trying to make up for their indifference? Diana turned the page over to find the signature.

Bernard Barrington (Colonel).

The name meant nothing to her.

    Shaky writing confirmed that Bernard was probably as old as he suggested:

    According to my GP I've outlived my appointed time, hence the need for me to salve my conscience. I must admit that curiosity has also got the better of me.

I was once a close friend and admirer of your mother – greatly saddened to hear of her tragic death, but that was a long time after we'd gone our separate ways. It wouldn't have been appropriate to get in touch with you then.

Please let me meet you and then I can explain everything to you. I'm so hoping I've found the right address in Edinburgh and am not wasting my time. I'm soon going to be a short train journey away from your home, staying with my sister. I guess that's partly what made me think of seeing you before I pop my clogs.

So, Diana – lovely name – I would GREATLY appreciate it if you could phone me at the above telephone number. Or write. Anything to let me know you will see me. Can't say how happy this would make me,

Kind regards,

Bernard Barrington (Colonel)

PS Please keep this confidential. Something tells me you're a completely trustworthy person.

Diana re-read the missive, screwed up her face … then re-read every word again. 'How extraordinary!' she said to Thomas, the tabby sprawled in disinterest on the seat next to her. She glanced at the date. Three weeks ago. *Damn!* He might have moved on by now. Or even died. Her disappointment took her by surprise: did she really intend following up an invitation from a complete stranger? Supposing he was two sheets to the Cotswold wind? And what was implied by *"the last thing I want to do is hurt your feelings"*? If he'd fallen out with her mother that was all too long ago to contemplate. What would Edgar say if she pursued the idea? *'Good grief, never imagined you'd take up*

anything so bizarre. You don't know what sort of crank you might be dealing with. Bin it.'
She started to crumple the message. But something made her stop. What was the harm in trying the number? She dialled 112 and an operator made the connection.

'Stroud 42175,' answered a pleasant female voice.

Diana swallowed. 'Oh, I was hoping to speak with a Bernard Barrington, but I realise—'

'He has moved, but I do have a forwarding address and contact number for him. In Scotland. Would that be helpful?'

'Oh yes, that certainly would.' Diana scribbled down the information. Curiously, goosebumps tickled her arms. Composure and self-control were attributes she prized. She wasn't the impulsive type. Here she was feeling like a flustered schoolgirl caught in dubious circumstances. Absurd!

'Is there anything else I can help you with?'

'Um,' Diana stalled. She really wanted to say, *Tell me about Colonel Barrington.* 'No thank you. That's all I need.' She returned the receiver to its cradle, then smoothed out the crushed paper and added the updated address. He was right: his sister's village was only fifteen minutes away on the mainline.

All day long the letter played through her mind. Imaginary conversations bounced to and fro. Perhaps Edgar should be consulted? Yet, wouldn't that be breaking confidentiality? *Now you really are getting ridiculous.* She'd write. But as soon as she found a pen, she changed her mind. A phone call would be more anonymous. Neither her address nor number had to be revealed and Edgar wouldn't be involved.

The idea persisted. She picked up the phone.

'Hello, Helen speaking,' said an elderly lady in a quavering Scottish accent.

'Oh, hello. I'm not sure if I have the right number. Might a Colonel Barrington be staying with you?'

'He is. Would you like to speak to him?'

'Oh, yes please.'

'Who shall I say you are?'

'An acquaintance of an old friend. He doesn't know me.'

'I'll just see if he's available, dear. He's not too steady on his pins if he's still upstairs.'

Diana heard footsteps fading and then, 'Bernard, are you there? There's a young lady on the phone for you.' The voice paused for a reply. 'No, she didn't give her name. Said she knows an old friend of yours.'

Another pause, followed by shuffling on floor boards.

'Bernard Barrington speaking. Who might I have the pleasure of talking to?'

Diana took a deep breath. 'You wrote to me a few weeks ago, expressing an interest in meeting me. Said you were a friend of my mother's. I'm afraid your letter has only just arrived – it was re-addressed.'

Bernard hesitated. 'You must be Diana. So kind of you to phone. Look, I know it must seem incredibly mysterious but, it's a long story and I was hoping to meet you in person to explain everything. Do you think that's possible?'

'Might this be just one meeting for an afternoon, say, in Edinburgh?'

'Oh yes. That would be wonderful. It would mean so much to me. And I promise I wouldn't bother you again, that is, if you wanted no further rendezvous.'

'But, before we make the arrangements, could you offer me a little more explanation, Colonel Barrington?'

'Oh please, I'm Bernard. Not so formal, you know! I am a

relative of yours and it would be a pity if I died before we'd introduced ourselves.'

'But I'm sure my mother never mentioned your name.'

'There is a reason for that. I do assure you there is nothing underhand with my intentions. Please, let's organise an afternoon tea. That would be my pleasure. You suggest the venue and I'll fall in with whatever you decide.'

With diaries checked, all was settled for the following Wednesday afternoon.

Diana replaced the phone and gazed into space. A relative? Maybe he was the "missing ancestor". Whispers of family members lingered in her mind to that very day. 'She's so tall, Cynthia! Where does she get it from?' Perhaps Bernard was a second cousin twice removed? But he said he was a friend and he had something to put right.

She chewed on her nails, a rare and hateful practice of hers. Now her nail varnish would have to be renewed. What had she let herself in for?

Chapter 31

Diana's deliberations returned to her mother and Irene. Although no-one openly mentioned any indiscretions between her father and step-mother before Cynthia died, she suspected there had been a relationship. She guessed that her mother had been heading for the hotel where her father was staying on the night of the accident. It didn't take much to put empire-builder and mistress together. Harold and Reenie were married just over a year later, well, eighteen months then.

Diana exhaled heavily. If tongues of fire had leapt from her nostrils she wouldn't have been surprised. Her resentment towards the liaison simmered, even after so many years. She linked the affair to her mother's death. Perhaps the Colonel knew something about her father and GD, aka Gold Digger, as Diana referred to her source of contempt. But he wouldn't: he'd said Mama and he parted long before her death.

She parked and made her way through busy festival streets to St Andrew's Square and Harvey Nichols, her favourite department store. Now that the assignation was imminent, she almost wished the letter had never arrived. The Colonel could be a pseudonym for a fraudster, someone begging for a boost to his personal income. Curiosity, however, outweighed her fears.

A clock nearby struck three. Not really tea-time, but it was the hour for meeting Bernard. She wore the cerise dress prescribed for identification. The scarf draped round her shoulders hid their broadness, she hoped, while her shoes, always sensible, guaranteed she was no taller than Mary Queen of Scots. The last thing she would do was totter round in spindly stilettos like her step-mother. She took the lift to the balcony where a table had been reserved for them.

Not far from the entrance, an elderly gentleman stood up. Immediately Diana had a sense of déjà vu. Hadn't she seen him somewhere before? Though elderly, Bernard Barrington had that undeniable military demeanour, so, at least the title of Colonel was genuine. He was wearing an impeccable pin-stripe suit with the whitest of handkerchiefs just visible above the breast pocket. As he stepped forward, Diana imagined she had never before seen such a highly polished pair of shoes. Practically patent.

Bernard beamed and stretched out one arm, while he steadied himself at the table with the other. No time to be staring at feet as she allowed him to clasp her hand. She raised her eyes and looked into his. She noticed that even his nose possessed a soldierly air, sharp and aquiline, with a trim moustache completing the picture.

'Diana! You're as true as your name suggests – a Goddess of the Heavenly. Do take a seat, my dear, my legs aren't up to standing for long.' The stick, all but hidden from view, bore out Bernard's infirmity. 'I've wondered over the years who you might take after. It's not your mother. But how discourteous of me—'

Before he could finish his sentence, a mouth-watering spread of scones and jams arrived. 'Just the ticket! Can't beat a Scottish cream tea.'

Diana wished she hadn't eaten a Scottish lunch beforehand.

'You'd be hard pushed to improve on this view, too,' said Bernard, taking his eyes from Diana for a second to scan the city.

'I have to agree with you,' she murmured.

'I'll play "mother", no, "father," he said as he poured the tea, seemingly undeterred by a slight tremor in his hand. 'Now, you need some explanation, I know, but tell me a little about yourself first. You have a husband and children?' She recognised that for once someone else was commanding the conversation.

'Yes, Edgar, and Alastair, our son. We moved to Edinburgh shortly after our marriage. Alastair's twenty-four now, hoping to work in the Diplomatic Service.'

'And yourself?'

'Legal Secretary. Edgar's into finance.'

'I predicted you would do well. It's in the genes. *And* you have your mother's charm. How about your, er, father? Is he still alive?'

'Oh yes, but getting on. He's not far off eighty.'

'Did he marry again?'

'He did – to a gold digger, unfortunately. The fortune's in *her* hands now. Papa built up a very successful business. *She's* younger than me.'

Bernard looked at Diana with compassion. 'That must be intensely annoying. I thought Harold would flourish. He was clever, but a pretty woman – always a distraction! Are you close to your father?'

'Not really.' Diana surprised herself with her openness. It was out of character. What was it about her visitor which teased out so much personal information? Perhaps it was his chivalry; he was the perfect gentleman. And how did he know her father's name? 'Edinburgh's a long way from Essex to keep in touch,' she continued.

'But—'

'And GD, Gold Digger that is, took over in 'fifty-two. If I'm truly honest, we were never that close, but our relationship cooled after his wedding. However, he's still my father and we see him occasionally. I like to think he cares about Alastair. He is his only grandchild.' She thought Bernard's expression flickered at the mention of a grandchild. She sipped her tea. 'Now it's your turn. Your link with my family is—?'

He smiled again. 'We need to do justice to these scones. Come on, tuck in while I repay your frankness.' He wiped the spotless linen napkin over his equally clean moustache, as if stalling to find the most suitable words. 'I suppose that neither Harold nor Cynthia have mentioned my name?' He paused. 'We could remain just acquainted for this one event, like ships passing in the night, if that's what you would like. On the other hand,' he hesitated, 'I could disclose my connection. But if I do, it might cause you some distress. Would you like me to continue?'

Bernard gazed at her, his eyes pooling with concern. And a tinge of excitement? Distress? Hazel eyes? Connections? Her stature compared to …? Her knife, poised to spread the jam, clattered to her plate. The truth hit her like a frame in a horror movie, frozen at the flash of realization.

'You've guessed, haven't you? I've tried to drop little hints to soften the blow. I'm so sorry. I shouldn't have, but I couldn't … I hoped I might see you now, just the once. Then slip away, not saying anything. But you're so like me. It's uncanny. It's … I've never stopped thinking about you.'

Diana's head hummed. Had her brain separated from the rest of her, as if made of something insubstantial, ready to float wherever?

'Why? I mean how? Wait a minute – let's establish that

what I *think* you are saying is correct. Are you telling me that you are my ... *father?*'

'Forgive me, I am.'

'Well, some hasty mental arithmetic suggests otherwise. I was born prematurely something like seven months after ... my God, *prematurely,*' she gasped.

'Your mother and I were, let's say, drawn to each other from the moment we met.'

'Where and when was that?'

'At your grandfather's house, Cynthia's home. Peter, your grandfather, introduced us at one of his parties about two years before you were born. He was the instigation for my entrance to Sandhurst.'

'So, why—?'

'I was married.'

'Oh, I see, philandering, as from the beginning of time!' Diana turned her head to avoid the Colonel's gaze. 'So, after the wild oats, you just left the harvest to fend for itself. I can't understand how my fath— ... Harold Hartley, enters the scene.'

'To this day, I bow my head in shame. A broken marriage would have finished my career *and* Cynthia's reputation as well. It would have dragged Peter down with us. I couldn't face any of that. Neither could Cynthia. She ... I don't know how much she actually cared for me, either. It's hard to imagine now,' Bernard sighed, shakily smoothing his military moustache. 'I believe I was once a young and dashing army officer! A uniform always assists with attraction, don't you think?'

Diana pursed her lips. She faced her possible parent with contempt; silence held more power than a hasty retort.

'Well, your mother had an ardent admirer in Harold Hartley. Afraid he didn't quite make the grade according to Peter – grammar school boy, you see, but—'

'My mother duped my father into believing he was responsible?'

Bernard's shoulders sagged. His head nodded. She noticed the tremor in his hand increasing. 'I admit my departure was unforgiveable but your mother acquiesced. Harold was already smitten, possibly by more than Cynthia herself, and ...' He drew breath. '... all seemed to work out for the best.'

Diana stared at him. 'I take it that I'm the only person you've told?'

'Absolutely, my dear. Even, or especially, my sister has no concept what this visit is about today. My wife died last year which is why I felt you might be approachable after all. So, you don't think Harold ever, um, speculated?'

'If he did, he's certainly kept it to himself.'

'There's no need to reveal your paternity.'

'I shan't!' Ironically, she could hear her father's – adoptive, no, unconsciously hoodwinked parent – impatience with her abruptness. Her mother used to be equally curt when annoyed.

'I appreciate that my news must be quite shocking for you.'

'An understatement,' she said frostily.

'But, please, we tried to take the best course available to us and for you as well. I never stopped thinking about you. I repeat myself for good reason. If you can possibly forgive me and better still form a slight friendship with this foolish old man sitting opposite you—'

'I need time to assimilate everything.'

'Of course, but I have to add that time is not on my side. I have Parkinson's. I expect you spotted the shake and the shuffle.'

A third surprise hit Diana – a squeeze of regret that this new bond could only be short-lived. So, should she warm to Bernard? Not yet. Her wounds were still raw. But curiosity fuelled a flame of further enquiry

'Does Diana née Hartley have any siblings by any chance, half-siblings, of course?'

'She does,' Bernard smiled at her. 'Two of each.'

'And how many mothers were there?'

It was Bernard's turn to be slapped.

'Just my wife, Marion, and me. I wasn't unfaithful again and Marion was the best wife anyone could have.' His eyes moistened. 'I wondered if you might ask about your next of kin. They, too, are in blissful ignorance. I'd rather it was kept that way but after my death – it's up to you. If you think it appropriate, you can get in touch. Sadly, Jonathan died sixteen years ago. Marion never got over his death. Janice emigrated to Australia, but Michael lives near Edinburgh and Sheila is just south of the border. Would you like to see their pictures?'

Without waiting for a reply, he pulled from inside his jacket a leather wallet. As he dropped it to the table several photographs fell out. The topmost lay by Diana's plate; two children stared back at her, one was a boy of about ten, the other, clearly his sister, roughly two years younger. The girl sported an enormous bow just under her chin, but what really caught Diana's attention were her teeth: a slight Terry Thomas gap at the front was identical to her own at that period in her life. In fact, the child was virtually a replica of herself.

'Janice or Sheila?'

'Janice, my dear, and so like you to look at.'

'What does she do?'

'She's a vet. In Perth.' He indicated to a waiter that more tea was needed. But Diana glanced at her watch. 'I'm sorry, I've another appointment coming up soon. I've got to go in a minute.'

'We can meet again – we can go through the photographs at your leisure the next time. Please – I've so enjoyed being with my other daughter.'

She tore a page from her diary and scribbled down her phone number. 'Whatever you do, *don't* announce to my husband who you are. I will refer to you as an old friend of my father's. I suppose there's some truth in that!'

'I am so grateful to you. I knew you'd make me happy,' said Bernard.

'Well, you'll make *me* happy if you remain entirely confidential concerning your original sin.'

They agreed to reconvene at the same time and place a week hence, Bernard insisting that with a lift the top floor presented no difficulties to him. Diana couldn't deny her inquisitiveness over her brothers and sisters. Especially having been an only child until reaching her forty-eighth year. But, more importantly, she had to befriend the Colonel to ensure that he was utterly discreet. She couldn't risk the reality of her genesis spilling out in Harold's direction, or worse, in Irene's. It was an irksome fact that her father's will was mainly in Irene's favour. If he should learn that she was not his daughter ...?

Diana Wellstead had work to do. Her first contact would be Desmond, the son of her father's colleague, Roger. She and Desmond had grown up together. She knew that, with a little persuasion, Desmond would oblige.

ANDREA EMBLIN

*

As soon as she estimated Desmond was in from work, and she knew Edgar was not, Diana picked up the phone. She heaved a sigh of relief when Desmond's voice bounced along the cables, all the way from Grays. With the briefest of pleasantries, she launched into her conspiracy. 'It's not too much to ask, from an old friend,' she said as she set the snare.

'Not much!' groaned Desmond. 'You always managed to get your own way when we were children.'

'Would you have wanted your father to marry a gold digger and walk off with your inheritance?'

'But you don't know that she is, taking it all, I mean. Last time you spoke about it your father was leaving you quite a slice of the old cake. Besides, you've your own personal mint somewhere up there in Edinburgh.' Desmond chortled as if to smooth out a possible gaffe.

'Well, I still can't bear the thought that *Cedars*, my ancestral home, is destined for someone who ousted my mother.'

'Oh, come on, they tied the knot—'

'Don't give me that story about their romance *after* Mother's death. You read between the lines as much as I did. Your father would confirm it if he weren't so loyal to Papa.'

Bitterness soured the tip of Diana's tongue. *Cedars* was hers by ancestral right. But if either her father or step-mother knew that Cynthia had betrayed them … it didn't bear thinking about. Her childhood home, and more besides, would probably be lost to her. Unless—

'Diana, are you there?' shouted Desmond.

'Of course I am! Where else would I be? This is *so* important. All I need you to say now is that you'll do this one

182

small favour for me. Your name is on the list of invitations for the Hartley shindig and so is mine. I normally cough up some kind of excuse as to why it's simply impossible to join them, but this time I shall accept. It's high time I saw Papa again.'

'So, what is it?'

'I want you to be caught snogging Reenie.'

Desmond's ragged gasp filled her head.

'Bloody hell, Diana! What about my reputation?'

'Oh, fiddlesticks, you haven't got a wife to upset. Don't worry, I'll make sure I'm the only witness, apart from my camera.'

'My father?'

'He won't know – Papa would be too proud to mention anything.'

Diana polished her thumb over her fingernails, as if testing their sharpness. 'Desmond, for old times' sake. *And* that interest-free loan a few years ago. Remember?'

'Hang it all … what the hell … oh God, all right, then.'

'I knew you would! I promise to make it up to you. There'll be plenty of time to work out the finer details on the evening itself.'

After saying farewell, Diana hummed a catchy tune. What was it? *Oh yes, an old Perry Como: "It's a Good Day". Now where did I throw that invitation from Irene?* Partying was definitely on the agenda. As she rummaged through the bin the back door swung open.

'Life's not that desperate is it?' asked Edgar as he arrived home.

Diana jumped, with a small card between her fingers.

'Found it,' she said. 'Not anymore!'

Chapter 32

Cedars

16th September '68

Dear Lizzie,

Here I am again – said I'd write soon. Afraid I'm bored out of my mind now, but a bit unsettled, too – think I said Diana was coming to stay. Diana, the Ice Queen. Remember, that was the title you so aptly bestowed on her (and you being the most generous natured person in the world). Harold was pleased to see his daughter and she brought her husband with her. She hasn't changed. Just has more wrinkles than me. Divine justice. And perhaps her spitefulness has been honed a little more, which is worrying.

Diana's visit synchronised with Harold's cronies getting together. I'd slipped down to the pool for a breath of fresh air and instead I got – Desmond. He was plastered! Do you remember him? That stupid son of Roger's, Harold's work partner, flung his arms round my shoulders and tried slobbering over me. So you can guess – that was the very moment Diana happened to be "taking the air" in the self-same part of the garden. What a coincidence!

'Oh dear, am I interrupting something?' she said in that snobby tone of hers.

'For God's sake,' I said as I pushed Desmond away. 'Sober up!' I left him slumped on the grass.

'I don't think Papa would be too pleased to hear about his wife's escapades,' Diana hissed in my ear. Could have sworn she slipped a camera into her bag. I've been waiting ever since for Harold's wrath to descend. Knowing Diana, she'll be holding the episode over me, a sword of Damocles.

Thank God for The Avengers – just about to switch the next episode on. Are you following it?

Oh, there's Harold's bell ringing. Probably means he wants me to pour him another whisky. I'd better sign off – no doubt I'll need to pour myself one, too!

Much love to you all,

Reenie x

Chapter 33

'Now approaching a lunar sunrise ...' The Apollo 8 astronauts' solemn announcement on Christmas Eve reverberated from the Hartley's new colour TV.

'Oh, my Lord – they've made it!' Reenie exclaimed.

Harold adjusted his hearing aid and nodded. Then returned to his *Racing Post*.

Christmas consisted of cards largely from the sycophants, a huge glossy one from Roger and Desmond, plus a hamper from Harrods laced with many a martini. For one fleeting moment, she remembered the Desmond disaster at their last party. Thank God nothing had come of it. Her thoughts lingered over the cards Jenny used to send, full of humorous messages. How she wished they'd kept in touch. She buried her head in *The Millstone,* while Harold assessed his chances of a win at the next races.

So ... Christmas came and went, much like any other day. With January's arrival a frost trimmed the cedar tree more effectively than anything artificial.

'That'll do nicely. Thank you for putting the decorations away,' Reenie said to Lottie, who soon disappeared. The minimum of embellishments had been put up for just the two of them.

Reenie thought of the family her maid was returning to, then her mother who was staying with the Cornish aunt. It had been worth the effort to drive her three-quarters of the way there and the aunt had turned up for the last quarter to meet them. A whole month off! But Reenie's freedom stretched out like the princess temporarily released from the tower, constricted by the same ultimate boundaries.

She yawned. A light supper waited for them in the kitchen. It was a pity she couldn't phone Lizzie. Harold had been home lately for most of the time and he didn't like her making contact. Besides, they had snatched a conversation recently when he was out. Reenie had to admit it had heightened the dullness of her own existence hearing Graham with his friends in the background and Lizzie with hers calling in. Mr and Mrs, aka Lord and Lady, Hartley, were like her mother now: no-one dropped in on them. It was always "By appointment only". The clock ticked loudly behind her.

She leant towards the television, considering anything better than the quietness, when an unearthly gurgling broke through the void. 'Harold?' She looked across the room to see Harold clutching his chest, face contorted and turning puce. 'Harold!'

Groaning, he toppled sideways in the armchair, gasping for breath, spewing out his last meal. Reenie sprang over and attempted to prop him up, then flew into the hall, shouting, 'I'm phoning for an ambulance.' When she returned, he lay unconscious on the floor. Her brain scrambled in an attempt to remember her first aid as she loosened his tie with shaking fingers. The irony wasn't lost on her: all those years supporting life-saving charities and when the situation needed vital action, she had little more than a suspicion of what to do. To her intense relief, a bell soon clanged with increasing urgency, until headlights flooded the drive. 'He's in the lounge,' she called from the open doorway. Two uniformed attendants hastened through, instantly setting to work.

'Airway's clear,' said the first attendant.

'I've got a pulse,' said the other. 'What's your ... the gentleman's name?'

'Harold. Harold Hartley. Has my husband had a heart attack?'

'That's for the doctors to say, but—'

Harold coughed and spluttered, twitching back to life.

'Harold, you're in safe hands. We're taking you to hospital,' the attendant continued, lifting him on to a stretcher. Harold moaned, his eyes closed. 'You can come with us, Mrs Hartley, if you wish.'

Within minutes, Harold, semi-conscious with Reenie at his side, hurtled in the ambulance across Grays. She fingered the ruby pendant round her neck. It was strange how she'd worn it that day. It had been locked in the safe for years. Was it an omen – for good or for ill?

She sighed as if carrying the whole of Grays Thurrock on her shoulders. She *had* tried to love him, hadn't she? What would it be like to be without him? Completely alone. Her heart leapt, yet, to her shame, it skipped with a slight sense of release. Over the death of her husband? What sort of person was she?

Harold moaned again, perspiration rolling from his brow. Dutifully, she mopped his face with her handkerchief.

'A word or two from you might help,' said the first-aider. 'He can probably hear you.'

'Oh, yes, of course.' But the roar of the engine and furious clanging of the bell was overpowering. 'Harold, it's me. Reenie. I'm here. You'll be all right.'

'Put your foot down,' said the attendant, 'he's slipping.'

Reenie stared at Harold, his face the colour of his last betting slip.

Chapter 34

'Three days earlier everyone thought you were dying,' Reenie said to the mental image of her absent husband. 'And now look at you!'

She turned out of the gates of *Cedars*, driving slowly that morning towards the hospital.

'Mrs Hartley? Good news,' the consultant had said, walking with her into Harold's private room. 'After two worrying days, your husband is making excellent progress. But we need to conduct a few more tests. Minimising the possibility of a further heart attack is our priority.'

Guilt washed through Reenie. Was she disappointed that Harold might live for ... another decade? Had her ticket to freedom been tantalisingly waved under her nose and then just as quickly withdrawn?

She chided herself for such thoughts. Glancing at the houses, the contrast between the terraces and the Avenue was stark. Glimpses of vast homes secreted behind rhododendrons flashed past the car, whereas the occasional misshapen tree surviving by the terraces hardly compensated for the front gardens. A few feet square, the apologies for gardens were either gravel filled or weed-choked. Paint peeled off gates and doors, yellowing net curtains sagged in neglected windows. How many times had Reenie driven down this street yet never given the disparity a moment's attention?

Now it shouted at her. Was it subliminally linked to

thoughts of an imminent change in her life? Whatever happened to Harold, she had *Cedars* and a healthy bank balance. She cruised past the arcade Harold had built when they were first married. So much of the Hartley Kingdom permeated Grays.

Reenie's contemplations returned to Cynthia and the house. *Cedars* had belonged to Cynthia's father until he died. Was Harold destined to leave this world in the same manner as his first wife? Her shadow had never quite left the ancestral home, though for Reenie it was more a voice whispering accusingly in the background. She'd never met Cynthia, only heard her on the other end of the phone. That final conversation …

A car horn abruptly blared from the other side of the road. A woman yanked back a small startled figure from the pedestrian crossing. Horrified, Reenie stamped on the brakes. Tyres squealed. The engine cut out and the *Rover*, overshooting the stripes on the tarmac, juddered to a halt.

'Watch where you're ruddy-well going!' yelled the woman, still clutching the girl.

Shaking, Reenie wound down the window. 'I, I'm so sorry. I—'

'Sorry! I should think you bloody are!'

Out of the corner of her eye Reenie saw the driver on the other side of the road shake his head, mouthing, 'Women drivers!' and pull away.

'Lucky for you, me and my little'un's quick off the mark.'

'I just didn't see you. My husband's in hospital and—'

'We could all 'ave been joinin' him given one second less. Get your eyes checked. Come on, Sally.'

Reenie watched mother and daughter reach the Belisha

beacon without further mishap. So bright and obvious! How could she have missed it? Her legs trembled. She wondered at her carelessness, especially considering that not one stopper had been removed from anything in the cabinet that morning. Pulling into the kerb, she drew in a deep breath. Something made her glance behind. A burly, uniformed woman approached. *Traffic Warden!* Reenie turned the key in the ignition and moved on to the hospital.

*

Through the frosted window pane in the door to Harold's suite, Reenie saw the outline of someone else already at the bedside. The nurse leading the way swung the door open, to reveal Diana in the visitor's chair. Harold was propped up in bed with several perfectly laundered pillows embracing his head and shoulders. Colour had returned to his cheeks as he smiled at his daughter. A conspiratorial smile? Or was that Reenie's creativity continuing to wreak havoc with her sanity?

'Hello, Irene,' said Diana, rising from her seat, proffering her hand. Reenie grasped it briefly.

'Hello, Diana. So pleased you've managed to reach Grays. Harold was hoping you'd be here soon. Have you just arrived?'

'I came as quickly as possible – tying the loose ends in Edinburgh first. Papa was finishing his breakfast as I turned up this morning.'

'Oh, you must be staying somewhere locally?'

'The Regent. It's close to Parkways.'

'If only I'd realised. There's always a welcome waiting for you at *Cedars.*'

Diana laughed politely, 'I think my coffee break is due –
give you two a bit of time together. I'll be back in an hour or
so.' The door closed behind her.

Reenie sat next to Harold, who stared at the ceiling. The
warmth reserved for Diana had deserted him. Unease
flushed a prickle of alarm through her as she cleared her
throat. 'Heart monitor still beeping nicely. How are you
feeling?' She pecked him on his forehead after placing a bag
on the cabinet. 'I've brought your journal and favourite juice
in today.'

'Hmmm, wish it was the fiercer variety – the juice, I mean.'

'I do sympathise, darling, but the stronger medication will
have to wait. Is Alastair coming down, too, to be with his
Grandpapa?'

'Not possible with his studies.'

A silence fell between them, emphasizing the throb of the
monitor and the gulf separating them. Another day stretched
ahead. In some ways, circumstances were probably more
difficult now that Harold was reasonably alert –
communication would be needed. Harold smoothed the
sheet across his chest and looked at Reenie.

'Diana told me about your smooch with Desmond at our
last party.'

'What!' Reenie gasped. 'How dare she insinuate … she
probably forgot to mention that Desmond was as drunk as a
duck in the cider orchard. Did she add that I pushed him off
me faster than she could repeat his name? Harold, how could
you say such a thing? And at a time like this!'

'Just ruminating. There is something else, as we're
mentioning things. I've always known what you said to
Cynthia on the phone – before she died.'

Reenie's blood drained to her toes. 'Why are you mentioning Cynthia?'

'Running through things in my mind. It happens when you've had a brush with *The Man with the scythe.*

'The man with … oh! Him. But, what do you mean– "what I said to Cynthia"? It's no secret. I told you about the row when it happened.'

'Some of it. Not *every*thing. But because I've worked out the rest,' Harold paused. 'Don't you remember I asked you not to tell anyone about that call?'

'I … I don't think I do.'

'*I* remember. Do you want me to complete the part you left out?'

Reenie's voice grew louder. 'I'm not sure that I like this discussion and I don't imagine it's doing your health any good, either.'

A sudden rattling beyond the room startled them and a nurse bustled in with the trolley. 'Come to take your blood pressure, Mr Hartley.'

'I think I'll go for a wander,' Reenie said, hoping to take the opportunity to escape.

'No need, my dear. I won't be long. I'll take your temperature, too, sir.' The nurse beamed at Reenie. 'He's doing so well, isn't he? Better colour. See how you cheer him up!'

Sensing that *her* colour had heightened, too, Reenie edged towards the door.

'Bit of an increase in the systolic today.' The nurse frowned. 'I'll check the meds with Sister and the doctor will be round later this morning. Meanwhile, no press-ups yet!'

'Chance'll be a fine thing!' said Harold amiably.

With temperature taken and records updated, the nurse departed.

Harold continued. 'Not you, we haven't finished yet. Got to get this off my chest. It's that phone call all those years ago bothering me. *Why* did you to tell Cynthia you were aware of Diana's parentage? That's what killed her!'

'But Harold! How did you …? I … it wasn't what killed her. The autopsy said her heart was weakened by the accident.'

'I knew it!' Harold snarled through clenched teeth.

Oh God, I've fallen for the oldest trick! 'But you didn't hear what Cynthia said to *me*! She threatened to publicly humiliate me throughout Grays, and that's putting it mildly. I had to think of something quickly. That was my only weapon. Not for one moment did I imagine it would kill her.' Tears rolled down Reenie's cheeks. 'If you've understood this for so long why haven't you said anything to me? I've had to live with it for all these years.'

'No point in excavating the past. Till now.'

'Now? Why now?'

Harold clamped his lips together, his eyes returning to focus on the ceiling.

'Harold! What are you implying?'

Before he could answer, the door opened. 'Mr Hartley, I'm Mr Lassiter,' said the consultant as he entered. 'You're due for a visit and Sister has expressed a little concern over the blood pressure.' His fingers touched his stethoscope.

'I'm slipping out for a while,' said Reenie, backing away from the bed. Could she hear Harold muttering that *Cedars* had to return to its original family? She blinked her tears away, guessing that the doctor thought she was upset over her husband.

'Mrs Hartley,' he called out.

Reenie pretended deafness and continued for the exit.

Chapter 35

I can't go back, Reenie thought. Crockery clattered. Laughter broke into the murmur of voices in the kitchen, then faded. How was she to face Harold and what he was suggesting? *Perhaps I could change his mind with a little persuasion?* Reenie shook her head, rolling a soggy handkerchief into a ball between the palms of her hands. She stood and gazed across the tables. Had she even been speaking aloud? Was she going mad? With a click of her handbag she dropped the unrecognisable handkerchief into a pocket, snapped the clasp and squared her shoulders. Time to return.

She took the lift to Harold's floor. One flight of stairs was too much for her legs at the moment. With her arrival, the same beaming nurse greeted her. Her smile jarred with the tension tightening every nerve Reenie possessed. 'Mr Lassiter asked Sister to explain your husband's latest condition. Do come with me to her room. She'll be with you in a moment.'

'Is he all right? Can't I see him first?'

'Well, he already has a couple of visitors, which is probably two too many!'

Reenie stared at the opaque glass. One figure was female, almost certainly Diana, and the other? As if willing the door to open, the silhouettes rose. One of them reached for the handle.

'Just a moment,' Reenie said, stepping into their certain pathway.

'Mrs Hartley!' said Nigel Hampton, Harold's solicitor,

nodding politely as he entered the corridor. Diana followed.
A thin smile creased the corners of her lips.

'Nigel! Since when have you called me "Mrs"? It's me,
Reenie!'

Nigel stared at his shoes as Diana took control.

'I don't think Papa can take any more at the moment. He's
too tired.' Her eyelids fluttered, as if underscoring a victory.

Reenie's pulse raced. 'That's not a problem. I've all the time
in the world to be at my husband's side.' She held her head
up, just as she did in her childhood, staring into Diana's eyes.
'But I hope neither of you are the cause of his tiredness. Stress
is the last thing he needs.'

'Oh, I can hear Sister now,' said the nurse.

Diana simpered, 'Don't worry, we're sure Papa feels some
relief already.'

Reenie turned her back on the duo and followed the nurse
into the office.

*

Once returned to *Cedars*, Reenie slumped in her favourite
chair. Exhausted. A glass of half sipped martini graced the side
table. She kicked off her stilettos and crossed her legs. A distant
memory surfaced of Harold delighting in the elegance of her
legs, the sound of silk stockings gliding over each other.
Incapable of thinking straight, let alone answering the phone,
Reenie merely glowered in the direction of a persistent ring-
tone and waited for it to stop. Peace at last. Her eyelids drooped,
sleep lulling her from reality. Then the phone rang again.

'Blast that infernal … better answer it. Could be Nigel
telling me all's well that ends well!' she said with a wry smile.

'Hello.'

'Irene. You're back. I've been worrying about you. How's Harold?' asked her mother.

'Not too bad, though the doctor is a little concerned today. After his excellent progress yesterday his blood pressure is right up again. I came home earlier than usual as he needs to rest.'

'Sorry to hear that, darling. Come and have supper with me tomorrow. I'm always on my own. I miss you popping in. I'm sure Harold could spare you for an evening.'

'I'll see how I feel, thanks, Mummy. I'm not much of a conversationalist at the moment.' Her mother's voice melted into a constant blur of chatter in the background as Reenie folded on to the hall chair.

'*Irene!* Are you there?'

'What? Oh, sorry. I'm just so worn out. I'll have to go to bed.'

'Of course, dear. Speak tomorrow. Bye.'

Reenie rested her head in her hands. For a moment she thought of the son or daughter she might have returned to. How different life would have been, especially if they'd been similar to Graham. She drained the martini and wandered upstairs to her bedroom, collapsing on to the eiderdown. *Cedars* seemed too vast and silent for one lonely mortal sprawled on the divan.

When sleep stole over her, the Ice Queen stalked her dreams, tailing her like a private detective. Even Nigel leered at her from one of the rose trees in the garden. Was he turning into a Cheshire cat? He was shaking a document which no doubt contained the vital instructions for *Cedars* to pass to Diana. Reenie pounced but the folder opened, releasing its papers, which twisted and turned, slipping through her fingers like spilt mercury, flying into the air, higher and higher...

She awoke with a start, peering into the darkness. Something was rattling the windows ... a storm was brewing.

*

Rain battering against the window pane woke Reenie again. In the half-light she glanced at her watch: five-thirty. Was that all? Another three and a half hours to wait before Nigel would be in his office, but it gave her time to work out how she would cajole him into supplying her with the vital information she needed. She'd known Nigel Hampton since her wedding day.

Eventually nine o'clock arrived. Without a moment's delay, Reenie lifted the receiver and dialled. 'Pick it up,' she growled at the phone. 'It's time you were—'

'Hampton and Co speaking. How can I assist you?' said Nigel's secretary.

'Hello, Jean, it's Irene Hartley. Could you put me through to Nigel please?'

'Oh, I ... I'm not sure. I'll just check if he's available.'

'Oh, come on, he's only just put his hat on the peg. No-one's seeing him right now. Just put me through.'

Reenie sensed the hesitation. She waited, listening for a break in the hum of a telephone on hold.

'Mrs Hartley?'

'Nigel, you're not still being old-fashioned, are you? It's Reenie. I was just hoping for a little help. Life has been difficult for the last few days.'

'Very difficult. I do offer you my concern for Harold's health.'

'So kind. Thinking of that concern, I w-on-dered if you could explain your conversation yesterday with Harold. I didn't quite understand it.'

'I'm afraid that would be breaking client confidentiality. You need to discuss such matters between you.'

'Yes, of course, we have ... a little. But Harold was so exhausted and—'

'Mrs Hartley, I have to repeat that whatever passed between Harold and me remains confidential. If you wish to know more, you must ask Harold.'

'Nigel – please. I'm asking you now as a friend. You and Angela have supported us since our marriage. As a *friend* —'

One sob escaped, probably just loud enough for Nigel's ears. 'I thought you cared.'

'It's not about caring, it's what's legal. I cannot *legally* divulge your husband's instructions. Now, I do have a client waiting for me, so – talk to Harold, do. I must go.'

The burr of a closed conversation rang in her ear. Reenie reached out for the box she'd placed on the hall table. 'Plan B,' she murmured. Fastening the ruby pendant round her neck, she left for the hospital.

Chapter 36

Harold had never enlightened Diana to the fact that he'd liaised with Reenie before their marriage for longer than she'd imagined.

'Are you sure, Papa,' Diana had asked when Harold announced their engagement. 'You haven't known her for long and … isn't she a lot younger than you?' At least she hadn't stated the gold-digging-obvious.

Harold ruminated after breakfast. 'It happens after Death's teeth have snapped at your heels.' That's what he'd told Reenie recently.

His mind switched back to those early days, when Irene Meadows first bewitched him. 'Anne Boleyn,' he muttered under his breath, 'but I'm no Henry the Eighth! As ancient as, though.' He glanced at his hands resting on the sheet. Still plump, but wrinkled, veins prominent like the road system round his housing estates. Old hands. They were past their sell-by date when he slipped the diamond ring on to Reenie's slender finger. He'd kidded himself that he was desirable; presumed Reenie loved him as much as he did her. *Come on – you* desired *her. Isn't that a bit different from love?*

A picture of Reenie in her heart-shaped top, straps slipping from smooth, polished shoulders, smiled at him. 'Not really,' he snapped. 'Showered her with riches and what did she do? Deceive me – almost had another child.'

He flitted back to Cynthia. When Cynthia found out about Reenie, she liked to twist that proverbial knife into her. That was why, though he suspected Reenie of saying something heinous on the phone, he chose to ignore it. But when she spilt the paternity conundrum to him, he guessed what the crucial retort to Cynthia's goading must have been.

Roger's son, Desmond, filled the frame in more ways than one: Desmond was large, certainly as broad as him and taller. A quiet fury rose through Harold. Duplicity again. Had his wife no dignity? If his daughter witnessed the debauchery how many others did, too? *Desmond* of all people. It was humiliating. For both of them. He gazed at where his wedding ring had been cut off when he arrived at the hospital. With his flesh enfolding the band there had been no other way to remove it. All that remained was a circular indent and even that was fading. Like his marriage.

Diana constantly shadowed his thoughts. She would always be his daughter and Alastair his grandson, no matter what Reenie said. Diana's husband was a bit of a prat, but she was happy, so happy, in fact, that she hardly left her eerie in Edinburgh to seek out her old man. Never mind, she'd travelled to Grays now, when it counted.

It was important to get things right. Trying to work everything out ... he dozed. Awoke. *Cedars* was Diana's by rights, handed down from Cynthia's father. And the rest? He dozed again, briefly. Nigel would be in. *Mustn't forget to mention ... final draft. Was that for signing this afternoon?*

Chapter 37

'I just want to see him,' Reenie said to the nurse.

'Of course you do, my dear, but he's asked not to be disturbed for the next half hour.'

'Why? What's happening?'

'A visitor – he has someone with him at the moment.'

'Is it the doctor?'

'I – I really don't know who he is. All I—'

'Well I'm his wife. If it's not Mr Lassiter—'

Reenie marched to Harold's bedroom door, abruptly swinging it open.

'Nigel! So, this is the reason for secrecy. Mr Hampton takes precedence over Mrs Hartley.'

Nigel studied his fingers. 'Harold asked me—'

'I'm sure he did.'

'For God's sake, you were asked to wait,' snarled Harold.

'Sorry, Mr Hartley,' said the nurse, bustling into the fray. 'I did … Mrs Hartley and er Mr—'

'Hampton,' said Nigel.

'We have concerns regarding our patient's blood pressure. Follow me please and let him rest now.'

'I'll be damned if I'm going to rest before—'

'Harold,' said Nigel, easing Harold's shoulders back on to the pillow. 'It's sorted. I'll bring the papers back this afternoon. Don't worry, old chap.'

He turned to Reenie and nodded politely. 'Mrs Hartley.' In

the next second he disappeared down the corridor, as inscrutable as a phantom fading through walls.

'This way,' said the nurse, trying not to sound agitated. 'You can see your husband after he's had a sleep *and* after I've given him the once over.'

Reenie sighed and conceded defeat, but only temporarily. 'I'll give my husband half an hour then I'm going in. You know how you said I cheer him up.' Smoothing the ruby at her neck with her fingertips, she reinforced the notion that Harold once had a softer standpoint. Surely, she hadn't used all her adroitness to become "Lady Hartley" only to lose it? It wasn't solely the fact that she'd exhausted every possible ploy to achieve her eminence and wealth; it was the endurance of tedium, isolation and the superficial that followed. When she had made a deal with Harold, the consequences hadn't been quite so obvious to her.

She stepped into the gardens, where a cigarette calmed her thoughts. The child she had lost hovered nearby, similar to Graham, she imagined. How much she would have relinquished her stargazing status for that child. It struck her as sharply as Harold's slap all those years ago. No, harder – the effect lingered on. "Rubies for my dream lady." That was what Harold had said when he gave the ruby pendant to her, while the jeweller confirmed that its possessor made wise choices. Hadn't she been destined for riches – "Lady Hartley"? It didn't mean losing them once grasped. Did it?

The Thurrock clock tower struck eleven. *Cheer up Hour. For both of us. I'd better slip in quietly before Nurse Smiley pounces.* Giving herself extra minutes to strengthen her resolve, she took the stairs to Harold's floor, where she beamed at the consultant passing her in the opposite direction. She *was* going to make Harold see reason. She peered round the familiar door. Then froze. Harold, white as Sister's starched apron, lay motionless, mouth wide open. She tiptoed to the bedside and touched his hand. So cold. The unthinkable crept into her mind. 'I must call someone,' she murmured aloud, as if to reassure herself she wasn't dreaming.

Harold opened his eyes.

'Oh!' gasped Reenie, clamping her fingers to her mouth.

He coughed. 'You didn't think the old goat had passed on to greener pastures, did you?'

'Harold! Don't talk like that. I've come to keep you company.' He grimaced. She plumped his pillows, tidied the sheet, even though it was impossible to improve on hospital neatness. The pendant swung towards him as she fussed around. 'Remember when you gave me this?' She leant closer to him, holding out the necklace. With the light glancing off the stone, it was as lustrous as when first given to her.

Harold grunted.

'Remember how much you loved me? That's why I'm wearing it. It's not just a piece of jewellery, darling.'

'Haven't seen it on you for ages.'

'Perhaps you haven't looked carefully,' she lied. 'We'll soon be celebrating our eighteenth wedding anniversary.'

'As long as the systolic stays down.'

'You'll have me to care for you. Let's not argue again. I promise you I've never been unfaithful. I've loved you from the beginning, despite some of our ups and downs.'

'More of the "downs" lately.'

'Well, let's concentrate on the positives.'

'You mean, think back to the sweet thing you were when you told me how much you loved me?'

'Yes, I'm still the same person.' This wasn't going how she'd rehearsed it.

Harold frowned. 'But all that other ... baggage ... has happened since. You can't turn the clock back.'

'Harold, you're exaggerating. Tell me what's been going on between you and Nigel.'

'I did tell you. You know *Cedars* will be Diana's when I die.'

'Please, not that. Don't do that.' Reenie held her breath.

'You were the one who pointed out to me that Diana wasn't my daughter. *Cedars* was Cynthia's. It was left to her when her father died. So, the rightful heritage should continue.'

'But I love *Cedars*! And ... the rest?'

Harold avoided her gaze.

'What else?' she persisted. 'What are you doing?'

'I shan't leave you destitute, but the bulk ... goes to my daughter and grandson.'

'Don't do that to me! Harold, *please*. I've given you the best years of my life. Everyone envied you when they looked at me. Can't you remember what people like Roger used to say?'

Harold's impassive face shocked her.

'Diana has poisoned your mind. She's like her mother and you had little time for her. I'm not so grasping that I need the entire Hartley estate, but I have grown used to my comforts.'

Was he so obdurate? Tears trickled. Had she wasted so much of her life for nothing? 'What must Nigel think of us? What will people say after ... I'm appealing to the person who once declared undying love for me. The person who bought this pendant and fastened it round my neck, who slipped this ring on my finger. For pity's sake, HAROLD!'

'Mrs Hartley? I could hear your voice,' said Nurse Smiley, unsmiling. 'Oh dear, don't distress yourself. That won't help

Mr Hartley, either. Take a break in the Visitors' Room, dear. Right, next BP reading, Mr Hartley.'

Unable to stem the tears, Reenie fled, leaving the hospital grounds altogether. She wandered aimlessly through the new estate, no doubt constructed by *Hartley Homes*. The rest of the world was happy or busy, chattering, propelling pushchairs laden with shopping; cars hummed; a child on a bicycle jingled its bell for no obvious reason. A young couple scanning the photos in the estate agent's caught Reenie's attention: his arm resting on his partner's shoulder, such a small gesture, yet sending a pang of envy quivering through her.

There was only one aspect of her life of which she was certain – her make-up was surely streaked and her eyes swollen with crying. A couple of tables on the pavement by a small cafe suggested strong black coffee, though outside was too public. She slipped indoors, welcoming the poor lighting, and lit her third cigarette that day. Now what? There seemed to be no way round a confrontation – nearly half a lifetime's work couldn't blunder into mere memories; not without a fight.

Two more cigarettes and three coffees later, Reenie dabbed at her features in the Ladies. A little rouge and redrawing of her lipstick camouflaged her low spirits, while her fingers scrunched the waves in her hair. Neither Harold, nor Nigel Hampton, Solicitor, should see her at her worst. She wasn't defeated yet.

'Parkways, please,' she said to the taxi driver when he pulled up to the kerb.

*

Nurses and doctors don't run. But they *were* as Reenie entered the corridor on the first floor of the hospital. Running to and from Harold's room. She glanced over her shoulder, just to check that no-one needed to overtake.

'Oh, hell's bells,' she shouted as she collided with Nigel. His briefcase flew out of his hand.

'Oh, Irene, you'd better—'

'Don't you "Better" me, Nigel Hampton!' A tornado stormed through Reenie.

'I ... I think Sister—'

Had Reenie misjudged something? Nigel turned and disappeared.

Simultaneously, Sister stood directly in front of her, a picture of concern. 'Mrs Hartley, you need to come to my room. Your husband has taken a turn for the worse. It's best you don't go in just yet.'

'What's happening?'

'We are doing everything we can, but ... Nurse Fletcher, please look after Mrs Hartley, will you?'

Reenie's stomach churned as the nurse steered her towards Sister's office.

Mr Lassiter emerged. He shook his head in Sister's direction.

Was Harold on his way out? And just after Nigel's last visit.

The timing was too appalling to contemplate.

PART 3

Chapter 38

September '69 Cedars

Dearest Lizzie,

I still find it difficult to believe that dear George passed away only two months after Harold. Just when you thought he'd beaten his dreadful illness. Life can be so cruel. Thank goodness you have Graham to help you. He's the best son imaginable – I could tell when I stayed with you in May.

That brings me to my next point – I'm going to move to the Cotswolds. I promise I won't be so close that I'm a nuisance, but close enough to be a help to you. It's my turn now – you've always supported me in the past. But you are right: Mummy wouldn't survive if I left her in Grays. I just can't do that. I thank my lucky stars every day that that awful re-drafted will never got signed. The tussle I had with Diana's solicitor! Still, in the end it was worth the struggle. I didn't mind losing a bit to the Ice Queen with that out of court settlement.

I digress. Selling Cedars, plus my bank balance, will ensure the lifestyle I'm used to. And it will mean I'll have enough to buy somewhere with separate rooms for Mummy. The sale of her house will help, but, rightly, she says what she leaves behind when she's promoted to glory should be shared between both of us, so it won't all be ploughed into my next house. I couldn't cope with living exactly under the same roof as Mummy – your advice taken on board – but with a dividing wall I think we could manage. So, it's Action Stations! Estate Agents are posting every possibility for the new home and, yes please, if you could keep a look out for me as well that would be wonderful.

Oh dearest Lizzie, I feel like a new woman. I can't wait to leave this place. If Neil Armstrong can land on the moon, I'm sure I can do the same with the Cotswolds – far more beautiful than a lunar landscape! I've been given a fresh start and this time I'm going to get things right.

Much love to you and Graham,

Reenie xx

Chapter 39

May 1970 The Cotswolds

'Damn this car. What's wrong with it now?'

Reenie pulled into a convenient passing place as the Hillman Convertible made an alarming thumping noise under her feet. The last of the cow parsley stood to attention next to the bonnet. It was a single-track lane with grass growing intermittently down the middle. She got out of the car and slammed the door in exasperation, then stared at the wheel. Flat tyre. So flat, the car tilted closer to the tarmac on the driver's side.

'Oh my God, now what am I going to do?'

It was pointless to glance up and down the lane or even towards the horizon – not a house was in sight. She'd have to start walking. But her heels weren't suited to a hike through the Cotswolds. She should have known better, having moved down three months ago. Sending a message out to a guardian angel, Reenie murmured, 'Whoever is out there, pl-ea-se send me a wayside pub! I'm not likely to find a telephone box nestling in a ditch.'

The countryside exuded everything that was good about late May: bird song from the hedgerows with the olive green of lively growth. Under a peerless sky, the world sparkled, emphasizing her new beginning, closer to Lizzie again after such a long separation. Reenie breathed in deeply, holding the fresh air in her lungs. When did she last feel like this? It was another world. She did miss the town and the city a little but with the car – when it was working – it didn't take too long to reach Gloucester or even Bristol.

Her heels click-clacked over the road, but not for long. To her dismay the rustic idyll crumbled as a pungent smell from a dairy herd wafted from beyond. Worse was to come: the cattle had relieved themselves across the entire width of the lane until the next bend. Cows lowed in the distance as if to claim responsibility for such opprobrium. She eyed the thick, green sludge, still steaming. Then laughed. 'If you will choose countryside over town you have to expect the inevitable.'

At that moment a more hopeful sound approached from behind. She spun round to see a *Range Rover* pulling in, close to her abandoned car. 'Is that *your* convertible with the flat tyre back there?' said the driver, striding towards her.

Reenie's eyes widened. 'It is, worse luck! And no telephone boxes round here.'

'Just leave it to me. Absolutely right, no facilities at all in this neck of the woods.'

'So kind,' she said, wondering at the plum he'd swallowed.

With the Burberry jacket flung off and designer shirt sleeves rolled up, her knight in exclusive armour fetched the tool box. There was something familiar about him. And the *Rover*. Hadn't she seen him leaving *The Crown* a little earlier when she'd stopped for lunch?

'Pardon me for appearing to intrude, but have you taken a holiday here?' he said as he found the jack.

'Oh no, I live here now. *Lynton Grange*, Bickersleigh. About four miles away.'

'Well, well, fancy that.' Putting the box down, the stranger reached out to shake hands. 'You must be Lady Hartley. I'm a near neighbour, Chris Pen*selle*. Delighted to meet you.'

'Of the two of us, *I'm* probably the most delighted! I'd no idea how I was to negotiate the cow pats.' Reenie beamed, realising she hadn't attempted to amend his misnomer. She shook hands, showing her appreciation of both his help and his brown eyes and tanned appearance. With an unexpected lurch of nostalgia, Reenie couldn't help thinking of Mawgan. He was roughly the same height, too. *After all these years,* she scolded herself. He looked so like him.

'Right, set to!' said Mr Penselle, lifting the spare wheel, then fixing the jack. 'Bloody-hell, pardon my French. There's a huge nail in that tyre. But we'll have it sorted in no time.'

As he laboured on her behalf, she chatted. 'If you live near me you must work locally, Mr, um, Pen*selle*?'

'Please, I'm Chris. Yes, that's right. I'm into design – interiors, you know. Might you and your husband be interested in some—'

'My husband died last year. That's why I've moved here. A complete change.'

'Oh, I'm *so* sorry. How stupid of me, blundering in. But you're too *young* to be widowed!'

Reenie, twisting her wedding ring round her finger, sensed a sudden glow to her cheeks. Should she transfer her ring to her right hand? A shock of wavy brown hair fell over Chris's forehead as he pulled on the wheel brace. His hands were strong, like his general physique, and obviously used to hard work. Spotting his fingernails chewed to the quick, she felt a flush of concern. Such a characteristic seemed at odds with his debonair style.

'Do you have children, Lady—'

'No, we didn't have any. I'm on my own. How about you?'
'Got to have a wife first! Well, one does normally.' He chuckled infectiously, dimpling his cheeks, eyes sparkling. 'But my bachelor pad suits me down to the ground.'
Returning his smile, she pondered over his single status. Though quite boyish in appearance, he was handsome and definitely old enough to be married with a family. And, despite his accent, so charming.
'All complete,' he said. With a final yank on the brace, Chris secured the last nut.
'You've saved the day. And my shoes!' she giggled. 'I really can't thank you enough.'
'No need, it was nothing. Glad to help. But, might I ask if your new home, um, might require any changes? A little updating on the décor? You're *very* different from its previous occupant, if you don't mind me saying.'
A mischievous look danced in her direction.
'Oh, I never met her. The agent dealt with the sale.'
'Hmm, widow, much older than you. When the husband died, her sister moved in, and then … something happened. They both switched to … somewhere else. Quite old fashioned – the widow, I mean – quaint for almost fifty.'
'Oh – fifty!' Reenie ruffled her hair.
'*The Grange* will be so much better with a new breath of life from someone younger like yourself. Oh God, I'm doing it again.'
'"Doing"?'
'Forgive me if I'm being, er, over familiar.'
'Oh no, don't worry. We *are* neighbours after all. Please feel free to visit. I'd appreciate some advice on the house. It needs a few serious alterations.' Her spontaneity took her by

surprise. 'I'm looking forward to redesigning my new home, but some help …'

'Would love to. That's awfully kind of you. Can't shake on it though,' he laughed again, gazing at his oil-streaked palms. 'Must get a duster to clean myself up. Then I can give you my card.'

Feeling strangely elated, Reenie slipped into her car. The bronzed hand, now wiped clean, quickly passed a folded card to her and she popped it on the dashboard. 'Thank you again,' she said.

'Delighted to be of service. Nice cars those convertibles and you've got the weather for it, too. Hopefully, I can be of further help vis-a-vis your beautiful home? I'll pop by one day.' He smiled as she pulled at the choke and turned the key.

'I'm Irene, by the way, but my friends call me Reenie.'

She waved goodbye. One glance in the mirror told her that Chris Penselle had stopped cleaning round his finger nails and was gazing at the Hillman as she glided down the lane. Or was he looking at *her*? Of course, she had omitted to mention that her mother had moved down two months ago to take up one of the many bedrooms in *Lynton Grange*. She hoped her mother wouldn't get in the way.

Chapter 40

'Mummy! Are you nearly ready? It's almost half past ten,' Reenie called sharply from the bottom of the staircase.

'Just coming, darling.'

Now in her late seventies, her mother still looked elegant. Immaculate in her new beige suit, with not a hair out of place, courtesy of the recent perm, she reached the hall.

'We'll be late for the coffee morning if we don't hurry.' Reenie raised her voice – her mother's hearing wasn't as good as it used to be. 'You know I'm not staying for long. The designer's calling to take a look at the lounge, sketching out some ideas for the refurbishment.'

'For the lounge? It doesn't need anything doing to it!'

'But it's not *mine*. We've already been over this.' Reenie huffed. 'It's somebody else's décor. And it's dated.'

'I do wish you didn't have to leave me at Vera's. I don't know anybody.'

'It's not for long.'

Together they walked the length of the house to reach the yard where the Hillman was parked. 'Vera has said she'll look after you. And I'll be back to pick you up. It's all in a good cause. You'll get to meet our neighbours.'

Seating herself in the car, her mother pressed her lips together as disdainfully as Queen Victoria had in her later years.

'You'll be introduced to Carissa, the lady who lives in that converted castle. Remember? Someone said she's related to a viscount.'

Her mother's lips relaxed and the car slid through the gates. 'I suppose you need some time to yourself to sort things out. It's just a pity she had to come at the same time as the coffee morning.'

'She?'

'The Designer.'

'Oh, well that's life. Can't be helped.' And I'm not enlightening her to the gender of our artist.

*

As Reenie returned, she admired the chimney stacks of her new home vying with the trees for pre-eminence. A grade two listed building, its mellowed Cotswold stone had a warmth to it that *Cedars* never had. The frontage was broken up symmetrically by a porch with steps to an imposing entrance. It hid the continuum of lupins to the right-hand side and the paving stones bordering them.

But most of all, once inside, she loved the light streaming through the sash windows on to the polished floorboards. Marilyn, the daily, assisted with keeping up the shine on everything. And Reenie prized the stunning views of the Cotswold hills framed from the lounge. Her mother had exclaimed over their isolation, but she didn't mind. For Reenie it emphasized the house's grandeur, as did the peacock occasionally strutting across the lawn. "My borrowed embellishment", she called Henry, who really belonged to the adjacent farm. To Reenie, his oriental symbol of beauty was the final clincher of class for her new manor house. She could even put up with his penetrating scream from the oak tree when dawn broke.

It was time for a hasty freshen-up. She flew to the cloakroom, 'Not bad for going on forty-nine,' she said to her reflection, thinking of her "elderly" fifty-year-old predecessor. Her ruby lipstick redefined the neat bow of her lips. That sounded like Chris's car. Hastily, she fluffed out her hair. It still bounced and waved, while the colours, so carefully applied, looked as natural as the original. With the doorbell chiming, she smoothed her blouse and headed for the porch, where, to her surprise, her pulse quickened. The bell rang again and in the next second, Reenie flung open the door. 'Chris! Do come in.'

Her designer, carrying a large portfolio, stepped inside. The same lock of hair, slightly sun-bleached, tumbled over his forehead. He pushed it back with his free hand, beaming at her.

'First things first, would you like a coffee before we get down to business?' said Reenie.

'Delighted, um—?'

'Please call me Reenie. And do take a seat in the lounge.' Leading him to an armchair, she added, 'It'll give you a chance to think over the changes we need to make while I'm brewing up in the kitchen.' She was glad she had removed her family portraits that morning. Harold's had dominated the room, while hers, painted twenty years ago, emphasised the aging process. She wondered what her mother would say, but really it was none of her business. They were only on display to pacify her mother after a shocked outburst when Harold's image was consigned to the attic. Sideways.

Now, where had Marilyn put the coffee and the percolator? That was the trouble with "Dailies" – they always put things back in different places. And she had to remember how the percolator worked. Marilyn had cleaned for the previous owners and wasn't bad at her job.

Soon, the aroma of freshly ground coffee embraced her and drifted down the corridor. With a plate of biscuits saved from the Harrods' Christmas hamper, and her waistline preserved simultaneously, she carried the tray into the lounge, setting it down on a nest of tables. Chris had been busy: *Liberty* wallpaper books lay open at relevant pages, with matching swatches of fabric sprawled next to them over the sofa and chairs. Colour charts for paint possibilities jostled for position.

Looking up from his notebook, he smiled, charm oozing from his eyes.

'Just drafting and scribbling a bit.' He dropped his pencil on to the page and steepled his fingers to his chin. She noticed how he rubbed his bottom lip thoughtfully. Had she realised how attractive he was when they met in that country lane?

'It all looks quite amazing. You'll have to talk me through it.' She sipped her coffee and avoided the biscuits, aware of how difficult it was staying focused on fabrics.

Chris gazed at her. 'That's what I'm here for.'

How was it that no-one had snapped him up already?

Reenie simply relaxed into his company.

The doorbell jangled and she glanced at her watch.

'Oh, my goodness, just look at the time! Someone's calling, just when I'm running late. Won't be a minute.' She found Marilyn standing on the doorstep.

'Sorry to bother you, but I left my cardigan behind – on that chair in the hall. I was just passing—'

'I'm in such a hurry. Just help yourself.' Reenie whisked back into the lounge.

With a brisk 'Thank you,' from the hall, Marilyn slammed the front door.

Chris had moved to the other side of the room, his portfolio reassembled. 'Nice that you've made friends already.'

'Oh, that's Marilyn, my "Daily".'

'Marilyn? Did she come with the house?'

'How did you guess?' Reenie laughed. She watched him turn to the window, twitching the curtains. 'I'll be changing those to the ones you've suggested.'

'Changing? Oh, yes, the curtains. I couldn't help hearing you say you were, um, late. I do apologise if I've kept you.'

Why did he seem so distracted, peering through the window? 'Don't worry, it's just that I promised to pick ... be at a friend's house, half an hour ago.'

'Well, if she's a good friend she'll understand. We've covered a lot of ground today, in more ways than one, Mrs ... Reenie.'

He smiled again and she wished that at her age her legs hadn't weakened.

'Now, I've given you my estimates. No huge sums, I have to say. Let me know when I can start with the decorating.'

'*You* can start? You do the decorating as *well* as the designing?'

'I do indeed. Essentially, I'm a designer but I like to see a job well done, from inception to completion, you know.'

So that was why his hands were at odds with his jacket and his whole appearance. How diligent he was. 'Oh, look, I've simply got to dash, but I'll phone you. That would be *wonderful* if you were able to sort this room out.' She picked up the car keys, delighted that Chris could possibly be with her for so much longer.

'Hope you don't mind, but I just need to "tether the donkey". Delectable coffee, but goes straight through!' Chris pulled a helpless face.

'Sorry, I should have … The cloakroom is—'

He'd already slipped into the hall and then into the passageway for the toilet, as if he knew where to find it.

'Damn, I'm going to be even later now,' Reenie said to herself. 'Let's hope Carissa's keeping Mummy entertained or the atmosphere in *Lynton Grange* will be strained this afternoon.'

Chris emerged and, simultaneously, they hastened to their cars. As she turned to wave, the peacock yelled and she jumped. 'Oh, he never gives me any warning!' she laughed as Chris swivelled to look in Henry's direction.

'So, he's still here.'

'*Still?* You knew about Henry?'

'Henry? No, I noticed him up there when I arrived. Well, it will be my pleasure to see you again soon.' His hand gripped hers. Its roughness reminded her of Mawgan's.

She watched the Range Rover turn to the right. Though important not to sound too keen, she decided she'd phone him the next morning.

Where could her mother be relocated yet again?

Chapter 41

Lizzie hugged Graham and then Rachel, his fiancée. The evening had flown by too quickly.

'Come back soon,' she said.

'Don't you worry, we'll be back. And Auntie Reenie's only a few miles away now. She has changed, you know. She's ... happier, easier to get on with.'

Lizzie smiled. 'It's wonderful to have her down here. But it could be a mixed blessing with Grandma in tow!'

Lizzie noticed that Graham hadn't mention Grandma. But she *had* noticed that Reenie had brought the drinks cabinet with her. She so hoped Reenie would stick to her promise not to drink too much in future.

Giving a final wave goodbye, Lizzie went back inside. 'Best move ever,' she murmured, thinking of how fourteen years ago they hadn't imagined George's redundancy would work out so much in their favour. It was more than a year now since George had died and it was still unbearably quiet. She opened the living room door, as if that would release his voice to her. Then she stared at his armchair, the one she couldn't bring herself to sit in, willing him to return to it, legs crossed, book in hand, his other hand round a mug of strong tea. Smiling at her.

The sweet fragrance of newly mown grass, heightened in the evening air, drifted through an open fanlight. That, too, reminded her of George, all six foot of him stooping over the flower beds to bring in bundles of delphiniums. She'd never imagined life could be so agreeable since the three of them settled in; the home with the name that symbolised their new path to contentment. Now the void in her life was impossible to fill.

Lizzie, hold me. I'll always love you.

Lizzie's eyes brimmed as she remembered George's last whisper to her before meeting with eternity. *I'll always love you. Always.*

She ran her fingers over his photograph with Graham in his school uniform – her favourite picture of them both. 'Dear God, if only you'd let me speak to George. I want him to know that I think of him as soon as I open my eyes in the morning.'

Abruptly, the telephone broke into her thoughts.

'Hinden Lacey 649,' she croaked wearily.

'Hello. It's me – Reenie. How are you?'

'Oh, I'm all right. I've just said goodbye to Graham and Rachel.'

'That can't be easy when they leave you. Hope you've had a nice weekend with them. Rachel sounds lovely.' Reenie paused. 'I've been dying to speak to you. About the house; well, really about someone who's coming to sort it out.'

'You mean convert the side into Mother's annexe?'

'Not yet. That's still on the agenda. This person I've mentioned has some amazing ideas for the lounge. And he's pretty amazing himself!'

'You *are* going to make the annexe, aren't you? Don't leave it or you'll both drive each other round as many bends as in the Cotswolds!'

'I know, but he doesn't do building, just design. Do you think you could come round tomorrow? See some of his ideas and even meet him. He's dropping by at eleven. I'd like your opinion.'

'Oh, I'm not really a designer. You're much better—'

'No, not the alterations, I meant an opinion on Chris, the person who's making the changes.'

'Oh!' Lizzie was speechless.

'Lizzie, are you there? Damn this phone! Li—'

'I'm here. Why do you need my opinion on someone who's decorating your lounge? I bet Mother has expressed her sentiments, hasn't she?

'Er, no, she hasn't – hasn't met him yet.'

'Well, she will tomorrow,' Lizzie said.

'Nope – she's coffee-morning again. OAP's in the village.'

'Oh.'

'Lizzie! Stop saying "Oh!" all the time. Just tell me if you can come.'

'Is he – the designer – a similar age to us?'

'Yes!'

Lizzie smothered a sharp breath, almost as sharp as Reenie's exclamation.

'Actually, he's a bit younger,' Reenie admitted a little sheepishly. 'But you still haven't said—'

'I'll be there. Don't worry.'

*

'Oh, you should have seen his designs – wonderful! Liberty fabrics, matching wallpaper, colours I couldn't dream up. It's all perfect. Your aunt can afford whatever she likes!' Lizzie said to Graham the following Sunday as he finished up the crumble.

Graham chuckled. 'I meant his *designs* on Auntie Reenie!'

'Oh!' Lizzie laughed. 'Sorry. Bit slow off the mark, I'm afraid.'

'What's he like?'

She paused, gathering her thoughts. She could hear George saying, 'Your Mum's always more than fair. She'll never run anyone down.'

'He's quite pleasant; falls over himself to be polite. Bit of a plum when he speaks, though.'

'Auntie Reenie doesn't seem to mind?'

Lizzie shook her head.

'What does he look like?'

'Quite tall, lots of wavy, brown hair. Sun tanned – must work outdoors as well as inside, I suppose. He's full of charm, especially with those brown eyes, and obviously has a talent for interior decorating.'

Graham raised his hands to the ceiling. 'And spotting a widow who's loaded! You haven't said how old he is.'

'Um, a bit hard to say, but he's probably … thirty-ish.'

'Thirty! Auntie Reenie can't fancy him then.'

'W-e-ll—'

Graham groaned. He stood up and put the kettle on. 'Auntie Reene used to stretch for the drinks' cabinet, but I think I'll make a black coffee. Despite Uncle Harold and everything else, I'm fond of my aunt. You can't seriously let her fall for him. He's got to be after her money.'

'She's not stupid. And when has she ever let me influence her choices?'

'She's always phoning you.'

'I know, but I'm just her sounding board. She usually—'

'I can't believe this.' Graham stirred the sugar into his coffee as if grinding granite. 'It's so obvious.'

'Look, Auntie Reenie is just finding her wings, after such a long time keeping them folded – no, squashed! She's still lonely and in need of friendship. If this – relationship – helps her to settle into Bickersleigh, I'm all for it. It'll probably fizzle out as quickly as it's started, when she's made a few more friends.'

'I think you ought to say something.'

Graham's comment sparked a flashback.

'I tried that once before,' she said, 'a long time ago, and it didn't work, so why should it work now?'

Chapter 42

Chris's smile brought a vitality to Reenie's existence. Little by little, Reenie's lounge was transformed, as was the hall, the dining room ... and her life. It was as if her very soul had slowly atrophied over two decades. When her arm grazed Chris's as she lifted the fabrics, a tingle tiptoed her spine. With the armfuls of flowers he brought into the house, she was revitalized. They were gone, those measured, cold times and she could start again. With her hair still luxuriant and in the latest fashion, her figure neat and skin pampered, Reenie felt the years lifting from her. Why shouldn't she think of herself as still attractive? Even so, she applied her makeup with extra diligence and tried to smile confidently at her reflection.

After a busy and warm summer's morning, Reenie suggested a break with cool drinks and choice Kunzle cakes. 'Ready, Chris?' she called from the hall with the tray in her hand. Before he could reply, her foot clipped a paint pot and, with a screech, she fell headlong into a bag of plaster. A cloud of pink dust exploded, settling like rose-tinted snow over and around her. Struggling to rise, she blinked at particles fluttering from her lashes. 'Not sure if pink suits me!' she spluttered.

Chris shook with laughter. 'Oh my God, you look ... amazing!' He knelt down and swept the powder from her shoulders. 'Don't get me wrong, but I could—' His fingers teased through her hair, then touched her brow and smoothed her cheeks, his brown eyes gazing into hers. In seconds she was twenty years younger.

'Don't stop,' she whispered as she closed her eyes.

'You're covered ... in layers—'

'Then ... they need removing.'

Gently, he dusted her arms; his fingers brushed over her breasts and then clasped her hands. She blew through her lips, moistening, softening them and giggled, 'It's a first for lipstick.'

'P'raps I should, if you ...'

She leant into him, 'I did say, "Don't stop".'

*

When the chrysanthemums declared the first hint of autumn, a few weeks later, Reenie's reverie on her burgeoning romance was cut short by the doorbell. 'Lizzie!' she said on opening the door. 'How lovely to see you.'

'Just passing by – thought I'd drop in to see the renovations.'

'Come in,' said Reenie, pulling Lizzie into the lounge and watching her face for a reaction.

Lizzie stared, open mouthed. 'Oh, my word, it takes your breath away!'

'I'm so pleased with it. Don't stand – have a seat.' Reenie pinched her mouth into an anxious smile. 'While you're here ... there's something I've got to talk about – quickly, while Mummy's resting in her room.' She drew in a deep breath. 'I've been dying to tell you – it's Chris – he's my "Mr Right". At last! But, do you think the age gap is a problem?' She stiffened, waiting for the blow.

Lizzie looked into her eyes. 'Well, I s'pose that depends on how much you love each other.'

'Of course we love each other! I'd like to think we'd be as close as you and George were.' Reenie couldn't bring herself to mention the wasted years with Harold.

'If Chris is your man, perhaps age isn't so important.'

'Not if it's nineteen years difference?' *Even twenty,* she said to herself.

Lizzie paused. 'Not if you truly love each other. Most people grab happiness when it comes their way. Don't let it slip through your fingers this time.'

"This time"? Was she referring to ... Mawgan? Shocked that Mawgan should still spring to mind, Reenie returned to Chris. 'He told me he didn't think about my age, especially as I looked so youthful.'

'But you are *sure*, aren't you, that Chris's intentions are—?'

'Chris loves me. I *know!*'

There it was again. Lizzie wasn't the only member of her family who seemed to distrust the one person making her life worth living. If only her fiftieth birthday wasn't calling her.

'Um, what have you gleaned of his background,' Lizzie continued. 'How much do you—?'

'He might seem a bit ... rugged, with his decorating business, but he's *County!* You've heard me say that before. Still, I don't care what his provenance is. He grew up in this part of the world; his parents sent him to boarding school, which he *loathed*, poor thing. His stories make me feel – was I about to say—'

'Maternal? That shouldn't be a problem, not if it's resolving a need for him. Why should it matter?'

'Of course it matters! The last thing I want is to be his mother.'

'You wouldn't be. Maybe just ... extra supportive from time to time. Have you met his parents?'

'They died a few years ago, and he's estranged from his sisters, half-sisters. I daren't question him about his family. He gets very touchy if I do.'

Lizzie looked concerned and Reenie took her hand, 'It's *Chris* who matters and if I can help him, I will.'

Lizzie smiled now. 'I'm just pleased that my little sister is happy at long last. See – I was meant to call on you this afternoon. But,' she glanced at her watch, 'I haven't got long. I'm meeting Rachel at four.'

All too quickly, Reenie was on her own again, but at least she could bask in thoughts of Chris.

*

Another coffee morning at Carissa's for her mother gave Reenie and Chris the freedom to explore both decorating and their new relationship.

'Chris, dearest, the dining room does look wonderful now, but …'

'But what?'

'I did have a few of my own ideas. I thought—'

'Reene! I'm the designer. I've transformed it.'

Reenie drew breath … and then said nothing.

'Time to celebrate all my efforts. Come on, I'll pour you another whisky.'

'No more alcohol, darling,' Reenie giggled. 'It's not even mid-day!'

'Just one small glass. Here we go – here's to the new room.'

Reenie raised her tumbler. 'And here's to us.'

'Shall we look at those other swatches for the hall?' said Chris.

'Not now. We've got an hour before Mummy gets back. So—'

They made for the lounge, closed the door and slipped on to the settee. Buttons and blouse slithered with ease, until Chris sat up with a start. 'Are you sure your mother's out?'

'Quite sure. I took her in the car hours ago.'

He breathed out and Reenie re-nestled.

'Darling, your Mama is a special lady, I know, but she can be a bit of a … problem. Sometimes.'

'Oh, she can't help it, but I must admit she does drive me up the —'

CRASH!

Something had toppled in the hall.

Chris leapt to his feet and Reenie followed.

'I knew it!' she heard him mutter. '*Somebody's* outside the lounge.'

Reenie's eyes widened as she reached the hall. Her mother stood guiltily by an antique vase in pieces on the floor. 'Mummy! Why are you here?' Hastily, Reenie pushed herself back into her clothes, being more concerned about her mother's listening skills than the fractured vase.

'I've such a bad headache. Carissa brought me back. Didn't you hear me? I've been lying down in my room.'

Damn, it must have happened when we were in the garage.

'I was just fetching my medication, dear. I'm so sorry about the vase.'

'You sit quietly on this chair, Mrs Meadows, while *I* fetch your pills,' said Chris, guiding her to a seat. 'I know where Reenie keeps them.'

Reenie beamed after Chris as he headed for the kitchen, then focussed on her mother. 'You might have let us know you were back.'

'Well, dear, I wouldn't have wanted to interrupt anything. Ah, there you are—'

Chris, ever solicitous, had returned with the pills and a glass of water. 'Let me help you up to your room,' he said, gently looping his arm under their eavesdropper's.

With a twinge of guilt, Reenie mounted the stairs, not far behind them.

'You should sleep like you've never slept before,' drifted from the bedroom.

Chris had such a smooth way of speaking. So calming. Although she'd only known him for a few months, Reenie realised she couldn't imagine life without him.

Chapter 43

Early October – where had summer gone to? Lizzie sighed, wishing Reenie's friendship with Chris hadn't raced ahead so quickly. She picked up her sister's postcard on the windowsill, gazing at the picture of the Italian Lakes and then back to the cryptic message on the other side.

Weather not quite up to expectations, but everything else is, including my special news!
Reenie x

Special news? Oh no! Reenie always kept her messages to the minimum. She'd chosen to tantalise with this one.

'What do you think?' she asked her mother.

'Sounds like bad news to me!'

'Do you think Chris has proposed?'

'And Irene accepted. She's besotted with him.' Her mother frowned.

'I know,' Lizzie sighed. 'She's only known him for about four months.'

'It's ridiculous, going away together when they're not even married, though heaven forbid that should ever happen!'

'Reenie's forty-nine! I don't think you can be telling her who she can and can't be going on holiday with.'

'Well, at least I'm staying with you while she's away. We can work out a strategy together.'

'Strategy?'

Her mother raised her hands to the ceiling. 'For making her see sense.'

'Oh, I tried that once before. Don't you remember? When I asked you to persuade her not to marry Harold. You said she wasn't persuadable.'

'That was different. Harold was highly eligible.' Lizzie noticed that her mother reverted to fingering the faint scar on the back of her hand, a reminder of the shattered teacup at Lizzie's mother-in-law's. Yet another jibe at George, her own choice.

Lizzie kept quiet. It was useless to argue. She might just as well get her mother to eat at the new KFC as coax her into a rational opinion of Reenie's first marriage.

'So, what are we to do?' continued her mother. 'I can't *stand* the man – he's evil!'

'Evil! From what I've seen of him he's—'

'A snake about to strike! Our neighbours don't think much of him, either.'

'What d'you mean?'

'Celine said something to me last week about him that I couldn't quite catch. It's not *what* she said, but how she looked. Something about Chris's parents owning – must have been "shooting" – the grouse. Frankly, I couldn't care less about grouse or Chris – I think he does keep a shotgun in the back of that monstrous jeep. I just sort of huffed to let Celine know *that man* is not my cup of tea, either. We can't let him worm his way into Irene's affections.'

'Nothing I say … at what stage is the plan for converting the house, making your own, self-contained space?'

'Oh, not that idea! Has Mr Pen*selle* been converting you instead?'

Lizzie frowned now. 'You just alienate Chris calling him by his surname. It's no use antagonising him; that'll only stick the two of them together more firmly than *Loctite*. And, no, he hasn't mentioned the project. It was decided when you bought the place to alter it. That's why Reenie took on such a huge house.'

Her mother snorted, 'Nonsense! Irene's used to a sizeable home. I've grown to like my room and have no intention of changing the arrangement. *He's* the interloper.'

'Don't get me wrong – I'm concerned about her marrying Chris. The age gap is huge, but he does make her happy. And he's always the perfect gentleman.' *Even to you*, she felt like adding. 'I do think you need your own place. With or without Chris. Reenie and you generally get on well together but I've noticed you're rubbing each other—'

'It's *him*. He's changed everything. You've got to help.'

'All right. I'll see what I can do. But I won't interfere. It's Reenie's life. That's what you said to me once before, over Harold, when I *did* try to interfere.' She stared at her mother still rubbing the scar. 'I just want her to make the right choice.'

Sitting in her fireside chair, Lizzie pushed the postcard back into her novel. She couldn't concentrate; the plot in her sister's life was ever more beguiling and she feared the more obvious outcome for Reenie than the fiction in her lap. Another cryptic message via an abrupt telephone call had bounced in the day before. Why had Reenie asked her to be at the station tomorrow as they returned from Italy? Reenie always took a taxi home. She ran over the conversation in her mind.

'Where are you?'

'London. Coming home on Sunday– on the train. It would

be so lovely if you could be at the station to meet us. Four-thirty, all being well. We'd like to take you out for tea, especially as we're asking a big favour of you – please hang on to Mummy for another few days. DON'T bring her with you and don't tell her we're home, not yet!'

'Oh! Is everything—?'

'Sorry, simply got to go now. Will you be there?'

'Yes, I ... I can manage it.'

And that was that. 'Your wish is my command,' Lizzie murmured to the burr of the telephone.

Throughout their brief conversation, everything Reenie referred to involved "we" and "us". Lizzie sank her head into her hands. So it sounded like she was going to be the buttress between the happy couple and their mother.

Quarter to three – she could see her mother glancing up at the clock, to her annoyance from George's chair. As she'd always deemed George to be inferior to the Meadows, her mother's seeking out *his* chair whenever visiting irked Lizzie. No, she wouldn't mention Reenie's telephone call.

The hand on the clock moved far too slowly, but it gave Lizzie the chance to rehearse possible scenarios: I'm thrilled for you both. But are you sure Chris is the man for you second time around? I'm only saying this because your happiness is paramount. She shook her head. It would have to wait for the appropriate opportunity: Chris would be with her today.

Three-fifteen ... three-thirty. At last. Lizzie placed her hand gently on her mother's shoulder. 'Sorry to disturb you, but I'm leaving now.'

'What? Oh yes, going to meet a friend.'

'Tea's on the table and I'll be back in a couple of hours.'

'Back with flowers?'

Lizzie laughed. 'Not that I know of.' She raised her voice. 'Back in two hours.'

'You keep mumbling. Everyone keeps mumbling. Is this acquaintance something to do with Reenie?'

'Bye, Mother,' Lizzie called without answering.

She locked the door behind her. If only Chris wasn't quite so young. Still driving the van George had used for work, she set out for the station, despite its rattling round corners. The contrast between her vehicle and Reenie's Hillman Convertible brought a smile to her face. Were they all driving back together to Bickersleigh? In the van? Graham was right: his Auntie Reenie *was* a changed person.

As the last space in the car park presented itself, Lizzie pulled on the handbrake and made for the station platform. Another wait. Her emotions see-sawed: one minute, swinging up with the pleasure of seeing Reenie again, the next sinking down with thoughts of a triumphant Chris at her side. The first thing she would look at was Reenie's left hand.

'It's coming,' a small boy shouted excitedly a few yards away.

A distant spectre loomed larger and larger until the four-twenty powered into its destination. Lizzie scrutinized the flash of faces in windows as the train slowed down and then, more easily, the passengers disgorging from doors flung open. There she was and how stylish she looked: white linen trouser suit, with neat, waisted jacket, surely Italian, together with the red leather handbag slung over her shoulder. A wide brimmed hat completed the picture with her wavy hair framing her still attractive features. She looked like a model. A red ribbon round the hat and matching lipstick completed the effect.

If only I looked half as good, Lizzie thought, as Reenie hugged her. One quick glance at the ring finger told her she would have to wait for an answer – gloves, as pure as the suit itself, covered the evidence sought.

'Lizzie, darling. So sweet of you to be here. Chris thought I shouldn't ask, but I knew!'

Chris stepped forwards, brushing his sun-bleached hair from his forehead and hugged her. 'I do hope we haven't expected too much of you.' Reenie was right: he was charm itself. So why ...? Was it purely the age difference and her concern about his motivation? She smiled back. The weather couldn't have been as poor as the postcard suggested – his deepened tan suited him, though it seemed to emphasize his youth.

'Reenie – you are stunning,' said Lizzie as she was enveloped in a haze of expensive perfume.

'She certainly is,' said Chris as Reenie gazed at him.

'Then I can recommend the Italian Lakes.' Reenie, glowing as if she'd reached the clouds, laughed. 'Now it's tea at *The Angel*. They're expecting a threesome. I hope my sister doesn't mind being our chauffeur?'

'Of course not, if you don't mind squeezing into the van. I'm not sure that your suit will be quite as white afterwards,' Lizzie chuckled. 'Then I can take you back to *The Grange*.'

'No need, Lizzie. Chris left his Rover at *The Angel*. Stephen, the proprietor, knows us well.'

The gloves stayed put. No matter how much Lizzie peered at the cover-up, it was impossible to identify a new engagement ring. She'd have to wait till the cake was passed round.

'Come on,' said Reenie when they arrived at the hotel, 'follow me.'

To Lizzie's amazement the proprietor hurried over, indicating a table with a cloth vying with Reenie's trouser suit for whiteness. But it wasn't fashion catching her attention: the champagne bottle in the cooler couldn't be missed, nor the large silver horseshoe embracing it.

'Congratulations, Mrs Pen*selle*,' said Stephen, turning first to Reenie and then to Chris. 'And to you, sir. We are delighted for you both.'

Lizzie felt her mouth drop open. For a moment it was impossible to close it.

'Don't look so shocked!' said Reenie.

Chris squeezed Lizzie's hand. 'I've not only got the perfect wife, but the sweetest of sisters-in-law.'

'So pleased,' Lizzie said, trying her hardest to sound convincing. The shock of Reenie's news left her stretching for the chair back. The proprietor fussed round them, pulling out seats and calling for the waiter, who promptly picked up the ostentatious bottle. Champagne at *The Angel* was in keeping with Reenie's life-style and this astonishing occasion.

'Tell me about the wedding,' Lizzie murmured.

'It was like a fairy tale. There's a castle overlooking the lake. It did take a bit of planning beforehand, but when Chris accepted me—'

'*You* did the proposing?'

Reenie's eyes sparkled like the champagne. By now her hat was on a side table, together with the gloves. A simple platinum ring on her wedding finger gleamed as she rumpled her hair in the same old way.

'We're made for each other. Cliché or not, it's true. Chris is a little on the shy side, so I did the nudging!' Reenie slipped her hand over Chris's resting next to hers. 'Why wait, I thought. Life's too short. Chris suggested the holiday. That's when I found out about the castle with its wedding speciality. It was in the brochure he gave me.'

'But why didn't you tell us?' Despite her question, Lizzie knew the answer.

'Mummy would have—'

'Had a fit,' said Chris, chuckling. 'It's all right. I do understand. It's hard to adjust at her age.'

'I'm afraid Chris is right,' said Reenie, '*You* know that. I wanted everything to go ahead without histrionics. No delay. I was quite sure of Chris. So – a *fait-accompli*. This way Mummy has to accept our marriage.'

'Absolutely,' said Chris, beaming at Reenie and then Lizzie.

Lizzie wondered if she'd covered up her unease when she looked at Chris. Did that smile reach his eyes? Whatever troubled her, or him, he was now her brother-in-law and so different from the previous one. The champagne cork exploded. 'Oh!' Lizzie screamed, her hand flying to her mouth.

'*Saluti!*' said Reenie and Chris simultaneously, with arms and flutes entwined. Cut glass chinked, bubbles popped, laughter mingled and the cash register at *The Angel* increased its sum total.

'Only half a glass for me,' Lizzie protested. 'I'm driving.'

'A full one won't hurt,' said Chris, pouring liberally. 'I'm going for a second.' Another twinge of anxiety gnawed at Lizzie. It was obvious it wasn't their first drink of the day.

Please don't rescind on your vow to drink less, Lizzie willed Reenie.

She listened to Reenie's descriptions, fuelled by excitement and alcohol, of their ceremony in a medieval castle. With vows exchanged and two witnesses from the hotel, sunlight had flooded over Reenie and Chris when they'd stepped outside. After the sombre interior, it was as if all the happiness in the world bestowed itself upon them. Bells pealed as they descended through steep, narrow cobbled streets embellished with colourful window boxes. Shoppers and holiday makers alike stopped to gaze and cheer them on to the lakeside where a festive meal awaited them.

Lizzie listened in awe. 'I've never known you speak so eloquently! How could you notice so much?'

'It was so beautiful. So romantic. I wanted to soak up each and every detail. It was everything I could have wished for.'

More bells for Lizzie, tolling in alarm. Hadn't she heard that last phrase once before?

Reenie continued in the same vibrant tone, 'I expect you're wondering about my engagement ring?'

Lizzie wasn't. She was more concerned about Reenie's life-changing choice, made so hastily. How were they to break the news to their mother?

'Lizzie? You haven't answered my question.'

'No, I wasn't thinking about jewellery, more about … Mother.'

'Well, firstly, the ring is at the workshop. It's antique and slightly too big. Chris chose it. So, our engagement's back to front. Next, Mummy will have to be told, but this is why we asked you to come on your own. We thought—'

'You could drop hints, little by little? Like the old dripping tap. My *wife's* suggestion,' said Chris, emphasizing his new relationship.

'Darling! Mummy *will* come round to liking you. I'm working on it.'

'So am I,' Chris grinned boyishly.

'We do need a few days to ourselves. Chris must feel at home before Mummy gets back. You don't mind hanging on to her, do you?'

Lizzie smiled obligingly and nodded. Then considered the original annexe plans, now more crucial than ever. But an extended wedding reception was not the time to pursue such a prickly subject.

Chapter 44

As Chris drove back to The Grange, Reenie couldn't wait to step through the door with the husband she'd yearned for. Years of being a lonely collector's item was a thing of the past. It was a pity Lizzie hadn't been convinced by Chris's sincerity. She knew that edge to her sister's voice when she'd said, "So pleased."

'That's a hell of a snake,' Reenie said as Chris slewed round a z-bend. Or was it her head swimming? They'd been celebrating on the train as well.

'Don't worry, I've driven down these roads all my life. I can't wait to put my feet up in the old *Grange*.

Reenie paused as she thought of Chris returning to her beautiful home. No – *their* home. Together.

'Penny for them, love-of-my-life,' he slurred as he tried to avoid a pothole in the road.

Hadn't Harold said those very words to her at the beginning of her first marriage? Only *that* husband hadn't needed any more pennies. 'Is that all my thoughts are worth?' Reenie replied.

'You, sweet soul, are worth more than anyone can tell!'

Reenie laughed. 'Whoa! Take it steady round these corners.'

Chris tipped back and guffawed. 'Stop fretting, you're entirely in my hands now.'

Roughly three miles to go before safety could be reached. Hopefully, the headline in the next issue of *Contact Cotswold* wouldn't be *Newly Weds Die in Head-on Collision*. That had associations, too, which she preferred not to dwell on.

'Well, you can give me a penny – no, a tantalising kiss – after I've told you mine.' Chris cleared his throat. 'When your Mama returns from Lizzie's, we will need to look into sorting an annexe for her.'

'I'll phone the architect tomorrow. But we can't be too hard on her.'

Reenie caught the conciliatory kiss blown in her direction. Instead of thinking about the lingering kiss to come, she pictured Marylyn cleaning the house to perfection. She wished Chris hadn't made her dismiss Marilyn. 'Believe it or not, I'm thinking about the dusting. You will find another home-help, won't you? Soon!'

'Of course I will. But we don't want anyone fussing round us for the moment. I want you just to myself.'

She looked at him with forgiving eyes. In every other way he was so attentive to her, not extravagantly like former times, but in all the little surprise presents, including the kiss to the nape of her neck and telling her how beautiful she was. Countless sweet devotions. If only her family didn't think he was after her money. He wasn't. He had his own cottage not far from *The Grange*, where his work was going well. After all, he could afford a *Range Rover* and designer outfits, although she wasn't sure how. And now she was in the picture, she could elevate him to, say, *Penselle Designs*. He'd be employing decorators in future rather than doing it all himself.

She reflected on signing the will before they married. There was nothing unusual about leaving him everything on her death, and another clause mentioned divorce. Well, that wasn't going to happen. But … the cottage he owned bothered her. 'My other thoughts were about your cottage—'

'It's my office – keeping my work separate from my love life, darling.'

'But it might be sensible if I have a key to *Retreat*, just in case.'

Chris frowned. 'Don't be silly! There wouldn't be a "just in case"! Look, if it makes you feel better, I'll have another one cut.'

She could tell he didn't want to. A furtive unease crept into her. She dismissed it as quickly as it had arrived.

He smoothed her knee affectionately. She glanced at his handsome profile and he beamed in return. She couldn't wait to run her fingers through his hair and tell him how much she loved him.

*

'Arrived in one piece!' Reenie said, flinging the front door open. She guided him over the threshold and, as promised, planted her lips on his.

'Mmmmmm. That lived up to my last drop of sexpectation, pardon the pun, darling wife!'

So why did he pull away from her?

'Where are you going to?' she asked as he strode purposefully down the hall.

'Cellar. Got to toast the bride once more *and* christen the new home with a bottle.'

'We've barely stopped imbibing all day! I did promise Lizzie I'd drink less from now on.' Nevertheless, he disappeared. She sank on to the settee in the lounge, head humming with exhaustion and alcohol. Something troubled her. What was it?

'Here we are, my lady-love.' Chris burst in, wiping a bottle with his hanky. 'Told you I'd find something.'

'But how did you know it was there?'

'All cellars have wine in them.'

'No, I meant how did you know where the *cellar* was?' An ordinary cupboard-sized door, set back from the stairs, opened to it. She'd never seen him go near the gloomy place. 'Oh, I'm used to these old houses. They've all got cellars. Come on, let's pop the cork.' He peered at the label. 'Bloody-hell, it's 'fifty-two!'

'Fifty-two. The year when she and Harold were married. Reenie frowned. 'Let's not have that one. It feels like a bad omen.'

'Nonsense!'

She watched Chris firing the cork and the wine gurgling into what looked like a tumbler. 'Where's yours?' she said as he passed it to her.

'Just watch.' He tipped a few spots of wine from the bottle on to the hearth.

'What on earth …?'

'I christen *The Old Lynton Grange* into new life, now named *Penselle Heritage*.' He kissed his fingers, lightly touching, not her, but the grate. Then he shook a few drops of wine over the stones. Taking a long swig from the bottle, he placed it on the coffee table and slumped half on top of her. 'You and me *ch*ogether. Don't mind if a poor old chap rests his head on your shoulder, do you, sweetheart?' He looked at her with tenderness and apology. 'My little joke didn't upset you, did it?'

By now her head was spinning. Didn't he forget to toast the bride? And the paltry joke *had* upset her. But it was no use saying anything – he was snoring. So much for consummating their love for each other on their first night back. She'd had different ideas for the occasion when they'd flown into Heathrow.

Why had that sense of unease returned? It wasn't the silly christening and bravado, not even the breaking of her promise to drink less. It was … the alcoholic fog lifted slightly and she could see Chris heading swiftly for the cellar.

It didn't seem like he'd guessed where it was.

Chapter 45

Propped up in bed waiting for Chris to return with breakfast, Reenie planned an evening get-together. 'Darling, I have asked you to have Graham and Rachel over several times, but you keep putting it off. We should be congratulating them on their engagement.'

'I am pretty busy and, you know, it's not always easy meeting so many new people.'

'But you had no problem befriending me on that roadside!' she reminded him.

Chris cupped her chin and kissed her, 'You, Sweet-pea, are different.'

Just as she and her mother were getting to know them, their neighbours seemed to be withdrawing from their circle. Reenie wondered at Chris's paradoxical lack of confidence when he had more charm, if he wished to use it, in his demeanour than her mother could muster for an entire lifetime. Still, she knew enough about him by now to use the most effective approach: 'That superb meal you cooked for us the day before Mummy came back – do you think you could conjure it up again?'

'For you I can do anything,' said Chris.

'Well, I do want to ask the neighbours round, but this time it would be for Graham and family.' Reenie gazed at Chris. He was still in his dressing gown, spoiling her with tea and toast beside the bed. That lock of hair falling over his handsome brow reminded her of the first time they'd met. He pushed it back irritably and screwed up his face.

'Shall we think about it? The work's piled high – back to the old slog, I'm afraid.'

He kissed the top of her head. 'Decided – shower, breakfast and – off to *Retreat*. Oh, forgot to say, this came for you today.' He gulped his tea and pulled out a dog-eared envelope from his pocket. 'Looks like it's been on its rounds before it found our new address.'

'Who can that be from?' Reenie started to open it as Chris disappeared. 'So, when can I arrange the meal for? I'm phoning Lizzie later,' she called.

'We'll talk about it when I get back,' he shouted from the shower.

She sighed. She wasn't going to let the subject drop.

Meanwhile, the curious missive begged to be investigated. Two addresses had been scored out, one of them being *The Cedars*. Someone had obviously delayed in finding its correct destination and the handwriting was just as mysterious. She tore at the flap.

Cornwall
26th August 1970
Dear Reenie,

Sorry to be contacting you only when I'm the bearer of sad news. I'm afraid Jenny passed away peacefully last week after a short illness.

'No!' Reenie dropped the letter. A cold tide seeped down her spine. 'Not Jenny!' She picked the letter up and tried to refocus.

I'd hoped she might pull through, but it wasn't to be. I know you and Jenny fell out, but you used to be such good friends – thought you'd want to know.

Just in case you wish to come to the funeral, it's at 2 pm on Friday 4ᵗʰ September at the old chapel.

Sincere good wishes to you and Harold,

Mawgan

Reenie blinked away her tears. She covered her face with her hands, in her mind's eye watching the two of them giggling together on their way home from school, sharing their homework when stuck, standing in for each other when an alibi was needed. Or discussing their preferences for the handsomest boy in town.

Not even fifty. How cruel life could be. The children would be devastated. And herself? The impossibility of ever renewing their friendship hit her like Harold's slap across her face. She fingered the sting on her cheek, then buried her head in her arms resting on the table and wept. She sobbed not only for her and her family's loss, but also for the impossibility of ever restoring their friendship. Feeling the wetness of her sleeve against her face, she raised her head and reached for the tissues. There was one thing she could do and that was write to Mawgan. The funeral had taken place over a month ago. Whatever must he think of her? When she had finished writing, she propped the letter against the salt cellar until she could find a stamp for it.

*

'Who's Mr Pedrick?' Chris asked on his return.

Reenie explained and Chris swept her into his arms. 'So sorry. For a moment I thought you were writing to an old flame.' He smoothed her hair and lifted her chin to look into her eyes with the sympathy that touched her heart. She leant into his chest. He smelt of the autumn garden, the chrysanthemums he'd just brought into the kitchen and somehow it brought solace with it.

'Hey, not saying anything? I'm not right am I – the old flame?'

She shook her head.

'Don't think I could cope with any opposition!'

Reenie looked up and he kissed her brow. Her lips softened to receive another kiss.

*

A week later, to Reenie's relief, the family party was arranged: Graham, Rachel and Lizzie would arrive at seven. Chris had spent some time in what he called his "pad" since their conversation about the gathering. His cottage, *Retreat*, he insisted remained as his extra dwelling for his business, especially since *Penselle Design* now had an injection of fresh promise: a substantial sum of money had been invested. At least on this particular day, Chris was home and in earnest over the preparations. 'Leave it all to me,' he said, 'and no peering into the dining room.'

'Keep it casual. I thought the kitchen would be all right,' said Reenie. 'Graham doesn't stand on ceremony. Young people don't anymore. Oh, and by the way, don't overdo the drinks tonight.'

However, by late afternoon things weren't going as well as she had hoped. While Reenie and Chris took a well-earned break with a cup of tea for a change, her mother huffed and puffed round the kitchen, fiddling unnecessarily. 'Only saying you haven't put the plates to warm,' she said, raising her eyebrows in Chris's direction. 'And don't forget – I tidied everything in here this morning.'

'How could I forget?' Chris muttered out of earshot.

'Irene – are you changing that dress?' she continued. 'I'm just going up to put something smarter on.'

Tension heightened for Reenie as Chris folded his arms and growled, 'What did I say? I've only got to turn my head and she's there, at my elbow, or yours. Constantly interfering. You know the old adage, "I didn't marry your mother". He checked on the roast and basted the potatoes. 'It'll be ready in an hour. Time for an aperitif. Maybe that'll mellow dear Mama when she comes down.'

'I know she's utterly exasperating, but try to imagine what it's like for her. Only four weeks ago she'd no idea we were getting married. It's quite a lot for her to take on board.'

Chris grimaced. 'The only "boards" she should be contemplating are the ones on her bedroom floor.'

'Shh! She'll hear you.'

'Irene?'

'Bloody-hell – see what I mean?'

The kitchen door opened.

'I forgot …' Her mother's gaze locked on to the drinks by the china. 'More spirits, Chris?' She raised an eyebrow at Reenie. 'Isn't this your third or fourth since lunch time, dear?'

'Special occasion, dearest Mama.' Chris thrust a sherry into her hand. She opened her mouth, then clearly thought better of saying anything, but her "Queen Victoria", as Chris called it, persisted. 'All's well,' he said as cheerfully as possible, 'Reenie's helping you back to the lounge, *aren't* you, darling.'

On her return, Reenie ventured into the dining room. She gasped at its transformation: the table had been set, with two polished candelabras in the centre, cutlery gleaming and arranged in multiples on either side of the placemats, together with two glasses per person, glinting in the light. Every item was reflected in the burnished surface of the mahogany table. The new, exotic curtains draped from floor to ceiling, had been bunched slightly on the refurbished floorboards, while a silver tea set, equally highlighted, sat ostentatiously on the sideboard. Chris had even thought to fill the decanters. Extra bottles, like soldiers standing to attention, ranged behind them.

'It looks amazing!' she called. 'Where did you find that tea set?'

'Rummaging round the attic,' he said as he joined her. 'Nice, isn't it.'

'Fancy the previous owner leaving it behind! I had no idea there was anything—'

'You weren't supposed to come in here yet.'

'Oh Chris, that's sweet of you to go to so much trouble. The only thing that concerns me is—'

'What's there to worry about?'

Reenie pointed at everything. 'Might it be a bit formal? It's only Graham and Rachel coming. I thought we'd be tucking into the dinner in the kitchen.'

'For God's sake, is there no pleasing you? Their first meal here. Thought we could make an impression.'

'Chris!' Tears unexpectedly brimmed. 'I … I didn't think you could—'

Instantly, he wrapped his arms round her. 'Sorry, my love. Don't know what came over me. I'm afraid Mama has rattled my last shred of ...whatever.' He bent over and gently wiped the tears from her face. 'How could I? Forgive me, darling.'

'No, it's me, I shouldn't have—'

'Shh!' He placed his fingers on her lips and stretched for a second glass of sherry. 'No Adam's ale for you. Drink up. You'll feel better for a drop more.'

She closed her eyes, while Chris's fingers massaged her shoulders. 'We're together and that's all that matters.'

Reenie breathed out slowly and brushed down her skirt.

When the doorbell rang, she at least felt their differences had been smoothed as much as her clothing. 'So lovely to see you all,' she said, adopting her hostess voice.

Lizzie stood behind Graham and Rachel, smiling at her. Graham was wearing his usual bell-bottoms, while Rachel wore smart trousers with a figure-hugging mohair jumper, adding a touch of class. A metaphoric instamatic still snapped for Reenie where fashion was concerned.

'Don't stand on the doorstep you three. Come in!' With hugs and kisses exchanged, Reenie led them inside. 'I've been dying to meet you, Rachel. Graham must have told you he's my favourite nephew!'

'Graham has cousins?' Rachel looked surprised.

'I'm afraid not, but if he had, Graham would still be the best,' chuckled Reenie.

Rachel laughed in turn. 'He's told me how much he likes coming to see you.'

Hanging coats on the stand, Reenie glanced back at the kitchen, hoping Chris would put in an appearance. 'Follow me. We've lit a fire in the lounge and Grandma is expecting you. I hope you've been warned, Rachel, about Grandma's "once over"!'

Graham smiled. 'Something smells good. You've been busy, Auntie Reenie.'

A deafening crash stopped everyone in their tracks. 'Bloody-hell!' reverberated from the kitchen and down the hall. Reenie clamped her fingers to her mouth.

'Don't worry, I feel completely at home now,' chuckled Graham.

So like his mother, always trying to put people at ease, Reenie said to herself. 'I'll have words with my husband! Not the best introduction for you all,' she laughed. 'This way. Grandma can't cope with delays.'

'I've been looking forward to this all week,' confirmed Grandma as the guests trooped into the lounge. 'And it's nice to have some time together without any meddling from—'

'Meddling from the chef, Mama?' said Chris, striding in to join them. 'Now that would never do!' He beamed at everyone, while *Mama* covered a scowl from her seat by the hearth. Chris ignored his mother-in-law, kissing first Lizzie; then pumping Graham's hand. 'Last but not least, my dear – you must be Rachel. Delighted!' He took Rachel's hand and pressed it to his lips.

Reenie linked her arm through Rachel's. 'As you can tell, Chris is my knight; rescued me from boredom to new life!'

'Well, *Chef* declares dinner is about to be served.' Chris slipped his arm round Reenie's waist.' But first, a little "warmer" before we start. White wine, sherry, whisky, G and T? I prefer fruit of the grain, but everyone to their own. Rachel?'

As if colluding with the matriarch, the log fire spat and hissed at the mention of spirits. Reenie hoped her mother's snort had merged with the combustion in the grate, while

Chris sorted the "orders" and then edged towards the door. 'Shall we finish the drinks in the dining room? Can't leave the galley for too long.'

Reenie took in a deep breath. She so wanted everyone to see Chris at his best.

Why shouldn't they?

Chapter 46

Reenie needn't have worried. She gazed at Chris, flawlessly hosting the party. A perfectly arranged prawn cocktail was passed to each of them. For a moment, her mind flashed back to cold consommé and ... Mawgan. Why did she keep thinking of her first love? Well, Chris was similar in appearance, so that was probably why, plus the arrival of the recent letter.

'There's enough cutlery here to sink the Titanic,' said Graham. 'I guess it's the smallest first for the cocktail?'

'Graham!' protested Lizzie. 'Don't mind my son.'

Making sure Chris had returned to the kitchen, Reenie said, 'I did tell him not to fuss.'

Nevertheless, the roast that followed met with cries of approbation, especially as the wine persisted in flowing. 'Wonderful meal,' said Lizzie, spearing a roast potato. 'You didn't say you'd married such an excellent chef.'

'Chris has many talents.' Reenie smiled, pleased at the opportunity to net her family's approval of Chris, while he looked on with a sense of achievement.

'He's a talent for sniffing out the spirits,' said her mother in her best stage whisper. Pointedly, she sipped an orange juice.

Graham skirted round the aside. 'Tell us about your decorating, Chris.'

'If you'll pardon me for correcting you, I'm first and foremost a designer, of interiors, that is. We employ our decorators where and when.' He topped up Reenie's glass.

'I'm hoping to do something similar myself,' said Rachel. 'How did it all start? I mean, did you know from your school days that this was what you wanted to do?'

'School days? What you wanted and what you did were poles apart in *Babbington*. No, natural genius, that's what got me going!' He winked at Rachel. 'Sorry! Couldn't resist that one. I suppose my first forays into design for someone I knew helped me to break into the market. Then it mushroomed, so's to speak – word of mouth can count for more than costly advertising. And *now* my beautiful wife is on board and we are *Penselle Designs*. Expanding, as you can see.'

Reenie pursed her lips. *Not too much of how I'm helping you!* She glanced round at her family. Were they warming to him? Thankfully, Lizzie had seated their mother the furthest away possible from her son-in-law. She blessed the heavens for the deafness of old age, then started to clear the plates, ready for the sweets. She tipped her head at Chris, who nodded back.

'Just there in the hatch. I'm afraid I had a bit of a disaster with the fruit salad. You probably heard me? Apologies for the French if you did! So, it's trifle or biscuits and cheese. Which is it to be? Rachel? Mama?'

Despite protestations about over-full stomachs, Chris quickly passed round the individual trifle bowls. Reenie reassured herself that her misgivings over the formality of the table and Chris's social skills had been unfounded. She could feel taut muscles easing, hear conversation gently buzzing and candlelight flickering as the evening closed in on them. A warm, gentle conclusion to the day, with the mellowing of spirits, enfolding her. Everyone would grow to like Chris, as she had done. Her life was perfect.

'Mother! Your lip's bleeding. Badly!' Lizzie suddenly cried.

Graham leapt to his feet, 'Grandma!'

Utterly confused, Reenie sprang up with him.

Her mother spat into a serviette. In the next second, something like a cherry stone clattered on to her side-plate. Her mother pressed the fabric to her mouth. 'In with my dessert!'

Reenie stared at her as she dabbed her mouth with the napkin. Crimson drops spread like blending splashes of watercolour. Simultaneously, her mother prodded the offending item on her plate: a splinter of glass. Reenie's spoons clattered to the table. The boundaries of time wavered as everyone, including Chris, gaped at the spectacle.

Lizzie broke the silence: 'Let's take you to the light where we can see what's happened. We need to make sure that's all it is.' She took hold of her mother's arm. 'We must check there's no more glass in your mouth.'

'Of course there's no more! I'd feel it if there was.'

Reenie rose from her chair and bent over the patient. 'You haven't swallowed any trifle, have you?'

'Definitely not. This wretched *shard* was the first thing that touched my mouth. I spat it out straight away.'

'Don't you think we should take Grandma to hospital?' said Graham.

'Oh, heavens above! When you've been through two World Wars like me this is nothing!' She pressed the serviette all the harder to the injury. 'What concerns me more is how a piece of glass came to be in *my* dessert in the first place? How did that happen?' Her gaze fixed on Chris.

Stung by the implication, Reenie felt a sudden flush to her cheeks.

'Mama! You don't think —' Chris started.

'It was an accident, for goodness sake,' said Reenie, determined to squash the insinuation. 'We all heard the crash in the kitchen. Chris knocked over the fruit salad bowl.'

'It's just *how* that glass actually got into *my* bowl, that's what concerns me.' The glare in Chris's direction intensified.

'Jeeze! I'll not be accused of attempted murder,' Chris exploded. He strode from the room muttering, 'Though there might just be one shortly.'

Reenie's legs trembled. How could it all go so wrong?

'Why don't you take Grandma into the lounge,' Lizzie told Graham and Rachel. 'We can go straight on to coffee, can't we?'

'Of course,' Reenie murmured, trance-like.

The flames from Chris's candelabras wavered next to Reenie, as if casting ripples of doubt over what should have been the final sublime touch. The entire crisis had certainly stolen the gleam from what was meant to be a perfect occasion.

Reenie turned to Lizzie: 'I can't believe this is real. What must everyone be thinking? I'm just slipping out to see what Chris is doing. I'm *so* sorry.'

'Don't think about me. Wait – what's that?'

Reenie's eyes widened. 'It's Chris – the *Rover.* He can't be leaving? Surely not?'

Horrified, Lizzie shouted, 'Quick! Stop him. He mustn't drive. He's way over the limit!'

Dashing outside to see the *Range Rover* lurch through the gates and swerve to the left, Reenie watched the headlights zig-zagging down the lane. She shivered with cold and shock. Not only did she fear for his survival on the road, but how could she face her family now?

'Oh my word, where's he heading for?' said Lizzie as she reached Reenie on the drive. She put her arm round her sister's shoulder.

'Oh, Lizzie, you shouldn't be so kind.' Reenie's tears flowed. 'If you'd shouted at me, I wouldn't be crying now. What do I *say* to them all? What will they think of Chris? And what the hell is he like behind that steering wheel?'

'Surely, he'll realise he can't go far like that.'

'He's going to his cottage. I can't think of anywhere else. It's about four miles away,' Reenie sobbed.

'Then he'll soon be there. It's not exactly busy on these roads. You can try phoning him a bit later. Right now, we need to get back in the warm and finish tidying up. That'll give Mother a chance to calm down and by the time we join them the air will have cleared. You'll see.'

'But how can I excuse him? I don't understand. Going off like this … it's unimaginable! I know Mummy has brought him to fever pitch today, but … oh, you haven't heard her.'

'I have – in the past, and not so long ago, either.'

'I've still got to tell the others—'

'Why don't you try something like, "Sorry everyone. Chris hasn't been at all well today. He's sent his apologies for all the trouble over the meal and he's had to … retreat. Terrible migraine, I'm afraid." Come on, let's make a start.'

Arm in arm they walked back to the kitchen, Reenie silently rehearsing her defence for Chris, though nothing sounded adequate. Besides, everyone must have heard his car roaring past. Did he have to desert her to cure a migraine?

*

It was midnight. The ringtone rang in Reenie's ear endlessly until she returned the receiver to its cradle, determined not to demean herself any further. After the initial shock, a slow, burning anger consumed her. How could Chris behave in such a puerile manner *and* in front of her family? He'd ruined everything. It would be difficult for him to recover even a semblance of acceptance now from any of them. As for poor Rachel – what must she think of the family she was about to join?

Reenie kicked off her Italian shoes, a reminder of their honeymoon only a month ago, and collapsed on to the bed, pulling the eiderdown round her. The catastrophe re-played through her mind. "What have you gleaned of Chris's background?" she heard Lizzie saying to her weeks before their marriage.

Not enough! She tried her hardest to excuse him – Mama *was* a problem. She had deliberately goaded him, not solely over the final catastrophe. Even so, he should have had sufficient resources to cope with it. How dare he abandon the party and now ignore her phone calls. A surge of fury swept through her, followed by bewilderment and deep disappointment.

But she missed snuggling into him, even though sometimes he eased away from her. In his sleep, of course. Not if he was awake. She stared at the moonlight sidling through the unclosed curtains, as if underscoring the sudden cooling of their relationship.

Insomnia took a firm hold. She could see her mother's disdain over the alcoholic intake that night and sense Lizzie's discomfort. Hadn't she asked Chris to hold back? But wasn't he doing his best to give their festivity a sparkle? Then her confession to Lizzie not long after moving to the Cotswolds came to the fore. "I'm determined to cut down on the spirits in future. That was all Harold's doing. With a fresh beginning I'm taking control of that side of my life as well." So, how successful had her pledge been? Could she blame Chris for *her* lack of will-power?

One, two, … three o'clock. *Maybe you need a small whisky after all, just to help you sleep,* said her tempter. She sat up, ready to pad downstairs to the cabinet, then realised Chris had left a bottle of Scotch by her bedside. Even the small glass next to it smiled at her. Chris could be *so* considerate, she thought as she poured the whisky. It was clear now. The evening had been spoilt by her mother after what had been a complete accident. How would she have liked it if … she drifted off to sleep and dreamt of guiding Chris back to her side.

The bed was still empty when she awoke at six in the morning. Like the new washing machine, her head was on full spin. She knew she had to visit the cottage and reconcile their differences.

Chapter 47

A peace offering was needed. However, arriving at the crack of dawn would be counter-productive. Reenie pushed a breakfast together. Speed was impossible while her head pounded, yet she had to be gone before her mother came downstairs. She couldn't cope with her that morning, or the questions about Chris's absence, so a note on the worktop about going shopping would cover for them both.

As she made up a flask of black coffee, she poured a first cup for herself and sat down with a cigarette. That was something else she thought she'd given up, she brooded, ready to tap the ash on to a saucer. The coffee reduced the swimming sensation behind her eyes, but the headache was unremitting. Perhaps one more Scotch to settle the pain? No, that was ridiculous. With her elbows propped on the table, one hand supported her chin, while the other held a Benson and Hedges. She closed her eyes. Like the alcoholic fumes which had fuelled the situation in the first place, Reenie willed yesterday's debacle to evaporate. An imprint had undoubtedly been stamped on everyone's mind.

She gulped down one more coffee, then showered and dressed. A pale forty-nine-year-old with puffy red eyes, underscored by two heavy shadows, stared back at her from the mirror. *So much for looking youthful!* She splashed cold water on to her face, followed by a vigorous rubbing with a coarse towel. Renewing her efforts at the dressing table, she reckoned years of practice had endowed her with skills hard to beat. She contemplated her labours after one final pat of the powder puff: the counterfeit gazing back at her was a reasonable success. Hopefully, Chris would look somewhat dog-eared after the excesses of the previous night. The clock chimed eight-thirty; time to put the hamper in the car and head for *Retreat*.

Floorboards creaked upstairs. Her mother! How could she forget the message? Hastily, she scribbled a few words and darted outside. She was off, driving down the winding lanes she'd grown to love. It was a grey November morning holding a promise of sunshine later and maybe a glimmer of the reconciliation she longed for. She flicked out her hair and forged ahead with a little more confidence.

Before long the car tyres crunched to a halt on the gravel parking space next to Chris's *Range Rover*. Scrutinizing the cottage, she climbed out of the convertible. As expected, curtains were still closed, but what did surprise her was a red Beetle half hidden at the side. Who might have called so early in the morning and how had they known Chris would be in? There was a telephone in the hall, but Chris wasn't up to making use of it, was he? It was so quiet. Even the birds slept on.

Then Reenie's stomach churned.

Chris had a lover.

All that rubbish about not standing for accusations. All along he'd planned a secret tryst with someone, and half her age. Was that why he'd been so liberal with the drinks, so she wouldn't notice? She slid back on to the driver's seat, her hand resting on the open door, legs trembling as a whirlwind of strategies spiralled inside her. Should she use the key in her handbag, the one she'd cut secretly? No, he would guess she'd gone behind his back. How about hammering on the door ... and give the interloper a chance to creep away? Might she hurl a stone up at the bedroom window, see who peered from it?

She pressed her fists into her eyes until psychedelic patterns filled her vision. The options were too degrading. Her lungs begged to scream, but that would split her head in two, so perhaps a swift entrance, straight up the stairs ...

'Hello, can I help you?' said an unfamiliar voice.

She turned. A young man with soft, pleasant features smiled down at her. 'Were you hoping to see Chris this morning?'

Could he be the owner of the Beetle? If so, he knew Chris well enough to be visiting before nine on a Sunday morning – the front door was ajar.

'I was,' she replied, 'though I don't think he's expecting me. The phone must be off the hook.'

The stranger chuckled. 'Case of having to be,' he said in a warm Gloucester accent. 'Must have had one-over-the-eight last night. Are you by any chance Chris's—'?

'Wife,' snapped Reenie, pre-empting any embarrassing misconceptions. It seemed strange how her role had reversed from her previous marriage. How unfair it was that people more readily accepted the age difference when the male partner was the elder of the two.

'Bobby Fielder,' said the newcomer. 'Very pleased to meet you. I'm a friend of Chris's. We sometimes work together.'

'Oh!' Reenie exhaled long and deeply, hoping her relief wasn't too obvious. She wondered why Chris hadn't mentioned him before. She pushed her fingers through her hair and stepped on to the driveway. Had Bobby noticed how her legs wobbled? 'That's strange I haven't heard Chris mention your name. Oh, I expect he has. Just me being forgetful. Were you calling about work this morning? No, it's Sunday, isn't it?'

Bobby shuffled his feet in the gravel. 'It is really a day of rest, but … we thought we might prepare some ideas, ready for the new week, like. Why don't you—?'

'Reenie! Fancy seeing *you* here. And you've met up with Bobby,' said a now sober Chris from the front door. 'What are you waiting for? Both of you, come in. 'Fraid I can't offer you any breakfast, but I can plug the kettle in.' Chris waved them inside with a magnanimous sweep of his arm, while his right hand gripped his forehead. He flinched. A network of fine red veins across the whites of his eyes told their story. She imagined he'd slept in his clothes, though his jumper was on inside out, minus his shirt underneath. Clearly, he hadn't been awake for long.

She reached for the hamper, her voice artificially bright. 'No worries, I've brought breakfast with me. I'm sure there's enough here for the three of us.'

'That's very kind of you, but really I must be going,' said Bobby.

'But, your plans,' said Reenie. 'You've only just arrived. Weren't you—'

'You two need a quiet repast together. Don't worry about work. Chris – the drawings? I think you took them upstairs,' Bobby added, turning his back on Reenie as he made for the Beetle. She could have sworn he opened his eyes wider at Chris.

'A hamper, Sweet-pea,' said Chris in exaggerated pleasure. He waved goodbye to his first visitor. 'How thoughtful. Not up to eating much at the moment, though, most dreadfully sorry.' He coughed as they entered the kitchen. 'Before we do anything else, I've got to apologise for last night.' He slumped on to a bench, smiling blearily at her, while she handed him a steaming mug of coffee. 'You are an angel and I don't deserve you.' He shook his head, his fingers sliding rhythmically across his brow.

Reenie shuddered. "Angel" reminded her of Harold, when they first met. How quickly she'd slipped from grace then. She waited for Chris's next comment.

'Guess Bobby saw no point in staying.'

'But how did he know you'd be here?'

'Happened to be passing … but I'm in no fit state for work.'

Reenie folded her arms. 'And in no fit state last night.'

'God, if I could turn the clock back! I so wanted to make everything perfect for you. Show them our marriage really is made in heaven. But Mama … something snapped inside me. You know I've told you socialising isn't my forte—'

'But you do it so well!'

'How about starting afresh today?' Chris's brown eyes gazed into hers, pleading like a scolded puppy.

'Christopher Penselle, you know how to melt my heart!' In the next second, she sat beside him with her arm round his shoulders. 'Don't let Mummy come between us,' she murmured, kissing his cheek. 'Don't ever leave me again like that.'

'It was inexcusable, but I couldn't take any more. You know, when we got married you did agree to giving us our own space. You vowed to keep Mama out of my hair. Don't for one minute think I'm blaming you, but it hasn't happened. She is forever having a go at me.'

'Tomorrow,' she said, sure the debacle had been as much her fault as his. None of it would have happened if she'd kept to her promise. 'We'll start on that annexe idea in the next twenty-four hours. But there'll have to be a bit of a time lapse before we see the rest of my family again. They're not going to forget last night in a hurry.'

'Was it that bad? Can't remember.'

'Lucky you!' laughed Reenie, giving his shoulder a gentle slap. 'Do you need any help here before we go back?' She looked round the kitchen. Two mugs sat in a polished Belfast sink and an old jacket she'd not seen before was slung over the side of a chair. Otherwise, the room appeared well ordered. In fact, it astonished her how neat and tidy it was, a far cry from the bachelor pad she'd imagined. Her gaze settled on the curtains and she gasped. 'Chris – your curtains! They're the same as ours in the cloakroom.' The self-same pair that came with *The Grange* when she bought it.

'Oh yes, bit of a fluke, hey. My mother gave them to me; must have shopped in the same place as your previous owners. Not really my style, but what can one do when mothers try to help?'

'You never talk about her,' said Reenie, seizing the moment.

'Well, today's not the best timing for mentioning mothers, darling.' Chris clamped his lips together. As always, he pushed the subject of his parents to one side. Why did he change the topic whenever she broached it?

She could feel him watching her as she switched back to him from the window. 'Remodelling the kitchen soon, you'll be pleased to know. Those flowers have definitely got to go. But right now, better bathe and shave before returning to your dear mama's lair.'

'Oh, don't say that – it's *our* nest! I'll run your bath while you finish here. Then I can scrub your back for you.' She stepped towards the hall.

'No – not upstairs!'

'Chris! You sounded like there's a body hidden in the closet! What's the problem?'

He looked sheepish. 'Sorry. Terrible bachelor mess up there. I'd rather you didn't take a peek at it.'

She laughed again. 'I shall close my eyes until I reach the bathroom.'

'I said, "No". Leave it! Look, we'll simply go as we are. Key's in my pocket. We'll leave together. Now.'

Taking her arm by her elbow, Chris steered Reenie out of the front porch, turning the key in the lock. 'You go first, I'll follow.'

She stared at him. 'What about the coffee? The hamper?'

'We'll take it back with us. Stay there.'

If darting was possible, Chris sped back for the breakfast. What was he trying to hide?

'Think we'd better go in my jalopy. You're not up to driving, yet,' said Reenie.

With a look of resignation, he sank into her passenger seat. Wearily, she started up the engine, hoping her mother would have returned to her room by the time they sloped indoors. Had they made progress in their relationship, she pondered as the car purred back? At least Chris had apologised. But why the hurry from *Retreat*? Why had that snap to his voice crept in? She wondered, too, how swollen her mother's lip would be now, less than twenty-four hours since the incident.

The convertible pulled into *The Grange*. Chris was out first, opening her door and pulling her into an embrace. His lips, so soft, so inviting, brushed over hers. 'Sorry, my darling,' he said. 'Please forgive me. I shouldn't have spoken so sharply.' Hand in hand they entered the house.

How *had* Bobby known Chris would be at the cottage?

Chapter 48

Pre-Christmas busyness was on Reenie's side. The incident, she hoped, had time to fade as other concerns took its place. And it gave Chris and her time to get to know each other. She hadn't idly entitled him as her knight; it was true, he had certainly changed her life for the better. Even when her mother sharpened her tongue for his benefit, Chris managed to grit his teeth. 'What's this I've heard about an architect?' her mother said a week after the party, pointedly dabbing at her lip. 'Surely you don't intend *desecrating* this beautiful old house by carving it up?'

'All in the melting pot, so's to speak, Mama.'

'Well, I like to be consulted, especially when it involves me.' Reenie watched him anxiously.

'When the time comes, Mama, we'll let you know. But I think it'll have to wait till the New Year.' He smiled at her benignly. 'Let me make you a coffee.'

Reenie looked perplexed, following him to the kitchen. 'I thought the annexe was urgent?'

'Yes, but a few more weeks won't make any difference.' The kettle hissed and Chris bustled round.

'But—'

'Let's just leave it for now. We've got so many other things to think about.'

There it is, that "edge" again. Or was he being extra kind, not wanting to bother her?

Mama puffed in her inimitable way.

*

Amongst the many things to consider was Christmas itself. Reenie and Chris were delighted when Graham offered to drive his grandma down to Cornwall for the festive season. Together at last without the fussing and, worse, the barbs in the background.

'No wonder you're so fond of him,' Chris said as she drew him closer for a celebratory kiss.

'So, it'll be us with Lizzie and family for Christmas Day,' she murmured.

Chris pulled back. 'I was hoping it would be just the two of us. Think how lovely that will be!'

'But Lizzie's expecting—'

'Darling, you haven't made plans without my considerations, have you?' A pained expression covered his face. 'You know, I still believe we need time to recover from the unmentionable.'

Reluctantly, Reenie agreed.

*

On Christmas Eve Chris worked late. Silence folded round Reenie as she stared at her carefully wrapped present for him and waited … and waited in the lounge.

'Sorry I'm so late,' he called to her on his return. 'God, I'm tired!'

He headed for the bedroom and by the time Reenie reached him, he was sound asleep. Had he saved romance for the special day itself, she wondered?

*

'Ter-dum-tee-dah!' Chris said when a grey dawn woke them. 'Close your eyes.'

Reenie did as she was told, a shiver of anticipation rippling through her as he kissed her eyelids. 'Stay like that till … Now! Open them!' A gift wrapped in silver paper, almost as vast as the hamper from Harrods, rested in his arms. 'Come on, my lady-love. It's present time. Had you forgotten?'

'Whatever— ?'

'Open it.'

Her fingers picked at the tape, then brushed against something soft.

'Go on, don't tickle it– rip it off!' Impatiently, Chris tore at the end she'd unsealed – a full-length sheepskin coat unfurled over her lap.

Her eyes opened wide. 'Oh, it must have cost a fortune!'

Chris looked at her adoringly. 'For you, I'd buy the earth. Stand up and put it on.'

In a daze, she felt soft leather glide over her hands. She sniffed at the sweet smell of new suede. A vast fringed fur collar hugged her neck, while the hemline was similarly decorated. Colourful embroidery curled below knee level, cuffs, like feathers, caressed her slender hands in a soft cream ruff.

Darting from the room, Chris returned with the long mirror. 'Take a peek.'

She stared at herself in disbelief.

Isn't it for someone younger? Reenie could still hear her mother's voice, even in her absence. *Mutton dressed as …*

Chris spun her round and laughed as she swayed into his

arms and they toppled together on to the bed. Poised on his knee, she nuzzled into his neck and kissed him. 'So thoughtful of you.' She turned to the bedside cabinet. 'This is mine for you – a lot smaller!' She placed her gift in the palm of his hand, 'but it comes with all my love.'

He gazed in amazement at the watch gleaming at him from its velvet case.

'It … it's an art deco *Reverso.*' Should she have gone for something more contemporary? 'I—'

'It's just what I wanted! You are the best thing that's ever happened to me and I love you with all my heart.' He kissed her over and over again.

Time, anxieties, considerations blurred as she melted into a cocoon woven in Paradise.

*

Sadly, Reenie's cocoon unravelled, little by little, with Christmas Day passing in an alcoholic fog. 'Another one, Chris? I did promise Lizzie—'

'It's Christmas!' Chris filled her glass or tumbler: cocktails, whisky, wine, gin and tonic, a snowball or two, even after-dinner port, reminding her of Harold and his cigar. She vaguely remembered Chris carrying her to bed. Daybreak brought a headache and Boxing Day another, then the realisation that passion hadn't featured for one moment. She didn't like to admit that their first celebration of Bickersleigh yuletide had not lived up to her expectations.

Chapter 49

When Lizzie suggested a family gathering at Stepping Stones on New Year's Day, Reenie leapt at it. She guessed they'd been invited in the morning to steer clear of any possible embarrassments, but, to her annoyance, Chris still wasn't keen, not when her family was involved. She justified their outing as she slipped her shoes on: 'You've had your own time at *Retreat*.'

'That was work.'

'On New Year's Eve?'

'Absolutely.'

Chris drew his portcullis down. Any more questions she knew would exasperate him.

'You look fabulous in your new coat,' he said, diverting the conversation. He gave her a peck on her cheek; then picked up two bottles of wine as they made their way to the car. He'd started to stash a few bottles in the cupboard on the other side of the stairs, closer to the lounge.

Reenie wrinkled her brow: 'Do you think we need *two* bottles?'

'One for your sister and one for us, well, you really, I'm driving.'

'Oh, you do encourage my bad habits!'

She glanced at Chris's fingers as he pulled at the *Range Rover's* door. 'Your nails! You've chewed them down to the quick.'

'It's *Mama Day* – bringing her back with us tonight, aren't we?' He sucked through his teeth.

'Don't! Please. At least you can't be worrying about spending the day with Lizzie. She's much too sweet.' Reenie stroked his arm as the car swung through the gate. 'You are still my knight, don't forget.'

'Never. Never forget, I mean. Oh, you have remembered what I said about today haven't you?'

'Remind me.'

'When I called from the landing?'

She looked at Chris. His eyes narrowed against the low glare of sunshine on the wet rise in the lane. Someone honked their horn behind them and Chris blasted back.

Before long the Rover pulled into the curb by *Stepping Stones* and Reenie realised she'd forgotten to follow up his question. It didn't matter – curtains twitched in the kitchen window and by the time she reached the path Lizzie was hugging her with a 'Happy New Year!'

Chris smiled in the background.

'And the same for you,' said Reenie. 'It'll be Graham's wedding in the summer, so you've got something special to look forward to. Are Graham and Rachel here yet?'

'Any minute now. Come in. It's too cold to hang about outside.'

With coffee and biscuits by a glowing fire, Lizzie's living room drew them in. Reenie kissed Graham and Rachel when they arrived and then her mother as she joined them, focussing her attention on her grandson. Chris moved to the other end of the room and Reenie followed him, willing him to ignore pointed comments. Though she missed her mid-morning tipple, Reenie knew lunch wasn't far away.

'Graham, dear, I've heard how well you are doing. Working hard. Not everyone applies themselves as diligently as you,' said her mother, glaring in Chris's direction.

Reenie's ears pricked up. They'd only been together for a few minutes. Her eyes flashed a *"Don't take the bait"* to Chris. 'Thank you, Grandma. In my final year now, so fingers crossed. Great to have a real fire, isn't it?' Graham poked at the logs.

Reenie watched Chris biting his fingernails, what was left of them. She tapped his wrist, at which he slid his hand inside his jacket.

'Don't mind if I add a little nip to my coffee do you, Lizzie?' Without waiting for a reply, Chris drew out a small flask, unscrewed the cap and poured into his cup. He reached out to do the same for Reenie.

'Really!' Her mother tutted.

'Problem, Mama?'

'Mother! It's New Year's Day. Let things be,' said Lizzie quietly.

Chris crossed his legs and sipped his coffee. He sighed with too obvious satisfaction; clearly the nip had improved the flavour. Reenie stretched for her mug as if nothing had been mentioned, and she had to agree it tasted like nectar.

'Did you ask Irene if she needed spirits at this time of day?'

Reenie's natural spirits plummeted.

'You mean, "Did you ask for *Mama's* permission first?"' said Chris.

'For goodness sake!' hissed Reenie.

'It's not *me* with a problem.' Chris turned to Graham. 'You know that walk you mentioned, just getting my wellies.' He gulped down what was left of his drink and strode to the door. 'Won't be a moment.'

'A bit of fresh air will do them good,' said Lizzie after the door closed behind Chris. 'You can't keep men cooped up for too long.'

'Cooped up?' their mother snorted. 'Would like to tie *that* one up!'

'Mother! Come on, everyone, I'll show you in a minute what I've been doing to the dining room,' said Lizzie, 'when we've finished our coffee.'

The atmosphere in the lounge hung as heavily as the clouds over the cottage. Even the clock ticked extra loudly. Reenie fidgeted with her engagement ring. Maybe they should leave sooner rather than later this afternoon, but they hadn't anything to be going back to, other than Chris sloping off to his office. Why was he going there so often?

And why was he taking so long to fetch his boots?

Lizzie turned to Reenie: 'You're not usually so quiet. Tell us about Christmas.'

'Oh, there's nothing to say really.'

In the next instant, the front door burst open. Rachel screamed. To Reenie's horror, Chris straddled the entrance, wearing a tweed jacket and wellington boots. But it wasn't Chris she was staring at. It was the shotgun in his hands. Trained on her mother.

Chapter 50

'Put it down!' Reenie yelled.

Chris laughed. 'No need for histrionics, darling. Sorry, Rachel. Didn't mean to scare you.' He lowered the gun. 'Was going to ask you to pass me an apple, Graham, old boy. Thought we might balance it on Grandmama's head.' He laughed again.

'What the hell …?' Graham started to say. 'Grandma, are you okay?'

For once, Grandma was speechless.

'Pass me the gun,' said Reenie.

'God almighty, you don't really think it's loaded, do you?' Chris opened the magazine and shook it. 'See – empty. Trouble with you lot—'

'Not another word!' said Reenie.

'—is that you've no sense of humour,' Chris persisted. 'All right, hands up! I've broken the golden firearms rule, but I knew it wasn't loaded.'

'*We* didn't! It was enough to give Mummy a heart attack, let alone the rest of us. Whatever got into your head?' Still, Chris held on to his gun, smiling defiantly.

Graham rubbed his grandmother's hands, as if to kick-start her circulation, while Lizzie poured her another coffee. For a split-second, Reenie envisaged them massaging her mother's heart back to life.

'Oh, come on, Reene, I spoke about the New Year's Day Shoot this morning. What do you think I was going out to the *Rover* for?'

'Get him away from me,' quavered his target.

Reenie stepped into the door frame. 'We'll just take a walk round the garden.' She guessed it was the best way to remove both the offender and the lethal weapon. She steered Chris out to the path, insisting he put the gun against the wall and then placed her hand on his brow.

'What's that for?' he said, pushing her fingers off irritably.

'Just checking your temperature. Wondering if you're hallucinating.'

'Bloody-hell! I s'pose you're going to tick me off again, only this time not in front of everyone else. It was only a bit of harmless fun.'

'Fun! Killing your mother-in-law with shock.'

'She just gets my goat! Knows how to press the button that tips me over. Anyway, your mother is the toughest old bat I've ever known. It was obvious I was coming in with the gun, at least to you.'

'How could I possibly—?'

'I called to you about the shoot, this morning, from the hall. Said I'd bring back something for supper.'

'So, you intended slurping a quick coffee and then leaving us for the rest of the day. That's a fine social visit.'

Chris shoved his hands into his pockets. 'You didn't complain when I told you.'

They paused. Reenie remembered their brief conversation in the car. She should have questioned him then, though she felt sure he hadn't mentioned his plans.

'You're the one who says we should mix with the community. The New Year's Day pheasant cull is a Bickersleigh tradition – been involved from way back. I was coming in to take Graham with me. Then I just couldn't resist

… thought Graham might like the party livened up. And you four could gossip to your hearts' content about the appalling new husband at *The Grange*. *Mama* would certainly fuel the banter.'

'Oh, Chris.' Reenie's eyes smarted. She blinked back the tears threatening to spill over.

For a moment Chris looked contrite. He squeezed her hand. 'Look, I'll make it up to you.'

'Too late!' She licked the salt from her lips. 'It's too late.'

'No, I'll stay here while you get Graham. Let it all blow over. I've got spare wellies. We can still go together.'

'Go?'

'To the Shoot! I'm expected. If I don't hurry, I'll be late.'

Reenie pressed her nails into her hands. 'Do you think he'll want to join you? After what's happened?'

'I'm waiting, ten minutes. After that, I'm off.'

Reenie watched him sit on the wall, the offensive weapon propped beside him. Then he pulled his rucksack from his shoulders and rummaged, no doubt checking on the ammunition everyone had feared. Could she hear him grinding his teeth? *So … he'll wear his teeth out, along with his fingernails. He's certainly wearing me out!*

Yet another social fiasco. She returned reluctantly to the gathering in the cottage, knowing it had to be faced. A glimpse of Graham and Rachel slipping out to the back garden confirmed that Chris would be on his own at the shoot. So, not much had changed after all. She could hear each member of her family thinking, *he's like a child. And a gold digger!* She paused at the living room door, gathering her last whisper of courage.

Chapter 51

The weeks trudged by monotonously after Chris's disgrace on the first day of 1971. Reenie considered it strange how he now seemed to bat away any decisions about separating her mother's accommodation. Nothing had happened, other than *dear Mama* becoming more reclusive. Chris took up her breakfast, always encouraging her retreat. She emerged from her bedroom at lunch time and returned mid-afternoon most days and Reenie popped her supper into her room. A polite truce was attempted by Chris, but in reality, the atmosphere between mother and son-in-law remained as spiky as a hoar frost.

February was probably Reenie's most depressing time of year, with days still short and gloomy. Like an all-enveloping dark cloud, it settled over her. Lizzie rarely visited, Graham phoned occasionally, nobody else contacted them. The coffee mornings she had once found so helpful withered.

'Why don't *you* invite the neighbours ?' Lizzie said when she phoned her.

So, Reenie did, but everyone had an excuse.

'That's just the way the cookie crumbles,' said Lizzie, soothingly. 'It's probably all this rain. People hide indoors. Try again when the weather's nicer.'

Reenie sensed there was another reason for the distance their neighbours kept, though she couldn't quite see through her disappointment. Meanwhile, the glacier round her mother's room, or her very presence, crept insidiously between her and Chris. Reenie needed to plan something special, something to cheer them up. Something to melt the ice-flow. She checked the date for her hairdresser – the thirteenth. But the fourteenth of February shouted at her: how could she forget? And it was a Sunday.

'I'll book a table at *The Angel*, my namesake. Early afternoon. They're bound to put on something festive for Valentine's Day. It'll remind Chris of our honeymoon,' she murmured to herself. A romantic surprise. She chewed the end of her biro, considering the present of all presents for Chris. It was difficult. There wasn't much they didn't possess. Tickets for the theatre? She picked up the phone and dialled. If anything more personal came to mind it could be bought later.

*

After two more tedious, rain swept weeks the fourteenth arrived. Reenie had actually managed to buy another present for Chris – lilies to be potted in his beloved greenhouse – and then had accidentally left them at Lizzie's. They would have to be collected later that day. She took pains to set out a pleasant breakfast table and, to save Chris, took up her mother's tray a little earlier.

'Any plans for today?' asked Chris, ladling marmalade on to his toast.

'Not really. How about you?'

'Spot of gardening.'

'What, in all this dreadful weather?'

'And I might have to pop into Gloucester this afternoon.'

'Oh!' He's got something up his sleeve after all. Could it be roses?

283

Chris curved his lips into his magnetic smile. 'Problem with that?'

Before Reenie could answer, the door flew open and her mother flounced in, her dressing gown rumpled like the frown on her face.

'Mummy! I left your breakfast on the trolley.'

'*Somebody's* been tinkering with the hot water again.' She glared at Chris. Then pulled out a chair and joined them at the table. 'You can pour me a cup of tea, Irene dear, while I'm here.'

'It's the Gremlins of the Grange, Mama. Never quite got shot of them, you know.'

Reenie nudged his foot under the table.

'Hmmm, a jinx is it? I have other suspicions,' Reenie's mother continued. 'P'raps you could *both* come up and take a look at the immersion after breakfast.' As if emphasizing her determination to root out the real evil, she tied the cord round her waist with a serious tug,

Chris raised an eyebrow in Reenie's direction. 'We were talking about plans for the day, weren't we, darling. How about you, Mama? I dare say a little more cleaning wouldn't go amiss. All that rain on the window panes!' He pulled a face of mock horror and Reenie stiffened.

Mama huffed. 'Well, you're right there. I cleaned them recently but you'd never know. I think the guttering needs fixing. It's as if all the muck gets thrown down on my windows in this weather.' She sighed again. 'I do wish you'd let the Daily work on my room. She keeps the brass beautifully polished in here.' She gazed approvingly at her copper bed-warmer and jelly moulds embellishing the one wall free of cupboards.

'All this huffing and puffing will get you nowhere, Mama, unless you actually sort it out.' Chris got up and delved into a kitchen drawer. 'Here you are,' he said, handing her some dusters and a bottle of cleaner.

'Chris! Mummy's not up to leaning out of windows. We have a window cleaner anyway.'

He shrugged.

'Oh! You know there's not a speck of dust in my room. It's the muck, I tell you, which should have been cleared from the gutter before winter set in. Your father—'

'We'll sort it. Don't worry,' said Reenie. 'And don't even think of opening windows.'

'That's right. No need to get them clean yet. Dawson's coming next month.' Chris smiled.

'Next month!'

This time Reenie kicked his foot.

'Where's that cup of tea?' her mother snapped.

'Just fetching one for you.' Chris sprang up, opening a cupboard door.

'Darling, what are you doing? The teabags are over there,' Reenie pointed.

'And the larger bag is sitting at our table,' he muttered. Reenie heaved a sigh of relief that his arch-enemy had left her hearing aid behind. 'Coming, Mama. Someone put the sugar in the wrong place.'

*

By the time the immersion was sorted, a simple matter of the trip switch being down, and *dear Mama* reassured, half the morning had gone. A flutter of anxiety quivered through Reenie. Had she heard Chris saying, 'You'll never get them clean!' Not those blasted windows again! Surely not?

Another flutter asserted itself. The roses had not materialised, neither had the hoped-for card. Reenie comforted herself with the knowledge that men tended not to go for the latter. It was a shame about the roses, though. Was he keeping it quiet for a little longer? To her irritation, her mother still managed to hover on the landing.

The telephone rang and Reenie jumped.

'Hello,' said Lizzie. 'I think you might have left something behind – a present you mentioned?'

'Trust me to forget it. I'll come over now, if that's all right.'

'Lizzie?' asked Chris. 'You're going over *now*?'

'Yes, something I need to do. But I won't be long.'

'Hmm – if it's anything like you two normally are, I'll see you after lunch.'

She hesitated. 'No, I'll have to tell you after all. As it's a special day—'

'Special?'

'Don't pretend you've forgotten, Christopher Penselle! You need to wear something smarter – your jacket or your suit.'

'Aren't I smart enough?'

'Always, but I'm taking you out for a late lunch.' She reached up to cradle his head and plant a kiss on his lips, one that could put him in no doubt about the depth of her love.

'Bloody-hell, have you been at the Scotch already?'

'Language!' called her mother over the banister before she disappeared into her room.

'Haven't had a drop,' Reenie giggled.

'Am I still banned from expressing myself in my own

home?' said Chris, ignoring Reenie's last comment. 'Oh well, it worked. She's gone.'

'Do you think Mummy looked a bit tottery?'

'A bit. She didn't have her stick, did she? But, funnily enough, she didn't have a problem with her hearing!' He glanced at his watch. 'Hadn't you better be going if we're out soon?'

'Mm, I must, but … the meal isn't till two.'

With one more kiss, a quick one this time, Reenie was on her way to Lizzie's. She hummed a Monteverdi tune which had played in their Italian hotel not long ago. If only she could turn the clock back. So much had happened since their wedding. Her mind returned to Italy, to their vows and then basking in the sun on the shores of the lake, sipping cocktails, Chris so attentive, so in love. Or was he? Had she fantasized? Snippets of conversation with Lizzie dogged her as she drove down the country lanes. A dull, wintry mist lingered over the tree tops and the tune died on her lips as her inner conflict shadowed her. Was it a case of the first flush of romance not lasting for ever? But did it have to be followed by a plodding friendship? She found herself speaking aloud, 'I didn't marry to have a boring acquaintance!'

Or someone who makes a joke of taking aim with a shotgun?

He's too young, her family would say. Obviously after her money.

She squared her shoulders and persuaded herself that the perfect opportunity had been seized to reignite the dying embers of their first passion. Valentine's Day. What could be better?

Chapter 52

Reenie pulled on to the grass verge by *Stepping Stones* and hurried towards Lizzie, waiting at the door.

'I've got the package here in case you need to fly,' said Lizzie.

'Lovely, but I'll have a quick coffee all the same.' Reenie hugged Lizzie and slipped into the ever-welcoming kitchen. She gazed at the window overlooking the back garden, though it wasn't the view which caught her attention. 'What beautiful roses!'

'Graham and Rachel gave them to me yesterday.' Lizzie gave her a wobbly smile. 'Said George would have wanted them for me.'

Reenie swallowed, wishing she could feel happier for her sister instead of sinking into self-pity. She cleared her throat. 'How thoughtful.'

'Have you told Chris yet about the meal at *The Angel*?'

'He knows we're going out but everything else is a surprise.'

'Sounds very romantic!'

Reenie couldn't help noticing the lack of conviction in her sister's voice

'Are you all right?' Lizzie continued as she peered into Reenie's eyes.

'Oh yes. Just thinking about everything.' In turn, Reenie looked more closely at Lizzie: dark shadows circled her eyes, while piles of washing sat on the table, waiting to be taken upstairs. The room looked more lived in than usual. Why hadn't the muddles registered when she walked in? 'You're tired. It's me who should be asking how *you* are,' Reenie said. Lizzie sighed, rubbing her face as if to wipe away weariness. 'I don't know when I've felt so exhausted. The doctor thinks I might need a hysterectomy. He's just put me on the dreaded consultant's list, but if it restores my energy, the sooner they sort me out the better.'

'Oh no! You should have told me. I could have helped.'

'There's not much to be done here. It's probably nothing. It's missing George which is more of a problem. People say it gets easier, but I've hit a bad patch at the moment.'

Reenie placed her hand over Lizzie's resting on the table. 'Come over tomorrow.' But she recognised the fleeting expression in Lizzie's eyes: Chris was the deterrent. 'We can go out somewhere – that tea shop in Gloucester.' Starting to bite her nails, Reenie hastily pulled her fingers away. Chris's habits were catching.

'That might be a good idea. But hadn't you better go now?' Lizzie sighed.

'I'll stay a bit. Show me the Christmas photos you told me about.'

*

Reenie put her foot down on the accelerator, as much as the lanes allowed. Chris was right: she had stayed longer than intended and now she was late. There would be no time to make-up and dress carefully – she liked to take off the years as much as possible. The ruby in her engagement ring winked at her as she changed gear. Had she adjusted to Chris's choice of gem by now, she mused?

CRACK!

A startled pheasant flew into the windscreen, as sharp and loud as Chris's shotgun. Reenie's brain seized. She slammed on the brakes, swerving on to the verge and into the hedge. Blood and feathers stuck to the windscreen, while twigs and branches cradled the bonnet. Shaking, she got out to inspect the damage.

'Stupid creature,' she shouted at the mutilated body. 'You could have killed me. At least the car looked undamaged, albeit a little scratched. She braced herself to wipe a duster over the kamikaze remains, retching at her efforts; then stuffed the revolting cloth into the hedge.

Still trembling, Reenie got back into the driving seat and reversed off the bank, muttering to the elements as the wipers attempted to clear final traces. 'Of course, it *wouldn't* be raining, would it!' A feather clung to a corner of the screen, quivering. Increasingly, foreboding wrapped its tentacles round her. Why couldn't she shake off the pessimism clawing at her? She breathed in slowly and deeply. This *was* going to be a special day; she would make sure of it.

*

Damn, the wind must have closed the gate, thought Reenie as she was about to turn into the drive. Trust that to happen when she was in a hurry. Abandoning the car at the roadside, she leapt out to open it. Rusty hinges complained. She hesitated. Was that the wind moaning in time with the gate, or was it just another job for the handyman?

There it was again.

There wasn't a wind. Of course, there wasn't – the mist

hadn't cleared. Even the birds were mute on such a dank morning. She stared in the direction of the disturbance.

'Chris?'

Silence.

She stepped forwards. Wait, someone *was* moaning.

'Who's there?' Her heart skipped. The still atmosphere exaggerated the sound of her heels clicking on the tarmac as she strode towards the house. She stopped to peer across the front lawn. Another moan? It was coming from the side of the house, to the right. Someone was hurt but hidden from view. She kicked off her shoes and sprinted across the grass, turning the corner where the path skirted the house to what Chris called the West Wing.

'No!' she gasped. Her mother lay spread-eagled on her back on the paving stones, her dressing gown open, fanning like a partial parachute. One leg jutted out, at odds with the rest of her. 'Mummy!' she called. 'Mummy. I'm here now. How did you fall?' Kneeling beside her, Reenie desperately wanted to cradle her in her lap, but should she be moved? Her eyes were closed. Could she hear? Blood pooled round her head.

What should Reenie do? Something made her look upwards; perhaps it was the duster lying nearby. The bedroom window was wide open and a curtain flapped partially over the sill, as if to say, 'I tried to stop her.'

Reenie's head reeled. Chris, where was he? The phone. How could this be happening? Torn between abandoning her mother to summon assistance and staying put to comfort her, she sobbed, 'Mummy, I'm just going—'

Her mother's eyelids fluttered, then opened, her lips barely moving as she tried to speak. Reenie bent closer.

Chris? Was that what she saying?

'Chris is on his way,' Reenie said. Her mother's face filled with horror.

Dear God, even in extremis, Mummy can't bear him being near her. But he was needed. 'Chris!' she screamed. Gently, she released her mother and stood up. The race of all races stretched ahead – if only her legs hadn't disconnected from her brain. Somehow, she careered to the back of the house, crying for Chris, hoping she'd collapse into his arms. Wherever he was, 999 had to be rung. No time to search for him. She dashed through the open door and snatched up the telephone.

'It's my mother. She's fallen from her bedroom window … badly injured … yes, it's *Lynton Grange*, Bickersleigh.'

Footsteps. Reenie jumped.

'Chris! No,' she said to the receiver, 'th-that's my husband.'

'What's going on?' Chris asked, his brow puckering.

'Front garden!' she shouted. He stared at her in amazement.

'It's Mummy – she's fallen – from upstairs! Her bedroom.' His eyes opened wide. Then he dashed towards the porch.

'Thank you,' Reenie whispered to the emergency services after their confirmation that someone would be with her very soon. She replaced the phone, still shaking, and tore after Chris.

Outside once more, Reenie dropped beside him, both of them crouching next to the casualty, whose eyes had closed. Chris's face creased with concern.

'I'm with you, Mummy,' Taking her mother's hand, so limp, so cold, Reenie squeezed it gently. 'Oh, Chris!'

'Hang in there, old girl. Listen! The bell. The cavalry's coming.' He slipped off his jacket, pushing it solicitously under his mother-in-law's head.

'Careful! Oh, do be careful.' Though she could hear the

alarm growing louder and louder, Reenie's world shifted on its axis. Time lengthened. Seconds became hours. She stared at the lifeless face, willing a glimmer of existence into it, willing her mother to speak, to make the faintest sound. 'Dear God, please let her live,' she whispered as the ambulance pulled into the drive.

A blur of activity followed. Efficient. Almost reassuring.

'The patient's name?'

'Avril Meadows.' Reenie answered questions in a trance and Chris interjected when numbness overcame her.

'One, two, three, lift,' she heard the driver say. Her mother, now so fragile, was hoisted upwards, strapped to a stretcher.

'She *is* going to make it isn't she?' Chris asked.

Did the stretcher bearer shake his head? Had Reenie imagined him saying, 'I'm afraid we can't get a pulse, sir.'

'Would your, um— ?'

'My wife.' Chris frowned.

'Your wife like to sit with the patient?' said the other attendant. 'You could follow on in the car, sir, to the hospital.'

She couldn't quite hear what he said next but his expression spoke for him. Her heart dipped. Surely not?

'We'll travel together, I think. That would be best,' said Chris, taking command. He slid his arm under Reenie's and the ambulance was gone before their feet touched the drive.

'I'll help you get your shoes back on,' she heard him say, as if his voice floated down to her from a distance. So gentle. So thoughtful.

'Passenger seat for you this time, my angel.' He steered her into the convertible. They must have walked down the drive and crossed the road then. She shivered uncontrollably from head to toe.

'Your keys, Reene? Where have you put them?'

'I d-don't know.' As if feebly attempting consolation, her damp clothes clung to her. 'I don't r-remember anything.'

'I'll get the spare set. And a dry coat. Back double quick.'

Why was it so dark and dismal? What time of day was it? And why was Chris taking so long?

All at once, he was back and they were off, heading for Stroud, speed limits ignored.

'Do you think Mummy …?' Reenie's voice quavered, too shocked to cry or suggest the unspeakable.

'Remember what I've always said, she's a tough old bird, but I don't know how hopeful we can be.'

'Whatever possessed her?'

It was the argument – that stupid argument over the dirty window panes.

And Chris had started it.

*

'Yes?' Reenie asked in the hospital visitor's room as the ward sister entered.

'Oh, please don't get up. I'll sit down, too,' said Sister Johnson. 'You have a friend with you?'

'My husband,' Reenie said sharply.

'You have the best support then. I'm afraid, Mrs Penselle, the news is not good.'

Reenie gripped her fingers together so tightly it hurt, as if pain might postpone the dreaded news.

'It was impossible for your mother to survive such a fall, my dear. I'm so sorry. She died before she reached us.'

'No!'

'Darling,' whispered Chris, kissing her brow. He held her hands between his and she gazed at them. How badly bitten his nails were! Strange she should be concentrating on something totally irrelevant. 'So sorry,' she heard Chris say, echoing the nurse's words.

Reenie drew sufficient breath to speak. 'Can you tell me when she died, I mean, I hope she didn't pass away when … I left her to phone for help?'

'The ambulance crew believe your mother died as they arrived.'

Chris stroked her hand. 'She knew you were there. That's what mattered.'

Another nurse popped her head round the door. 'Nurse Baker, could you bring us two cups of tea please. How do you like your tea, Mrs Penselle?' she asked.

'White, one with sugar, one without,' said Chris.

'Oh, there's no need—'

'There's every need,' Sister Johnson said. 'You don't have to rush away. You're still in shock. If you want to ask me anything then feel free to do so. You know, if you would like to see your mother it can be arranged.'

'Oh, I don't … I can't—'

'Reene,' said Chris, 'I don't think now is the time. You can see dear mama at the undertaker's. I should be taking you home.'

'Oh, you will, by the way, be receiving a visit from the police,' said Sister Johnson.

'The police!' Chris jerked backwards.

'No cause for alarm. It's standard procedure with every sudden death. They'll just want to ask a few questions before you leave.'

'I can't believe this is happening – Mummy, gone. I'll have to tell Lizzie and Graham.'

'You can use the hospital pay-phone, if you wish, my dear.'

'Oh no, I couldn't do that. I must go and tell her. Properly. Not over the phone.'

'Ah, here's Nurse Baker with the tea. I expect you'd like some time to yourselves once the police have gone. They'll be with you in a moment. If you want to talk to me, I'll be on the ward. But remember – *no* rush, take your time.'

Reenie found herself alone with Chris in the unfamiliar, windowless room. It had that hospital smell of hygiene, while someone had attempted to make it homely with the ever-recurring print of van Gogh's sunflowers in a cheap plastic frame. Too dazed to even discuss her feelings, Reenie's brain froze. Why wasn't she crying? Was it because of the shock Sister mentioned? Shouldn't she be doing something?

'I can't stay here. Lizzie must know.'

'Let's go then; no point hanging back.' Quickly, Chris drank his tea, while Reenie glanced at a sad pot plant on the table and poured her builder's brew into it. Maybe it would cheer up it up. What was it? Mother-in-law's tongue! It was no consolation to her. But, didn't they have to stay for … what was it? Her mind misted as much as her eyes.

'Chris?'

'Over to the lift and down that ramp to the car park. We'll soon be at Lizzie's, my love.' Chris, steered Reenie out of the bleak, disinfected room.

Wait a minute, wasn't this a different way out?

With her altered sense of time and reality, Reenie found herself being guided to the car yet again. Chris opened the passenger door, then pointed at the package on the backseat. 'What's that?'

'Oh, it was a present for you – for Valentine's Day.'

'Darling!'

Reenie's floodgates were released. She turned her face to Chris's shoulder and howled. He pulled her into his arms, smoothed her hair and kissed the top of her head. She could hear him saying, 'Don't stop – let it all out.' His murmurings embraced her like his arms. 'But we'd best be off.'

She dropped into the passenger seat. 'Oh I must let the restaurant know why we didn't turn up.'

Strangely, she realised as Chris wiped away her tears, they were literally closer together than they had been in a long while.

'Couldn't we just stay here, together, like this? Don't let's move off yet. Didn't the nurse say—'

'Best to get to Lizzie's right now. Besides, I didn't have time to put the roses in water.'

'Roses?'

'Red ones. For my angel. You didn't think I'd forget, did you?

He turned the key in the engine and they sped out of the car park.

Chapter 53

'Where were you, sir, when the accident occurred?' asked the policeman not long after Reenie and Chris had returned from Lizzie's.

'Probably in the greenhouse,' said Chris.

'And you heard nothing?'

'Absolutely nothing, Constable. Look, we have been through this already.'

'It's *Ser*geant, Mr Penselle. And we do need to double-check everything. I'm just running through your answers with my colleague. I know this is painful for all of you, but after such a serious accident we do have to be quite sure of all the circumstances.'

'That's all right. We understand,' said Reenie, linking arms with Chris. She could tell the interview had aggravated him. But the police, she sensed, harboured a greater irritation. She should have stayed at the hospital. The nurse had told them to. Instead, they'd driven to *Stepping Stones* to break the news to Lizzie, who had insisted on coming back with them. Though grateful for her company, Reenie had to admit to herself that the police presence in the lounge felt like an invasion of their privacy. It was the last thing she needed. All she wanted to do was curl up in a ball on the settee and shut reality out of her life.

Even worse was the attitude of the officers, as if they were speaking to the accused and the Penselles were on trial. Didn't they have sufficient evidence by now? The garden had looked like a crime scene on their return and then their helpful police force had combed *Lynton Grange* as if set in an Agatha Christie novel. 'Not allowed upstairs?' This is getting ridiculous,' Reenie had exclaimed as a policeman guided her into the lounge. But Chris *had* hurried them away from the hospital. He must have been as confused as her with the shock.

What *had* he been doing in the greenhouse that morning? The sergeant brought Reenie back to the present with a jolt. 'And you, Mrs Penselle, were coming from your sister's when you found your mother on the path?' She nodded and he turned to Lizzie. 'You have confirmed that your sister was with you this morning, Mrs Simmonds?'

'I have.'

'Tell me again, Mrs Penselle, why you think your mother was cleaning windows on a damp February morning?'

Reenie drew breath. 'One of Mummy's favourite phrases is "Cleanliness is next to Godliness". I know it's difficult to imagine, but my mother is fastidious over keeping everything immaculate.'

'Always has been,' murmured Lizzie.

Thank you, dear Lizzie. No need to mention disagreements now.

'She wasn't depressed?'

'No. She's not ... that kind of person.' Reenie's heart dipped; they were talking of their mother in the present tense. If only that was possible.

'Any medication, drugs?'

'Blood pressure tablets, that's all.'

'And everything was harmonious in the household – no arguments, no differences of opinion?' said Sergeant Banting, looking at Chris.

'Good God, you don't think I murdered my mother-in-law, do you? We have our moments, but generally are on the best of terms.'

'Oh, Chris!' Reenie wove her fingers together.

The sergeant sighed. 'As I told you these are routine enquiries after a sudden death. We appreciate how distressing it is for you.'

Tears trickled down Reenie's cheeks as Chris spoke. '*Mama*, Mrs Meadows, was bent on cleaning those blasted windows. We tried our damnedest to put her off, but she's not one to be dissuaded.'

'Not even at seventy-eight years of age?'

Chris's royal "we" didn't escape Reenie's attention. Surely, he had …?

'Not even at seventy-eight,' confirmed Lizzie. 'Our mother has never been any different.'

A pause followed while the policeman's pen scribbled furiously across his notepad until the door handle twisted and Lizzie jumped.

'Ah, PC Moore,' said the scribbler to his colleague re-entering the lounge. 'I've almost finished here.' He smiled at the trio and it reminded Reenie of the crocodile in Peter Pan. 'Any further questions?' he asked his colleague.

'Yes, Sir. Mr Penselle – the shotgun in the, er, second kitchen: is that where it's usually kept?'

'The shotgun!' said Lizzie.

'In the back kitchen? Occasionally,' Chris hesitated. 'In the cupboard, with a lock, of course. Or sometimes in the cupboard in the garage. That's always kept locked.'

Reenie raised one eyebrow, but quickly dropped it when she noticed the sergeant's gaze rested on her. She couldn't help recalling the New Year's Day debacle. Surely Lizzie would be thinking of it, too.

'Would you corroborate that, Mrs Penselle?'

'Um, yes, I would.'

'And can you, sir, confirm it's kept unloaded?'

Chris raised his hands, 'Good grief, it's *never* loaded, not unless I'm out on a shoot.'

'You have a licence for the gun, sir?'

'I have.'

'If you wouldn't mind …'

'I'll fetch it now.' Thankfully, Chris soon returned with an envelope which he passed to PC Moore.

'We appreciate your co-operation,' said Sergeant Banting, nodding at each of them in turn. 'Obviously, there will have to be an inquest and you will be called to give evidence. We may need to clarify a few points over the next week or two. Is it your intention to stay here for the duration?'

'We couldn't entertain the thought of leaving our home after all that's happened,' whispered Reenie.

'In that case, I must repeat that the said bedroom must be left undisturbed. We do offer you our sincere condolences and if we can assist in any way don't hesitate to contact us. You have your link number?'

'It's in my address book, thank you,' said Reenie.

Chris stared into space.

'Thank you for your consideration,' said Lizzie, her face pale with the strain as the police retreated.

Chris wandered over to the drinks cabinet, 'Double Scotch for you, Sweet-pea? What would you like, Lizzie?'

'Nothing, thank you, Chris.'

Could Reenie detect a slight grittiness to Lizzie's voice?

'Oh, come on,' Chris said to the tune of spirits filling a glass. 'We all need something today.' He poured two of his favourite "fruit of the grain". Reenie wept again as she realised that for the first time since her marriage her mother wasn't there to remonstrate with him.

'I'll have mine when I reach *Stepping Stones*,' said Lizzie. 'I'm driving you all back with me in a minute. Graham and Rachel are coming over with a take-away. We can't starve ourselves, even if we feel like it.'

'But—' said Reenie.

'Please, just come. You can pack an overnight bag if you like. It might be best for you both to have at least one night away from the house.'

Reenie frowned. 'I think we have to stay.'

'No, you don't. If it worries you, ring that number and give them mine for the night. I can't imagine they'll ask any more questions before tomorrow.'

'Sounds like a good idea,' said Chris.

Reenie wasn't sure of anything. She felt exhausted. Her head swam.

'Tip that glass up, I'm topping it up.' Chris was at her side again, alcohol glugging into a glass that looked bigger than her usual tumbler. She slumped back into the settee. Was Lizzie staring at her fiercely? Surely, she wasn't taking over from ... Mummy? *Oh God!* The grandfather clock chimed six. How Reenie wished they could turn its hands back to six am. Start the day all over again. 'If only I'd stopped Mummy!'

Lizzie put her arms round her. 'Don't! There's no "If only". It's no good saying that. It's happened. And we all know what Mother was like, so don't start blaming yourselves. I'm just surprised you didn't hear anything, though, Chris, but it still wouldn't have saved her.'

Blame, pondered Reenie in her stupefied state. She couldn't shake off the image of Chris finding out the dusters in the morning. "We tried our damnedest," he'd replied. And why had he said the gun sometimes lodged in the back kitchen? She had never seen it there before.

'Angel,' said Chris. He leant over her so closely she could smell the spirits ... no, it was body odour. He must have sweated buckets through the day. Was he nudging her whisky hand? She looked at her glass: it was full. Hadn't she just drained it? What was that? Lizzie? Was Lizzie ... shaking her elbow?

'Reene! You'll never manage to walk down the path at this rate.'

'Just let me be. I can't move now. Tell Graham ...' Reenie slipped her head on to Lizzie's shoulder. Sleep, that's what she needed. Sl-ee-p. She closed her eyes. The comfort of obliteration.

'One more sip?' said Chris.

'No!' shouted Lizzie. 'Please – it's not helping.'

'Doctor Chris orders, just for today. Can't do better for shock, dear Lizzie.'

But Reenie sensed that "tomorrow" would become "today" and the day after ... and after?

She thought she heard Lizzie saying, 'You promised.'

Reenie drifted into oblivion.

Chapter 54

'I can't believe you said that to the policeman,' said Reenie the next morning, wishing she hadn't woken up. Chris, dressed for work, glanced back at her as she tucked the sheet under her arms.

'Least said, soonest mended. Wasn't that one of Mama's sayings?

'But to tell them we were the most harmonious of families!'

'For the sake of a quick conclusion, there's no need to mention the argument we had.'

'*We* had! It was between Mummy and you!'

'Well, the last thing we want is the police thinking there was something suspicious about your mother's death. It's best to keep things simple. It was just as well that Lizzie was with us. She confirmed Mama's fastidiousness with cleaning. God, you'd think that now dear Mama has departed we wouldn't be having these arguments anymore!'

'How could you? Have you really just said that?'

'No, not really. Sorry, darling. It's time I left for work.'

'Don't leave me! I—'

He didn't wait for her to finish. 'Please don't go,' she whispered to the door banged behind him. She tried not to dwell on another flash of temper. He had been so supportive through all her troubles. But the recollection of her mother and the duster were all too vivid.

Reenie scanned their room. Merely moving her eyeballs sent stabbing pains through them. No wonder she had no recollection of reaching her bed. She looked down at her jumper, sweaty and creased, the one she'd pulled on twenty-four hours ago. An overpowering hospital smell lingered on, churning her stomach with its associations. She glanced at Chris's pillow – not a dimple dented it. He must have slept somewhere else. If only they'd stayed at Lizzie's.

'Damn,' she groaned. 'I'll have to strip the sheets as well. They must stink of disinfectant.' She considered asking the Daily to see to them, but the thought of yet another busybody intruding changed her mind. 'I don't want anyone else snooping round, looking for the spot where—' She couldn't bring herself to complete the sentence.

She'd have to cancel Mary this week; the cleaning could be left for a while.

'I miss you, Mummy, even if you did wind us up.' Reenie's tears dropped on to the dishevelled bedspread. Chris's clothes and her skirt, stockings and dressing gown sprawled across the floor; breakfast lay untouched on the bedside table, along with several empty whisky tumblers. 'Oh Mummy! You would have been appalled by the state of this room. Standards are slipping! I so hope you've got your duster with you in heaven. Can't imagine you being happy there without one.'

She wept again, her head pounding all the more. 'I let you down. Should have got that annexe in straight after our wedding. Lizzie did warn me.' She reached out for a glass, which was empty, of course. To her surprise, a brand-new bottle of Scotch stood by the lamp. Chris must have pulled at the seal to make it easier for her to open. 'Oh Chris,' she sobbed, 'I do love you!' Quickly, she twisted the cap off, telling herself it would only be taken as self-medication. She could have a little more, with her coffee mid-morning.

At that moment the telephone rang. Grateful for the extension, Reenie staggered over and lifted the receiver. Dear Lizzie, she mused, so caring.

'Hello, is that Irene?'

Reenie's head spun. The only person who called her Irene was Mummy!

'It is,' she whispered.

'It's Vera. Vera Standing. I'm phoning because I've just learnt your terrible news. I'm so, so sorry. Your poor mother, and poor you having to cope with ... with everything. If there's anything we can do to help, please let us know.'

How did her neighbour find out so quickly? Jungle telegraph, Harold would have said.

'That's kind of you. Mummy used to enjoy your coffee mornings.'

'We were pleased to have her. She was such a sweetie. I'm sorry now that we hadn't seen her for a while, but we've had so much going on.'

'Don't worry, it's much the same here.'

'Look, why don't you pop round for a coffee this week – when you feel able to? Wednesday?'

That'll give her time to have the silver polished.

'Or the end of the week?'

'I'm sorry. I'm afraid I'm not up to socialising yet.'

'My dear, I do understand. I'll phone again on Friday. See how you are then. And please, if you want to talk to someone, I'm only a couple of miles away.'

'Thank you so much.'

Once the receiver was down, the silence of *The Grange* hit Reenie like the cold blast from the door just slammed shut. It was strange how she used to yearn for her mother to give them space but now she was gone ... In her confusion, she tried to remember what she was doing when the phone interrupted. Oh yes, "the little nip" as Chris called it. Her hand slipped as she poured the nectar into a glass. "Can't complain if it's slightly over full," she imagined him saying. She swallowed. Couldn't risk any spillage. Then she took another swig. And another.

That's better, darling Chris. You do think of me.

She curled up on the bedspread, the warmth of her alternative remedy caressing her, dulling the pain in her head, lulling her to sleep. Her glass rolled over the bedding and fell noiselessly to the floor. Not a drop of spirits moistened the carpet.

*

Chris came home in the evening, his usual blithe and blustery self. Reenie gazed at him reproachfully. 'Chris, how can you be so cheery? Mummy died only yester—'

Chris wrapped his arms round her. 'Darling ... one just has to keep going. I'm no use to you if I'm all down in the doldrums.'

'But I've coped with another visit from the police, the funeral director, the vicar. It's endless.' Reenie's eyes welled up again. She didn't tell him how two of her visitors phoned several times before she responded.

'There's no-one better than you to deal with all that, such an improvement on me. I'd just get in the way! And now I'm home; I'm here to take care of you.' His deep brown eyes, still so handsome, locked on to Reenie's. Any antagonism on her part melted. She forgave him for leaving her to cope on her own and continued to drown her sorrows, especially when Chris said he would be working late the next day: 'Can't let the client down, I'm afraid. There's such a rush on at the moment.'

*

When the new day dawned Reenie took herself to task. She had a lot to get through, which meant being reasonably alert. The funeral director was calling that afternoon and with so much to occupy her, the hand on the clock ticked faster than the previous day. Mary wouldn't be in to tidy up, so that left her a few more jobs to cover. As requested, the door to her mother's room was kept locked and for that she was grateful.

At some stage she would have to make an effort to look presentable. Paracetamols would keep her headache under control and by mid-day another gin and tonic would ease her depression. The persistent ring-tone of the phone jarred as much as the alternating oppressive quietness. There it was again. She lifted the receiver.

'It's me – Lizzie. I can come over today to help run through arrangements with you, if you like.'

'Oh, I think I'll be all right. But tomorrow would be good. There'll be more options then to sort through.'

'You're sure?' Lizzie hesitated. 'It's that promise you made to me. Please don't back-slide.'

'God above! I might be taking just a little more spirits than usual at the moment. Mummy was very close to me.'

Silence cut through her gin-soaked self-protection.

'I'll see you tomorrow. Ten o'clock.' Lizzie cut the call.

What had she done? Reenie said to herself. After all the

support Lizzie has given you. Snap out of it! Ring her back. Now!'

Instead, she showered and put on the dress Chris most admired her in, taking pains with her appearance and the make-up that would soon need replenishing. Despite the nausea she felt with the mere smell of food, Reenie recognised the need to start eating properly soon. It was lunch time – overcoming her abhorrence of the kitchen was on the agenda. Striding purposefully down the hall, she steeled herself as a key rattled in the front door.

'Chris?'

'Home, Angel,' he answered as if their world hadn't changed. In his arms was a bouquet and a bottle of wine. 'You looked so washed out this morning, I've brought you something to cheer you up!'

'Oh, don't set me off again.' She blinked at the gathering tears and took the gifts from him.

'Thought we could de-stress over lunch with a merlot old Hodges recommended to me.'

'That's so sweet of you, but … might it be a bit celebratory under the circumstances? I don't think Lizzie would approve.'

'Lizzie? What's she … ? She's not a reincarn … Sorry, didn't mean it. A splash of red wine is nothing. It'll just lighten those little hammers drumming away inside your pretty head.' He pulled her into him. 'A big kiss from your husband and then you can tell me what you've done so far. Reene! You're trembling!'

For the second time that day, she found it impossible to speak. The old Chris, so solicitous, stood before her and a surge of emotion swept through her like the champagne effervescing on their wedding day.

'Come on.' Chris took hold of her hand, kissing the back of it, and on, up her arm. Then he led her to the lounge. 'Can't have you getting into a state. Sit down, legs up.' He manoeuvred her on to the settee and lifted her legs to rest them on a cushion. 'I'll bring a snack in here. We can eat in comfort'

She wiped her tears from her cheeks. 'Please stay like this,' she whispered as she watched him disappear through the door, her whole being aching with longing. If only he would find her as irresistible as he was to her.

Though her head sank on to the settee, her body refused to relax. Chris soon returned, holding the wine and a glass, 'Just pouring you a modest aperitif, my darling. Settle those demons!'

Chapter 55

Friday evening and the demonic hold had not released its grip. Reenie heaved a sigh of relief when Chris returned earlier than usual, hugging her tightly.

'Anything doing today?' His brown eyes searched hers.

'Police called; said we'd soon be hearing from the Coroner about the inquest. They explained some of it to me. And they mentioned something else.'

'Something else?'

'Yes. Damn, I hope they're not back again,' said Reenie as the doorbell rang. She hurried to open the door and stared in amazement. A huge bouquet, held by a young girl, filled the entrance.

'Mr and Mrs Penselle?'

'They're for us?'

'Mr and Mrs Penselle, *Lynton Grange*, that's right.' The delivery girl smiled at Reenie and relinquished the flowers.

'Thank you so much.' Reenie closed the door and turned to Chris.

'Hey-ho – a secret admirer? You kept that quiet,' he chuckled. 'Who's it from, old girl?'

'Not so much of the "old". It's from ...' she opened a small card, "*With our sincere condolences, Vera and Gerald Standing*." How kind of them!'

'Hmm, very kind.' Chris was finding his slippers in the cupboard. Had she detected a peevish tone?

'You could sound more appreciative. Actually, Vera phoned earlier in the week and invited me over for coffee.'

'Vera Standing's for coffee? You're not going, are you?'

Reenie glanced at Chris rising from the cubbyhole. 'What a frown on your face! You can't possibly mind me going to Vera's!'

'*Actually*, I do. She's an old windbag. I bet she can't wait to poke her nose in here.'

'That's so uncharitable. She's invited me to *her* house, so there's no intention of nosing round our place.'

'She can still "nosey", so's to speak, when she gossips.'

'How can you say such a thing? You don't even know her.'

'You forget, my origins are not far from here. There's not much I don't know about anyone within a five-mile radius of Bickersleigh. So, I'd rather you didn't meet up with Vera, either at the Standing's mansion or, even worse, at our place. There's more to her than meets the eye.'

'But Mummy went there when we first arrived.'

'That was different. And Mama was deaf as a post.'

'So, let me get this right: you're telling me who I can and can't see in my own house?'

'For once, I am. In *our* house!'

The hostile expression on Chris's face startled Reenie. She pushed her hair behind her ear, giving herself time to work up a reply. But he was already heading for the kitchen, leaving her clasping Vera's present. 'I'll put the dinner together,' he called back.

I will go to the Standings'. Christopher Penselle is not dictating to me! Then she remembered. She'd forgotten to tell him about the police. Well, if he couldn't be civil, she wasn't going to enlighten him.

*

A flutter of anxiety in Reenie's stomach took her by surprise as she approached Vera's front porch the following Monday morning. *The White House* lived up to its name. Why should she feel nervous? It certainly was palatial, but she had chatted amiably to Vera in the past when dropping her mother off. And it wasn't as if mansions were beyond her experience. She smoothed her fingers over her skirt, as if to augment her acceptability. If only she could take a hasty nip from the flask in her handbag, a recent addition from Chris, who said it would give her all the confidence she needed. But somebody might see if she pulled the hipster out now, so, perhaps she could sidle into the cloakroom.

The front steps beckoned her forwards, but before she had time to touch the bell, Vera flung open the door and extended a welcoming hand. 'Irene, do come in. Such miserable weather today! I'm so pleased to see you.'

'Thank you, Vera. It's kind of you to think of us. Please – I'm Reenie. Though Mummy always called me Irene, no-one else does.'

'Reenie it is, then, dear. Come through to the lounge. Phyllis, my sister, is joining us.'

After initial commiserations, everyone skirted round mention of accidents, demise, and Avril Meadows. Bone-china rattled; stilted conversation stumbled. With a sense of alienation, Reenie wished she was home again. Three wasn't an ideal number, especially as her hosts were virtual strangers. And she hadn't managed to take that vital nip.

'I beg your pardon,' Reenie said when she realised her mind was drifting. She was so tired.

313

'I was just saying, we must introduce you to more of our neighbours, now that you are settled into *The Grange*. Mustn't let tragic circumstances cloud your future,' said Vera.

'That would be nice, getting to know people,' Reenie replied.

'Of course, it can't have taken much "settling" for Chris, can it – I mean, being back to his childhood roots?' said Phyllis.

'Oh yes, that's right. I came from Essex to the Cotswolds, but Chris has been here all his life.'

Reenie noticed Vera shooting her sister a sideways glance.

'Let me see,' continued Phyllis, clearly missing the warning. 'He moved out of The *Grange* to his cottage about six years ago, wasn't it?'

Vera cleared her throat. 'Do have another biscuit, Irene, um, Reenie.'

'*Who* moved out of our house?' asked Reenie. The familiar hammers morphed into a mallet.

'Chris. I'm talking about Chris. How wonderful it must have been for him to feel he was back where he belonged, in his childhood home.'

Too stunned to speak, Reenie's hands trembled and she slid them under her legs. *Moved out of The Grange!* She released her fingers to push her hair behind her ears. She had to say something. 'Yes, he's happy. It, um, it all worked out for the best.'

'Of course,' said Vera soothingly. An awkward silence followed. 'More coffee?'

'Oh, no thank you. I couldn't take any more coffee or biscuits.' Reenie yearned to escape.

'Vera, I think the heat could do with being turned down. Reenie's looking quite flushed.'

'Please don't worry about me, but I must admit I'm still feeling out of sorts since Mummy's accident. I … I think I should be going back soon.'

With a few sympathetic clucks from the sisters, Reenie stood up. Her head reeled as she bent over to retrieve her handbag. She straightened, but the room spun round with rings circumnavigating Saturn inside her head. Her vision closed down as her legs gave way and then … black-out.

When she came round, Reenie was stretched out on the sofa, while Vera fanned her with a magazine and Phyllis proffered yet another cup of something in her direction. 'Do drink up, dear – it's sweet tea this time. Will help to up your sugar levels.'

Reenie fingered her forehead. It was as she imagined – clammy. Her blouse had been opened at the neck and clung to her. How embarrassing!

'Don't try to say or do anything,' said Vera. 'You just stay there until the doctor arrives.'

'Doctor? Please, not a doctor. I'm just hot and tired. I really shouldn't have come out today.' She eased herself into a sitting position. 'I must get home. It's too soon after Mummy's passed away.'

If only she could get at that shot of whisky in her bag.

'Of course, we do understand, don't we, Phyllis? But I'll drive you back. You're in no fit state—'

'I shall be fine in a minute or two.' Despite her condition, the full implication of leaving the car outside *The White House* glared at Reenie like fatal evidence abandoned at another crime scene. The last thing she wanted was Chris discovering her visit. 'I really don't need a doctor. You have been so kind to me, but,' she breathed in deeply, 'I just want to get home.' In desperation, she even gulped down the sugar-laden tea and smiled.

'You win,' said Vera. Reluctantly, the doctor was cancelled and Reenie helped to her feet and then out to the car.

'Oh no,' groaned Reenie from the driver's seat, 'I've left my handbag behind.'

'Don't worry, I'll fetch it,' said Vera. 'It'll give you time to pick up a little more before you turn the key in that engine.'

Reenie watched Vera return post-haste. 'How are you feeling now?' she said as she handed possessions to her through the open door, but the clasp caught on the handle and the bag flew open, its contents tumbling to the tarmac. All eyes swivelled towards Reenie's personal possessions.

'Here you are,' said Vera, scooping everything up until the final item dropped into Reenie's lap. It shone under a weak February sun – the silver hip flask. 'Drive with care,' Vera said.

'Thank you,' Reenie replied in a small voice. She wouldn't be returning to *The White House*.

The car glided on to the road. Could she return to *The Grange*? What if Chris was there? He sometimes came back for lunch. Could she face him? She couldn't. Not yet. Everything had changed again. *Well, what have you gleaned of Chris's background?* An image of Chris as they returned from their honeymoon filled her mind. He was kissing his fingers, touching not her, but the cold stones of the hearth: "I christen *The Old Grange* into new life, now named *Penselle Heritage*."

'You bet it's bloody *Penselle Heritage*,' she said to her absent husband. How could he deceive her like this? It was all too obvious: out of the haze, missing pieces of the jigsaw started to fall into place – Chris's uncanny empathy with the house;

how he knew where the cloakroom was and then the cellar. And that bottle of wine the previous owners had left behind. *Oh, don't forget the curtains, the matching pair in Retreat.* Then, there was the Daily, Marilyn, who knew all about Chris. She had been dismissed.

Other pieces from the puzzle assembled, juggling for precedence in their eagerness to fill the gaps. Even that blasted peacock he'd recognised. The two sisters who sold the house to her – who were they? What had happened to Chris's inheritance? How had he lost the house to … relatives? It was a Mrs Anderson who was the vendor and she never met her or her sister as the agent had dealt with the sale. Had they even existed or, horror of horrors – that new raised bed Chris had been tending …

Don't be ridiculous!

The chimneys of her home loomed ahead. Reenie slowed down, amazed she'd covered several miles without recalling any of it. Chris's *Rover* was in the drive. Her foot touched the accelerator and the *Hillman* moved on, past her gate, past *The Grange* and on to – where? She had no idea, but it couldn't be the place she called home.

Chapter 56

The sun disappeared and rain clouds gathered, as if emphasising the darkness overshadowing Reenie's life. The protective bubble she'd so carefully blown around her had burst. Everyone else was right: Chris had married her for *The Grange* and the bank balance that went with it. How could she have let herself be taken in by the oldest trick – his charm, good looks and declaration of undying love?

Too shocked to cry, Reenie felt the thrum in her head give way to a floating sensation. She drove in some trepidation, pulling over to let a tractor pass. Any faster might leave her in a ditch. Disbelief jockeyed with reality. She'd forfeited her wealth like a dowry for a deceitful husband. Or ... maybe he really *had* loved her, but couldn't bring himself to mention the fact that her house once belonged to his parents, knowing the revelation would finish his chances?

Is the Pope Catholic? One of her father's sayings for a change.

She took a right turn to the next town, where a visit to the estate agent might shed some light on the conundrum. It was no use asking the neighbours. She pulled into the first car park and took a little fortification from the silver flask. Her resolve was as shaky as her legs. Wouldn't they recognise her at *Rumbold and Sons*? It was about a year ago when she'd first ventured into their sales' embrace. So, what was her plan? What should she say? It was important to be prepared, yet her mind was so muddled. Should she back out – blaze out the questions directly with Chris?

Before she could decide, the agency gazed at her from two multi-faceted eyes, a proliferation of photographs filling the double bay windows. She pretended to peruse the houses on offer, but peered between them. The shop, looking much the same as the last time she'd visited, was devoid of clients. It was Monday lunchtime and one of the dullest months of the year – they would have time to assist her with her enquiries. She took the problem by its devious horns and entered, heart thudding.

'Good morning, madam. How can I help you?' asked the sales assistant.

'Actually, I'm doing some research on a property.' Reenie smiled and a spark of recognition lit up the assistant's face.

'Mrs Hartley, of course! I remember – we sold *The Grange* to you, let me see, it must be nearly a year ago? How are you getting on?'

'Oh fine, thank you. It's Paula, isn't it? Actually, I'm keen to find out more about my house – doing a sort of, er, historical search. I wondered if you might be able to help me. Perhaps I've arrived when you aren't too busy? You acted on behalf of the vendor, a Mrs Anderson.'

'That's right, we did.'

Reenie imagined Paula could never have forgotten her beautiful home.

'Did she have a sister living with her?' Reenie asked.

'I think she did. Her husband died a few years previously and then she said her sister came to stay.'

So far, the story tallied with the one Chris told her when they first met; he'd been so obliging with changing that wheel. She even wondered if he had engineered their first meeting – a nail found in The Crown carpark, working its way over to her tyre?

'Can you tell me who Mrs Anderson bought the house from? I'm told it belonged to the Penselle family.'

'One moment, I'll ask Bill. He's new here but Bickersleigh is his old stamping ground.' Paula opened the door behind her and called for her colleague. Reenie soon found herself sitting opposite a quizzical William. Perfect – he knew the house in question, but had never met Irene Hartley. Two customers entered at that point. Even better. They provided her with confidential cover while Paula was occupied.

Reenie looked at Bill – middle-aged, slightly bald, but hopefully not too crisp and business-like. She praised him for his expertise on his knowledge of the village.

'Thinking of settling in Bickersleigh? It's very small. I don't think we have any properties on our books.'

'Oh, I'm just doing some research at the moment. Paula hasn't mentioned that?'

'What would you like to know?' Bill asked a little smugly.

Reenie swallowed. 'The previous owner of The Grange – a Mrs Anderson – was she related to the Penselle family?'

'She was – the eldest daughter, who married *Mr* Anderson. I remember his passing away – lung cancer. Very sad. She inherited the house after her parents died.'

'But there was another daughter and a son, wasn't there? The son didn't inherit *The Grange*, or part of it?'

'I believe not.' Bill's lips tightened.

'That's strange!' The buzz of conversation opposite Paula had finished. Chairs squeaked on the flooring and the customer left.

'If you stayed long enough in Bickersleigh you'd soon uncover a wealth of gossip. The Penselles were familiar faces there, including the *son*.' The disparaging emphasis Bill

adopted was all too apparent. 'In fact, Mr Penselle, *the son* …
but I don't really think it's my place to go down that road, Mrs,
um, did Paula say Mrs Hartley?'

'Mrs Hartley!' exclaimed Paula, joining them from her
desk. 'I've remembered – you married recently. You're Mrs
Penselle now, aren't you?'

Bill's chin dropped, his mouth a perfect ellipse. Reenie's
world imploded in embarrassment for the second time that
day. Her legs weakened. Though supported by a chair, she
knew she had to get away.

'That's right,' she answered in a small voice, looking down
at the cushion flooring. Carpet would have been so much
more professional, she considered, as if her thoughts could
deflect acute humiliation. It was her chair's turn to squeal.
The silence that followed in *Rumbold and Sons* was as heavy
as the mud no doubt sticking to her new husband and now
herself. It was solely Irene Hartley who hadn't been able to
see it. She turned and strode out of her place of shame as
boldly as her limbs allowed her.

*

"A wealth of gossip"? So why had Chris been disinherited and
what had happened to his parents? The elevated flowerbed
refused to be erased from Reenie's mind, no matter how
much she tried to vanquish the absurd. Her ruse had been
rumbled before she'd managed to ask the vital question. What
was she to do now?

Wearily, she made for the car, now her only refuge, as long as
she could bring the hip flask to her lips. Chris had filled it the
night before. She slipped into the passenger seat and pulled the

silver deliverer from the front pocket, a sense of comfort seeping through her veins as the whisky trickled down her throat.

Just a sip– to keep me going.

A flashback of their sublime wedding day slid into view. Tears diluted her next quaff. I'd have married you even if I'd known about your past, if only you'd been honest. If only you'd told me everything.

Are you sure?

Was there anyone more stupid than the late "Lady Hartley"? Everybody else was fully aware of the situation *and* the reason for Chris's parents cutting him off. Why else had the neighbours shunned her since their marriage?

By now alcohol was dimming her clarity of thought. She wept again, finishing the last tissue in the box, then rested her head on the steering wheel and slept.

*

Reenie awoke to a tapping on the car window. Startled, she looked up to see a middle-aged woman with a scarf round her head peered at her and mouthing, 'Are you all right?'

'Oh, yes, thank you.' She wound the window down. 'I've been feeling poorly and so tired recently. Just had a cat nap in the car park.'

'Well, if you're certain you're feeling okay I'll be on my way, dear,' said the Good Samaritan.

'No, wait! Are you local?'

'Yes, my dear.'

'I … I've just found out that Mr and Mrs Penselle – old family friends – died some time ago. Such a shame.' Reenie turned her mouth down at the corners.

'Real shame. They weren't very old, neither. Yes, I knew who they were.'

'Can you tell me what … I mean how they died?'

'Well, Mr Penselle had a sudden heart attack. His wife was heart-broken – took a holiday that summer and then *she* met her death.'

An involuntary shiver spiralled down Reenie.

'Electrical fault where she was staying. It was properly investigated by the police – pure misadventure, poor lady.'

Reenie gripped the side of her seat.

'So sorry,' murmured the Samaritan, 'but I best be going or I'll miss my bus.'

'One more thing. Their son – why didn't they get on?'

'Now I'm not one to stick my nose in where it don't belong, but—'

'Yes?'

The stranger put her hands on her hips and gave Reenie what she could only describe as a "knowing look". Then she clamped her hand to her mouth for a moment before saying, 'There it is – I shall miss it!'

Before Reenie could utter another word, her informant dashed towards the approaching bus.

Reenie wanted to scream. Instead, she clenched her fists and leant her forehead on the cool window beside her. *Unbelievable!* What had the woman implied? Surely not? At least she didn't have to worry about bodies in the garden. Did she? What about the mother dying from an electric shock? Reenie shivered again. Where was she to go from here?

Somehow the old Reenie emerged: she stepped out of the car, shook out her crumpled clothes and ruffled her hair. Then she drew in a deep breath. Climbing back in the driving seat,

she was determined to get the better of her situation. She
swung open the mirror above her and took out her make-up.
Vastly improved, she checked for the bottle of dubonnet on
the back seat; that would keep for supper. She had decided
not to confront Chris as yet, but rather play the innocent wife
and see what could be unearthed before she revealed the
truth to Chris.

Chapter 57

Reenie glanced at the calendar: March 14th. An appointment with the doctor coincided with the day of her mother's inquest, but she decided to keep to it as it was early that morning and her headaches were increasing. Telling Chris she was popping into town for flowers, she headed for the surgery. She wished she could pour out her heart to Dr Richards, but he wasn't the warmest of physicians and she knew composure was needed for what lay ahead. With the briefest of descriptions and mention of migraines, she listened to his response.

'Mrs Penselle, I appreciate how difficult life has been for you recently. The easiest thing in the world would be for me to prescribe anti-depressants without further ado. However, I notice this is your first visit here and I think a thorough MOT might be in order.'

She left with a punctured arm from a blood test and a prescription for sleeping tablets. Once home, Reenie slipped the pills into her bedside drawer, wondering if they might be needed after the day's proceedings.

She hadn't told the doctor how stressful it was maintaining a pretence of being an innocent and loving wife. Her charade had been for a month now, while Chris lavished presents on her and told her how much he loved her. Did he harbour suspicions? Almost relenting under his charm, she constantly reminded herself of his deception. Her concerns had to be kept to herself while she dealt first with her mother's funeral and now the coroner's court. It was important she didn't disintegrate before all formalities were completed. Ever watchful Lizzie sensed that all was not well, but Reenie hoped her sister put that down to their mother's death.

'Why aren't you wearing your engagement ring any more,' Chris asked her as she put her handbag on the table.

'No need to spoil it with constant wear. Mummy wore the band out on hers by doing that.'

But she slipped it on as she changed her dress. He might wonder if his token of love had abandoned her finger altogether, and she needed to sound less clipped with her answers. She chose her next outfit carefully, giving herself a respectful, professional appearance, yet not too sombre, or worst of all, aged. Gazing at herself in the mirror, Reenie chanted: 'Mirror, mirror on the wall—'

'The fairest of them all certainly isn't you, Irene Penselle.' She wanted to shout "Meadows" in return, but knew that "Penselle" was there for the time being. 'But I'll try my utmost to be reasonably fair and at least closer to forty than fifty.' Were the lines round her mouth deepening? She felt sure the puckers in her brow were etched more clearly, so she flicked a few wispy curls of her new hair style over the culprits. She didn't want to give Chris the slightest opportunity to gloat.

Another version of the fairy tale rhyme came to mind:

"Mirror, mirror on the wall," it tells the wicked ... prince? "You've bagged the richest, and the oldest of them all!"

She would definitely defy the aging process.

'Are you ready?' the wicked prince called from the bottom of the stairs.

'Just about, darling.'

326

*

Reenie shuddered. It was like being in a law court. Lizzie, Graham, Chris and she were all called as witnesses, sitting opposite the coroner for the inquest. Reenie appreciated Mr Nicholson explaining that it was an investigation rather than a trial, but, nevertheless, waiting to be questioned, along with the police sergeant who Chris had annoyed, set her stomach churning. Chris rested his hand over hers and she stared down at it. Was it possible he meant it?

Quickly the "who, when and where" of Avril Meadows' death was established. The policeman confirmed the details of his report, which suggested accidental death with the evidence of the glossy, and slippery, magazine on the floor, the polish and the duster and no sign of force upon the body. Chris testified to being in the greenhouse at the time. There was no-one else as far as he knew in or around *The Grange* when the accident had occurred.

'And relationships within the family were amicable?'

'Yes,' said Chris.

Reenie bit her lip.

'Now we return to the "how". This is the aspect which is most puzzling,' Mr Nicholson deliberated. 'From the autopsy it was determined that Avril Meadow's bloodstream contained a quantity of propranolol which probably caused some dizziness. A double-dose suggests an absentmindedness not unusual for a 78-year-old.'

An ice-cold shiver surged through Reenie. Her mother was never absentminded. She had been a lot of other things, but forgetful wasn't one of them. An image of Chris reaching up to the cupboard for tea bags on that fatal morning dropped on to her retina. The tea bags were always stored on the worktop and he knew that. Mummy's medication was in the cupboard, fresh from the chemist.

'Calling Irene Penselle to the witness box.'

The coroner continued, '*But*, a woman of her age leaning out of an open window in order to clean it? On a cold February morning?'

Reenie tried not to tremble. Reliving the tragedy was almost more than she could bear and taking the oath made it all the more fearful.

'Mrs Penselle, can you explain how your mother might have been cleaning that bedroom window?'

'I can. She was utterly obsessive about cleaning. All her life.'

'And had she mentioned her intention that morning?'

Reenie felt her eyes brimming.

'She had. She said ...'

'Take your time.'

Reenie cleared her throat. 'She said how dirty her windows were and she couldn't wait for the cleaner coming so much later.'

'Thank you, Mrs Penselle. I might ask your sister to corroborate that.'

A second picture of Chris goading *Mama* in the kitchen, reaching for the duster, sliced through Reenie's mind with surgical precision. But Lizzie affirmed Reenie's account without a single hint of doubt and Mr Nicholson decided that, although this was difficult to imagine, it did appear to be consistent with their mother's character. His pen scrawled across papers, while a high-pitched hum whistled through the top of Reenie's head. How much longer was this going to take?

'Thank you everyone for your clear answers.' A concise summary of circumstances followed. 'I have reached the conclusion that Avril Meadows' death was accidental. The verdict is death by misadventure.' The coroner looked over his spectacles at them. 'You are in no way to hold yourselves culpable for her tragic death.'

Reenie breathed out slowly. Chris gripped her hand once more. She glanced at Lizzie and Graham, who seemed to have gathered some composure and maybe a sense of catharsis.

Except for herself. Whisperings in her head distracted her, lurking like prowling hyenas. They should have been snapping at Chris's heels, but it was her they targeted, ready to pounce on her last shred of happiness. Was that why she had kept silent about the medication? But that would be so wrong. How could she live with herself if ...? And how could she live with the person who ...? Was such monstrous conjecture on her part pure inventiveness? Should she reveal her suspicions? The consequences were too dreadful to contemplate if she was completely mistaken. Somehow that seemed worse than the terrifying possibility.

But you know how he hated her.

Surely, he wouldn't resort to ... murder? Not my Chris. Please God, let this nightmare leave me.

'Come on,' said Lizzie, 'time to set out to that restaurant for a late lunch. It's only a short walk.'

Chris slipped his arm through Reenie's and she flinched at his touch.

'Are you cold, my love?'

'Just a little.'

'You look pale and you've been so quiet,' Lizzie said to Reenie.

Chris attempted a chuckle. 'Not like you, to be so quiet, I mean.'

Reenie didn't reply. Her family skirting round their mother's dislike of the new son-in-law was all too obvious.

'But the inquest has thrown out a few more questions for me,' Lizzie continued. 'Because Mother had only just opened her blood pressure tablets, it was clear she'd taken double the dose when she got up.'

'Not obvious,' said Chris. 'She could have lost one.'

Why was he so quick to answer?

'Probable, then,' said Graham. 'A lost tablet was never found and her blood test suggested too much propranolol. That's what made her dizzy.'

'It was *so* unlike mother to muddle her medication, though.' Lizzie frowned.

A look of disbelief covered Chris's face. 'I must admit I thought Mama was getting a bit dithery of late.'

'Oh, I don't think so,' Lizzie paused. 'And the magazine on the floor by the window – totally out of character. We all know that!' She stared at Chris as she spoke.

'Never crossed the coroner's mind Grandma could be so fussy,' said Graham, missing his mother's pointed implication.

'Never crossed *my* mind she would contemplate *Shine-easy* in February,' murmured Chris.

And it never crossed the coroner's mind that you hated Mummy with a vengeance. That YOU handed her the polish! Goose-bumps prickled Reenie's arms. She wondered what Lizzie was thinking.

'Auntie Reenie, are you all right?'

'Oh, yes, let's think of something else now. I'm glad we've decided to stay out for lunch together – away from our homes for a bit longer, away from things reminding us of that … that terrible scene.' Her voice caught in her throat.

'If you don't mind me having the last word,' Lizzie started to say. Both Graham and Reenie burst into laughter. 'What have I said?'

'That was so "Mummy" – having the last word,' said Reenie.

'Well, perhaps she is then. I was just going to remind us of the summing up. You are not to blame yourself, Reene. Mother was lucky to know how much you always cared for her, and that's what matters.'

Another explosion from Reenie's flashbulb. This time it was the look of terror on her mother's face as she lay on the path, when she told her Chris was coming. Releasing herself from Chris's support, Reenie squeezed Lizzie's hand. Tears welled again. 'No-one could have a sweeter sister than you.'

By now the restaurant welcomed them. Reenie gazed across the room at Lizzie sinking into a seat. How could she have been so self-absorbed when her sister looked grey with tiredness and possibly pain?

'Should have booked *The Angel*. Far superior,' Chris muttered to Reenie as they hung up their coats.

'This isn't a celebration and superiority is irrelevant,' she snapped.

Chris raised his eyebrows and clamped his lips together. He moved on to biting his nails. Reenie could see there wasn't much left to whittle away.

Chapter 58

Somehow Reenie knew she had to approach Chris's deceit over the house. Annoyingly, her efforts at uncovering his secret had failed – visiting the town, hoping to bump into her informer again, would all prove hopeless. She guessed asking Bobby anything would fly straight back to Chris. With the exhaustion following the last few weeks, she could barely face up to what those suspicions had first whispered. Doubts crept in, especially when Chris was so attentive.

She sipped a gin and tonic to calm the turmoil in her head and the telephone rang.

'Reene?' said Lizzie, 'I've something to tell you.'

'Oh … right,' Reenie took one more sip. 'Yes, um, go on.'

'I've been … you're not drinking are you, Reenie?'

'Lizzie! Mind your own business!'

'But it's only eleven in the morning.'

'Oh for God's sake, I can't cope with this now.' Reenie slammed the receiver down. Then regretted it. Lizzie wasn't well and she had been about to reveal something important. She stared at the glass in her hand, filled with more gin than tonic. But, surely Lizzie should realise she needed something for her frayed nerves?

Reenie slumped on to the sofa, indignation and shame blending together like the drinks Chris so frequently made for her. When had Lizzie ever lost her temper with her? She should phone back and apologise but, somehow, she couldn't manage it. With ears buzzing, Reenie sensed outlines in the lounge blurring. It was eleven thirty now and her head ached. Her faculties were fudged.

'Hello-ee. Are you there, darling?' Chris was back, no doubt with something else to pot-up in the greenhouse. As he appeared in the doorway, another posy of flocks in his arms, Reenie hoped he hadn't overheard the phone call.

'Sweet-pea, what's wrong?'

That was the thing about Chris – he could be so sympathetic. How could she face living in isolation in her vast home, especially having experienced something similar for two decades in *Cedars*. All that conjecture about her mother's death, Chris's parents and his motivation for marriage – was she right? Or could she even side-step his deception over *The Grange* if he … loved her as much as their home? Loneliness stared hostilely from a husbandless void.

Stroking her hand, Chris sat beside her, gazing into her eyes. 'What's it all about, darling?'

She turned into his chest and sobbed, 'I've let Lizzie down.' A sense of relief washed over her as her story poured out. She blew her nose, while Chris gnawed on his fingernails. He ripped his finger from his teeth and spat out the smallest shard, like the sharpened tacks her mother used to shoot at an offender. His eyes smouldered and a quiver of fear rippled through Reenie.

'Your family, damn them all! They do nothing but interfere. I know one shouldn't speak ill of the dead, but *Mama* did her utmost to stand between us. And now your self-righteous sister is taking her place!'

'She only—'

'I haven't finished! I thought Lizzie was a little more

sensitive. She should understand what you've been through and that a few spirits are helping you to recover.'

'You don't think I'm over doing it, then?'

'Of course not! It isn't going to last for ever – just tiding you over till you feel like your old self.' He clasped her hand between both of his. 'You're trembling! Those bloody Meadows make me so angry! But I mustn't.' With a gentle caressing of her fingers, Chris folded her into his arms, rocking her gently and kissing the top of her head.

'Is that the perfume I gave you? You smell as sweet as your name-sake. You were right to be cross. Forget the whole bloody lot of them.' His breath grazed her cheek as his lips brushed her brow.

Reenie's eyes misted. This was how they were meant to be. 'But—'

'No "buts", darling.' He released her to look into her eyes. 'We'll make up for it tonight, what d'you say, with a party.'

'We don't know anyone!'

'We do, but none of those meddling maniacs are coming. Bobby will, though. I'll give him a call.'

'Just a threesome?'

'Why not? We can still make merry – *and* with moderate encouragement from another perfect chateau-neuf I bought yesterday. Stuff the whole blasted lot of them I say.'

She sat up straighter, as much as her befuddled state allowed. 'You're the perfect tonic! What shall we cook?'

'Over to your chef for that one. *You* just make yourself look pretty – I mean even prettier. I can go shopping this afternoon.'

'No, I'll do that. It's the least I can do.'

'Don't think so, darling – too much booze!'

So, Lizzie was right. She was in no fit state to slip into the convertible. Especially if Chris endorsed her statement.

'You curl up on that sofa. Doctor's orders, and I'll bring you some magazines to read.'

The word "Doctor" jolted her memory. She'd had a call from the surgery to make another appointment tomorrow – to pick up the results of her blood test? Her eyelids felt impossibly heavy. Nestling into a cushion, she started to drift off ... magazines ... Chris was bringing her some. What was it about them? There was something significant about magazines ... and Mummy. A late morning nap was just what she needed.

*

A tardy afternoon sun startled Reenie into wakefulness. Had she been asleep for that long? She glanced at her watch – two o'clock! But her head felt clearer. The magazines lay undisturbed on the coffee table, so she flicked through them – all *House Beautiful* or similar. Not one of Chris's hunting, fishing and shooting journals, thank goodness.

Clattering noises from the kitchen indicated party preparations underway. A party for a trio. At least Chris was trying to do something positive. She'd only met Bobby a few times but he seemed to be a pleasant fellow and he had a soothing effect on Chris. She wasn't the only one who had tensions to release. Hadn't Chris's bluffness at the inquest been a cover for his insecurities?

Or was she making the usual excuses for him. Wasn't she about to sue for divorce? This evening Chris was being nice to her and that was all she could cope with for the moment.

Struggling to her feet, Reenie made her way upstairs to the bedroom. Serious work on her appearance was calling her. Perhaps she could view the evening as a time to celebrate their togetherness, even if it was to be short-lived *and* shared with a third person. She appreciated that Bobby was a long-standing friend of Chris's, in fact, probably his only friend. She couldn't think of anyone else.

By the time she had performed her usual make-over, there was just the table to set and a quick tidy of the lounge. She descended to the hall as Chris approached and he whistled his appreciation. 'My wife's quite a corker, I'll have you know. Love the suit.' She smoothed her sleek, black flares which fitted her still narrow hips so perfectly, while a stripy top completed her entrance.

'One twirl, then,' she laughed as she spun round with renewed confidence. Such a feat would have been impossible earlier on. The heels on her shoes weren't quite as high as some she wore, but they nevertheless added to her elegance. She tapped over the floorboards into the lounge, where the fire was hungry for an extra log. It crackled as she threw it in, then burst into flames as if symbolising that the next few hours promised to inject a little more life into her troubled existence.

*

The last cork on the third bottle of Barolo popped. With Lizzie's words still echoing, Reenie heard the glug of yet more wine filling her glass. Feebly, she protested, but Chris only had ears for their guest.

'Sorry, Sweet-pea. You were saying something? We'll polish off with a small port, what d'you say, Bobby?'

Reenie felt her brain shutting down. Had Chris and Bobby drunk just as much? They were babbling away as if a new day had just dawned.

'We'll take the port round the fire in the lounge,' said Chris, pushing that lock of hair away from his forehead. With lights dimmed and the glow of the fire, she nodded again. It was cosy and the evening had been warm and affectionate. What was more, it was good to hear Chris and Bobby laughing together. Mirth had been a stranger in *The Grange* since ... before Christmas? Reenie's eyelids opened sufficiently to check on the time.

'Dear God, it's nearly midnight! I had no idea. Are you having coffee before you turn out, Bobby?'

'Not before I've helped clear the table,' Bobby smiled at her.

She yawned, then apologised. 'I don't think I can stay awake.'

'No need,' said Chris. 'Why don't you roll out on the settee like you did this morning? It's your treat today, don't you agree, Bobby?'

For the second time she found herself sinking into the cushions, Chris lovingly wrapping a blanket round her. Consciousness swapped with that delicious floating sensation, semi-awareness enveloping her as much as the blanket. The lights snapped off as dying embers sputtered. Chris and Bobby moved out. Could she hear dishes rattling on their way to the kitchen? Muffled laughter again, by the stairs. Chris and Bobby were in the kitchen, weren't they? She strained to lift herself from her stupor.

Too late. The car, Bobby's Beetle with its unmistakeable roar, could be heard in the distance. So why didn't it sound right? Never mind, sleep was all that mattered now. She snuggled into a pillow. Oh, so kind, so thoughtful of Chris; she sighed as all sensibility deserted her.

*

Something thudded upstairs. Reenie fought off her tiredness, but the room swam round as she opened her eyes. What was it? The house creaked. Nothing unusual in that. A wave of nausea rose from the pit of her stomach and she shivered. The fire was lifeless and she could just make out the blanket lying in a heap on the floor. The effort of stretching out to the table lamp sent a surge of pain from the nape of her neck to the crown of her head. Clamping her cold fingers to her brow, she paused, then pressed the switch. Sixty watts flooding the settee blinded her for a few seconds, but peering at the clock told her it was almost four am. Another three hours before sunrise. Another three hours sleep at least, in her own bed.

She pulled down the stripy top which had twisted and risen to her armpits. How uncomfortable her clothes felt and her mouth was as dry as the chimney flu. It was a pity her glass was empty. She ran her tongue over her palate and lips in an attempt to moisten them. A cup of chilled water from the fridge – that would solve the problem. But her aching body, longing for a comfortable slumber, won. Reenie tiptoed upstairs, her hand grasping the polished banister to steady her. A mattress, with the bonus of a warm husband, were priority.

Chris must have left the landing light on, a blessing she realised as she headed for the bedroom, yet, that was strange – a shoe straddled the threshold. It wasn't Chris's. Too large. She clutched her head. If only it didn't throb so much.

A sense of foreboding filled her, but she pushed it to one side as she tugged off her top and trousers. She'd almost reached her goal despite her lack of balance and queasiness. Shivering in her underwear, she couldn't wait to slide between the sheets. If she could just lie down and obliterate all feelings. She pushed the door open. A beam of light stealing across the carpet fashioned a pathway across Reenie's side of the bed. It did more than illuminate a tangle of clothes thrown over the eiderdown.

She gasped. Not a hint of doubt could be entertained now over Chris's intentions when he married her.

Chapter 59

Reenie reeled backwards, then crumpled like her outfit into a heap on the landing. Slowly, the door swung back against the offending shoe. The vision of Bobby Fielder, bare shouldered, head nestling on Chris's, scorched her retina.

'No, no,' she muttered, pulling her legs into foetal position. She wrapped her arms round her knees, rocking to and fro despite the nausea churning her stomach. 'How could you? How could you make love to me when your real desire was for … for another? A man! I loved you with all my heart. What sort of idiot have I been? Prepared to take you back despite all the revelations?'

What sort of wife would guess her husband's interests were in his business partner, his *male* business partner and it was nothing to do with entrepreneurial projects? A flashback to *Retreat* on the morning after her row with Chris reminded her of the mysterious appearance of Bobby on a Sunday morning, and Chris's unwillingness to let her upstairs. The brushstrokes on the incomplete painting were finishing their task and it wasn't a picture to hang in a gallery.

She could hear Lizzie saying, "Are you *sure* Chris loves you?"

'Bobby,' said Chris from *her* bed. The mattress creaked. She sat still and listened, like that morning outside the cottage. Should she burst in on the lovers, create mayhem, shock them in a split second?

But … shouldn't she consider her next move carefully? A lot was at stake and not solely her marriage.

'Bobby, wake up. It's gone four. You'd better go,' whispered Chris.

Reenie grabbed her clothes and stole to the lounge, tugging the unwilling top back over her head with trembling fingers. No time for trousers. She clambered on to the settee, still shivering, throwing the blanket over her.

Bobby was obviously leaving as stealthily as she'd descended – not a single floor board protested. She visualised him carrying the enormous shoes as he skulked down the hall, Bobby Fielder the quiet Deceiver. The back door squeaked, betraying his clandestine departure, followed by a click of the latch as it closed behind him. Before long the *Beetle*, no doubt parked at the back of the house, purred past her window, sweeping him away from his lover. No wonder Chris was keen to hold on to *Retreat*!

Reenie sat up and pulled on her trousers, straining to hear the slightest sound from Chris. When silence prevailed, she stumbled out to the kitchen, well away from his earshot, and reached for the kettle. Without black coffee it wasn't even possible to think. Still shaking, she floated, like an out-of-body experience she'd read about. Was she imagining the film of mist before her eyes? She blinked, then looked down and the creases in her trousers wobbled into focus. Or was she in that sci-fi movie where the victims were frozen in perpetuity? No, they did come back to life, she consoled herself, though drastically changed. Might that happen to her? She massaged her fingers, first her left ones, then her right, as if that would kick-start re-entry to the world.

The kettle boiled. Fortunately, the whistle, which would have screamed her wakefulness to all four corners of the house, had been lost. In a miasma of disbelief, she discovered herself sipping black coffee, yet had no recollection, beyond lighting the gas, of making it. On the worktop next to her stood a glass of water and a packet of paracetamols. She stared at her left hand and a tablet card from the packet gazed back at her. Vaguely, an image of swallowing the headache relief sifted through her mind.

As caffeine seeped into her blood stream, Reenie's head began to clear and she remembered her sleeping tablets. Had a pill found its way into her wine last night? An ice-cold shiver crept down the length of her spine at the implication, so she poured herself a second coffee, resisting the temptation to add something stronger to it, and lit a cigarette. How she yearned for her mid-morning double scotch.

By now the navy-blue sky was lighter. Daylight was imminent and Chris would soon be up, looking for her. He'd go to the lounge and she was in the kitchen, but did that matter? She was entitled to wake up, despite what she'd been imbibing the day before. What *did* matter was how to approach him. Did she want to behave as if nothing untoward had taken place – shelve the blazing row until she could cope with it? She covered her eyes with her fingers, tears slipping through and trickling down her cheeks. 'I can't manage this,' she sobbed. With shoulders heaving, weeping renewed the drumming in her head – belief in Chris's love for her was inconceivable now. That was as transparent as the dawn brightening the vista through the window.

She lit a cigarette. Important decisions had to be made. It was six o'clock and she had roughly two more hours to rehearse play-acting until Chris's affectionate face put in an appearance. A charade yet again would be necessary. Feeling confident Chris would be up late, she sighed with relief that several appointments had to be attended that day, her first the visit to the surgery at ten. She would disappear an hour earlier, leaving a note on the table to explain her absence, and move on to a protracted period of shopping. That would take her to lunch time before the necessary performance started. She chewed on her thumb nail, then quickly dropped her hand. Too much like Chris. The rest of the day would be for other enquiries. She blew her nose and added one more tissue to the pile on the table.

It was a pity she couldn't change her dishevelled clothes. She sniffed her sleeve: 'Chanel Number 5, you've been eclipsed by whisky and nicotine, with just a whiff of body odour. Nonetheless, you'll have to do.' She shuddered at the thought of the doctor smelling her presence, but waking her husband was a risk not to be taken. 'Husband!' she snorted as she staggered into the wash room – the room opposite the kitchen where Chris's shotgun had been found. *How can I even think of him as my husband now?*

Stripping down, Reenie washed in Lifebuoy and rubbed herself dry with an old tea towel. What had Chris reduced her too? Even in her childhood, her mother would never have used washing soap for personal hygiene. She shook out the same top and trousers, reluctantly climbing into them yet again. No deodorant and surgeries were usually hot. Still, fingers crossed, she wouldn't be there for too long. Thank heavens spare make-up could always be found in her handbag – another trip to the hall. She grabbed her bag like a thief. Unable to risk opening a creaky cloakroom door, she touched up her face with a pocket mirror in the kitchen.

Seven o'clock. How slowly time passes when misery dogs you. What could she do for the next two hours? An early departure might arouse Chris's suspicions. On the spur of one totally insane moment, she rummaged through the cleaning box for the first time in her life, pulling out the *Duraglit*. It was normally the Daily's job to burnish anything in *The Grange*, but she determined to hone her polishing skills before breakfast. Donning the gloves, she rubbed at a copper kettle on the table as if her life depended on it. There was something satisfying about first blackening the vessel and then being responsible for revealing the rich lustre underneath. She scoured the surface, having chosen a clean duster from that same fated drawer, until the kettle gleamed like the sun on the native sand bars of her youth.

She paused to admire her handiwork before stretching out to pull down the brass bed warmer. 'Your turn,' she said, yanking out another clump of wadding from the tin. 'Mummy, you'd have been proud of me.' More blackening, then triumphal gleaming. Duster after duster hummed across the metal, each one being discarded once rendered useless, and while she scoured, the rhythm Reenie adopted sparked a flow of thoughts. By the time she finished, her arm ached, but sunlight glinted off an assortment of utensils now repositioned round the room. The parody wasn't lost on her, for, though her arm had suffered, she had drawn up a strategy for her situation. It wasn't shining like the pans, but at least there was a glimmer of hope under the murkiness. Just as she'd taken control of the dusters, so she would over her predicament.

The pleasure she derived from such a menial task took her by surprise, as did the sunshine. It was turned eight o'clock and closer to her time for departure. After the doctor's, she would be dropping into her solicitor to check on their will made just before their marriage, followed by the solicitor dealing with divorce. Visiting her bank manager was also on the 'To Do' list. If she had time, she'd drop in on Lizzie to apologise for being so rude in their last phone call.

She stared at her efforts admiringly, pulling off one of the gloves and twisting a stray lock of hair behind her ear. The jelly mould was still smeared – perhaps one final rub?

'Bloody-hell, what *are* you doing?' said Chris from the kitchen door.

She spun round, the cloth tumbling to the floor.

'What've you been doing, old bean? Your chin's black and your nose is as red as a lamp lighter!' said Chris, gazing blearily at Reenie and then in amazement at the gleaming pots and pans. 'And you look as guilty as hell! You aren't hiding something are you?' He laughed, his innocent schoolboy giggle.

She rubbed her chin. 'Don't know what came over me!' She succeeded in smiling weakly, until the pile of soggy tissues caught her eye. 'I think I must have a cold coming. Can't stop blowing my nose. Don't worry, I'll sleep in the mirror room tonight.' She glanced at him. His "morning-after" appearance was obvious. No doubt the bags under his eyes were as puffy as hers.

Quickly, she dropped her gaze, picking up the duster and crossing to the cupboard to tidy it away. It wasn't possible to sustain an interest in the puppy eyes once so attractive to her and, besides, she didn't want him reading the conspiracy behind hers. He slumped on to a chair, resting his elbows on the table, forehead in his hands.

'God, that steam roller's run over my head again. How's yours?' he groaned.

'Not brilliant. But I've a doctor's appointment this morning, then a spot of shopping and meeting up with Lizzie later. Probably be out for most of the day.'

'Jeeze, it's all right for some! Any coffee in the pot?' He lifted the lid as if straining a tendon.

'I'm just getting ready.' Ignoring his question, she slipped into the hall. She guessed their argument about Lizzie had been forgotten. She breathed in slowly and deeply. Nine o'clock and enough time after all to sort herself out.

And time to check the sleeping tablets before she left. She fled to the bedroom, averting her eyes from the rumpled evidence of closure on her marriage. Tugging at the bedside drawer, Reenie pulled out the white cardboard box from the chemist. It had been opened and not by her. Her fingers tore at the box. This was going to be the confirmation of Chris's guilt, one more bullet to fire at him, one more hate-nail in his coffin. He'd drugged her for his fun-filled night with his choicest partner. Shaking the cards over the bed, disappointment took her by surprise.

No pills were missing.

'Damn, damn, damn,' she whispered to the walls as she stuffed the medication into her handbag, determined that a second opportunity should not be offered. Then she ripped off her unbearable clothes, replacing them with clean jumper and trousers, the first reasonable outfit to meet her fingers as she rifled through her wardrobe. She squared her shoulders and ran the palms of her hands over the soft cashmere wool. 'I never imagined I'd love you quite so much,' she whispered to the jumper. 'There might still be a touch of Lifebuoy about me, but at least I'm clean.' With that, she thrust a deodorant stick under the soft knitwear and hastened to the door in a final cloud of Chanel.

As she reached the bottom stair, she wondered if a complete card of tablets was missing, She would check later. She snatched her jacket from the cloakroom and made for the front door. Her handbag held everything she needed and it would mean avoiding Chris, hopefully still lounging around in the kitchen. 'Bye,' she called, unable to utter the word "darling" as she slammed the door behind her.

Despite her longing to run to the garage, Reenie controlled the impulse. Chris might be watching. She strolled past the kitchen, waving casually and then noticed the convertible parked outside. *Damn!* She'd forgotten to put it in the garage and it always complained after being left in the cold. 'Not too much choke' she could hear Chris saying before Christmas. 'You'll flood the engine if you overdo it for the poor old girl.'

'Come on, my beauty,' she coaxed the engine as it coughed and spluttered. But no amount of persuasion from her would work; the engine whirred slower and slower until it cut out altogether. 'Oh God, no, please – no!' she moaned. From the corner of her eye she glimpsed Chris approaching.

'How many times … out you get, I'll see what I can do,' he said. 'You'll have to wait a bit. She's flooded. I've told you—'

'I know!' she said through gritted teeth as she struggled on to the drive.

'We'll have to wait a bit before I turn the key. Did you say you're going to the doctor's? What for? You hadn't mentioned an appointment to me.'

'Nothing much. I'm still getting those headaches since Mummy died.' Reenie stared into the car, unable to meet his gaze.

'Bloody-hell, he only needs to check your alcohol levels.'

'Don't lecture me on alcohol! You were the one—'

'Reene! I was joking. Just thinking of last night – you know, a one-off.'

Did he mean her drinking or his fornication?

He placed his hand on her shoulder, squeezing her gently. Instinctively, she flinched and he looked at her quizzically. 'There is something wrong, isn't there?'

'Certainly is. If this blasted car doesn't start soon—'

'I didn't mean that.'

'Well, I did. Can't you—?'

'I'll drive you in. I can wait till you're out.'

Reenie's gaze fixed on the steering wheel, as if to will it into action. 'Try it once more. Please.'

He slid into the driving seat and she held her breath. One splutter, two more. It wasn't working. What in God's name was she to do now?

'Reene, she's not going to—'

With a contradictory wheeze the car sprang into life. 'Thank heavens,' she sighed as he handed the driver's seat back to her.

'Don't forget, you've got sleeping tablets already,' he said. 'You put them in the bedside drawer.'

So, he did know where her medication was kept.

She wound up her window and accelerated out of the drive. Her thoughts returned to the doctor's telephone call yesterday. 'Doctor Richards would like to discuss the results of your blood tests with you. Could we make that ten o'clock tomorrow morning?' said the bossy receptionist. All the intrigue had pushed the message to one side. Now it forced its way to the forefront of her mind, a Jack-in-a-box, but unlike Jack, it refused to be squashed into obscurity.

Why had he contacted her? She'd made an appointment for next week. He must have known that.

If there was nothing wrong with her results, he would have waited.

Reenie clamped her teeth together for the second time that morning.

Chapter 60

Reenie stared at the poster in the doctor's surgery. A heavily pregnant woman smoked guiltily while her unborn baby, visible for the sake of the message, wrinkled its face in disgust. "DON'T" she read.

In an instant, she jumped back to her first marriage and the baby she had longed for. How different things might have been. She pictured herself with Graham in the park in Grays, then superimposed her fictitious child over his semblance. It might have been a daughter, a friend for life, brought up with the freedom to ... marry for love? But she *had* married Chris for love. Or had she? Was she so desperate she'd clutched at—?

'Are you next, dear?' asked an elderly lady who couldn't stop wheezing. A dated mackintosh covered her vast physique. Reenie guessed she was there to sort the asthma out, but how would she extricate herself from the small wicker chair? A poor choice of seating?

Irene Meadows had, she said to herself, made a poor choice of husband. *Twice!* That was more serious.

'Sorry to bother you,' the patient persisted, spluttering into her handkerchief, 'but do you think you are next?'

'If only,' said Reenie. 'I've been here for at least half an hour. What number are you?'

'Twelve, dear.'

'Oh, then I'm next. I'm eleven.' Reenie crossed her legs impatiently, holding an image of the lady tottering in with a wicker carapace attached to her ample posterior.

'Mrs Penselle for Doctor Richards.'

'At last!' She beamed at her elderly companion. 'You won't have to wait long now.' She trusted her consultation would be quick as, apart from a broken heart, there wasn't much wrong with her.

Despite her conviction that the consultation would soon be over, Reenie's confidence drained as she entered the doctor's room. The huge desk and Doctor Richard's expression were hardly welcoming.

'Ah, Mrs Penselle, do take a seat.' She shrank on to the leather chair opposite her physician, who pored over the papers spread before him. 'Let me see, the blood tests.' He raised his eyes to look over the rims of his glasses. 'I'm very concerned about these results. Coming straight to the point, I noticed the tremor in your hand with your previous appointment, so included an extra test. I'm afraid ... the level of alcohol in your bloodstream is probably causing some damage to your liver. In fact, I would say *severe* damage.'

She dropped her gaze to study the gold-leaf pattern embellishing the top of his desk.

'I need you to think very carefully and give me an honest answer. How much alcohol do you consume on a daily basis?'

With that sinking sensation, Reenie moistened her lips A flush of shame crept upwards from her neck. 'Um, I usually have a glass of wine with my lunch and another with our evening meal. Oh, and I,' she heard her voice fade to a whisper, 'I sometimes have a port to follow.' She gathered enough strength to glance up at her inquisitor. 'I do like a martini occasionally, too.'

Doctor Richards gaze unnerved her. If his eyes had been drills, she would have felt them piercing her brain. She squirmed and the chair squeaked, as if compounding her guilt.

'That's still over the limit if it's continuous, but I don't think it's as much as you are actually admitting to. The indications are that your alcohol consumption is considerably higher, so much so that it has created a dependency in you.'

Her fingers gripped her bag on her lap. 'It's true I've been drinking a bit more lately. You know that my mother died and—' She stopped.

'I do understand. You were prescribed a mild sleeping tablet to help you relax, but the evidence suggests your habit has developed over a much longer period of time. We need to tackle the problem post-haste.'

'But I really don't feel ill at all! Perhaps a bit tired, but not under the weather. I only came in for the test results.'

'Fortunately for you this has been revealed by those very results. The symptoms for cirrhosis of the liver only manifest themselves when,' he hesitated, 'it's too late.'

'Too late! What do you mean?'

'Mrs Penselle, cirrhosis is a killer. Once the liver is permanently damaged there will be nothing more we can do to help you. And the end is *not* a pleasant experience! Now, I'm going to put you in touch with the nearest AA group.'

'AA! Alcoholics Anonymous? How ridiculous. I'm not an alcoholic!'

Doctor Richards fingered the notes and then handed her a piece of blank paper. 'When you return home think very carefully and write down every drink you had yesterday. Record every drop of alcohol passing your lips today, and tomorrow and so on. It is crucial that you are totally honest with yourself – the first problem an alcoholic has to overcome is to recognise their condition. The next thing for *you* to understand is that unless your predicament is arrested – promptly – you won't be with us for much longer!'

In the pause that followed, Reenie listened to the surgery clock ticking. Was it emphasizing the reeling in of her lifeline? With each tick, it shortened. Every reverberating second heightened the diagnosis that each glass of her self-medication was killing her. Doctor Richards passed over a leaflet, plus an exposition on alcohol and liver function. 'Here is the information you require to help you. I strongly recommend that you contact the number given here,' he pointed to an address. 'Make an appointment to see me next week, same day, same time, roughly speaking, and we'll see where we go from there.'

With a scraping of his chair on the linoleum, her physician extended his arm to shake hands. Was it also to confirm what Harold used to call "A Done Deal"? The interview was over, with her chair matching the doctor's scuffing. Before she could pose another question or comment, she was outside the surgery, shaking. Was it with fury over the doctor's suggestion? Or fear of isolation from any form of support? The leaflet was for alcoholics. Not for her.

Or was it possible the finding was correct? That was enough to make anyone shiver. There was no need to read about the absence of a liver; she knew what that meant.

She tottered towards the car park, her mind spinning. Hadn't she got enough to cope with? Where was that blasted car? Did amnesia come with a crumbling liver? Bleary-eyed, she searched for her convertible, feeling totally foolish at yet another stupidity until she found it. She slumped into the driver's seat with relief and peered upwards to the mirror. A stranger's face gazed back at her: drained of all colour, virtually devoid of make-up, flesh sagging under eyes and jaw line, hair limp and dishevelled. A fifty-something-or-other visage, going-on-sixty, stared back at her.

Reenie closed her eyes. Did it matter anymore what she looked like? She fumbled in her handbag until her fingers felt the cool, smooth surface of her silver flask, her comforter. She lifted it to her lips, bathing in the reassuring warmth diffusing from her throat. The quivering taking over her body subsided with a few more sips and she snuggled into the driver's seat, dredging up her plans for the rest of the day. The solicitor, Cambridge's, specialising in divorce – that was who she had to see next, if only to arrange a meeting. Maybe he would be able to consult her at some stage in the day. Just one more drop.

A piece of white paper fluttered from her lap.

'Hell's bells,' she groaned. 'Not that blasted arrangement for a guilt complex! Just a few swills don't count.' The offending form was tucked back into a side pocket in her bag, still pure white. Taking a final defiant swig, Reenie relinquished the flask to its usual safe place.

*

Lunch at *The Royal Oak* was a grateful interlude before Reenie took up an appointment with her solicitor. She wasn't hungry – how could she be when tension fed her appetite, but it gave her time to mull over the doctor's words and think about her strategy, letting the shock of reality sink in.

It also gave her the opportunity for further fortification. One small glass of white wine hardly counted; it wasn't very strong. Besides, if she was going to take the advice seriously a final ingestion was essential. Final? That was serious. Washing down the smoked salmon sandwiches with her last mouthful of sauvignon, she intended to record the drink as her first of that day. And possibly her last? At least Lizzie would be pleased with her. She smoothed her trousers as if banishing the slightest wrinkle might also eliminate her memory of losing her temper the previous day, especially as Lizzie was going into hospital in the near future. In her exasperation at the time, Reenie realised she'd missed hearing the date. She picked up the glass again, glanced round to make sure no one was watching, and then attempted to squeeze out an ultimate trickle of clear ambrosia.

After so much contemplation, it was time to make a few notes in readiness for Mr Cambridge. She soon covered her napkin in bullet points for her defence or even attack. With another hour to kill, plus one husband, she made her way to the Ladies. The vigour with which she brushed her hair stung her scalp, a self-flagellation for being so stupid, so beguiled by an imposter. But it released a sense of determination to redeem her situation as much as possible.

*

'It's just not feasible to move out of my home as yet,' Reenie explained her circumstances as simply as possible to Mr Cambridge. It wouldn't be easy to abandon *The Grange* and she was bent on establishing exactly how her mother plunged to her death. Absentmindedly, she twisted her hands together; it was crucial that Chris didn't suspect her change of mind in both respects. A knock on the door interrupted her thoughts. 'Ah, Johnson, the will Mrs Penselle requested. Thank you.'

The document from the Cambridge vaults lay before her. 'Of course, my own practice is in divorce, but if you wish to consult a colleague on your will you are welcome to make another appointment.'

'If I could have a copy, please, I might take up that invitation at a later date.'

The afternoon had by now worn away. Dusk approached and Reenie was exhausted. 'Mrs Penselle, er—'

Mrs Penselle! How she hated the name now jarring her fractured nerves. She squared her shoulders and took in a long, deep breath. 'I'd appreciate it if my consultation was kept strictly confidential.'

'Of course. It's our business to be completely confidential.'

'*I* will have to be the person making contact with you in the first instance. Anything else at this stage would alert my husband. I will be in touch regularly.'

She clasped her hands with an underlying sense of a contract being confirmed. Her weary steps took her out, past the bank, now closed, as she trudged back to the car. Sadly, she hadn't managed to fit in a discussion with her bank manager; it would have to be scheduled a few days hence. She pondered over Mr Cambridge's counsel: 'Almost certainly the courts would divide your home and other assets equally between you.' Still shaken, she resolved to put up a fight. How could what was entirely hers be carved up so liberally in Chris's favour? Why should such a gold digger take more than his share after a mere few months of artifice?

But, wasn't that what *she* had done when she married Harold? No, that was different. She'd liked and respected him, supported him throughout their marriage, decorated his arm whenever they attended functions and had been the perfect hostess for their parties. He might have imagined she'd had an affair – if wishes came true – but she hadn't.

Even so, she see-sawed. Harold didn't have to cope with her mother like Chris and she *had* been a problem. Chris's point was valid: she should have tried harder to give them their own space. If only ... but Harold would never have considered ... murder?

'Oh God,' she moaned, 'I can't believe I've married a murderer. He's not *that* bad!'

You don't still love him, do you?

'Not possible.' She shook her head. 'I've just remembered Bobby.'

At last the car welcomed her back again. Sliding behind the steering wheel, Reenie caught the brown envelope containing the will as it fell on to the passenger seat. Her fingers shook as they pulled out the evidence of a legal formality she couldn't recall, neither the wording nor her signature. A vague recollection on the night of their engagement tried its hardest to define itself, but she guessed their celebrations blotted out anything tangible.

There wasn't much to read; just that on her death everything reverted to Chris. And if the youthful Mr Penselle should die before her? 'Chance would be a fine thing,' she snorted to the dashboard – everything would be inherited by Irene Penselle. She guessed that sounded reasonable, though she was shocked that she hadn't thought to leave anything to Lizzie and Graham. Now that the scales of infatuation were vanquished, she wished her family had been included.

So now, if they were to divorce, she was prepared to do

battle. Mr Cambridge had pointed out that she would have to remain in the marital home, otherwise it might fall entirely into her husband's hands. So, a home-coming had to be faced, but it was imperative that Chris had no inkling of her new understanding. There was much to do, including her visit to Lizzie, which she hadn't managed either.

The convertible hummed downhill. Why was it so unsympathetic? It always sounded contented despite her darkest moments, unless, of course, the carburettor flooded. Invisible arms almost sprang from behind her to take control of the steering wheel and sweep her past the gates of *Lynton Grange*, but she knew she couldn't, especially as it would be easier to be in situ before Chris arrived. She turned into the drive. 'Damn Christopher Penselle,' she yelled at the windscreen.

The kitchen light was on. He'd beaten her to it and was bound to ask why she'd been out all day.

Chapter 61

'Thank goodness for that,' said Lizzie when a cancellation at the hospital summoned her for her hysterectomy. She packed her bag and made for the hospital on the same afternoon, telling Graham she would let Reenie know all about it when she returned and was on the mend. By then, she hoped, Reenie would also have recovered from her irritable spell.

However, when the consultant visited her on the morning after her operation, Lizzie sensed that all was not as expected. 'Mrs Simmonds,' he began, 'your operation was partly exploratory – heavy fibroids were suspected.' She nodded, keeping her gaze fixed on her physician. 'I'm afraid when we opened you up it was clearly a problem with another cause.' At this, his words blurred for Lizzie. 'When I reached the uterus,' he hesitated ominously, 'the "fibroids" proved to be a tumour. A malignant tumour.'

Lizzie's heart missed a beat. 'Are you telling me … I've got cancer?' she whispered.

'I am, Mrs Simmonds. Cancer of the uterus.' He paused again. Was he giving her time to assimilate the unthinkable? 'But the tumour has spread to your ovaries. It can be very difficult to diagnose, which is what happened in your case.' The nurse moved closer, taking hold of her hand and Lizzie wished it was George.

'So, the treatment? Is there any?'

'I wish I could say there was, but it is, I'm afraid, an inoperable tumour. It was best left intact, especially as it had spread. We will be offering you palliative care, which includes pain relief, of course. Nurse Freeman is our expert here and will talk everything through with you.'

A stunned silence caught Lizzie's tongue as Mr Chapman prepared to move on to his next patient. 'I'll leave you in Nurse Freeman's capable hands.'

'Oh, please don't go. I want to know ... how long have I got?'

'That's something I don't normally like to predict for my patients.'

'But you do have some idea. Please ... am I likely to see the summer through?' Graham and Rachel's wedding was at the forefront of her mind.

'It might just be feasible. Cancer doesn't always follow the rules.'

*

Lizzie mulled over the consultant's words as she watched the dawn break over her garden, sitting on the bench near the pond and dressed in her warmest winter coat with a blanket tucked round her legs. It was the multi-coloured, many-squared blanket she'd crocheted for Graham when he was small, renewing fond memories of the three of them. Early April at five o'clock in the morning still had a bite to it, though the dawn chorus which first roused her, followed by the almost imperceptible lightening of the sky, made the encounter worthwhile.

The sun rose in a pink haze and a carpet of primroses responded by opening to greet the new day. Frogs croaked in the pond, announcing latent amorous activity and more swarms of wriggling tadpoles under the lily pads. How Graham used to love watching them with George, scooping them out with his seaside net to study the onset of legs and shortening of tails, always returning them, under George's insistence.

It was nearly two weeks since she had been told of her condition: not very long to come to terms with such news, especially after imagining her hospital visit was to restore her to good health. And especially as she felt reasonably well. That was the cruellest aspect. She remembered how she didn't believe George was slipping away, even when he was so obviously suffering. When he died, she had been shaken to the core with disbelief and grief. Now she was thrusting Graham back into the same situation merely two years later. No wonder sleep eluded her.

She had always loved the sunrise. It seemed to herald promise. Despite her bad tidings, it still had the same effect that morning. Almost. With such a spiritual embrace, reluctance to let its suggestion evaporate stole over her. She stared at her fear of the unknown. Could this dawn be a foretaste of heaven? Thoughts of her childhood crowded in: Sundays in the chapel, mother pinching her, fire and brimstone pitched from the pulpit. That wasn't her God. Whoever or whatever her God was, the beauty of the world around her declared a Creator far beyond and infinitely greater than the chapel experience.

As far back as she could remember, a sense of Something, Someone greater than humanity watching over her, had existed. And it still did. A visit to the ancient church in the village, where she liked to slide into a pew occasionally mid-week, might help. Its quietness filled her with a presentiment of prayers covering centuries and that intangible mystique intrinsic to the atmosphere.

'I do believe this isn't the end,' she found herself murmuring. 'This could be the beginning of … of something better?' Wasn't that what the priest had said at George's funeral? Or had she imagined it? Was this life the first part of her journey, like the caterpillar to the butterfly? Would she see George again? How would she find him and might she somehow watch over the grandchildren she so longed to see? Why did she have so many doubts and so many fears every time she felt a measure of composure had been reached?

'We'll fight it together. You know what people say, you mustn't give up,' Graham said when he brought her back from the hospital. Dear Graham. He would be working from *Stepping Stones* two days a week and on the other three, he would return as quickly as possible. And Rachel was already like a daughter, a cheerful, positive soul. Lizzie had smiled at Graham, as if acquiescing, but to herself she said, 'I'll fight it at least to your wedding in July.'

Now the sun was higher, breaking through the mist. Dewdrops like pearls glistened on cobwebs, while a blackbird sang in fortissimo. Graham and Rachel would be up soon, wondering at her sitting in the garden and probably asking when she was going to speak to Reenie.

Poor Reenie, trapped in yet another loveless marriage, thinking she had no idea of its nature and drinking her self-deception into permanency. Or was it solace for a subliminal recognition of her mistake? Lizzie so wanted to help her.

"Once you have recognised your dependency, I'll be there to support you." That's what she had planned to say when she phoned. Now it was hardly applicable. The row was a product of Reenie's problem, so she no longer held it against her and, hopefully, Reenie had forgotten it.

Then there was that sneaky, appalling thought that Chris might even have hastened their mother's death. Too dreadful to contemplate, Lizzie pushed the idea to the back of her mind.

'You must be frozen out here! I was just bringing breakfast up to you. Porridge is ready,' said Graham with an enquiring gaze from the back door. He slipped his arm under hers and they walked back to the kitchen. Was she really quite so wobbly? 'Oh, by the way, I finish early tonight if you'd like me to be here when Auntie Reenie arrives.'

'She'd love to see you, I know, but I'll have to see what she says when I phone.'

'Don't leave it, Mum.'

'I won't. I just needed an interval for the dust to settle after our argument, time to adjust before speaking to her. I'm ready now.'

Chapter 62

With a lurching heart, Reenie picked up the phone. What if it was the solicitor? Chris was still in the hall.

'Bickersleigh 260.'

'Hello. It's Lizzie.'

Reenie released an audible sigh. 'Lizzie! Lovely to hear your voice. Oh dear, I should have called you before now. Are you able to come over today?'

'I could, but Graham has the van. I was hoping it could be the other way round – you to me.' Lizzie paused. 'I've something important to tell you.'

The front door slammed behind Chris.

'Oh, that sounds interesting,' Reenie tried to keep her voice buoyant. She'd kept it up for over a week now. 'I'd love to come over. Shall we make it soon?' Guilt seeped through Reenie. She'd been so immersed in her own predicament that their disagreement had been squashed into a dark corner. She still had no idea when Lizzie was going into hospital and an apology was owed.

'Don't hang about. Jump in the car now,' said Lizzie.

'Okay. I will. I've, um, something to tell you, too.'

Lizzie laughed. 'Sounds like we're going to be busy. See you in a minute. Bye.'

No longer bothering with immaculate make-up, Reenie was ready, wishing she didn't feel quite so exhausted. It was only nine-thirty, a bit on the early side, but a sense of urgency in Lizzie's voice spurred her on. She hoped her "something" was a pleasant revelation. Might she have found a new man? That was doubtful – Lizzie still hadn't got over George's death. *Her* story was pretty grim. She hadn't decided quite how much to reveal, but the first thing she had to do was say sorry.

*

Half-conscious that she was sitting on the window seat in *Stepping Stones*, Reenie heard her cup rattle in its saucer. Lizzie took it from her.

'I can't take it in. Not you, please, not you,' whispered Reenie after Lizzie had broken her news.

'That's much how I feel, but I guess there's no reason why it shouldn't be me. I'm not the only—'

'There's every reason! You are the most loving, trustworthy person in this world. You've done nothing but good to all living creatures. There's no reason for you to be taken from us. I'm not going to let it happen!'

Reenie sprang out of her seat and hugged her. 'Everybody loves you,' she murmured, leaning back for a second, hands on Lizzie's shoulders, to look into her face and kiss her damp cheeks. She clasped her again, wondering how she could release her.

Gently, Lizzie unclasped Reenie's arms and slid back on to the seat. 'I need to talk about Graham and Rachel. I've got to be realistic. The surgeon didn't spare me the details. I've … I've probably just few months left.'

The crockery on the dresser swam out of focus as Reenie fastened her eyes on it. Desperate to stay composed for Lizzie's sake, she peered towards the family photo on the piano, but that, too, buckled through a blur of tears. She blinked, wiping the back of her hand over her face and in a distant voice she said, 'How could I have been so mean to you, when you tried to tell me about your op? If only I hadn't been so bloody pig-headed!'

'Hush! That's irrelevant now.' Lizzie brushed away the lock of hair that had fallen over her forehead. 'I've got to say it – it wasn't the real you. It was all that alcohol speaking for you. Wait a moment, it *is* relevant, but—' Lizzie stopped.

'Keep going. I think I know what you want to say.'

'I want to help you. It's more important than ever now that I'm open with you. Time isn't on my side and I want you to see that you're drinking too much and … and it's *changing* you!'

'Not for the better, either,' added Reenie. She seized the opportunity to revisit the surgery with Lizzie, though she omitted some of the details. 'I am trying to cut down. But Dr Richards does exaggerate!'

'Have you contacted AA?'

'No! I think I can manage without them. I'm not an alcoholic. Yet.'

'Have you thought about the cause – what makes you go over the limit?'

Reenie sighed. How she yearned to let spill every detail of her discoveries concerning Chris, even her suspicions over their mother's death. But was she ready to expose her foolishness in all its depravity? Not quite. Besides, it wouldn't be fair to Lizzie, not since learning what she was coping with. Reenie gazed into her eyes, certain that Lizzie was bound to recognise the sadness pooling in them. 'My marriage is … a travesty,' she said looking down at her knees. So, the truth was out. It felt like half the rubble under the new garden terrace had been shifted from her shoulders.

'I'm so sorry. I had a feeling that was the root cause. What are you going to do?' It was Lizzie's turn to rest her hand over Reenie's.

'It's my own silliness. My troubles are nothing compared with yours. I shouldn't really be talking about myself at all.'

'Yes, you should. It was me who asked. With the sand in my timer nearly running out, I want to see my sister happy in her life. So, do you think Chris encourages you to have the extra drink?'

'Maybe, since Mummy died, but it's not going to last. I'm filing for divorce. You're the only person who knows so far, apart from my solicitor. Even Chris is in the dark at present.'

And I've got another agenda to sort before he finds out. 'I daren't leave the house, either. I … I just don't trust Chris if I do.'

'You can stay here.'

'Thank you, my love. But you don't need me interfering at this stage. I probably won't start proceeding immediately. I don't think I can cope with it all right now.' Reenie straightened her skirt. 'Enough of me. Rachel and Graham deserve some attention. You know how fond I am of them.'

*

Reluctantly, Reenie embraced Lizzie; at the end of the day. *Lynton Grange* beckoned with a brooding finger. 'I can be instantly on the phone or fifteen minutes away in the car. I'll call again tomorrow,' Reenie said. She glanced back over her shoulder as she waved. Did she imagine Lizzie looked frailer, with that slight yellow tinge?

As she drove down the lanes, all she wanted to do was park in a lay-by and howl. She pictured Lizzie's appearance. Didn't the literature the doctor gave her indicate she was liable for similar colouring with cirrhosis? Her mind switched for a few minutes to herself. But she was in control of *her* situation, wasn't she? Another finger of guilt tiptoed down her spine – the white sheet of paper was no longer quite so clean, even though not every drop of spirits had been recorded. Things got in the way when the pen was poised.

And now she had to brave Chris. Yet again. He would be home for supper, no doubt his usual convivial self. Did he suspect her plans, and not just the divorce? One or two barbs hadn't escaped her attention, probably when he thought she was under the influence. She parked the car by the garage, preparing herself for another tortuous evening, one she felt even less like enduring since learning of Lizzie's illness. She reached up for the key under the paint pot on the shelf.

Something was different.

Her skin prickled. She slammed down the garage door, locked it and made for the kitchen.

'Darling. Just in time,' said Chris, pouring her a double scotch. 'Any soda with this?'

'What are we celebrating today?'

'Oh, aren't we the one with the poker face? Do we have to have an excuse for a good time, Petal?'

So, it's "petal" now, is it? Does he envisage the Sweet-pea wilting under his influence?

'Certainly not,' said Reenie, taking her glass before her handbag had left her shoulder. Chris had that furtive look, the one he tried to hide in ex-public school bonhomie. She knew him well enough to recognise the symptoms. And something *had* been different about the garage, but what it was escaped her as much as her ability to refuse a drink.

Chapter 63

'Sorting the washing,' Reenie called out after supper. Any excuse to reduce the time spent in Chris's company. Staying in the back kitchen wasn't ideal, but it was better than another half hour with her husband and after that it would be vital to check the bedrooms for clean towels. Anything to avoid him. She could see Chris had already been ferreting in the anti-room, wellies left in the corner, old garden kneeler—

"Mr Penselle – the shotgun in the, err, second kitchen: is that where it's usually kept?'

"The back kitchen? Occasionally. Or sometimes in the garage."

The exchange between Chris and the policeman jolted into Reenie's deliberations. "*Sometimes*" in the garage? *Always* in the garage, in the cupboard with the glass window, next to the paint pots, but it wasn't there now. *That* was what troubled her when she went for the key. Dear God, what was he up to? She knew he had those weasel eyes again.

She chewed her thumb nail. Then sauntered into the lounge and sat opposite Chris, swilling her last drop of whisky round and round in her glass. 'The shotgun – I hope no-one's stolen it. It's not in the garage.'

'Aha, Mrs Penselle/aka Holmes the Detective, I see,' Chris chuckled.

'Where is it, Chris?'

'Took it out for cleaning and then, you know those noises we heard in the night last week—'

369

'I don't remember any.'

'Well, there were. And I never got to the bottom of it. So – just for absolute security – I've put it under our bed.'

'Under our bed! For God's sake, I don't want to sleep with a gun beneath me!'

'You're not sleeping in our room at the moment anyway,' said Chris huffily. 'Your cold seems to be lingering.'

'Well, it won't linger indefinitely. Whatever's got into you?'

'When that burglar stands at our bedside, you'll be only too pleased for me to point a shotgun at his head. We've no neighbours. Who would there be to come to our rescue?'

Reenie folded her arms and stared across the room at him. 'We have an alarm, with secure locks. There's also a telephone on the chest of drawers. That's enough security for me.'

He glared at her now. 'Are you undermining my authority here?'

'What do you mean, *your* authority? I just don't like a gun under the bed!'

She heard him swallow. His cheeks flushed and he crossed his legs, a sure sign he was bridling his temper. 'I'll bring it down tomorrow, if that makes you happy. But don't blame me if an axe murderer breaks in and there's nothing I can do about it.'

A palpable silence filled the room until Chris got up and reached for the drinks' cabinet. 'See your glass needs replenishing.' He pulled out the customary bottle. 'Brandy for a change?' Without waiting for a reply, he poured into a tumbler and put it next to her. She could hear Lizzie remonstrating.

Next, he turned the television on. Instantly, his focus switched, with a loud guffaw, to *The Odd Couple*, an appropriate programme, it seemed to Reenie. At least it diverted his attention.

'I'll be back in a minute,' she said, her fingers wrapped round her drink. He hadn't poured an extra one for himself, so, *he* intended staying sober. With her high heels abandoned at the foot of the stairs, she padded up to their bedroom, determined to remove the firearm. She crouched on the carpet and stretched her arm under the bed on Chris's side. Expecting to feel the cold metal of a gun barrel, she pulled out a couple of dirty hankies and one retired sock. Was he winding her up? Another of his stupid stories?

With one more thrust, Reenie's fingers touched something hard. It felt like a book. How curious – Chris never read. She tugged at what was possibly a tome and a Readers' Digest *Medical Dictionary* emerged. She remembered the special offer in the paper, laughing with Chris and saying how she'd be certain to have every complaint at least in the Cotswolds once she began to dip into such a manual. So, he had succumbed. What for? She sat half cross-legged on the carpet, television burbling in the background, bursts of laughter drifting upwards.

With it nestling in her lap, the book fell open naturally, where a page had been folded at the corner. She paused at the first symptom, the words swimming together as if a malign finger stirred a cauldron of ailments. It couldn't be coincidence. ALCOHOL POISONING. In a flash of Hitchcock proportions, a picture of Chris waving a merlot filled Reenie's vision. It was after the inquest, when he came up from the cellar, trousers dripping wet after wading through the flooded chamber. He'd insisted on pouring more wine for her, despite her protests, despite the previous bottle.

And the gin and the scotch they'd polished off? Was it on a pretext to celebrate something? She couldn't remember, but other recollections of Chris's encouragements decanted, including her mother's exclamations, "*Irene! More spirits? Isn't this your third or fourth since lunch time?*"

The half glass of brandy sat beside her on the carpet. Still in shock, Reenie grasped it. She clutched the bedspread and stood up. It only took a few shaky steps to the en-suite where she tipped her addiction into the wash-basin, watching it spiralling downwards, regret and relief draining through her in similar fashion. 'I'm not handing this house to you on a plate, Mr Penselle. Or should she say *in a whisky tumbler*? Who needs AA when their husband's intentions are suddenly so blatant?'

Yet, what pierced her more keenly than any loss of possessions was Mr Right's betrayal. The person she had yearned for, the partner she loved unconditionally, had masqueraded feelings of tenderness towards her from their very first encounter – the now familiar winding lane with her car abandoned on the grass verge. Yes, she had seen the *Rover* at *The Crown* beforehand where, no doubt, that nail had somehow become embedded in her tyre. How her pulse had quickened as Chris beamed at her when he changed that wheel.

Was her life with Chris a game of alcoholic whist? She turned up each of his "tricks": *Lynton Grange*: player's (Mr C. Penselle's) childhood home; wealthy widow now in possession of said house, arrives on the scene; she's hooked by his charm – marriage is the price he must pay; long-standing relationship with so-called business partner remains a secret; other secrets maintained by dismissing poor

Marilyn, and withdrawing from society; *Mama*, initial obstacle, falls to her death from upper floor. Nobody notices that trick. Nobody suspects the significance. Next move: the will obviously works in favour of the lead player surviving the ultimate obstacle, Reenie's finest card, her ace of hearts, already trumped.

Why fear a weapon upstairs? Chris's final decider was a more subtle solution. Reenie devoured the details on the page shouting at her from her lap. She had been feeling tired recently – due to stress? What about her weight loss? She didn't feel like eating with so much worry in her life. That was all. That was why her skirts were loose about her waist. She'd congratulated herself on keeping such a trim figure when approaching fifty.

But the doctor said she probably wouldn't feel ill until it was too late. And now? Were her symptoms imagined? CIRRHOSIS in bold, black capitals on the next page stared brazenly back at her.

'I guessed you'd be up here!' said Chris from the doorway.

'Oh! You made me jump,' Reenie slid the book into its hiding place behind her.

'Not nearly as much as Axe Man would have,' Chris laughed.

She turned to face him, hoping he hadn't noticed the hasty concealment.

'I'll take the gun away tomorrow, Reene. Promise. Sorry I've been a bit of a bear tonight. Come and eat that supper I'm making for you. It'll be like old times again?'

Reenie steeled herself. Little did he appreciate how close to the truth he was when he addressed her as Mrs Holmes. There would be no divorce before all evidence was thoroughly scrutinised. She smiled at Chris, 'What's on the TV tonight, darling? I could do with a thriller. Something to keep me on the edge of my seat!'

On reaching the doorway, Chris hugged her. She wondered if he'd noticed her overpowering revulsion to his embrace. For a moment he stood back at arm's length. 'You look quite fragile tonight. Is everything all right?'

'Not so bad. Let's go and have that meal.'

Telling him about Lizzie wasn't possible. It would open the flood-gates and leave her totally vulnerable. And she certainly couldn't bring herself to discuss the devastation of what used to be her heart.

Chapter 64

Reenie moved back into their bedroom. A cold couldn't last for ever, but neither could her predicament. The knowledge that a resolution must be found kept her going, while her secret card was about to be dealt.

Initially, she thought the hardest part of the pretence would be slipping under the bedcovers, but in her heart, she guessed Chris's dwindling interest in anything physical would make it bearable. All along she had kidded herself over the clumsy pawing, speedy conclusions; the excuses, "Not tonight, darling. I'm exhausted!" or "Busy day tomorrow". How she'd persuaded herself there was a perfectly good reason for postponements, that next week, or even next month it would all come right.

Dwindling interest? It had never existed. Like sandpaper glancing off an open wound, the pain of perfidy dogged her every waking moment. Alcohol, her dual tormentor, beckoned simultaneously, dulling reality, which included the imminent loss of Lizzie, the one person who'd loved her all her life. Unconditionally. The thrum in her head from several glasses over the limit was welcome in comparison to facing the future. Bottles left in conspicuous positions lured her on: *just a few sips, that's all you need.* Hastily, she replaced them in the cabinet, but merely opening the doors invited her to even greater choice. Yet more vintages vied for her attention. When she turned away, hands shaking, they leered at her: *You'll never manage without us.*

I can and I will! He's not getting away with it.

Mysteriously, the spirits soon reappeared. The worst was when Chris poured her a drink. The musical glug of a glass being filled, the sparkle multiplied within crystal diamonds set her entire body on edge.

'Mother Nature's cure! Join me in one,' he called from the lounge with his return from work.

'Mother Nature?'

He laughed. 'Well, fruit of the grain.'

'Go on then – just a little tonic.' A fever of yearning pricked out beads of perspiration on her forehead and her fingers tingled, but as they made their way to the kitchen, glasses in hands, she found an excuse to slip behind for something. That was when whisky exchanged for water secreted in a recycled bottle, or when the oriental fig swayed fractionally. She created a range of strategies. The hardest part was carrying them through. *Go on, just one lick, a taster won't do any harm,* her demons whispered.

Trembling, the headaches, uncontrollable sweating, the craving for one tiny drop racked her from head to toe. How much more could she endure? Just as the rigours of abstinence were about to crush her, Lizzie's voice tiptoed into her mind: "*You can do it! Please try for me. I want to see you back to normal before ... I meet my Maker.*"

'I *will*. And I'm not letting you go. Not that easily.'

The fern in the hall received yet another "pick-me-up". Was it her imagination that the plants looked cheerful at her expense, or that the yukka had a noticeable tilt?

*

A week after she implemented her resolution, Reenie found Chris staring at her. Had she spoken aloud to the pot-plant when she returned from the cloakroom? Wasn't she aware of whether her silent voice had lost its inscrutability? 'By God, that was a speedy "downer". You must be ready for a top up?'

'Later.' She hoped Chris hadn't noticed the quiver of regret in her reply.

It was Lizzie who kept her going, of that she was certain. Now that Chris knew of Lizzie's condition, but not her own, Reenie could phone every morning and visit almost every day without questions asked, no matter how much he loathed her family. If only there was another reason, anything but her sister's slow wasting away.

'Give my love to Lizzie,' Chris said each morning when Reenie left for *Stepping Stones.*

She blinked back the tears and stepped on the accelerator.

*

The next morning Reenie's visit to Lizzie was brief. Unbelievably, her bank had bounced her cheque to the solicitor. 'I've been with them for almost thirty years and never before been so embarrassed!' Reenie said to Lizzie. 'I'll have to sort it and go into Cambridge's to apologise. I can't believe the bank could make such a stupid mistake.'

'What did Chris say?'

'He'd left for work before the letter arrived. It must be due to this blasted decimalisation. The banks can't cope with it.'

'Neither can I,' Lizzie laughed. 'Sorry you've got to leave so soon, but it's best to put a mistake like that right asap. I'd come with you if I didn't feel so tired. Anyway, the nurse is calling this morning.'

Reenie gazed at Lizzie and hugged her. She looked so frail. 'I'm taking you out for a drive through the countryside and a coffee in that tea shop tomorrow morning. I'll give you a ring before I leave to see how you feel.'

*

Lizzie always had a calming effect on Reenie. By the time she reached the bank her financial feathers had been smoothed sufficiently for her anger to be under control. After all, there were bound to be a few hiccups after Decimalisation Day.

The bank manager, as ever, demonstrated an envious equilibrium. 'Ah, Mrs Penselle, do take a seat. I have checked the statements and—'

'So, I take it the mistake has been corrected?'

'I'm afraid,' he coughed into his fist, 'there is no mistake. There are insufficient funds in your current account to cover the said cheque.'

Reenie gasped. 'I don't understand. We can't have spent that much last month!' What had Chris been doing? It had to be his decorating business. 'Well, we have a substantial deposit account with you. We've always had one. I would have thought that might have been taken into consideration. After all, I've been one of Bingley's best clients for roughly the last thirty years.'

Mr Monkton raised his hands to press his fingertips together like the well-known cathedral spire, elbows on the writing pad, index fingers touching his bottom lip. Then, resting his hands on his desk, he continued, 'Indeed, you most certainly have been a highly valued client.' He shuffled the papers in front of him. 'I have your deposit account statements here as well.' Pausing for a moment, he passed the documents to Reenie. 'It does appear that you are also unaware of your husband's withdrawals from your joint deposit account over the last three months.'

'My husband's?' Reenie's blood curdled. 'I … I think … just a moment while I study the figures.' She took her glasses from her handbag and her eyes travelled over line after line of steady withdrawals until a final "Account closed" in bold black print stared at her like a defiant teenager. Were her spectacles in the right position? She adjusted them on the end of her nose. The words and figures confirmed her first reading, eventually blurring out of focus with incredulity.

Drawing in a deep breath, she turned to the current accounts. The pattern repeated with a mere six pounds and thirty pence remaining. 'Is it possible there's been a mistake here?' she asked in a small voice.

'I'm afraid not. I have personally triple checked your accounts since your phone call this morning.'

Still in shock, Reenie couldn't bear to look at the manager. His presence bore down on her like an executioner with passive correctness awaiting the criminal.

'I'll make sure the balance is put right and the cheque rewritten. In future could you let me know if you feel there are any discrepancies? That would be helpful.'

'Certainly, Mrs Penselle. But when one sets up a joint account, it is assumed—'

'It is a joint account, I know,' she jumped in, 'but such massive changes to it! I just think someone might have considered it more closely. But, I can see I should have examined the post properly myself.'

At this she succeeded in glancing upwards. With a fleeting smile, as weak as a faded watercolour, she added, 'I'd better go home and deal with the matter!'

Mr Monkton stood up to indicate closure to the interview. The corners of his mouth pinched into what might be described as a smile. 'If we can be of any further assistance, please don't hesitate to contact us.'

*

Still seething, Reenie marched out of the bank and headed for the car. No matter what she tried to prove about Chris or salvage from her generosity to him, a few pounds in the bank was impossible to live on. How did he think she wouldn't notice?

But she *hadn't* noticed.

She dwelt on how blind she'd been over so many aspects of their marriage. Infatuation had a lot to answer for. The entire afternoon yawned ahead of her. Chris wouldn't return till six-ish and she had no idea where he was working. How was she going to kill the next six hours? How was she *not* going to kill Chris? The time certainly couldn't be swallowed up by retail therapy.

Returning to the house always set the Alcohol Demons on her, baying for her liver. Or they took the softly, softly approach: *Just pour yourself half a glass. Think how that will give you the strength to tackle anything!* But she needed to go through the bureau before Chris stood on the threshold. Steeling herself for an afternoon of solitude compounded by temptation, Reenie stepped into her home.

It didn't feel like home anymore. It even smelled different – Chris's gardening and decorating influences, she guessed. Her footsteps echoed round the cavernous hall until she reached the study and the Chinese rug. Perhaps the thick, silky pile had colluded with Chris in keeping his secrets. He rarely used the room, but then the rug silenced any footsteps. She ran her fingers over the brocade curtains they had chosen together. It seemed like another era. Sighing, she sensed the enigma that was *Lynton Grange*; Chris knew most, if not all of its secrets.

Stillness was broken with a sudden creak. 'Chris?' she called from the doorway. No reply. Old stones and woodwork habitually creaked when you least expected it. *Now for the bureau.* To her disappointment paperwork was minimal. 'Her eyes focused on the photograph gazing at her from the top of the bureau: their wedding day in Italy, Chris's arm round her waist, eyes locked on to hers, beaming his predatory smile she now realised. She turned the picture down on its face, then trawled through every scrap of paper a second time. Not one item referred to their bank accounts or any enterprises Chris had possibly taken up.

'I might have guessed,' she whispered. 'He'd keep it all at *Retreat.*'

She considered letting herself into Chris's cottage, but the risks were too great. She would tackle the subject after supper, when his defences were down. Time to make for the kitchen. Reluctantly, she stood the photograph up once more. Nothing could hint at the real fiasco her life had become.

*

'Well, old bean, that wasn't a bad meal at all,' said Chris, wiping his mouth with his napkin. 'And all laid on just as I walked through the door. Can't complain at that, can I?'

'Certainly not.' Reenie controlled her flinch as she spoke. 'But I have one, a complaint I mean, and I need an honest answer. A cheque I wrote last week bounced today.' She paused for effect, staring into his face, at which his left eye flickered, while his fingers pushed back the familiar lock of hair. 'So, I went into Bingley's to sort out their mistake. It wasn't a mistake. I've seen our accounts, current and deposit.'

'Bloody-hell! You might have given me warning.'

'Warning!'

'I was just about to explain everything and you have to—' His face switched to the hurt look, 'start snooping.'

'What?'

'Sorry, wrong word. I mean, now I'll have to tell you about my surprise, my treat. I thought you might trust me enough to—'

The telephone rang, catching her off guard. 'Leave it,' she shouted as Chris turned to answer it. He ignored her.

'If it's Bobby Fielder stealing my thunder …' Chris's footsteps could be heard returning. With his brow puckered, he pointed in the direction of the phone. 'It's for you – Graham.'

The thrum in Reenie's head quickened. 'It must be Lizzie,' she said, hastening to reply.

'Graham? Is your mother all right?'

'I'm afraid not. The nurse insisted on Mum being admitted to hospital today. I left work early and managed to speak to a doctor. I think you should come in.'

'I'll leave straight away. Will my timing fit in with visiting hours?'

'I don't think the hospital will be keeping to visiting hours.' Graham's voice cracked. 'Just come.'

Chapter 65

'Oh, Graham, thank you for meeting me here,' said Reenie, hurrying through the main entrance to the hospital.

'Well, I knew no-one would be in Reception at this time. Where's Chris?'

'He's at home. I wanted to come on my own. How's your mother?'

'She's asleep at the moment. The morphine's taken effect, thank God. I'll take you to her. She's in a room on her own, just off the main ward.'

Together Graham and Reenie made their way to Lizzie's bedside. The corridors, white tiled walls, blue doors and highly polished linoleum, gleamed under the artificial light. They were endless, almost soulless, too, if it weren't for the occasional oil painting breaking up clinical monotony. Nurses passed by; an auxiliary rattled a night trolley, while the hum and clank of a lift jarred on Reenie's nerves. All other visitors had left. She grasped the hand rail and followed Graham up one more flight of stairs.

'Rachel's with her father until tomorrow. We didn't imagine Mum taking a turn like this so soon. In fact, I thought she looked a little better yesterday. She seemed to be rallying.' Graham shook his head in disbelief.

'None of us imagined this. Tell me what the doctor has said.'

Graham stopped at the top of the stairs. He rubbed his fingers over his face. 'Mum is fading. He doesn't like to say exactly how long she's got, but, probably no more than a couple of days.'

'Oh, Graham!' Reenie hugged her nephew, then took his hand between hers as they continued their journey.

'Don't be too kind! I've got to keep going – for Mum. She's been asking for you.'

Reenie blinked back the tears. 'Has she?' she squeezed out in a broken voice.

'The pain got so bad they upped the medication and Mum drifted off again. Here we are.' Graham stopped outside a single door and peered through a small window set into its frame. 'She's still asleep.'

'You've been here for hours. Why don't you take a short break? I'll sit by your mum. She won't be on her own.' Reenie crept into the room, draping her jacket over the back of a chair before sliding on to it. She smiled at Graham, reassuring him as he left the room.

'I'll be back in half an hour,' he said.

Though asleep, Lizzie's breathing was laboured. Gently, Reenie stroked Lizzie's drip-free hand, gazing at her face, thin and drawn. Flashbacks from a past era to the living room in Lizzie's small, terraced house in Grays, then in the park with Graham, panned out before her – laughter, anxiety rolling away unbidden, even a sense of mischievousness woven into their camaraderie. A tear trickled down Reenie's cheek. 'Don't leave me,' she wanted to say. 'How can I live without you?' The monotonous click of the drip emphasized the inevitable marking of Lizzie's finite existence. Reenie brushed a hankie over her sister's damp skin. The floodgates couldn't be opened. Not yet.

As if sensing Reenie's presence, Lizzie stirred. She sighed

and her eyelids fluttered, then opened. 'I knew you'd come. I … I've—'

'Hush, sweetheart. No need to say anything until you're ready to.' Reenie bent over and kissed her forehead. 'I'm here to stay, as long as you need me. Graham has just nipped out for something to eat.'

'Remember those cream cakes you used to bring us in the old days?' Lizzie looked up at her and smiled back. 'Memories! They're funny things. What should make me think of cakes?'

'Not so strange. They're memories of good times spent together. I just wish I'd brought you more, metaphorically speaking. All those years—'

'Stop! You've always cared about me. That's what I wanted to talk about.' Lizzie flinched as pain washed over her. 'I thought I'd got longer, but, maybe I haven't. It's Graham … and Rachel. Promise me you'll look after them. I know they're not children, but they're still … so young to be left parentless.'

'Of course I'll be there for them. That goes without saying. It's taken me over half my lifetime to realise how stupid I've been, but at least I can recognise now whose love is genuine. Graham is like a son to me and I'll help him as much as I can. Just as you've supported me – throughout. And Rachel is included equally. Unlike his aunt, Graham's made a wonderful choice in his partner.'

She brushed her fingers through Lizzie's hair. 'Would you like a drink?'

'I'm all right. Talking of drink—'

'No need to. I've given it up. That's what you meant, wasn't it? It's past history, hard work, but, it's water, or should I say "spirits" under the bridge. So, you know I'll be Graham's best auntie.'

'And an adoptive grandma when the children arrive?'

'Definitely, though I couldn't possibly replace you. I … I think you'll be a bit like George. Remember how you told me he seems to be with you? I'll be a Grand-Aunt and you'll never be … far from us.' She straightened her mouth as it puckered.

'I'll do my utmost to watch over you. That's *my* promise,' murmured Lizzie.

Reenie squeezed Lizzie's fingers. 'Graham's his own self, of course, but he's like a part of you, and to me, the child I almost but never had. You both helped me over that more than words can tell. I promise to treat Graham and his children like my own. Oh God, I hope what I'm saying isn't coming out all wrong. I love you so much.'

'Wrong? No!'

Reenie could see a wave of pain striking Lizzie again. 'Should I call for the nurse?'

'Not yet. I haven't finished and she'll dose me up again. Then I'll … when I sat in the garden at sunrise not so long ago, I had such a sense of something far greater than … me … and my small world. I can't explain, but I do believe in Something beyond … beyond what we can see and touch. For now.' Lizzie drew a feeble breath. Beads of perspiration moistened her forehead. 'It made me feel at peace, despite the diagnosis. But then … the doubts crept in.' Lizzie's voice softened to a whisper. 'I worry about how I'll find George.'

'With the love you had for each other, there won't be a problem.'

'You do believe in heaven, don't you?'

'I believe that if anyone deserves to be there, it's Lizzie Simmonds.' Reenie swallowed, her mind in turmoil. 'I only wish I could say the same of myself,' she added and then wished she hadn't. These precious moments were about Lizzie, not her.

'Don't! You've got so much to offer – being the grand-aunt for starters. I don't think you realise … ohhh!' Lizzie cried out in pain.

'I'm calling the nurse.'

But Sister was already gliding in with Graham behind her. 'We'll increase the morphine now, Mrs Simmonds. It'll make you more comfortable, dear,' said the nurse.

Reenie's stomach lurched, goose-bumps spreading from her spine. She turned from the face she loved more than anyone else in the world, blinking away hot tears, steeling herself to cope as the nurse busied herself. A sea of lights blurred; then sharpened through the window, piercing the darkness into a map of the city below the hospital. Apart from the street lamps, every one of them represented a family going about their usual routine on a Thursday evening. So normal, so unaware of Lizzie's last hours. It didn't feel right that the glow from their window made up part of that pattern, yet theirs was anything but normal. She wanted to shout to each pin-prick, 'It's not fair! Why should you keep going as if nothing is happening?' Why should the rest of the world continue in the same old way while Lizzie was dying? Couldn't somebody save her, at least keep her with them a little longer? She still had things to say, things she could do to show her how much she loved her, things to make up for her past.

Reenie swivelled back to Lizzie, whose eyes were closed, her breathing laboured. Their precious conversation had exhausted Lizzie. Gradually the speckled map beyond the hospital diminished as each family finished its day, underscoring the impossibility of hindering the passage of the night. Only the street lights remained, a tangle of necklaces on black velvet. Together, Reenie and Graham sat on either side of the bed, Graham's face as pale as the hospital blanket covering his mother. 'We're staying with you,' said Graham. Reenie knew the effort it took to keep his voice steady.

Softly, she caressed Lizzie's hand. 'We shan't let you be alone.'

*

The pale grey of dawn foreshadowed a new day and Reenie stared at the skyline. Could it be a new day without her sister? She gazed once more at Lizzie: each breath seemed gentler, her face more relaxed. Could it be possible …? Was Graham aware? Slumped in the other chair, on the opposite side of the bed, he rested his chin on his chest, head nodding in a few minutes of snatched sleep, fingers twitching over his mother's.

The door opened and Sister re-entered, feeling again for Lizzie's pulse. Startled by the movement, Graham awoke, eyes bewildered, fearful of facing reality.

'I think the time has come for you to say goodbye,' Sister murmured.

Reenie's stomach twisted. *Let Graham kiss his mother first.* Then she leant over Lizzie and kissed her other cheek.

'Love you, dear Lizzie. Always.'

'Mum!'

For a moment, Lizzie opened her eyes, but whatever she saw was far beyond them. Her eyelids dropped and with two faint breaths, she slipped away from them. Neither Reenie or Graham moved, other than taking up Lizzie's hands for one last time. It seemed right to keep holding her, despite the sense she had crossed another threshold.

'Oh Mum, I can't believe I'll never speak to you again,' Graham sobbed.

'I'll leave you to have time together undisturbed,' said the nurse after she confirmed her patient's death. 'When you are ready, please feel you are welcome to stay in the visitors' room four doors down.'

Reenie sat there, enveloped in silence. Numb. Had Lizzie found the tranquillity she'd spoken of? She looked peaceful, her mouth relaxed into a slight smile. Eventually, Reenie stood and stumbled round in a daze to hug Graham.

'Do you think Mum knew we were with her? She couldn't seem to see us.'

'I'm sure she heard us. She knew. And you are the greatest comfort she could have.' She hugged him again.

'When she looked up ... do you think—?'

'She saw your father?'

Graham nodded.

'I think so.'

They clung to each other and wept. Reenie's tears fell till her body ached. Why was crying supposed to make you feel better? She wiped her cheeks with the heel of her hand. 'I'm coming back with you to *Stepping Stones*. You'll need some assistance with all the phone calls and arrangements to be made. Your Mum would want me to be with you; only, of course, if both you and Rachel are happy with that.'

'Thank you. We ... we would like that.'

Somewhere in the recesses of her mind Reenie recognised

there was still much to sort between Chris and her, but for the moment more important circumstances took precedence. She had another promise to keep.

Chapter 66

Chris seemed to accept Reenie's need to stay with Graham until after the funeral. He joined her for the service in the small parish church, followed by the burial next to George. Close to the bluebell woods, seemed appropriate. Reenie trembled as she dropped a morsel of soil on to the coffin, followed by one lily of the valley. The light thud of earth on wood, continued by Graham's and Rachel's, lanced through her like an arctic wind and she shivered uncontrollably.

Chris stood at her side, a travesty to her raw emotions with his shallow pretence of sorrow. His subterfuge was blown, though only she was aware of it. However, in her anguish, all his intrigues were pushed to the smallest corner of her mind. She was glad she hadn't raised the spectre of his involvement with their mother's death before Lizzie slipped away.

After refreshments in the church hall, Reenie waved her farewells to relatives and acquaintances she barely knew and returned to *Stepping Stones* with Graham. The garden and lanes were lined with celandines closing up for the night. How Lizzie had loved the spring flowers. She was pleased the sun had broken through the clouds for her that afternoon. Two solid weeks of rain previously had compounded Reenie's grief. Even though she'd come back from the churchyard, it was still difficult to believe Lizzie wouldn't be arranging bundles of daffodils and tulips in the kitchen, along with her favourite lilies of the valley.

She glanced at her watch: Six o'clock. *Lynton Grange* could wait no longer for her. The crockery was washed up in what was now Graham's kitchen, her suitcase packed. Her heart felt as empty as the kitchen without Lizzie. Drained of her last drop of energy, she kissed Graham and Rachel goodbye and reluctantly drove home. Was it her home? It wouldn't be for much longer.

For some inexplicable reason she parked the car in the lay-by hidden from the house; it didn't have to be obvious she was back. She was relieved that Chris had the inevitable client to seek after Lizzie's funeral – facing that first footfall past the front door with Chris at her side was too painful to contemplate, a trigger for too many reminders of their first entrance after their wedding.

She pushed at the wrought iron gates opening on to the vista of lawns and shrubbery, camellias in final bloom, and the fateful paving stones under her mother's bedroom window.

'Damn,' she said, looking at the key in her purse. 'Only the front door key. Now I'll have to pass the one place I hate more than anything else on this God-forsaken estate.' Crossing the lawn, she noticed how immaculate it was. Had Chris combed it, blade by blade? It was as smooth as Harold's old billiards table in *Cedars*. Ridiculous. Where was the sense in spending your life manicuring lawns? She stepped on to the "baize", taking pleasure in each puncture mark delivered by her stilettos.

Once inside, a strange sense of alienation encroached, as if she'd passed from the warmth of Lizzie's cottage into an inscrutable stately home. Her fingers reached out for the light switch and instantly, a glimmer from the chandelier picked up the gleam of opulence: the two Chinese vases on their polished marble pedestals, the third having been smashed by her eavesdropping mother. Guilt-edged picture frames bordered meaningless portraits, tokens of another ancestry; no connection with hers. A couple hung there as part of the house sale, from Chris's past. All along, he'd known who they were. Others were bought in a couple of auctions a few months ago, enhancing Chris's country squire image he had so carefully cultivated.

With the shock of recognition, Reenie realised it meant nothing to her now.

She wandered down the hall and into the lounge, scanning its contents and the decor, the Liberty's wallpaper with matching curtains. How she'd flaunted, with Chris's connivance, what Harold had left her. Much the same as she and Harold had achieved in *Cedars*. It had mattered so much then and now … it meant *nothing*. For one brief moment she even sensed the comfort of the sagging chair embracing her in the Pedricks' cottage so long ago. The coldness of *The Grange* contrasted with the wave of nostalgia and with *Stepping Stones*. Was it something to do with the occupants as well? She sank into her chair. 'Lizzie,' she murmured, 'I do miss you so!'

An empty silence shouted at her.

She thought she knew what it felt like to be devastated, but in the stillness her loss, a tidal wave of misery engulfed her. She'd never forgotten being bowled across the Cornish sands by such a force of nature, unable to lift her head above the churning spume pounding over her. Until Mawgan's hands wrapped round her waist. It was happening again – the panic rising, snatching away her last breath.

Oh, Lizzie! I always thought I had so much more than you,

when in fact it was the other way round. None of this matters. It's … pure nothingness. She clutched her head. As long as I've sufficient to pay the bills, enough to set Graham up in his own business … that's all I need. I know you'd be pleased with that. That's what I'll do – after the divorce and finances are sorted.

Leaning, exhausted, into the cushions, she closed her eyes as the throbbing in her head blotted out any other sounds. Chris had to be told a divorce was imminent. She winced. He wouldn't be pleased. Separating him from *Penselle Heritage*, his slip of the tongue for *her* home, would probably be the worst blow of his life, especially as he'd only just succeeded in securing his childhood dream, but it had to be done. He could keep half of his blasted palace, but he wanted it all. That's why he'd married her. Perhaps dear Bobby Fielder might come to the rescue, though hadn't she been inadvertently funding him as well as Chris?

She thought for a moment that she could hear Chris's car drawing up, then gazed across to what had been her mother's chair. *Oh yes, my other pledge is to dig a little deeper into exactly what happened when you took that duster upstairs.* An undercurrent of concern for her own safety tugged at her.

She groaned. A drink *would* put it right.

'Hello, Petal'

Oh God, it's "Petal" again.

Chris smiled at her as he entered the lounge. 'Tiring day. Stay there. You don't have to move a muscle. I've got you a take-away – Chinese.'

'You're very late. Did you celebrate today's successes – with Bobby, of course?'

'Of course. Bobby deserved a little liquid refreshment. I like to show my appreciation.'

It didn't take much for Reenie to guess what else had taken place. She reined in a tell-tale huff. 'Don't think I could manage a meal tonight, Chris.'

'Well, it's in the oven, keeping warm. You might feel up to it later. Gin or scotch? That'll perk you up.'

She didn't answer. She watched him as the glug of spirits into glasses stirred up an indescribable longing. He put the Tempter on the coffee table next to her, then looked down at his brogues. 'I ... I know you wanted to talk about ... various things. I can explain it all to you.'

Briefly, Reenie closed her eyes. 'I'm not sure if I can manage it tonight. How about—?'

'Suits me,' he shrugged. She could tell he was struggling to supress the real Chris under his skin. He hadn't finished. 'Just thought you might consider what it's been like for me on my own all this time, worrying about everything.'

Hmmm, on your own? 'Well, you might spare a thought for *my* feelings. I've just returned from Lizzie's funeral.'

He pushed his hair from his forehead and sipped his whisky. 'I know it's been a difficult time for you, but it's always about your damn family.'

'At least I have one! Where's yours? I never hear anything about them.'

Chris's hands twitched. 'That's below the belt.'

She stared at him. Distaste glared back. For her. Or was it contempt for the wife he'd totally hoodwinked? Sparing a thought for his feelings was more than she could cope with. 'I'll fetch a cardigan,' she said, stumbling out to the bedroom. There it was, still round the back of the chair by her dressing room, but she didn't remember leaving her red handbag out. Nor her box of sleeping tablets, lying on the cushion next to it. She checked. Hadn't she only taken a couple of pills roughly three weeks ago? Five were missing. A shiver of fear crawled down her spine. Maybe she'd swallowed them in extremis and then forgotten. No! Had he spiked her drink? But she'd watched him pour it. Perhaps she'd left the pills in the bedside cabinet.

She pulled the drawer open; then gasped. It was empty. All her jewellery was missing. A quick search in the most obvious places increased the pounding behind her eyes. Not one earring glimmered in the lamplight.

As if draining her bank account wasn't enough.

The goose bumps on her arms reminded her that she'd come up for her cardigan, apart from escaping her husband. She slipped it round her shoulders, remembering how her mother had liked this one. "Never leave till tomorrow what can be done today," she could hear her saying. Questions had to be asked. Avoiding them would solve nothing, and she guessed a start could be made by locating the missing jewellery.

She bathed her eyes in cold water to reduce their puffiness. Weeping at the graveside had brought no relief, just a headache and swollen face. But she pulled back her shoulders and drew in a breath until she felt her ribs ready to explode. Slowly, she exhaled. *I might even broach the window incident after all. Let's see.*

Feeling increasingly vulnerable, Reenie crept down to the lounge and peered furtively through the door. The hairs prickled on the back of her neck. A hum in her ears intensified until the hall spun round and round. Was that Chris coming over? And possibly the clatter of metal on floorboards?

Her last flicker of vision vanished into blackness.

As she came round, Reenie heard Chris saying, 'Bloody-hell –you passed out on me, old girl. Just for a few seconds.' With his face a few inches from hers, his breath smelt of whisky. She shrank back, then cringed when he clasped her hand. Ignoring her reaction, he lifted her shoulders. If only her head didn't swim so much.

'Here you are. Sup up.' He pressed a cold glass to her lips. The same stimulating scent of whisky seeped into her nostrils, followed by the splash of liquor warming her throat, soothing the tensions refusing to release her. A quiver of euphoria shot through her body.

'Told you before, you needed a touch of the old spirits. You've probably been on the wagon while you've been away.'

'W-what happened?'

'You fainted. Whole day's been too much for you. And you should have eaten that meal I brought you.'

She moaned and he mopped her forehead with his handkerchief. She noticed he'd taken her slippers off. Then everything came back to her, including the image through the door.

'Another sip. Come on.'

'No. I … I'm all right. Just put it on the table.' Slowly, she pulled herself up and scanned the room. 'Where's the gun? You were cleaning it again, right here.'

Chris rolled his eyes. 'Oh God! You weren't upset by that old rabbit popper, were you? Never crossed my mind. Got bored waiting for you.'

'But why's it back in the house? You know I hate it in here. It's meant to be under lock and key.'

'Look, I'm sorry if I got irritable. Today of all days. I just get tetchy when families are mentioned. Anyway, I'll put it in the hall ready to go down to the garage. Promise.'

Promise! Like the time you promised to love me for the rest of my life! Well, I've made one to my mother and to Lizzie. 'I was a long time upstairs because I was combing the house for my jewellery. The boxes have disappeared.'

'Into safe keeping. You didn't think I'd … I told you before, any burglar would make straight for it – the most obvious place.'

'Where is it then?'

'You don't doubt me, do you? They're hidden in the cupboard under the stairs, in that old cutlery canteen of my … the old cutlery canteen.' Chris narrowed his eyes. 'Do you want me to get them? I've hidden them extremely well, so it would mean pulling umpteen things out first. *And* when I'm on my beam-end.'

'No, it doesn't matter.'

'Just to make a point – I thought I heard something earlier today. That was when I brought the gun in. Can't be too secure, you know.' He topped up her glass. 'Drink up, darling.'

She did as she was told, just a sip. Oh, how she'd missed the magic.

Don't Reenie, for my sake, don't do it. Lizzie's voice stole between them.

With shaking hand, Reenie placed the glass on the table, close enough to reach easily. It had given her just enough courage to ask another question. 'Our accounts at Bingley's. I need—'

'Thought you'd get to them! If you can wait till tomorrow evening, I'll show you all the paper work. It's at *Retreat.* Doing something special for you. A careful investment. 'Fraid I overspent a bit, though.'

'But why didn't you tell me?'

'It was going to be a surprise. A really good one.' He gazed at Reenie. His contrite eyes were back.

'What surprise, Chris?'

He twisted his fingers together. 'Look, you've had a terrible day. Let's not argue. I can show you everything tomorrow. *Penselle Designs* is taking off. For both of us, of course. It's just that ... I didn't want to worry you before it was all sorted. Now – food, drink, TV, that's what we need tonight.' He moved over to the television, switching on a film. A blast of gunfire assaulted Reenie's ears and she shrank further into the settee.

'Can't get away from firearms today. Sorry!' he said, laughing weakly. He turned the volume down and fetched the take-away from the kitchen. She picked at her meal, aware that she hadn't started to probe her mother's accident, while *A Fist Full of Dollars* played across the screen. Chris had watched it before. Though over half way through, the film still held him in thrall. She decided to bide her time, especially as Chris by now was on his third whisky.

She topped up his tumbler and then couldn't resist lowering the level in her own. 'Chris,' she murmured. By now he'd shifted her legs to the floor and snuggled in beside her. She stiffened and hoped it wasn't noticeable.

'Mmm?' he asked, his plate abandoned on the rug and his glass in his hand, eyes fixed on Clint Eastwood.

'Never mind,' she said as she stood up. 'Won't be a moment.'

Closing the door behind her, she padded down to the back kitchen and picked up a torch to scan the cupboard under the stairs. She'd have to be quick. And quiet. The stairs might mask the said cupboard from view but not from any sounds.

Her gold and diamonds might as well have been brass curtain rings for all she cared now, but she needed to establish if this was yet another of Chris's deceptions.

She sneaked towards the new depository. To her annoyance, the latch creaked. But Hollywood was louder. With her pulse quickening, Reenie flicked on the torch. Blackness retreated to the corners, revealing extra gin, wine bottles and one Scotch stashed at random in the entrance. Immediately behind them, high-rise stacks of magazines threatened to topple over the minute her hand brushed past. Perhaps if ... gently, and on her knees, she pushed the bottles to one side. Now she could direct the light beyond the journals. She peered into the gloom – something was in the furthest corner. She could just ... *crash!* A sea of glossy magazines surged round her, tipping over the spirits simultaneously. Another volley from the Wild West exploded from the lounge.

'Get him, the bastard!' shouted Chris.

Rubbing her moist palms over her thighs, Reenie leant over the top of the cascade and peered into the furthest recess. To her surprise, an old cutlery canteen topped a sagging cardboard box. So, had Chris been telling the truth after all? With the torchlight on the box, she squinted. Surely it hadn't been touched for years? Cobwebs competed with Miss Havisham's. Gingerly, her fingertips reached over to the clasp. She shuddered. Was it the stickiness of cobwebs bringing out a rash of goose-bumps? Possibly, but worse was the fear of discovery. Holding her breath, she turned the clasp and lifted the lid. Vaguely, something else rasped in the background, but her attention centred on a faded blue fabric nestling inside. Nothing else rested in its folds, not even when she lifted the cloth to check underneath.

He was lying.

Reenie seethed.

In seconds, the horror of the last six months swept through her mind like a whirlwind: Chris vowing to love her above all else when the house was his main objective, Bobby Fielder established as his other half, her bank accounts boosting the lifestyle he loved equally well. Oh, so cleverly he'd removed the first Daily just before their wedding, the person who knew his history. Even worse were her mother's accusing eyes; her death had not been an accident. What about his own mother's demise? Was that the tragedy the police confirmed?

How she had deceived herself! She had to get away, that night, before something unexpected – accidental, of course – took her life, too. With the quantity of alcohol he'd consumed, it wouldn't take long for Chris to fall asleep. She'd go back to Graham and Rachel or even drive to a car park for the night. Drive anywhere, as long as she was well away from Chris. She could arrange to meet him somewhere neutral in the morning – drop the divorce bombshell then.

'Reene?' Chris called from the lounge.

She jumped, dropping the torch with an alarming clatter. His mood would change in an instant if he found her in the cupboard and then she would never wheedle the truth out of him about her mother. Hastily, she switched off the torch and tucked her feet in, tugging the door to. To her annoyance a magazine left the door slightly ajar. Shaking from her head down, she slid into the corner.

'Reene? Where are you?'

His footsteps were on the stairs now. So close. Clasping her fingers together, Reenie squeezed them as if pain would mask her presence just three strides away. To her dismay, he scuffed back over the floorboards, then paused, inches from her.

'Hmmm, a *Bordeaux* '58. That'll do nicely. Old girl won't be able to resist! Now, did I put it here or in the cellar?'

Could he hear her heart drumming against her rib cage?

'Nope, it's in here, I know.'

Light from the hall flooded past her, as did Chris's arm.

'Bloody-hell, it's a mess in here.' He grasped the only upright bottle as her nose began to tingle. She pinched her nostrils, terrified as a sneeze gathered momentum. Another round of gunfire rattled from the lounge. 'Hell's teeth, I'm missing the best part,' he said and she sneezed into her cardigan as he returned to the Wild West.

Thrusting open her hide-out, Reenie's cramped body unfurled. A sense of determination took over as her trembling fingers smoothed her black dress clinging to her legs. Guessing the police station might be her first port of call the next morning, she couldn't leave before she'd at least tried to prize vital information from Chris about her mother's death. She pushed a strand of hair behind her ear. She was only safe while he was ignorant of her intentions. Possibly. But she did know how to sweet-talk him, especially when he wasn't sober. He wasn't going to win. She wouldn't let him.

Only a few hours ago she'd watched Lizzie's coffin being carried out of church and now she was tackling the man who until recently had been her Mr Right. With more obvious footfalls, she approached the lounge yet again. A fatuous jingle announcing the efficacy of Tide rang out from the TV: "You know you can trust Tide!"

'But not Chris!' she whispered as she entered the lair. She cuddled up to him on the sofa.

'Can't miss the end. Only ten more minutes,' he said, still focused on the screen. 'Time for one more drink before bedtime. Blot everything out, Sweet-pea.'

Reenie stroked his knee, 'Not quite everything, darling.'

Chapter 67

Reenie watched Chris turn the TV volume down to a slight babble in the background. She clutched her whisky, bracing herself not to swallow more than a few drops at a time. She had to be *compos mentis*. Chris's hand now rested on her thigh, his right curled round a glass like hers, the only difference being that his was almost empty. She slipped over for the bottle. 'Let me top it up for you.'

'Oh, I've poured out two of the best red. Bordeaux. They're on the cabinet,' said Chris. Nevertheless, he accepted the extra scotch without protest. His eyes had that glazed look, his body signalling saturation point.

She slid beside him again, caressing his hand, 'You've been so good to me. I'm sorry if I haven't always appreciated it.' Mustering her courage, she prepared her performing skills. There were two imposters in the room at this point.

'Don't worry, Petal.'

'But I do! Sometimes I think of Mummy and how you put up with her. She was such a tyrant and you coped so well.'

'Jeeze, never thought I'd hear—'

'I should have supported you more.' Her stomach turned over. 'It wasn't *your* fault she was so crabby. She goaded you into doing things out of character. Like taking aim at her on New Year's Day. Some people would have understood if you'd carried it through!' She disguised the wobble to her voice in a giggle and then glanced round the lounge: the shotgun was on the hearth. Her heart missed a beat.

'Must admit it wasn't easy holding back, old bean.'

Reenie wove her fingers together. 'She nearly finished us, didn't she?'

'Well—'

'So, when Mummy complained about her windows, you had such an ingenious idea. You've always been clever. It's a pity others haven't recognised it. The police *almost* did. Until I covered up for you as I couldn't believe you'd been *so* inventive!'

'What?' Chris's slurred speech sharpened.

'Remember when I tried to tell you? They came back and asked me lots of questions about your relationship with Mummy, your possible movements on that morning in February.'

'Don't re ... call.' Chris shook his head.

'I never got round to telling you. I told the police that apart from the occasional tension between mother and son-in-law, you got on pretty well. I think Lizzie would have toned down the aggro and they didn't ask Graham. So, you watched Mummy through the door-jam and the minute she reached outside with her duster you skated in and pointed the shotgun, like you did before. And that glossy – *slippery* – magazine of yours was already at her feet.'

Chris raised his hands. 'It had simply dropped from under my arm.'

'And you *simply* aimed that weapon, at the critical point. I'm sure you didn't mean anything. Just like before. But ... how clever!'

Bemused, Chris looked across at the fireplace.

She drew breath. 'Of course, you knew Mummy would be a bit dizzy in the first place – that extra blood pressure tablet from the kitchen cupboard, when you made her tea? It wasn't a mistake on *her* part, was it? A masterly stroke. Who would have thought of it? But it saved our lives.' She stroked his hand again. 'Our own little secret, darling.'

'Do I need a hearing aid? Are you actually saying you didn't mind the old bat popping off suddenly?

Crossing her ankles to steady the tremor, Reenie raised an eyebrow. 'I'm congratulating you on seizing the moment.'

'*Carpe diem*,' murmured Chris.

'Assisting with that situation, that's what I mean. I'm not as imaginative as you, but I think I've worked it out. Haven't I? What would our lives have been like if we'd continued the way we were going?' She patted his knee. 'Don't worry, I haven't told anyone.'

'Bloody-hell … didn't think you'd … I mean, didn't think she'd really … no-one's-ever put me on a ruddy pedestal before. Why didn't you tell the police of your detective work – 'bout dear Mama's pills?'

'It's only just come to me. But it *is* true, isn't it?'

He rose slowly from the settee, rubbing his fingers over his forehead. She gazed at him, then lowered her eyes. Was he as shocked as she thought he might be at her revelation? Why wouldn't he admit it? What did she have to say for him to answer her question?

He pressed his lips together; so reminiscent of his victim, and turned to face her, tapping the side of his nose. 'Now, that would be telling.' A slow grin spread across his face. The confirmation she looked for? Time halted, suspended in an alcoholic haze.

She nudged the conversation, 'Don't you think we should be honest with each other? Isn't that what marriage is about?'

'You could be right, but it takes … how honest have you been with me?'

'I beg your pardon!'

'Come on! Second thoughts, I need to tether that donkey before we go any further. And my head's thudding like a drill.' He shambled towards the door. With his unexpected departure, Reenie found her legs trembling all too conspicuously.

She stood up, listening, then paced from one end of the lounge to the other, her fingers clenching and unclenching. *I can't take much more of this. What was he insinuating with his last comment: "How honest?"?'*

It didn't take long for him to return, the same crooked smile underscoring the true nature he'd concealed from her. Reluctantly, Reenie sat down, waiting for one of his barbs to follow a loaded question. She knew the pattern now.

'Raise a toast, Petal.' Chris lifted the wine glass nearest to him.

'Who to?

'Us, of course.'

Wasn't he going to mention her dishonesty again? She watched him, tension tightening to snapping point.

'A toast to *us*.' He swayed over her, touching the rings on her marriage finger. 'Diamonds are for ever, you know.'

'It's a ruby,' she snapped, then wished she hadn't. Had he got wind of the divorce?

He ignored her, gulping down wine as if it was water. 'Whatever! Good enough for Bond – when it comes out. Can't wait to see it. You and I – we're a bloody fine double-act, that's what!'

"Double?" Had Chris been duped into thinking she'd

colluded with him, hastened her own mother to her death? Shocked, she wondered what to say next. Her head began to spin again; she bent over, wriggling her feet into the rug – another faint would be disastrous. What about the gun? *Breathe in, slow and deep. Don't let him notice how nervous you are.*

But Chris was sinking into a torpor.

Perspiration trickled from Reenie's hairline. She stretched for her glass, knowing that would help; her throat was so dry.

'Old bean,' Chris murmured, settling his head on her shoulder before the nectar could touch her lips. 'Talk later, Mrs Holmes. Jeeze, you're so …'

Before she could discover her worth, he was asleep, his hand twitching on her knee, a pulse rippling through him, followed by flickering eyelids. Loathing filled her as much as fear. How she longed to push away the limb responsible for so much anguish, now resting insensibly on her, but she had to be sure he was unconscious. Her slightest movement was impossible for the moment. His breathing deepened… *at last!*

Although she guessed Chris would be unconscious for most of the night, she couldn't wait to throw off the mantle of stupidity. Even worse, of murder. The sooner she bolted, the better. Little by little, she eased herself from him, simultaneously pushing the cushions under his head until her release.

She massaged her aching back, pain spreading from support given to the person she now detested. Quickly, she rubbed her legs and stumbled into the hall, then up to the bedroom. Flinging a suitcase on to the eiderdown, she yanked haphazardly at clothes in the wardrobe, dropping them into the case, adding shoes, a handbag, cardigan, make-up and a damp towel from the bathroom. She swept the alarm clock and one bottle of Armani off the bedside table, pulled stockings and underwear from the chest of drawers. Her heart raced as she slipped on a light jacket, hands shaking.

Car keys? Where were they? On the table. In her jacket pocket now. With the quickest means to escape secured, she scrabbled through another drawer, desperate to find some money stuffed into a corner. 'I don't give a damn about this God-forsaken house, stocks and shares, savings. That's what you were always trying to tell me, Lizzie,' she sobbed. But she needed something, if only for petrol.'

To her disappointment, nothing came to the rescue. She would have to leave hoping the fuel would last. She slung her handbag over her shoulder, and tiptoed down to the hall, clutching her suitcase and shoes till her knuckles whitened. A photo of Lizzie with her family smiled at her from the corner table and she snatched it up, thrusting it into an ever-bulging handbag. Ready to jump into her car.

What about *his* car? Weren't his keys on the coffee table? If they went missing he couldn't follow her, not even the next morning. He would guess she'd go to Graham.

She peered through the lounge door-jam, much as she supposed Chris had done when spying on his first victim. At that moment he rolled his head and sighed. Had he sensed she was there? How wise was it to enter a viper's lair, especially at this stage? Gently, she lowered her possessions to the floor. With her eyes fastened on Chris, she crept into the lounge. His keys stared back provocatively from the table. A few more tiptoes and … they were in her grasp, her fingers threaded between a potential clink of alarm.

For a second, she gazed at Chris, looking so innocent, so young, still handsome with that tumble of wavy hair. Then the gun stared back at her from the hearth. That had to go, too.

One step, then the next, so carefully, she inched towards it, closer and closer. With one stretch of her arm … the snoring stopped and she froze. Sidling past Chris wasn't an option after all.

Run!

Scarcely aware of her movements, on reaching the door, she glanced back. Recharged, the scotch-soaked rumblings spluttered into life as Chris's lips opened wider. It wasn't safe to try again.

Then she remembered one item that couldn't be left behind. It took the form of another promise.

Was this madness?

Five more minutes. It had to be done.

Chapter 68

How could she forget? *The box!* The contents would provide her and Graham with some ready cash. Reenie could sell it tomorrow and then at least she'd have something to provide for her in the interim. Where was it? Lodged in ... an antique chest shoved into the attic bedroom. Chris had pushed it out of the way and the last thing she had wanted was a reminder of Harold and her first marriage.

Shifting her luggage to the foot of the stairs, by her abandoned shoes, she dropped Chris's keys into her handbag next to the case. She raced as lightly as possible up the first flight, slowing for the second twisting staircase. It wouldn't take long and Chris was sound asleep. Even so, she took care to seal the door. She tugged at the top drawer. Reluctant to open, it creaked and juddered, protesting at being disturbed after such a long hibernation. 'Sh!' she muttered. Frantically, she gripped both sides of the drawer. Like a bird startled from a garret, it swooped out, scattering memorabilia on the floor. Why on earth had she saved so much rubbish, she wondered, as she rifled through the clutter?

And why had that one vital item disappeared?

Maybe the third drawer? Her hands slid across and down the back until her fingers curled round the hidden object. Cocooned in a layer of dust and the palms of her hand, she blew at the surface and for a second watched the dust motes swirling in the lamp light before they settled on the woodwork. It hadn't been touched for years. She turned the

411

little key left in the lock. Her ruby pendant, the jewel encapsulating her past, gleamed at her. So it was still there. "As priceless as my beloved," Harold had said to her as he'd clasped it round her neck. "Rubies for my dream lady."

Despite her predicament, a wry smile crept over her face. 'Beloved!' she snorted. She snapped shut the lid. 'You'll do nicely for now.'

But first she had to escape.

She listened. Could she hear something? Only her heart drumming loud enough to wake a drunkard. 'Irene Meadows has moved on,' she said shakily to herself, dropping the box into her skirt pocket.

Hurry!

Dusk slid into darkness. Reenie's stomach churned as her stockinged feet hastened down to the last stair. Light streamed from the lounge where the door gaped at her; its sharpness in the gloomy hall served as a reminder of Chris's proximity. She wished he hadn't stopped snoring. And she wished her warm coat was wrapped round her, but creaking hinges at the cloakroom weren't an option. The thin jacket would have to do. She shivered in anticipation of the cold air about to embrace her, but also in recognition that she was literally yards from freedom. Or ... a picture of her mother's distorted body spread across the path filled her vision.

Keep going.

She picked up her shoes. Something was out of place: the cellar door was wide open. A musty smell of dank stonework drifting across instantly jolted her memory: a few weeks ago she'd stuffed several pounds under a brandy bottle. Exactly what she needed and it would only take seconds to grab.

Leaving the suitcase, she stole over. But with her first step into the cellar, her toes recoiled. A flooded vault yet again! She should have realised that after all the rain for the last fortnight. She reached up for the light switch, then thought better of it – she knew exactly where the notes were stashed: on the first rack to the left-hand side. And maybe Graham would appreciate the brandy, too.

With fingers gliding over the wall ...

BANG!

The door slammed shut, instantly plunging her into darkness. A key turned in the lock and footsteps receded, followed by unmistakeable laughter.

'Chris!' she screamed on hands and knees, feeling her way back up. She hammered on the door, her heart thudding in time with it. 'Chris, I'm in here.' She yelled again. 'Let me out – NOW! Let me out!' What if he genuinely wasn't aware that she'd crept into the dungeon? 'Oh God,' she moaned. She'd been as quiet as the biblical thief.

And if he was fully aware?

Either likelihood was equally terrifying. She dared not put the light on. Practicalities had never been her forté – they'd never been needed – but she did know electricity and water didn't mix. *And* she knew the wiring in the cellar was almost antique. With dwindling strength, she hurled herself at the door until it burst open as if propelled by a hurricane.

'Well, well, what have we here?' Chris, with the key in his hand, sneered in mock surprise, as she crumpled at his feet.

She scrambled up, humiliated, water pooling at her feet.

'Good job I heard you, Petal. Could have been there for days. Weeks! "Lady of the Manor discovered three weeks too late". Headline in local rag?'

'Shut up, Chris!' She brushed her skirt down, then raised her eyes to glare at him. Had he deliberately locked her in?

'What were you doing down there, my pretty maid?'

'What do you think I was doing? Changing my dress? Fetching a pick-me-up, of course.'

'Oh yes, despite a full cabinet. And the suitcase?'

Her mind raced. 'Sorting some of Mummy's things. It's high time ... Chris?'

He laughed again. Then stretched for the shotgun resting against the banister. Reenie gasped. 'Put that bloody thing away. I've told you how I hate it.' Surely, he was too sozzled to remember their conversation less than half an hour ago? Dear God, he'd better not remember how he'd convicted himself.

Nor see the terror in her eyes.

'Worried? What have you got to worry your sweet head about? Secrets? Let me help you. Open the case, Love-of-my-life.'

'This is getting stupid. I don't have to answer to you. Go back to sleep and we'll sort everything in the morning.' She thrust her hands into her pockets. He mustn't see them shaking. Her fingertips touched the box holding her pendant. Somehow it gave her courage, a fraction.

'Go back to sleep?' he snarled, 'I'll go back to sleep when I've sorted my wife.' His eyes blazed. He kicked the case into the stairs, where it bounced and, to Reenie's horror, flew open, scattering her clothes between them.

'Mama's possessions? I don't think so!' Seizing her shoulder with his free hand, Chris shoved her towards the cellar.

'I can explain!'

He pushed all the harder. One glance told Reenie he was beyond reason. Could she kick the gun from his grasp? She didn't have to: it clattered to the floor as he grabbed her with both hands, yanking her round to clamp his arms across her chest. 'No!' she rasped. Her heels drummed over the polished floor, chilled air reaching out to claim her. He turned. The entrance to the cellar, now a shark's smile, beckoned, its teeth the rows of once inviting bottles.

'Thought you could get the better of me, damn your eyes,' he shouted.

She struggled, screamed, shook her head. All useless. Chris was ready to erupt, ready to scorch and destroy.

He hesitated and Reenie seized her chance. 'Please, you're h-hurting me. We can talk about this. You've had your fun. Now let's ... why don't you go and see Bobby. He understands you.'

'Too bloody right! You're talking sense at last. I will see Bobby, but not until—'

With one last heave, he propelled her into the cellar. She shrieked, hitting the flood water headlong. Its coldness took her breath away. Frantically, she scrabbled round to lift herself, find purchase, anything on which she could haul herself up and out. Worse even than the water was the thought of Chris turning the key again.

'Did my ears serve me right? Was that a splash? Fancy the water being so high. Remember the last time I sought refreshment for my sweet-heart?' His voice echoed round the cellar. 'Thinking of running to the police were you? Don't bother. You'll be an accessory to the ... whatever, up to your neck, just like you are now. Ha! I could turn the tables on *you*, instead.'

Sliding to the far side of a wine-rack, Reenie took cover behind it. Hiding wasn't an obvious answer, but neither was rushing for the exit. She heaved on her arms and slid into a slight alcove above her. Soaked and shivering, at least she couldn't drown. The stream gurgled in from the grating, masking her shuffling into position.

Stream still rising? Her brain numbed almost as much as her legs, remembering how high the water could rise. So Chris had options. If only she could think straight. Sweet-talking him wasn't working, neither was pitting her slender frame against his. What if she could persuade him to follow her? Lure him in? She clutched at a shelf, then a bottle, teeth chattering. Perhaps if she sounded half dead, he might start looking for her? 'Oh,' she moaned. 'Chris! I think I've broken … oh!'

Framed in the doorway, a silhouette of his head and shoulders dwarfed the entrance. 'Reene?'

She stayed mute. Was he wondering if she'd gone the same way as his mother-in-law? She whimpered slightly again.

'Reene?'

Hardly daring to breathe, she gripped her weapon all the tighter. *A bit further. Just a bit.*

Heavy shoes scraped on the tiles, one step down …

Could he hear the thrum in her head?

'Jeeze, it's ruddy Wookey Hole in here.'

His feet splashed into the water. 'Where's that blasted switch?'

Peering between the gaps in her hideout, Reenie could just make out his arm searching for the switch. Instinct took over.

'No!' she howled.

Chapter 69

A blinding flash lit up the cellar. Chris screamed and fell, hitting his head on the wall before splashing into the water. Blackness swallowed Reenie up. With a sudden flare, flames spurted along the cable draped like a Christmas decoration from the door to the fluorescent strip. So, it wasn't to be death by drowning after all. She forced herself to look at Chris – fallen on to his back, partially submerged, his grotesque juddering stilled. The light from the blaze lit up the whites of his eyes. Unmoving. Petrified. Might he be merely knocked out? She lurched down from her shelf, wading through the flood waters, and tugged at his shoulders.

It had all happened so quickly.

Inexplicably, she tugged again, but he was too heavy and one upward glance told her the flames were taking over. Dancing tongues, eager to consume, licked across to the light and round the door frame, her only exit.

Remembering a film she'd watched, Reenie tore off her jacket, dipped it in the water and draped it over her head. Golden ripples in the darkness quivered, then fragmented, closing round her equally shivering legs as she waded through. Something splashed at her side, but there was no time to stop. Drawing in a deep breath, she pulled a sleeve across her mouth and launched herself at the steps. Up, up she stumbled, eyes closed, heading for her only escape, heat pouncing on every scrap of exposed flesh. Coughing, spluttering, skin searing, she broke through the ring of fire.

Out and alive.

Next? Dash for bowls of water? From the kitchen? That was on the other side of the house. The cloakroom? Yes, but she'd have to race to the back kitchen for a bucket. Her jacket slid round her shoulders and she looped the sleeves together.

The fire brigade. Why hadn't she phoned them?

She sprinted down the corridor, immediately pitched into obscurity.

What had happened to all the lights? Would she be able to even find the phone? Her hands flattened along the wall, feeling her way. Got it! – the little table not far from the lounge. Now she clutched the wire leading to the telephone. Number nine? Impossible to see. Trembling, she counted round the dial. Nine – there it was.

'Come on, come on!' she shouted at it. Why wouldn't it ring? Her forefinger jabbed at the button again and again.

Nothing.

The entire house had shut down, apart from the hall lit up like Bonfire Night, crackling as if enjoying the uninvited. How could she expect the telephone to work? Careering into the wall, a picture crashed beside her. She dashed back to the fire. With a life of its own, the blaze sprang across the floor to tackle the shotgun. Next – the Chinese rug. She heaved at one corner, not quickly enough – her suitcase ignited. Leaning against the banister, the case formed a bridge to the first floor. Up shot the flames, devouring the wooden structure, a dragon released from captivity.

Get out before you fry! The car's in the lane.

She yanked the front door open and a blast of cold air sent her spinning backwards. But the furnace welcomed the draft with eager fingers, mocking her feeble efforts with a roar. A sheet of dazzling yellow gained momentum … from the top of the steps Reenie leapt towards the lawn.

In the next second, an explosion ripped through *The Grange*.

Reenie lay face down in a daze on cold wet grass, the coolness balm to her scorched hands and legs. She rolled over to soothe her shins as smoke billowed from the front door. The windows in the lounge, popping and cracking, glared at her with orange rebellion.

'Chris!'

There was nothing she could do for him now.

She had to reach a neighbour. Yet again she pulled herself up, this time hobbling down the drive. A strange, disembodied sensation took over – as if detached, her legs somehow carried her to the convertible left in the road. There it was, her deliverer. Plunging her hand into her jacket pocket, her pulse quickened. Frantically, she searched all pockets. The keys had gone. That must have been the extra splash she'd heard just before she'd leapt from the cellar. And the handbag with Chris's keys for the *Rover* had been left by the stairs.

Tears coursed down her cheeks. The only option now was to walk to the nearest house, over a mile away. Could she manage that? Could she even start on bare, blistered feet?

Turning her back on Lynton Grange, she nevertheless set out for the nearest house, tottering down sleeping lanes. She glanced over her shoulder to see an unnatural glow lighting the sky behind her; an explosion split the heavens over the peaceful Cotswolds. Might someone have heard or seen it by now? Acrid smoke from *Lynton Grange's* last battle, drifted in her direction, catching at her throat as if still determined to snare her.

'Chris, we could have been so different – why did you …?' she cried.

A surreal hum and crackle of destruction behind her replied.

Out of the darkness, a siren wailed, then another. She stepped from the verge to wave at a fire-engine as it hurtled towards her, then leapt back as it swerved past. Dazed, she stared at it disappearing round the next bend. Moments later, a police car, equally loud, tore past. Brakes squealed and an officer soon peered down at her from what seemed to be a great height.

'My house,' she croaked. 'It's my house.' She swayed and she felt his hands catching her shoulders.

'Anyone left inside?'

'My husband.' She gulped for air. Were her lungs closing down? Her throat stung as much as her hands. 'B-but I think he's … he's … oh God. It was the shock. It started the fire.'

Somebody wrapped a blanket round her, warmth attempting to melt icy layers, shivering bent on disassembling her very bones. Had she explained about the flood and the shock? About Chris lying in the cellar? Even if she hadn't, Reenie guessed no-one could penetrate the blaze.

Time fractured and warped like the rafters in her home. Maybe Chris had survived in the flood waters? No, that wasn't possible. When the ambulance crew prevailed, despite her protestations, the medics whisked her away – back to the hospital, the other place holding memories of deepest loss.

Nurses fussed, police interviewed, Reenie shook and wept. Why wouldn't they leave her be? Didn't they realise that even thinking hurt. After yet another grilling, an all-efficient nurse came to her bedside. 'Just a couple of tablets for you, Mrs Penselle. They'll help you to sleep.'

At last she could feel herself drifting – Chris's face, creased in rage, a wedding outfit and Italian lake, flames, suitcase, water splashing, drifting, drifting ...

*

'Mrs Penselle,' a man in a white coat said. So much white everywhere. Was she in heaven? Couldn't be – Lizzie wasn't there. 'Your nephew is here,' he persisted.

"No peace for the wicked", she could hear her mother saying. Too much hustle. Why didn't they leave her alone? She was in hospital wasn't she? A sweet perfume dulled her pain and she closed her eyes.

'He would like to speak to you. Now that you're awake, don't go back to sleep.' White-coated-Man touched her shoulder. 'That's it. Well done!'

"Penselle", the hated surname. If only her voice would work. She'd tell them. But what about *Mr* Penselle: where was he? In an instant, the nightmare of mere hours ago revisited her.

'No-o-o-o!' she screamed. A searing pain in her chest cut her short.

'Bloody-hell– you're getting better!' Graham said. He smiled at her and kissed her cheek. Reenie managed to smile back, especially when a huge bouquet of flowers at her bedside came into focus. So that was the aroma. Could she reach out and touch the petals?

'W-who?' she croaked.

'A little something from Rachel and me.'

'Oh!'

Every word took a painful breath; each one pierced her lungs like a surgeon's knife, while her lips were made of rubber as she tried to speak. A tear trickled down her cheek. Graham reached out to take her hand, then rested his on her shoulder when he saw the bandages.

'Long ... h-how long, I mean when—?'

'It's two o'clock, Auntie Reenie. The day ... after the fire.' He paused. 'I'm so sorry, but the doctor's asked me to tell you.' He hesitated once more and Reenie attempted to nod. She guessed what he was about to say. 'It's not good news. I'm afraid Chris ... didn't make it. If ... if it helps at all, someone said he must have died the instant he touched that cable you told them about. I'm so sorry.'

Reenie's tears flowed. Deep, uncontrollable sobs tore at her scorched lungs. She guessed Graham imagined they were for her loss. He had no idea she had lost Chris weeks before the fire, or rather, he'd never been hers in the first place. So why was she crying? Was it for herself in shock or in guilt over marrying the man who precipitated her mother's death? For the void Lizzie had left in her life? For the love she'd yearned for and never realised? For wasted, embittered breath that belonged once to a young man who had his whole life ahead of him? Their world could have been so different.

'Don't stop – Mum would have said it's nature's way.' Graham waited until her sobs subsided. 'You know Rachel and I will look after you. The doctor is pleased with your progress, though he knows you are still in shock. But I can take you home tomorrow.'

'Home? I ... I haven't got one.'

'Yes, you have – with us, Rachel and me. There's room in the cottage for as long as you need it.'

'The last thing you … n-need is a grouchy … aunt settling in.'

How were the bills to be paid until everything was sorted?

'Of course you can stay with us. Rachel's made up the bed and looking forward to having you. You'll see – it'll all work out. I'm going back to work, but tomorrow I'll bring you back to *Stepping Stones*.

'Graham—'

'Don't say anything. Just rest and get better.'

As he turned to go, he pointed to a box by the flowers. A small, velvet box. 'The ambulance driver said he found it lying next to you. It's locked, but you probably have the key. I thought it might be important to you.'

It is, but not for me anymore, she thought.

*

Once back with Graham on the road leading to *Stepping Stones* the next day, Reenie knew she wanted to see *The Grange*. One final sighting.

'Please take me there. I can't explain why. It's something I feel I have to do. Maybe it's what people call vanquishing old ghosts,' she said.

'Doesn't seem like a good idea to me. You know it's all cordoned off. Um … Chris was—'

'It's all right. You can talk about Chris.' She lifted her hand to tease it through her hair. Then realised how impossible that was with fingers cocooned in dressings. 'I shall be fine. It's my turn now to say "Stop worrying".' How strange she felt in borrowed clothing from Rachel. Not one item remained from her own wardrobe.

Reluctantly, Graham drew into the roadside when they reached Bickersleigh. Linking arms, they headed for the gate through which Reenie had fled only two days previously. Her legs wobbled and she was glad of Graham's support. Yards away, she could see the police tape and *Beware!* notices warning off the curious and even the owner. The air, redolent with the scent of destruction, gripped Reenie's throat once again. Her tongue furred with that taste from her childhood – the old coke burner in the village school after someone had stoked it. But *this* stoking had been the devastation of her home. Graham tightened his arm looped through hers. Neither of them spoke.

Lynton Grange loomed larger than ever. Perhaps it was due to its starkness, a mere blackened façade silhouetted against a blue sky. Why did the sun always shine after a tragedy? She guessed she was staring at a shell – clouds floated behind its sightless windows. Did they have to emphasise how lifeless the house was? Unexpectedly, panic gripped her as her eyes searched the garden, then the greenhouse, still intact. Was that Chris emerging with the shotgun? Her skin crawled. No, the rowan tree was casting a shadow, wavering in the breeze. It was difficult to believe that Chris was dead.

'Would you like me to go back to the car, Auntie Reenie? Give you a bit of space to … to be on your own?'

Reenie took a long, deep breath. 'Thank you. I think I'd like that.' Keeping her focus locked on her past, she heard Graham slip away.

'I didn't mean it to end like this. I tried to save you,' she murmured to Chris. 'Can't say why. You didn't deserve my loyalty.' She paused. 'But, I'd like to believe that once upon a time a tiny part of you really did love – let's say even "like" – me. I loved you with all my heart. Until you broke it.' Uninhibited, the tears flowed again. Searching for a tissue in the loaned pocket, her fingers struck the box with her pendant in it, a symbol of a failed affection from long ago.

She shook her head. 'No more deception,' she said to a robin eyeing her from the gate. 'For me this heralds a new beginning. The past is demolished. It's over. There can be no fighting over possessions – they're gone, with Chris.' The bickering, alcohol, her quarrelsome mother, the shotgun, embarrassments, disappointments, deceit – all gone. Ashes and a few charred walls served to symbolise their demise.

Insurance would eventually pay for the house and contents. In the meantime, she'd sell the pendant. The box nudged her hip, reminding her she wasn't quite destitute. Could she feel Lizzie's arm round her shoulder, like old times? 'Dear Lizzie,' she whispered, 'I promised I would look out to Graham and Rachel and that's exactly what I'll do.'

*

Welcomed and settled into *Stepping Stones*, Reenie felt the time had come to open the box. She turned to Graham. 'I lost the key I'm afraid. Do you think you could prize it open for me?'

He took a knife from Reenie's supper tray and the lid sprang up.

'It's your pendant Uncle Harold gave you. I remember you wearing it when we all lived in Grays.'

'Well, it's yours and Rachel's now. Whatever it fetches at the jewellers is to go towards your wedding present.'

'But you can't do that – it means a lot to you!'

'*Meant!* I've no need of it now. Besides, I don't know how much money Chris left in the kitty, so until everything is sorted – and you know how long that takes after a death—'

'You shouldn't even be thinking of our present at the moment!'

'As long as I have a roof over my head and enough to live off …' She smiled. How she had fought to save her possessions from Chris's clutches and now, none of it mattered. She considered what she needed to support herself for the time being, knowing she would sell Chris's engagement and wedding ring as well as the pendant.

'The sooner *Lynton Grange,* well, what remains of it, is sold the better. I could never go back there. I shall find a cottage not too far away from you. Whatever's left over will be channelled into setting you two on your feet with your own enterprise.'

Graham gasped. 'You can't—'

'Don't say anything. It will give me far more pleasure than staring at walls and furniture that can't possibly reciprocate the love you've always given me. And in a way I'll be doing it for your mother. It'll be my attempt to right past wrongs.'

Chapter 70

Wedding July 1971

Reenie gazed proudly at the bride and groom.

'And now I wish to remember my mother and father,' said Graham, glancing at his speech. 'I'd like to think they're watching over our wedding celebrations. Mum was so looking forward to this day and certainly appreciated my choice of wife.' He beamed at Rachel. 'So, thank you, Mum and Dad, for being special parents and for all your support and encouragement over the years. We miss you.'

'More than words can tell,' Reenie murmured, thinking especially of Lizzie. 'I bet they're listening in.' She blinked at a tear attempting to escape.

'Let's raise another toast to Mum and Dad.'

With a scraping of chairs over the tiled floor in *The Fountain*, all the guests stood, glasses held aloft. 'To Lizzie and George,' they said. Handkerchiefs dabbed at faces again.

Reenie smiled at her companions, Isobel and Geoff, new neighbours since her move but old friends of the Simmonds'.

'And now I'd like to thank my Auntie Reenie for all *her* assistance – the constant phone calls and smoothing out of last-minute hitches, the flower arrangements and our stunning cake. Mum would have been so proud to see how well you've coped since that terrible day and *very* grateful for your support, as, of course, both Rachel and I are.'

'Well said,' added Rachel's father.

Together with other family members, champagne flutes were lifted to lips once more. Reenie sipped her pressé.

'So good to see Graham laughing again,' said Isobel, turning to her. 'It's a bit of a cliché, but they do make a most handsome couple! And I know how much they've enjoyed their aunt's help.'

'But that's what's kept me going – they've helped *me* to recover. And *you*,' Reenie said, gazing at Isobel. 'I value your friendship probably more than you realise.' Isobel squeezed Reenie's hand.

Before long the guests began to mingle while a folk band assembled in the conservatory. Taking the opportunity to slide into a comfortable chair in the corner, Reenie watched the festivities without having to take an active part. Tiredness swept over her – only four months had passed since the fateful night which had almost killed her. She made a point of asking Graham not to mention Chris and nobody did. She poured herself another pressé, then mopped her forehead; it was still an exceptionally warm day. The temptation to soak up alcohol, strangely, had a new effect upon her: a sense of achievement, having beaten her tormentor.

'Can we join you?' More friends of Lizzie's who had welcomed Reenie to their fold, sat beside her. 'What are you doing tomorrow? Don't spend it on your own. Come and have tea with us.'

Reenie smiled at them. 'I would love to.'

*

Reenie returned to her reminiscences later that evening. She thought back to when she'd visited the jewellers.

Mr Melrose had promised her an evaluation for the pendant. 'Miss Meadows, do take a seat.' He had seemed uneasy, a sense of déjà vu hovering. 'Erm, the gold chain and mount is of value – as you no doubt know, gold never drops its price, but the stone—'

Bemused, Reenie looked up. Mr Melrose continued. 'I'm afraid the stone is a very clever substitute for a ruby. It's really quite … worthless.'

The tear in her heart, beginning to heal, had reopened. Yet … it was true, time could be a great healer. Her heart had almost knitted together again in time for the wedding.

She gazed at Graham and Rachel, at her friends, at the adoptive grandchildren of the future, at her days now spent with a purpose. *Lady Hartley,* she murmured, remembering her pretension when Harold had pinned his token of questionable love round her neck. A July birthstone, the assistant had said. One standing for riches. Well, Lady Hartley was a thing of the past. *This* July was filled with a different kind of wealth. The first such July in her entire life; a month minus the rubies but filled with potential for Reenie Meadows. This time the jewels were genuine.

Epilogue

July 1976

Reenie looked back over her years following Graham and Rachel's wedding with contentment. She watched Graham's business take off and at the same time became the adoptive Grandmother she'd hoped to be to the twins, Matthew and Duncan, followed three years later by Sarah Elizabeth. Their parents accepted their aunt's help with unequivocal relief. She was part of the family.

In the summer of '76 a holiday in Cornwall was booked. Graham expressed a desire to explore his family roots and the beaches beckoned to the children. Several virtually unknown relatives were visited on their way down and then the rugged coastline of Cornwall welcomed them. For Reenie one particular memory outshone others.

Occasionally, she slipped away from the family to walk the coastal path or sit on the headland she'd wandered over so long ago, gazing over a turquoise sea. She was lucky – the sun didn't always shine over her childhood vistas. 'You need a bit of space for yourselves and I like time to ponder over past associations,' she said to Graham and Rachel. They seemed to understand. She found a bench in the perfect position, sheltered by a bank of gorse and overlooking the bay. Gulls wheeled overhead, colours jostled for supremacy, the surf sucked at the shoreline far below her. Reenie stared at the hollow a little to the right. Wasn't that the dip by the cliff where she and her first love had once nestled?

Reenie told her friends that the surge of recollections left her oblivious to the person who slipped on to the bench beside her, but she turned when she heard that longed for voice say, 'Rescued a maiden from a wave like that one a long time ago. Any chance of a second time?'

About the Author

Although Andrea graduated from art college and followed this by many years of teaching, she always had a yen to write. This she took up in earnest once semi-retired. Her passion for writing has been fuelled by her love of history, travel and coastline (and even cream teas), having lived on the Isle of Wight and having strong connections with Cornwall. She is married to Richard, and enjoys family time with their three children and four grandchildren.

andreaemblin@yahoo.co.uk

If you have enjoyed this book, please consider leaving a review on Amazon and Goodreads for Andrea to let her know what you thought of her work.